Beyond Reality
Complete Collection

#1 Outback Hearts
#2 Flaming Hearts
#3 Frozen Hearts

by Susan Stoker

Table of Contents

Outback Hearts

Beyond Reality
Book 1

by Susan Stoker

Chapter One

How in the world did I end up here? Sam thought to herself.

'Here' was Australia, the 'Outback' more specifically. It was almost a year ago that an article in the local paper announced there was going to be a new reality show set in the Australian Outback and they were looking for twenty to thirty-five-year-old women to audition. The ad was pretty vague and didn't say what the show was going to be about. Beth had found the ad and one night, over several margaritas, Sam, Beth, and Christina had sat down together and each had filled out an application. It was a lark, something they did for "fun." The ad requested that each application had to be accompanied by a headshot and a full body shot picture. They figured since it was for television they wanted to make sure they didn't have any really ugly people picked. Months went by and all three had forgotten about the applications.

Then a couple of months ago Sam got the phone call. It was the producers informing her that she'd been chosen to come in and interview in person. When she showed up, there were about one hundred other women there. Most of them looked like models. Sam had always been self-conscious about her weight. Beth and Christina were both slender. Beth was about five feet ten inches tall and Christina was a very petite five feet three inches. Sam was an average five feet six inches and weighed about one hundred and fifty pounds. She wasn't really fat, but she also wasn't skinny either. So she figured that with all these model look-alikes there was no way she was going to make it to the next round…but after a panel interview, a group interview with some of the other perspective contestants, a one-on-one interview with a psychologist, and a thorough medical exam…it turned out that she was one of sixteen women chosen for the show. And they still hadn't really said what the show was going to be about.

So, here I am. Sam thought. She'd taken two months leave at her job—luckily, she had a great boss and lots of leave saved up—and gotten on a plane to the Outback. The producers hadn't told her much about the trip, except that there might be some camping involved. Sam had seen enough reality shows in her lifetime to know that "some" camping probably meant they would be spending the entire time in the wilds of the Outback. She thought back to a reality show a few years back where one guy "Jack"—*which wasn't even his real name*, she thought to herself with disgust—had to pick from a bunch of spoiled rotten debutants which one he wanted to spend the rest of his life with. She, Beth, and Christina had watched the show and laughed at all the women who complained about where to plug in their hairdryers and about the icky bugs. They couldn't see why anyone would want to degrade themselves to be on a show like that and they didn't understand how "Jack" could see past all of the "glamour" to really get to know any of the women.

Sam loved camping and didn't mind—indeed hoped—they'd get to spend some time outside, communing with nature. She didn't mind being dirty and enjoyed being outside. So with that in mind, she packed a carry-on suitcase full of clothes appropriate for camping and another backpack with essentials.

Sam was brought to a hotel room from the plane and told that tomorrow she would meet the other contestants and the day after that their adventure would start. She was handed a packet of information about the show and the "rules" they had to follow. Her name was written on the packet, but instead of Sam, her name was written "Sammi." When she asked about it she was told that it was just a part of the show.

Sam sat down to read the information she'd been given. The notes on the show were short and vague:

You have been chosen as one of sixteen women to be on a reality show about dating, love, and real life. One by one, contestants will leave the show until there is only one left. You are not allowed to ask to be kicked off. The last remaining contestant will win.

And that was all it said.

"Whatever," Sam mumbled to herself. They were certainly being as vague as possible about the whole thing. Sam was a bit cautious and suspicious in nature. She remembered the other reality show she and her friends had watched, where the entire show was a lie. There was only one person who didn't know, and it was all based around him. She wondered if this was the case here as well.

Now that she thought about it there was another reality show where the women went to Vegas and the rich man got to choose one of them for his wife and they had to get married right there on the show. Of course, it ended badly. Sam remembered an interview with that "winner" saying she'd agreed to be a contestant because she wanted a free trip to Las Vegas. Sam hoped that wasn't what she'd gotten herself into.

Sam went on to read the "rules" of the show. They went on for pages and pages, most of which were legal things like "contestants aren't allowed to agree to share any prizes" and things like that. There were also provisions like, "contestants will agree to be taped at all times and will not engage camera personnel in conversation." Sam thought to herself, *This sounds more and more like Survivor.* She figured there wasn't anything more that she could do tonight and decided not to worry about it until tomorrow.

Chapter Two

Sam got dressed in a pair of jeans and a V-neck sweater then put on the nametag that was included in the packet she received the night before, and winced. She still didn't like the fact she had to go by "Sammi." She hadn't been called Sammi since she was twelve years old and she moved to a different school. She'd decided it was more "grown-up" to be called Sam.

She entered the ballroom in the hotel and saw there weren't that many people there yet. There were little cocktail tables evenly set up around the room with long white tablecloths over them and a rose in a vase sitting on each one. There was also a bar in the corner with a man wearing a full tuxedo standing behind it waiting to take drink orders. A few people were milling around and clustered in groups, talking. Sam had never been comfortable just walking up to people and talking, so she went to get a soft drink from the bartender and sat at one of the little tables.

The room quickly started filling up. The women who were wearing nametags were all beautiful. Most were tall. All of them could have been models. For what seemed like the hundredth time, Sam mumbled, "What am I doing here?" She didn't belong. She knew it, and it seemed like everyone else in the room knew it also. They'd see her and then do a double take as if to make sure they were seeing her correctly. Sam knew she wasn't wearing the appropriate outfit. Most of the other contestants were wearing short skirts or dresses, with their hair in fancy upsweeps and perfect made up faces. In contrast, she'd dressed comfortably. Sam knew this was going to go badly.

Soon one of the producers got up on the podium in the front of the room. He seemed to be the person in charge. Sam remembered he'd introduced himself to her as Eddie.

Eddie dramatically announced, "Welcome to the Outback. We are so pleased to have you all here. We know this is going to be the best reality show to air on television back in the States and you're all going to be stars!"

At that, the room broke out into spontaneous cheering and clapping.

Oh brother, Sam thought, *this is really over the top.*

Eddie on the podium continued, "I'd like to take this time to introduce all of our lovely contestants..."

With that he started calling the women up to the stage one by one. "Katie from New York City, Brandi from Phoenix, Kimmie from San Diego, Ashley from Toledo, Cindee from Albany, Lori from Colorado Springs, KiKi from Miami, Courtnee from Pensacola..."

Sam was starting to feel a little sick. All the women were lining up on stage and it seemed like they were automatically doing the "pageant pose" where one leg was a bit forward, their hips were swiveled, and their hands were on their hips. Most of them had long hair that was either flowing around their shoulders or up in an elegant updo.

The man continued his dramatic introductions. "Candi from Greensboro, Jennie from Billings, Missy from Los Angeles, Sammi from Albuquerque..."

Sam walked up on stage and stood next to Missy and stood there with her hands clasped in front of her nervously. She felt very awkward and out of place. She was a bit shorter than Missy and weighed about thirty pounds more. She felt like a beached whale next to all the other women. She knew she wasn't obese. In fact, she was probably the most normal sized woman in the room, but compared to the others she definitely stood out. Missy was wearing a white miniskirt which showed off her mile long legs. Seeing them, Sam suddenly wondered if she had even remembered to shave her own legs before getting on the plane. She had to remember to do it tonight before the show started, just in case.

"Wendi from Las Vegas, Nikki from Seattle, Amy from El Paso, and last but not least Kathi from Knoxville.

Remember these faces everyone, these are our new contestants for our show called "Love in the Outback."

It was even worse than she could imagine. Love in the Outback? Good lord. Hopefully they'd reconsider that name before this stupid show ever aired. Sam wasn't even really sure she wanted to find love. She had a great job that she enjoyed most of the time. She had great friends, she had a great rental house….she was content with her life for the most part. "Why did I let them talk me into this?" Sam mumbled as they were herded off the stage.

The rest of the morning was torture. All the other contestants were busy talking amongst themselves, already figuring out that Sam didn't fit into "their" crowd. Sam bet they were all rich. They talked about places they'd been to, stores they'd shopped in, and clothing they'd brought with them…all of which meant nothing to Sam.

Later that night, lying alone in her hotel room, Sam thought about what her game-plan was going to be, then rolled her eyes at herself. She figured she'd be one of the first people kicked off the show. After all, who would choose *her* over the other women? She wasn't as pretty, didn't have any fashion sense, was heavier than all of them, and most of all she didn't *want* fame as most of the others seemed to crave. She was content to fade into the background…not search out attention. She thought about some of the women she'd met that day. Missy and Katie had hit it off right away, formed their own clique, probably because they were from the "big" cities, LA and New York. Kiki and Courtnee had also paired up, probably because they were both from Florida.

"Wait a minute," Sam said out loud to the empty room. She sat up and started writing down as many names of the other women as she could remember…Brandi, Katie, Cindee, Candi, Amy, Kathi—even her own "name," Sammi. Sam groaned out loud. It couldn't be…it was beyond cheesy, beyond anything she could imagine…all of their names ended with the "ie" sound. Wendi, Nikki, Missy…it was going to be too embarrassing to be on this show. Sam flopped back on the bed and for what seemed like the millionth time that day, cursed Beth and Christina for getting her into this.

Chapter Three

Alexander David Sanders III watched the closed circuit television in his room intently. He wasn't quite sure how he'd gotten into this situation. Last year he was approached in a local bar and asked if he would pose for a picture for a production company who was looking for reality show contestants. He wasn't interested in doing anything like being on a reality show, but since he was with Craig and Pete, and they egged him into it, he posed. Apparently, the producers liked his picture and called him in for a round of interviews. He only went to the interviews because Craig and Pete dared him to do it and assured him he'd never get chosen.

Two more rounds of interviews after that, he'd made the cut and was chosen. Alex wasn't really sure what he was chosen for until they flew him out to Australia. *A freakin' dating show.* Alex thought to himself. He'd never live it down. He liked women—hell, he'd dated more than his fair share of ladies back in Austin. He never had to worry about finding a date on a Friday or Saturday night for that matter. He wasn't sure how he made it to where he was now, but he didn't have any choice…he was locked into the contract and he had to go through with it.

Alex was told there would be sixteen women who he'd be choosing from. Some weeks he'd be deciding who would go home, and other weeks the ladies themselves would choose. The producer also told him that other weeks there would be a competition and the "loser" would leave. At the end of the show, there'd be one lady left and that was supposed to be his "girlfriend" and hopefully future spouse. It was utterly ridiculous. How was he supposed to get to know sixteen women enough to know who they really were in a few weeks? He'd watched enough dating reality shows to know the women acted very differently to each other than to the "bachelor." He knew some would only be there to be on TV.

Alex wasn't sure he even *wanted* to find a girlfriend. He knew the producers were going to tell the women that he was a rich cowboy who owned a huge spread of land back in Texas, which wasn't quite true. Yes, he did own his own piece of land and had a few cows and horses, but it definitely wasn't a "huge spread" and he definitely wasn't rich. He wasn't hurting for money, true, but it wasn't like he was a millionaire or anything.

Thinking back to the concept of finding a girlfriend on a reality show, he *was* a busy man and sure hadn't been able to find someone to love back home, so maybe he should give this reality show thing a chance. He figured if it didn't work out, he'd have a great vacation in Australia, spend some time with beautiful women and maybe drum up some business for himself when it was all said and done.

So here he was, in the Outback, in a hotel room, watching closed circuit television. When he arrived in Australia a few days ago Eddie and the other producers sat him down and explained how the show would work. This show would be a bit different than others because he'd have 24/7 access to any of the tapes of the women or locations that he wanted. He'd see what the contestants did when they weren't around him. He could see their "true nature" when they were around the other contestants. He could see what they looked like without makeup on, he could see how they interacted, and most importantly, he could hear what they said about him when they weren't around him. When Alex heard that, he became almost excited about this adventure he was about to go on. He knew how to manipulate people with the best of them, and it was going to be great to see how, and if, these women tried to manipulate him.

So he was in his room, watching the "get to know you" function that the contestants were required to attend. It was his first chance to see the contestants before they met him. He kept his fingers crossed that they'd be beautiful. He'd seen one reality show where the "bachelorette" was introduced to the contestants and they were all unattractive, slightly awkward men. He wasn't a snob, but he didn't know if he could handle that, even with a signed contract.

At first the room was pretty empty. There were a few people milling around. Once the room started filling up he could pretty much guess which women were the contestants and which were a part of the crew. There were redheads, blondes, brunettes, and even one woman with long, straight black hair. Alex relaxed a bit. Thank God, they were all good looking! He watched as Eddie got up on stage and started introducing the women one by one.

"Katie from New York City, Brandi from Phoenix, Kimmie from San Diego, Ashley from Toledo, Cindee from Albany, Lori from Colorado Springs, KiKi from Miami, Courtnee from Pensacola…."

The women all lined up on the stage. Alex chuckled as it reminded him of the "Miss America" pageant he'd been forced to watch when he was younger.

"Candi from Greensboro, Jennie from Billings, Missy from Los Angeles, Sammi from Albuquerque…"

Alex sat forward in his chair and leaned in closer to the screen. That last woman…Sammi…she didn't look like the other contestants. For one, he hadn't noticed her earlier when he'd been watching everyone mingle. He wondered where she'd been. She was also dressed much differently than everyone else. She had on a pair of jeans. They weren't torn or ratty, but looked well-worn and comfortable…something she certainly didn't look like. If Alex wasn't mistaken, it looked like she was blushing. It was hard to tell from the little screen he was looking at and the distance the camera was from her, but it was definitely surprising. The producer was continuing the introductions…

"Wendi from Las Vegas, Nikki from Seattle, Amy from El Paso, and last but not least Kathi from Knoxville. Remember these faces, everyone, these are our new contestants for our show called "Love in the Outback.""

Alex groaned. *Man, that name sucks.* Hopefully he could talk to them and get them to change it. Alex watched the women walk off the stage. His eyes kept going to the woman in the jeans. He bet she felt self-conscious and out of place. He couldn't remember her name, but because of her differences she'd caught his eye. It was definitely going to be an interesting few weeks.

Chapter Four

The next morning, Sam went downstairs with her two bags to gather before meeting their transportation. The other women slowly started entering the ballroom they were to wait in. Most were dragging their bags and they all had at least two full sized suitcases, plus numerous other small handbags.

I hope we do end up camping, Sam thought to herself viciously, *it would serve them right if they had to haul their bags all over the Outback.*

Eddie came into the room and gleefully announced, "Okay, everyone, our transportation is here, but there's room for only one bag for each of you, plus one carry on. You'll need to go through your belongings and make sure you only bring the essentials that can fit into one suitcase. You have ten minutes before we'll be leaving."

The look on everyone's face was priceless. Panic, sheer terror, moved through the women like a stadium full of fans doing the wave. Sam watched as the women flung their bags down and started throwing their clothes out and around them, searching for what they thought they *had* to have.

"Should I bring my silk camisole?" Candi asked no one and everyone as she shuffled through her clothes.

"I *have* to bring my hair dryer and curling iron," Wendi shrieked as she tried to stuff more and more of her belongings into one suitcase that was already full to the brim.

"This isn't fair!" wailed Kimmie. "Why didn't they tell us this last night?"

Sam was leaning against the wall, enjoying the discomfort of everyone when Missy looked up and noticed that she wasn't unpacking.

"What's wrong with you, Miss Bitch?" she asked nastily, getting the attention of most of the other women in the room. "You only brought one suitcase to begin with? What, can't you afford designer clothes? Probably not since you wore those horrible jeans last night and have them on again today. Are we going to have to look at you in the same clothes every day until you're kicked off? Hopefully you brought clean underwear!"

With that, she started to laugh hysterically at her own joke. Her laugh was loud and braying. Sam looked around and saw most of the other girls were either laughing outright or at least smirking as they continued to rifle through their own belongings. Sam finally answered Missy.

"I figured since we were going to the Outback we'd probably not have the opportunity to wear much Gucci or Prada, but if we do, I'm sure you'll point out my deficiencies." Somehow Sam made it sound offhand and flippant, when inside she was hoping the first person would be kicked off before the bus left, and that it'd be Missy.

Eddie came back into the room in exactly ten minutes and started trying to herd everyone out of the room. It looked like a disaster area. There were clothes everywhere. Some of the women were still trying to close their suitcases, which were bulging at the seams with way too many clothes. The random TV employees had to help zip up and close suitcases before they were herded out to a large bus. Sam chuckled. She knew many of the other women were hoping they'd be brought to the place they'd be staying in stretch limousines. Or maybe like the other reality show that was set in the Outback, they'd be skydiving to their destination. But a bus...how plain, how...normal!

Sam overheard the women speculating the night before about what the house they'd be living in would look like. In most of the other reality shows she'd seen, the house was beautiful. There were always tons of bedrooms that looked like they were sets for a magazine. There were usually fish tanks and a professional chef-kitchen as well. Sam hoped they wouldn't all be in the same room. She could barely tolerate most of the women for the time the introductions took place last night, there was no way she'd be able to handle living with all of them 24/7!

With their bags stowed under the bus, everyone took their seats. Sam always liked to sit in the front of a bus. She could see where they were going and ever since she'd seen the movie *Speed* she imagined that if the driver was ever killed or injured, she could heroically take over and save the day. Silly, but she was a romantic at heart. She'd watched that movie a hundred times. When Keanu and Sandra had slid out of the bus together, lain in the dirt and stared into each other's eyes…whew…that was her favorite part.

Sam looked at the driver. She couldn't really tell what he looked like. What was obvious was that he wasn't Keanu Reeves. She huffed a laugh at herself under her breath. As if a movie star would be driving a bus in the middle of Australia.

When the signal was given by a woman standing outside, the bus driver started up the bus and drove off. The producer wasn't onboard with them, but there was a woman with a camera. The show had started.

* * *

Sam was dozing off when she heard "Hey, Sammi."

She looked over to her left and one of the women…Lori from Colorado Springs, Sam thought, was talking to her.

"Hey, Sammi, where do you think we're going? When do you think we'll get to meet the guy?" At least one of the women was being friendly. Sam was starting to think she'd be a total outcast.

"Um, I'm not sure. I think these shows are all about making us try to guess stuff. As for when we'll meet the guy, we'll probably meet him before we know we're meeting him. These reality shows love to give the guy a sneak peak of his pickings." Sam laughed at herself and then couldn't stop herself from saying next, "Do we know that we're competing for a *man*? Maybe it's a woman."

Lori looked horrified, obviously that possibility hadn't occurred to her.

"I'm just kidding, Lori. I'm sure it'll be a guy." Sam had to remind herself to try to rein in her sarcasm. Not everyone appreciated it, and she didn't think the other women would be like Beth and Christina and join in.

Lori looked relieved that Sam thought they'd be meeting a guy after all and nodded her head, then said, "You're probably right about when we get to meet him. I'd better make sure I look all right then, never know when he'll pop in."

Lori proceeded to take out a small pocket mirror and repair her already perfect makeup. *At least she was semi-friendly,* Sam thought to herself, *even if a little self-absorbed.*

Alex tried to control his smirk. Driving the bus wasn't hard. Not that he'd ever done it before, but he was given a short and fast lesson the night before. He was to drive the women to their lodging. He was able to watch all the women climb on the bus and overhear their conversations. Most were complaining about the fact they had to leave some of their shoes and fancy clothes behind. Others were complaining about having to travel by bus. He knew they expected something fancier. Some of the women didn't say anything as they climbed on board.

Once again he noticed that the woman called Sammi stood out like a beacon of light in the darkness. She wasn't wearing designer clothes and he didn't think she was even wearing makeup. She certainly wasn't model beautiful, now that he could see her close up, but she was easy on his eyes. She didn't flaunt her body as some of the other women did. In fact, it was hard to tell what she looked like under the baggy T-shirt she was wearing.

Since Sammi and Lori were sitting in the seats closest to the driver, Alex could overhear their conversation easily. He almost broke his cover when he heard Sammi's comment about him maybe being a woman. He changed his laugh to a cough at the last second. He wasn't above using sarcasm on occasion and it was refreshing to hear someone being real. Sammi did have the producers pegged, though. She'd obviously seen enough reality shows to know some of the tricks. But he thought that even she'd be surprised to learn that he was the "guy" they would meet later that night. He wondered if any of the other women had any idea about what was in store for them. He'd bet Sammi had some ideas.

They'd been on the bus for a couple of hours when he pulled up to a desolate area that had been scoped out in advance. Alex heard one of the women say, "Oh no, please tell me they aren't going to dump us here in the middle of nowhere!" Eddie, who'd been following the bus in an air conditioned limo, climbed aboard the bus and announced that each woman was going to do an introductory video for the bachelor. The order in which the videos were taped was the order the bachelor was going to watch them.

Before he could continue, Jennie called out, "I want to be first!" And just like that pandemonium erupted.

There were shouts of, "No fair!" and, "I want to be last" and, "That's dumb!" Finally Eddie quieted everyone down and explained that the order the bachelor would watch the videos would be determined by the women themselves. They had to work together and come up with a way to figure out who would speak first, second, and so forth. They had twenty minutes to work it out.

Sam heard Eddie chuckling as he left the bus. It was obvious the producer was loving the angst he was causing and was already imaging how it would play off on television.

Missy immediately stood up and said, "Okay, everyone, we need someone in charge and I think I'm the best person." Sam rolled her eyes as Missy continued. "So I want everyone who wants to be first to go to the front of the bus. Everyone that wants to be last, go to the back of the bus. If someone doesn't care, go to the middle of the bus."

Sam thought it was actually a good way to at least start the process. After all, they only had twenty minutes to decide. Sam went to the middle of the bus. She honestly didn't care. She didn't think the guy would even notice her with all the other women. There were two women who came to the middle of the bus with her. Amy and Nikki also claimed they didn't care where they went in the video introductions. There were eight women who wanted to be first and another five who wanted to be last. They figured they'd have the best chance to be remembered by the bachelor.

The bickering continued. Sam sat in the middle and halfway listened to both sides of the bus. She glanced up at one point and found the driver intently staring into the mirror over his head. Sam chuckled to herself. *Must be quite a sight to see all these beauties with their claws out.* It seemed as if the back of the bus had figured out their order, but the front was still pretty heated about whether Missy or Jennie were going to be first. Eddie came back on board and told everyone to get off and to line up in the order of who was going where. Sam, Amy, and Nikki didn't know where they were going, so they just got in the middle of each group and figured it was good enough. Missy finally got her way and stood at the front of the line with a smirk. The producer told them they were going to get back on the bus and do the videos one at a time with the camera operator.

Sam waited patiently for her turn. She squatted down in the shade of the bus and closed her eyes. It was a bit warm outside—a lot warm if you listened to the other women—but it was very peaceful, which was something Sam wasn't used to. Finally it was Sam's turn. She'd heard all about the things the other women said in their video. They'd bragged about how they knew they were going to catch the guy's attention with their videos. Sam still had no idea what she was going to say. She'd thought about it the entire time she was waiting for her turn, but still hadn't thought of anything witty or eye-catching. As she stepped on the bus she saw the bus driver slumped in his seat with his hat pulled down over his eyes. It looked like he was sleeping soundly. *Those other videos must not have been that exciting.* Sam chuckled.

Sam sat down on the seat as the camerawoman settled across from her. "I'm not really sure where to start," Sam said to the camerawoman, whose name she finally learned was Kina.

"Just introduce yourself and tell the bachelor what makes you special," Kina responded. Sam took a deep breath and when she saw the red light on the camera started.

"Hi. My name is Sammi and I live in Albuquerque, New Mexico. I'm not sure what I'm really supposed to say here, it's like a blind date…really blind on my part since I have no idea who you are." Sammi shifted uncomfortably in her seat and cleared her throat as she continued.

"I'm not sure what you'd want to know about me. I'm thirty-three years old and I rent a small house in the Four Hills area of Albuquerque…oh…I forgot…you probably don't know where that is. It's on the east side of the city near the Interstate. Um, I love animals, especially dogs…in fact, I have three…two basset hounds and a bloodhound. They're all rescues, I got the bassets from Arizona Basset Hound Rescue and their names are Blue and Albert, and the bloodhound I got from the local shelter and his name is Duke…um…I'm not sure what else interesting there is about me…I'm not allowed to talk about what I do for a living, so um…"

Sam looked around the bus for some inspiration as to what she should say next. Of course, all she saw was the bus seats and the driver, who looked like he was snoring in the front seat.

"Um…so I like to sit in the front seat of the bus…I usually won't ever sit further back than the second seat and it's all because of the movie *Speed*. It had Sandra Bullock in it…anyway, so in the movie, Sandra's character saved the day when she took over driving the bus when the driver was wounded. I've always thought that would be something I could do, so just in case, I sit near the front so I can take over…"

Sam paused, then looked at Kina and asked, "Can I say cut?"

Kina looked up from the viewfinder, cut the camera and said, "What's up?"

"Okay, I know this is supposed to be reality TV and be live and all of that, but that story just made me sound like the biggest dork in the world…can we please rewind it and let me say something else? I'd just die if the guy heard that."

Kina chuckled and said, "Sure, some of the others wanted to re-do their bits too, not a big deal."

Sam sighed with relief and said more to herself than to Kina, "Okay, now I just have to figure out what I *do* want to say."

Kina lifted the camera back up and the red light came back on. Show time.

"Okay, so you know where I live and that I live with three fur kids…I guess one question that sometimes gets asked in awkward moments when people don't know what to say to someone is 'what would you do if you won the lottery?' Let's see…I'd most likely quit my job, I'd tell you what I do, but then the producer would have to kill me." Sam chuckled at herself and then continued, "But I'd want to do something. There's no way I could just sit at home every day. I'd go stir crazy. I would probably donate money or put money in a trust of some sort for some of the rescue groups that help animals and dogs. There are so many unwanted dogs and the rescue groups do so much with so little. It'd be nice to be able to spread that wealth around a bit and be able to help more animals." Sam laughed. "I probably sound like a do-gooder, but it's not my fault…you try thinking of something interesting to tell someone you've never met! I hope you have a good time with this show, and that you meet someone you could consider spending the rest of your life with. I'm looking forward to meeting you."

Sam looked into the camera expectantly. Kina turned it off and lowered the large lens. "All done?" she asked.

"Yup, I suppose that's as good as it's going to be," Sam responded, blushing. "Just promise you'll edit that stupid story out before it gets shown on National TV!" Kina laughed, as Sam wanted her to, and she got up and stepped off the bus. After she left, Kina met Alex's eyes, which were now open and looking in the mirror over the driver's seat again.

"That was interesting," Kina told him. "Much different than the other ones."

Alex agreed, Sammi not only looked different, but she was a breath of fresh air. Most of the other women talked about how they liked to shop and where they liked to eat, and all of the important people they knew. Some almost stripped off their tops and showed their cleavage throughout the video. And that story about the bus…Alex knew Sammi would be mortified to know that he was the "guy" and that he'd heard that story. He'd already heard a short version of it when she was talking to Lori in the front seat, but hearing it again made her seem a bit more "human" and down to earth. Everyone had fantasies and in a small way Sammi was ready to fulfill hers. Alex sighed…not too many more of these videos to sit through and they'd be on their way.

After a couple of hours, and after each of the women got to record their introduction, they were finally on their way again. Sam had a headache. Listening to the other women was exhausting and irritating. They asked the same questions over and over and had the same complaints. It was too hot, when would they get there, where were they going, when were they going to meet the bachelor…why couldn't they just go-with-the-flow? The producers would bring forth the guy when they were darn good and ready, and not one second earlier.

Finally, they pulled up to what looked like would've been an old Girl or Boy Scout camp if they were in the U.S. There were a few trees and what looked like a fire circle and three small buildings.

They all filed off the bus toward the buildings. The two outer buildings were large open rooms that were filled with bunk beds. Obviously they'd reached the end of the bus ride. This was where they'd be staying. The other smaller building was the toilets. There were two toilet pits with two small sinks. There was also one shower head that looked like it had seen better days.

There wasn't a lot being said by the other women. It was obvious this was not what they expected or wanted. Sam laughed inside. It was perfect. It was what she'd somewhat expected and it was hilarious now that she'd met the other contestants. The sound of the bus starting up and driving away had all the women turning toward where the bus once stood. All of the luggage was sitting on the side of the road. It looked like it had been abandoned, except for the fact that most of it was designer brands. The women went and collected their bags, then started to drag them toward the bunks. There was some discussion about who would sleep where, but most of the women were tired, hot, and cranky, not caring much at the moment about where they'd sleep.

Alex drove the bus about five miles down the road to where the main camp for the show was set up. Since he'd be allowed to see any footage of the women that he wanted, the show decided they might as well save some money and let him stay in the main camp with the other television personnel. It was a bit better than where the contestants were staying, but the bunk beds were still in evidence. Alex was allowed his own small tent a bit off to the side of the rest of the production company.

Alex went to his room and lay down on his bed to think about the first day. The women were everything he could've hoped for. They were beautiful, slender, and easy on the eyes, but after listening to them talk to each other and having to listen to their boring conversations all day, he was ready to turn his back on the entire project. What did the people that cast this show do? Give an IQ test and only choose women who scored low? Sure, they were all pretty, but he'd reached a point in his life where he wanted more. He wasn't sure he was ready to settle down and get married yet, but he also needed more than a pretty face, he wanted intelligent conversation as well. Not all of the women were horrible, he conceded, but man, this was going to be a tough road.

While Alex remembered the crazy videos, his mind went back to Sammi. He didn't even know her, but her face kept coming to his mind. She had a funny sense of humor and a crooked smile. Alex had never believed in love at first sight, and he still didn't think he did, but there was just something about her that he couldn't put out of his mind.

Suddenly, Eddie knocked on his door and walked in. "What'd ya think, Alex?" he boomed. "Quite a field to choose from, huh?"

"Uh yeah, they certainly are interesting," Alex mumbled.

"Here's the thing," Eddie said with a sly smirk on his face. "We're going to start off the day tomorrow by kicking one of them off."

"Already?" Alex exclaimed. "I haven't even met them officially yet!"

"We know," Eddie cackled. "We're going to pretend it's a random thing, but we want you to choose tonight who you want gone. You're going to have most of the choices throughout this process, even if the women don't know it, so think about it and let me know in about an hour who it's gonna be, so we can set it up." And with that he was gone.

How am I going to choose? Alex didn't really know these women, and he was supposed to get rid of one already? But then he knew. He'd sat through the video and couldn't believe Wendi was saying the things that she was and that she'd practically invited herself to move in with him after the show was over. She'd also insulted and belittled some of the other contestants in her video as well. He didn't think he could even pretend to like her when he met her for real. Wendi had to go. Alex figured maybe it was because she was from Vegas, it was a cutthroat kind of town, and Alex had no desire to even go down that road. When the producer came back about an hour later, Alex told him his choice and Eddie left, already talking on the phone with someone, organizing Wendi's exit.

Tomorrow would definitely be an interesting day for everyone.

Chapter Five

The next morning was interesting. There were sixteen women trying to cram into the small bathroom building, all trying to use the mirror to do their hair and makeup, not to mention the rush for the shower…until they found out there wasn't any hot water. Most of the women decided they didn't need a shower after all. Sam found the entire situation pretty amusing. Since the shower wasn't being used because there wasn't any hot water, Sam took a quick dunk and washed her hair. She then went back to her bunk, got dressed, brushed her hair, twisted it up into a barrette, and she was ready to face the day. It took her about half an hour to get ready, so she was ready quite a bit ahead of the others. She decided she'd explore a little around the campsite before things got started. The cameramen and women were busy filming the women who were still trying to get ready and didn't notice when Sam slipped out of the camp.

Sam observed that their camp seemed to be at the bottom of a slight rise. She started walking up the hill to see what was on the other side. When she got to the top she stopped and stared…it was beautiful. It'd be the kind of place she'd love to build a house. She was staring out at the Outback. She couldn't believe she was actually here.

The sun had already come up and everything had a slight orange tint to it. There were rolling hills, trees, open spaces that looked like desert, and there was even a creek or river or something in the distance. The sounds of animals were loud. She had no idea what animals were making the sounds, but it was beautiful. Sam sat down on a nearby rock. What an unbelievable sight. If nothing else, she was glad she'd been chosen for this silly show just so she could see this. Sam sat there just drinking in the sight of the land in front of her for a while, when suddenly she heard a commotion back at camp. She reluctantly rose and started back down the hill. It looked like the show would be getting started today after all.

When she arrived back at the camp the other women were running around frantically. Eddie was there. Courtnee told Sam as she ran past that they had five minutes to meet at the flat open space near the fire circle. Finally all the women were lined up in two rows around the host of the show. This was a man they hadn't met before. His name, they were told, was Robert. He was tall and good-looking in a movie star way. He didn't interact with the other women until the camera turned on him and Eddie said, "roll." Suddenly, his entire face lit up in a wide smile.

"Welcome, ladies. I'm Robert. I'll be your host for this dating journey you're about to embark on. Later today you will meet the bachelor and I'm sure you'll be impressed and excited." Robert paused dramatically, then continued, "But first there is one piece of business we have to attend to. As you know, at random times during the next few weeks one of you will be leaving the show." Some of the women let out disappointed moans as if on cue.

"I know, I know," Robert commiserated, "but it can't be helped. In fact, one of you will be going home today, right now as a matter of fact."

There were shocked gasps from the group of women. Comments like, "No way!" and, "I can't believe it" and, "That isn't fair" and, "We haven't even met the bachelor yet" were heard.

Sam couldn't help it. She laughed out loud at the ridiculousness of it all and got quite a few glares from the other women.

"I know you're wondering how this will be done since you haven't even met the bachelor yet. Since we want

this game to be as fair as possible and since most of you
don't even know each other, we're going to draw names out
of a hat. If your name is drawn, you're safe, if your name is
the last one left, then you'll be going back home."

It's perfect, Sam thought, *totally random and
objective.* She wondered if this would be her last day in the
Outback. She didn't really care about the guy, after all she
hadn't even met him yet, but it was such a beautiful place,
it'd be a shame not to get to see more than this little
campsite, especially after her time on the rise. Another part
of her, a part she wouldn't admit to if asked, wanted to see
the guy. She figured all women had a fantasy of being
chosen above others, and she was no exception. She shook
herself and forced herself to pay attention.

"Okay," Robert continued, "Here's the hat. I'd like
for each of you to come forward and take your name and
place it into the hat." The hat was a big ten gallon cowboy
hat. The names were elaborate name plates that were the
kind of thing that would sit on someone's desk at work. They
were black plastic with big white letters.

What a cheesy prop. Sam thought as she got in line to
grab her nameplate and put it in the hat. *I guess I won't be
crumpling up my piece of paper.* She placed her name in
with the others. Sam had a trick she used in various raffles
that she'd participated in. She knew that if you crumpled up
your ticket, it was more likely to be chosen because it would
feel different than the others in the mix. There was no
possibility of these plastic pieces being crumpled, though,
darn it.

Slowly, Robert started calling out names.

"Katie, Nikki, Kimmie, Cindee…" After each name
was called the camera zoomed in on the woman as she
stepped away from the others and walked to a separate
platform. Robert continued, "Lori, Kiki, Courtnee, Kathi,
Missy, Candi…" Sam thought she saw Candi actually tearing
up as she stepped to the new platform. *Give me a break.* Sam
thought. *She doesn't even* know *the guy yet!* Five more
names to be called. Sam started to get a bit nervous. She

really didn't want to be the first person to leave the show. It was too much like getting picked last at kickball when she was in elementary school. She didn't want to be the first loser. "Amy, Brandi..." Sam held her breath. "Sammi..." *Thank God.* Sam thought as she took her place on the other platform.

There were now only three women left on the other platform. All three looked like they were going to cry.

"Ashley," Robert called as he pulled one more piece of paper from the hat. Ashley squealed and ran over to the other platform and hugged Candi. Sam inwardly rolled her eyes at their antics. The only two women who were left were Wendi and Jennie. Sam couldn't help but feel a bit sorry for them. It certainly wouldn't be any fun to be in their situation. Finally, after making a dramatic speech about fate and choices, Robert pulled the last name out of the hat.

"Jennie." Wendi would be the first contestant to be leaving the show. Wendi didn't say a word. She just turned around and walked toward the bunkhouse. Robert didn't look like he knew what he was supposed to do in response. Sam figured they were probably supposed to all go over and console Wendi and it was supposed to be a big cry fest. *Whatever.*

Eddie and the other staff assisted Wendi in packing her belongings and she was whisked out of the campsite fairly rapidly. The women weren't sure what they were supposed to be doing next when the producer asked them all to climb back on the bus. They all trudged back to the bus they'd ridden in yesterday like good little contestants. Sam, once again, claimed the front seat. She absently noticed that today's driver was a different man than the one who'd driven them to the camp the day before. He wasn't nearly as buff as the first driver. Sam shook her head at herself. Really. Now she was lusting after the bus driver? She needed to get a life!

They were driven to an area next to a small river. It wasn't too far across, maybe about twelve feet. Sam wasn't sure how deep it was as the water was a bit murky. When they got off the bus, Robert was once again standing around.

He'd ridden in a separate car and was getting his face makeup touched up. *So much for reality.* Sam thought snidely.

The women were instructed to stand in their two lines again on a portable podium that was set up for them. Once they were all in place, Robert stepped up to his place in front of the podium and started to speak.

"Today is the day you'll meet our bachelor. He's looking forward to getting to know you. He's watched all of your videos and is anxious to meet you. Instead of having a large meet and greet, as is normal for shows like this, today we are going to have a contest." Most of the women groaned. "*Some* of you will get to meet him today. The others will have to wait until another day. I'm sure you all know how important it is to get to know the bachelor, since in the future he'll be deciding who stays and who goes."

The women immediately started talking to each other. Robert allowed this for a while as it was a good dramatic effect to his announcement.

That's sneaky. Sam thought to herself. *Make us compete against each other to see who'll get to meet him first and make an impression.* Sam decided there was no way she was going to get into a pissing match with the other women. There would be plenty of time for her to meet the guy and she wasn't going to get caught in the middle of any catfight. That had never been her style and it wasn't going to change now.

Robert continued his speech, "Each of you will have ten minutes to follow the path," Robert said as he pointed to a wide swath of dirt that continued along the river. "At the end of the path there's a large barrel filled with water. You have to reach in and grab one fish, then bring it back down the path and place it into your pail here. Since there are fifteen of you, we will run in heats of three. There is only one barrel and there are twenty fish in the barrel. The eight women that collect the most fish will get to meet the bachelor today. The rest of you will go back to the camp and meet him at a later time."

Complete silence greeted Robert at the end of his speech. But then the women started talking amongst themselves, trying to come up with the best strategy. *This is so corny, but it ought to be funny to watch these women run in their heels!*

The heats were announced. First up would be Kathi, Nikki, and Missy. Heat Two would be Candi, Kiki, and Cindee. Heat Three would be Kimmie, Katie, and Amy. Heat Four would be Sammi, Jennie, and Courtnee, and the last heat would be Lori, Ashley, and Brandi.

Eddie and other TV employees quickly got the first heat ready to go. The course was already set up so it wasn't long before Kathi, Nikki, and Missy were off and running along the path. Since the other contestants couldn't see what was going on at the barrel it was a surprise to see Missy coming running back with a fish...and soaking wet! It looked like she'd dived headfirst into the barrel. The other women giggled uneasily, knowing their turn would come in the not too distant future. Not far behind her was Nikki, and she was also wet. The race continued. Missy was obviously determined to get the most fish. The final total at the end of the ten minutes was Missy with eleven fish, Nikki with six and Kathi with only three.

Heat two and three were much of the same. Candi, Katie, and Kiki had eight fish each. Cindee had four, Kimmie and Amy each had six. During heat three, Kimmie and Amy were both racing back to their buckets with their last fish and time was quickly winding down when Kimmie slipped on the path and almost fell into the river. Her fish went flying over the path and Kimmie went sprawling after it. She was fine, and she was able to get up and deposit her fish in her bucket before time was up, but it was a sobering moment for everyone. She could have really gotten hurt. By now, the path was wet from the earlier heats and was starting to turn into slippery mud. It wasn't inconceivable that someone could come around the corner and slip and fall into the river. It wouldn't be deadly, the river wasn't that deep, and wasn't moving very swiftly. There also weren't many rocks around the side of the river, but it certainly wouldn't be a pleasant fall.

It was heat four's turn. Sam, Jennie, and Courtnee were racing down the path toward the bucket. Sam suddenly understood why the women were all wet when they came back with their fish. The bucket was filled to the rim with water and was about three and a half feet tall. In order to reach the fish that were "camped out" at the bottom, you had to lean all the way in and put your head under the water in order to reach the fish. Jennie was the first to arrive at the bucket.

She soon had her first fish and was heading back to the pail to deposit it. Courtnee was next and she also came up with her first fish and was off and running. Sam was in no hurry to get her fish and head back. She stood there, looking down at the fish in the barrel. It was actually kinda sad. She knew that fish were killed every day, but this was different, these fish weren't going to be eaten, they were being killed for a stupid TV show.

Slowly, Sam took a deep breath and reached in and grabbed one of the fish. It was surprisingly heavy and very slippery. She heard Jennie running back up the path for her second fish. Sam headed down the path toward her pail. She didn't want it to look like she was deliberately not trying to win, but this was ridiculous. She put her fish in the pail. Then she picked up the pail and walked toward the river. She bent down and filled it with water, then carried it back to the clearing. If she was going to have to collect these fish, she was going to keep them alive until the ten minutes were over and then she was going to set them free into the river again.

After about eight minutes, most of the fish had been collected. Jennie and Courtnee were neck and neck in the fish department. There were two fish left in the barrel. Sam retrieved one of them and was headed back down the path toward her pail when Jennie and Courtnee came running up the path. They were both determined that they were going to get that last fish. Whoever got it would be the heat winner with eight. As it happened, Sam, Courtnee, and Jennie reached the bend in the path at the same time. Sam couldn't move out of the way fast enough and when Jennie brushed past her on her way to the barrel Sam lost her balance and slipped down that same slope that Kimmie almost went down. But this time, Sam went sliding into the river.

It's cold, was Sam's first thought as she went under. The water wasn't very deep, maybe about four and a half feet, but it was freezing. Sam looked up at the path and saw Kina pointing her camera down at her. *Great, just great, I know this is going to make the show.* Since the fish she'd been carrying was long gone, having been dropped as she tumbled into the river, Sam looked up at the bank and tried to climb up. She figured out pretty quickly that she wasn't going to be able to get back up to the path the way she'd come. It was pretty steep and covered with mud and rocks. Sam knew there were rocks under the mud because she could feel her side throbbing. She'd obviously scraped herself on those rocks on her way down. In order to get out of the river she'd have to go upstream and see if she could make her way back to the clearing and climb out that way.

She heard Jennie and Courtnee go running back down the path making enough noise to wake the dead. It sounded like Jennie had retrieved the last fish because Courtnee was bitching that Jennie had cheated as she followed her down the path toward their pails. They didn't even notice her down in the river as they were concentrating on the sound of Robert's voice counting down the time.

With Kina still filming, Sam started making her way back upstream. It was slow going since she slipped on hidden rocks every few feet. Sam was really starting to get cold. She wished she could ask Kina for help, but she knew the rules…she had to pretend the cameras didn't exist. Finally, she made her way to the clearing where everyone turned to stare at her.

"What are you doing?" Brandi asked incredulously.

"I thought I'd take a swim," Sam replied sarcastically while climbing out at a slope leading down into the river, dripping water all the way up the bank. When no one said anything else, Sam finally said, "I slipped." She then turned to Robert and asked, "Are all my fish counted?" When Robert answered affirmatively, she walked to her bucket, picked it up and walked back to the stream.

"What are you doing now?" Brandi asked again.

"What does it look like?" Sam responded with a bite to her tone. "My fish are counted, there's no need to let them die needlessly." And with that she emptied the pail into the river and watched her four fish swim away.

The last heat went off without a hitch. Lori and Brandi each retrieved eight fish and Ashley got four. The women who'd get to meet the bachelor that day were Missy with eleven fish, Candi, Katie, Kiki, Jennie, Lori, and Brandi, who all had eight fish, and Courtnee who had retrieved seven fish. Sam didn't really care. She was cold and wet and she knew she'd scraped her side pretty good on her way down the incline into the river. All she wanted to do was get back to camp and take a shower, even if it was a cold one, then get into clean clothes. But Robert had another surprise up his sleeve.

"Okay, ladies, everyone did a good job in collecting their fish. If the eight of you who retrieved the most fish would come with me, it's time to meet the bachelor." At his statement words of protest rang out.

"No *way*," Missy complained loudly. "I'm sopping wet, my makeup is gone and my hair looks horrible. This isn't fair...I want to go and change first." The other ladies agreed. Robert stood and looked at the group of women. They really did look bedraggled. He smirked.

"Okay, you have a choice, the eight of you who collected the fish can either come right now to meet the bachelor, or you can go back to the camp and meet him first thing in the morning. If you choose to meet him in the morning, the other seven women will go right now and meet him. It's up to you."

Sam laughed inside. These reality shows really were full of twists and turns. She wasn't sure what decision the winners would make. She knew they really wanted to meet the guy first, but they also wanted to make a good impression and showing up as they were wouldn't do that. But on the other hand, they really didn't want anyone *else* to be able to get to him first. It really was going to be a tough choice. Sam hoped they'd let their greediness get the better of them. She really, *really* wanted to go back to camp. It wasn't that she didn't want to meet the guy looking like she did, she was just cold and miserable. And fixing that came before a man. She probably wouldn't have been so cold, but the sun had disappeared during their little competition, and with the loss of the sun went the loss of much of the heat of the day.

The eight women were huddled together a bit away from the camp. The ever-present Kina hovered as close as she could with the camera. Sam tried to ignore her, she hadn't quite gotten the hang of ignoring the cameras, but she figured by the time this show was over she wouldn't even think twice about them being around.

The women who hadn't won the contest could all hear a bit of the conversation the winners were having every now and then, but for the most part they were being pretty quiet, all things considered. Finally Missy stood up. Since she retrieved the most fish, she obviously felt like she was in charge.

"For the record, we don't think this is fair. We won the competition fair and square and you tricked us," she said loudly. "But we've decided that we'd rather put our best foot forward tomorrow morning and meet the bachelor then. The *losers* can meet him now the way they are."

Of course the last was said with such distain it was impossible to miss. So the eight winning women climbed back on the bus and were taken back to camp. The seven women that were left standing in the clearing giggled nervously. They weren't happy at having to meet the bachelor looking like they were either, but they were a little less wet, except for Sam, than the others because they didn't retrieve as many fish from the barrel.

They were instructed to sit and wait. Next thing they knew there was a team of people setting up a table and mini-work stations. The fish were brought out by a crew of chefs. The chefs immediately started preparing them to be cooked. Sam laughed. *We're going to have quite the meal! At least the fish didn't die in vain.* It was hard to get excited about it, though, since her jeans were molded to her body with river water, her side hurt from where it was scraped, and she was so cold. She was glad the fish would be eaten—she assumed they'd be cooking the fish from the contest—and not just die for the sake of the contest and the show.

The women sat together and watched the meal being prepared. They tried to finger comb their hair back into some semblance of a hairstyle. Because of the dry air their hair was mostly dry when they heard from behind them, "Hello, ladies."

It was the guy!

Chapter Six

The women all abruptly stood up and turned around. It was time to meet the bachelor. Sam slowly stood up and faced the man she'd been calling "the guy" in her mind. He was tall, about six feet tall. He was wearing a pair of gently worn jeans and a blue long sleeve collared shirt. He had on cowboy boots and a cowboy hat. Sam couldn't really see the color of his hair, but his eyes were a deep chocolate brown. He had what looked like laugh lines around his eyes.

The ever present Robert spoke then, "Ladies, I'd like to introduce you to our bachelor, Al. Al is from Austin, Texas, and owns his own ranching operation outside of the city. He's thirty-eight years old and has never been married. He likes to hunt, fish, camp, and work with animals. He's an expert horseman and I feel confident he'll keep you safe out here in the wilds of the Outback. I'll leave the seven of you to get acquainted. In four hours I'll return to take you back to camp. Ladies. Al." And with that, Robert turned around and left the clearing.

Alex thought it was amusing that first of all, they'd shortened his name. Never in his thirty-eight years had anyone ever dared to call him Al. He guessed the producers wanted to try to preserve some of his privacy when the show finally did air. At least that was what he hoped, otherwise he had no idea why they'd shorten his name to something ridiculous. He also chuckled at the spin they put on his life. He did like to hunt and do the other things Robert said, and he was an expert horseman, but he knew with the outfit he was wearing, it would produce erroneous assumptions about what he did for a living.

Ashley immediately walked over to Al and introduced herself.

"Hi, my name is Ashley. I'm from Toledo, Ohio. It's great to finally meet you. We've been very excited, you're even better looking than I could've imagined. It must be great to own your own ranch!" Alex chuckled to himself. He knew that with that introduction they'd assume he was rich and owned a big ranch.

"Nice to meet you, Ashley," Alex responded neutrally.

One by one the other women lined up to meet Al. They all said where they were from and gushed on and on about how happy they were to meet him. Finally, it was Sam's turn. She held out her hand, shook the guy's hand and simply said, "Sammi" by way of introduction. Alex's mouth turned up in the corners.

"That's it?" he asked with a smile.

"Yup," Sam replied. "What ya see is what ya get."

With that Alex took the time to look up and down Sam's body. He noticed her jeans seemed to be wet, while her hair was dry. He couldn't help but notice her curves. Her jeans were molded to her body, allowing him to see that she was all woman. The blouse she was wearing was also clinging to her body. Sam had her arms crossed defensively in front of her, but that just pushed her breasts up, making them more noticeable. Alex didn't usually ogle women, but damn, this woman had a body that was built to be ogled. His eyes made it back up from his perusal of her body to her face and saw she was blushing. When was the last time he'd seen a woman blush from just a look?

His mind went back to the fact that her jeans were wet. None of the other women's clothes were clinging to them as hers were. None of the other women seemed to be as soaked as she was. And now that he thought about it, when he shook her hand, it was ice cold.

"You seem to be a bit wet," he said with one eyebrow raised up in a question.

"Had a little incident earlier, it was nothing," Sam replied, turned around and went back to sit on a log. She was too embarrassed to get into it. If she hadn't been so clumsy and if she'd paid more attention to what was going on, she wouldn't be in this situation now. She was also embarrassed at the way Al had looked at her. She wasn't an idiot. She knew with her clothes wet, they'd cling to her. She couldn't interpret Al's look, though. She wanted to believe that he was looking at her in a flirty way, but she couldn't fathom it. As was typical for her, when she was embarrassed she retreated into herself and it usually came across as disinterest.

The other women quickly tried to manipulate Alex's conversation. Alex couldn't wait to get back to his tent and watch the tapes of what happened that day. Somehow he just knew there was more to this meeting than the women were letting on. He thought the women all looked nice, he just couldn't put his finger on why they looked different than yesterday when he saw them on the bus. As part of the "meet and greet," Alex was required to spend one-on-one time with all the women. He started with Cindee and then met in quick succession with Amy and Kimmie. They were all pleasant. He didn't have any real positive or negative thoughts about any of them so far.

After speaking with Kimmie, it was time to eat. Sam was starving. It seemed as if shivering used up a lot of energy and probably calories as well. Fish wasn't her favorite food, but at the moment she was starving and would eat anything. The platter of fish was passed around and everyone took some of the delicious smelling meat. The chefs had outdone themselves!

Sam was so hungry she just dug right in. She'd taken two large chunks of fish from the platter. It was quiet for a bit and slowly conversation started back up. Sam wasn't interested in what the other women had to say. It seemed the longer she sat out in the clearing, the colder and more miserable she got. The lack of sun and the lateness of the day made the weather cool off quickly. This was ridiculous. Eddie knew she fell in the river, why wasn't he helping her get dry clothes? She knew this was supposed to be a reality show, but so far there hadn't been too much reality from her perspective. She finally looked up and noticed everyone else had finished eating. She was the only one left. Oh well, she was hungry and she wasn't going to let the meal go to waste. Hell, they'd probably give them rice and beans to eat back at the camp!

Alex didn't want to be rude and continue his one-on-one sessions with the women until Sammi had finished eating. He thought it was unusual that she was actually eating. It was his experience that most women, when in the company of a man, just picked at their food or ate very little. Not Sammi, she'd taken a large helping of the fish and was eating it with a look of pleasure on her face. Finally, Sam pushed back her plate.

"All done," she said with a smile.

One of the chefs came and took her plate. Before he could back away, Sam touched his sleeve and said quietly, "Thank you, honestly that was the best fish I've ever eaten, whatever spices you put on it really worked well...and I don't even really like fish!"

The man laughed and said, "I'll pass the compliment on to the other chefs as well," then he backed away.

With that, Alex knew it was time to finish up the one-on-ones. He talked with Kathi, Ashley, and Nikki, and then it was time to meet with Sammi. He'd been looking forward to talking with her for some reason. He wasn't sure why. She was an odd woman. She didn't seem to fit in any better today with the other women than she did yesterday. She seemed nice enough, but he wasn't sure what to think about it all yet. He looked up as Sammi came around the tree. They were sitting a bit away from the other women in order to give him privacy as he spoke with each lady. Sammi sat down on the log about three feet away from him. Alex was surprised. All the other women had sat so close to him, they were practically in his lap.

Sam sighed. She knew this was going to come. She didn't really want to be last, but she was tired and cold and didn't feel like fighting the other women for when she would meet with him. She had to be careful, though, because Kina was right there with the camera and she didn't want to look like a pathetic loser on national television.

"Hello, Al," Sam said.

"Hello, Sammi," Alex replied.

"Good fish, didn't you think?" Sam asked.

"It was great," Alex answered.

God. Sam thought to herself. This was *not* going well. She sounded like a complete dork.

She laughed self-consciously. "Sorry, Al, I don't really know what to say being this is the first time we're really alone." With that she laughed and motioned at the camera a few feet away.

Alex laughed. "Yeah, a bit awkward. Where are you from? You never told me anyway."

"I did tell you," Sam responded.

"No, I distinctly remember you telling me your name and that was about it," Alex said with puzzlement. Where was she going with this?

"I told you in my introduction tape…didn't you watch them?" Sam asked with a smile on her face.

Alex knew that he was caught. She was right. He'd forgotten all about the tapes. He didn't need to watch them, he'd been there.

"You're right, I'd forgotten..." He searched his mind to try to remember where she said that she lived. "Albuquerque, right?"

"Yup, good memory, Al," Sam replied. "I'm surprised you can keep us all straight with our names and all."

"What do you mean?" Alex asked.

"Come on, you can't really tell me you haven't noticed," Sam asked incredulously.

"Noticed what?" Alex asked, honestly confused.

In a sing-song voice Sam answered, "Samm-i, Miss-y, Kath-i, Kimm-ie, Lor-i, Brand-i…get it now?"

Alex threw his head back and laughed until his sides hurt. He'd honestly not even noticed that all of their names ended in the "ie" sound. It was utterly ridiculous.

"I'd thought that perhaps *your* name would be something like Charlie or Bobby," Sammi said with a laugh.

And with that Alex howled with laughter again. "That would be really over the top, huh?" he asked with a grin.

Sam relaxed a bit. It seemed like Al had a pretty good sense of humor after all.

"Come here," Alex said, patting the space next to him.

Sam looked at him with her eyebrows raised and he could see the distrust come over her body. She stiffened and sat up straight on the log. He stifled a sigh, knowing he'd just made her uneasy again and ruined their camaraderie.

"I'm not going to make a pass or cop a feel," he told her gently. "I just feel like I'm shouting at you sitting all the way over there."

Sam slowly scooted over closer to Al. She could feel the warmth emanating off of him, but maybe that was because she was still cold, sitting in damp jeans in the shade. She shivered.

"Are you still cold?" Alex asked, taking her hand in his. "Holy cow, you really are cold, aren't you?" he exclaimed, looking into her face a bit closer.

Sam pulled her hand away from his and said, "I'm fine."

"You're not fine!" Alex exclaimed and went to grab her hands back, and in doing so brushed his hand against her leg. "Your jeans are still soaking wet!" he said in shock. "How long have you been walking around with wet clothes on? Tell me it hasn't been the entire time!" he demanded.

"Why do you care?" Sam bit back. "I'm fine. I said I'm fine, I'll change later." And with that, she got up and walked back into the clearing. She didn't know why it bothered her so much. Probably because she didn't like to admit to anyone any kind of discomfort or pain. She hated being sick. Always had. Hated relying on others to help her. She was an independent person, one that didn't like to be catered to. When she was little she saw girls all the time faking illnesses or injuries to get sympathy or to get out of doing different jobs. She swore she'd never be like that, and she hadn't. She only went to the doctor when she had to and she never liked to admit that she was in need of help.

But another part of her was angry at herself. Sam was attracted to Al. He was handsome. He was everything she'd ever dreamed about when she lay in bed at night thinking about finding someone to spend her life with. She had no idea why she'd been so ugly to him. There was nothing she wanted more than to snuggle into his arms and have him warm her up. But she wasn't the kind of woman men wanted to snuggle up to. She knew it. Her history had proven it time and time again. She convinced herself the only reason Al wanted to get close to her was because of the damn show and so he'd look better on camera. She sighed as she walked toward the other women. She was confused and hurting. Al confused her. Her *reaction* to Al confused her.

"Done already?" Nikki sneered when Sam reentered the clearing.

"Yup," was all Sam could get out.

She felt Al come up behind her. She was tempted to lean back against him for a moment, but common sense prevailed and she ignored him as she headed to sit back on the log with her knees drawn up, her arms looping around them.

The rest of the time seemed to drag by for Sam. She watched as the other women went through a dance with each other of trying to manipulate Al's time and attention. He did his best to try to talk evenly with everyone. Sam noticed every now and then that his eyes would meet hers, but she'd quickly look away, blushing. She didn't feel that she was on an even playing field with him and it made her feel vulnerable, which she hated. He was so obviously out of her league it wasn't funny. He owned his own ranch and was probably richer than she could imagine. Why would he look twice at her when there were all these other beautiful women to choose from? Sam wasn't feeling sorry for herself, she was just being realistic.

Finally, Robert and Eddie came back into the clearing and announced it was time to go. Alex could tell the women wanted to say goodbye individually to him, so he stood a bit away from the group and allowed each of the women to come up, make small talk, say how much they couldn't wait to see him again, and kiss him briefly. Some kissed him on the lips and others kissed him on the cheek. He was amazed because it was obvious the women felt as if it was okay to kiss him so intimately even after knowing him for sure a short time.

Once again, Sammi was last in line. She walked up to him, held out her hand and quickly, before he could say anything, told him, "Look, I'm sorry about walking away earlier. I'm not having a good day. I know I didn't make a good impression and I'm sorry about that. I'm tired, wet, and yes, cold, and all I want to do is go back and get into some warm clothes. I promise to be on my best behavior the next time we meet." Finally, she looked up and meeting Al's eyes, gave him a shy smile. God, he was gorgeous. What she would do to start over with him. Hell, what she would do to have met him in a normal situation and not on this stupid reality show.

Alex grasped Sammi's hand with both of his and tried to infuse some of his warmth into it. "It's okay, I didn't have any right to pry and I was out of line. How about if I promise to only talk about the weather and other non-threatening topics next time?" Alex asked with a smile.

Sam smiled back and said, "Deal."

Alex slowly raised her hand, kissed the back of it and let her go. He watched as she blushed a fiery red and turned away to climb into the bus.

He couldn't help but notice that she had the sexiest back-end he'd ever seen as she stepped up into the bus. She filled out her jeans in all the right ways. He'd never really thought about what "type" of woman he was interested in, but seeing Sammi step up into the bus did something to him. Alex felt himself get hard as she rounded the corner and sat down in the front seat of the bus. He took a deep breath to try to calm himself down. He'd forgotten about her penchant to sit in the front seat and wished he could tease her later about it, but he wasn't supposed to have seen that part of the tape she'd made. He thought it was interesting that she was the only one who hadn't kissed him. She wasn't even trying to catch his attention, but ironically she had by being herself. He wanted to watch the day's tape more than ever now. He wanted to know what had happened that day to make Sammi's jeans soaking wet.

Chapter Seven

Alex pushed play on the tape that Eddie gave him of that morning's contest. He knew there were several different cameras taping the women at any given time, but the tape he had in his hand was from the camera that had been on the path. He could see most of the competition because of the angle of the camera. He watched as Kathi, Nikki, and Missy raced down the lane. Missy was the first one back on the path. He had to laugh at his first glimpse of the women after their encounter with the barrel. They were dripping from head to toe, looking like bedraggled little kids. Missy raced back and forth and was obviously determined to have the most fish.

The next two heats were much of the same. He could just see the barrel the women were diving head first into and he could barely see the clearing where they were putting the fish into pails. The camera was right on the curve in the path.

The next heat was Sammi's heat. Alex watched as Jennie, Courtnee, and Sammi raced up the path. He laughed at the look on Jennie's and Courtnee's faces as they raced by. They looked determined, to say the least. Sammi was running, but it seemed to Alex that she wasn't trying very hard. The tapes were actually getting pretty boring just watching the women run back and forth. Most of the way through the fourth heat Alex finally saw why Sammi had been so cold and wet. The camera was focused on Jennie and Courtnee running back up the path. They were jostling each other to get to the barrel first. Alex couldn't see exactly what happened because the camera suddenly pointed toward the sky, but the next thing he saw was Sammi looking up at the camera from the river. He could put together the pieces and he assumed that the two running women had knocked Sammi off the path and into the river.

Sammi was standing in water that was up around her chest. She was looking up at the camera as if to ask for help, but knew none would be forthcoming. Alex's hands clenched at his side. Damn it, the other two women didn't even stop! Soon he saw Sammi make one attempt to climb up the side of the riverbank only to slide back down again in the mud. She then started to make her way upstream. Every now and then she'd look up at the camera. He chuckled at the words that were coming out of her mouth. Oh, she was muttering to herself, but some of what she was saying was loud enough to carry to the camera.

Alex heard Jennie and Courtnee run past the camera, screeching as they headed toward the clearing, but they didn't stop to help Sammi. The camera stayed focused on Sammi as she struggled to get upstream and to the clearing. Obviously, the camera operator knew where the real "money shot" was. Alex watched Sammi finally reach the clearing and get to a point where the water was only at her knees. He watched her climb out of the water, go toward one of the pails, grab it and go back to the river only to dump out the fish. He laughed then. She wasn't kidding when she'd told him she liked animals on her video tape.

Alex continued to watch and learned how the "losers" came to be the ones to meet him that day. He thought it was pretty clever of the producers, but he also made a mental note to make sure he didn't underestimate them in any way because he knew they could always turn around and do the same sort of thing to him. What he couldn't believe was that not one person offered Sammi a towel or gave her any sympathy for falling into the river. He would've thought—no, hoped, that at least some of the other women would have been sympathetic enough to care about Sammi and what had happened. Unfortunately, not one of them offered an ear, a hand, or any type of assistance.

The camera operator seemed to know that Sammi was cold because she kept panning in very close to Sammi's chattering teeth and shaking body. Alex sighed. There was nothing he could do. He wasn't even supposed to be watching the tapes for God's sake, but he wasn't the kind of man who usually let a woman suffer, even if it was only something as small as her being chilly.

Alex suddenly had to know if Sammi had managed to warm herself up and if she was all right. He was also curious to see what the other women had talked about when the ladies he met today went back to camp. He knew he'd be meeting them the next day and he wanted to have some idea of what to expect from them. Alex wandered out of his tent and over to the production tent. Eddie was still there and Alex told him, "I'd like to see a tape of what went on when the women got back to camp." Eddie didn't seem to mind and asked one of the editors for the tape.

Alex wasn't sure what to expect when he sat down to watch it. He figured the other women would be jealous, and he was right. There was a lot of interrogation that went on. The women that he didn't get to meet today asked all sorts of questions about what he looked like, what he was wearing, what he said, if he kissed any of them. Alex was surprised when Nikki claimed they'd kissed during their one-on-one session. He just shook his head. It was definitely going to be interesting to see the dynamics unfold in the ladies' camp.

The fact that he could watch these tapes was probably one of the only reasons he was still on the show. He couldn't imagine trying to wade through what was real and what was fake if he didn't have the tapes to watch. He counted himself lucky in that sense. The last thing he wanted to do was have feelings toward one of the women and then find out that it was all a lie. Eddie was a sneaky bastard and seemed to know how to push and just how far to go to make good TV.

Alex tried to catch of glimpse of Sammi on the tapes of the camp, but he didn't see her anywhere. He watched as the camera in the bathhouse caught the ladies brushing their teeth over the sinks and washing off their makeup, generally doing what women did to get ready for bed. The cameras didn't show the bathrooms at all, only the sink area, thank

God. There was no way he wanted anything to do with any type of "peeping Tom" kind of thing. He still didn't see Sammi anywhere in the group, and he found himself really looking for her.

Finally, the light went off in the bathroom camera. He knew that that camera was hooked up to the light. When the light went on, the camera started taping. Eddie and the other producers had purposely blocked all the natural light from the building so even in the middle of the day, the women had to turn the light on if they wanted to see in the small dark building. It was one more sneaky thing that had been orchestrated on the show. Alex knew he should never underestimate them. This camera was also one that Alex didn't think the ladies knew about. If they had, he was sure they'd be playing to it and watching what they said to each other and about him. He sure had gotten an earful about what his butt looked like in his jeans and about their speculation about the size of his package.

He was about to call it a night when the bathroom camera suddenly came on again. The time stamp on the video said that it was about two hours after the other women had left. It was Sammi coming into the bathroom. She looked behind her as she shut the door. It looked like she was trying to see if she'd been followed or if there was a camera anywhere around. Alex found himself leaning toward the small TV, trying to get a better view of the woman. He didn't even try to kid himself and say that he wasn't interested in her. He was.

Sammi was carrying a small case. It looked like a cosmetic bag. Alex watched as Sammi went over to one of the sinks in front of the large mirror. She looked around furtively one more time, and finding no one, took a deep breath and lifted up her T-shirt on her left side. Alex gasped at the same time that Sammi said, "Damn." There were giant scrapes down the entire length of her side. Alex watched as Sammi lowered her shirt and reached into her cosmetic bag. She brought out a tube of something and lifted her shirt again. Because of the camera angle, Alex could see everything she was doing. She started to smear what looked like a lotion on her side. Alex sucked in a breath at the same time that Sammi did. It had to hurt. *She must be putting antibiotic cream on it.* Alex thought to himself. Smart, but he was still mad that Eddie knew about this but hadn't done anything. It was ridiculous and dangerous. Getting an infection while in the middle of the Outback wouldn't be good.

Alex watched as Sammi finished spreading the cream on herself and put both her hands on the counter and leaned against them. She closed her eyes, dropped her head and took a deep breath. Again, Alex's hands clenched into fists. She was in pain, and obviously trying to breathe through it. He wanted nothing more than to take her into his arms and hold her to help her work through that pain. Alex watched as Sammi stood as still as a gazelle in the sights of a hungry lion and remembered what her body looked like. He swallowed hard. He was supposed to be thinking about how hurt she was, but the only thing he could think of was how silky her skin looked. He thought about how Sammi was all woman. She wasn't stick thin, he couldn't see her ribs, but he knew she'd be soft, and he'd be able to hold on to her and feel the give in her body, as a woman should feel. He finally shook his head and willed Sammi to feel better.

Finally, he saw her take one last deep breath and look up at the mirror she was reflected in.

"Get a grip." He heard her say out loud. Sammi then pawed through her cosmetic case and pulled out her toothbrush. She brushed her teeth, packed up her case, and left the room. As soon as the light turned off, so did the camera. Alex pushed eject and went back to the production tent.

"Why haven't you helped her?" Alex demanded of Eddie after bursting into his tent.

"She didn't ask for it," he responded and went on, "besides, she signed the contract. She knew what the risks were when she agreed to be on the show, she can't touch us."

Alex left the tent. He couldn't believe all Eddie was worried about was being sued. He'd surely seen the scrapes. Why didn't he care and why didn't he do anything about it? Alex figured there wasn't much that he could do about the situation at this point. If he admitted to Sammi that he knew about her being hurt, she'd know that there not only was a camera in the bathroom, but he had access to watch. He didn't want anyone's behavior at the camp changing because they knew he was watching them. Besides, it was written in his contract that he couldn't say a word about it to anyone. He would just have to deal. If Sammi was strong enough to grit her teeth and push through her pain, the least Alex could do would be to honor that strength and not bring attention to her pain. It might kill him, but he'd do it.

Chapter Eight

The next morning, the women's camp was a hub of activity. The eight women who'd won the competition the day before were going to meet Al and were very excited. They were running around, trying to make sure they wore the correct outfit, their hair was just right and that the outfits they'd chosen were appropriate. Sammi once again retreated to the overlook up the hill. Her side didn't hurt as much this morning, but she knew it'd be tough to do any sort of strenuous exercise without it being painful. She knew she wouldn't get any sympathy from anyone, and besides, it wasn't as if she was going to get any kind of tropical disease from the scratches…at least she hoped not. Sammi turned back toward the camp just in time to see the bus pull up and the eight giddy women climb aboard. She shrugged and turned back toward the amazing view of the Outback. She was sure she and the other women would hear all about the visit with Al when the ladies got back to camp later.

* * *

Alex watched as the bus pulled up and the women almost tumbled out in their haste to get to him. He braced himself as all eight women surrounded him. They were all almost talking at once. Finally, he laughed and said, "One at a time, ladies."

One woman leaned up and kissed him on the cheek, closer to his lips than he was comfortable with, and said, "Hi, I'm Missy."

One by one, the other women followed suit. Alex felt like he was going to suffocate with all the different perfumes the women were wearing. The smell of the perfume was overwhelming and completely out of place in the beauty that was the Outback. He heard their names as if he was in a box…"Lori, Jennie, Kiki, Candi…" He remembered the conversation the day before with Sammi about everyone's name ending in "ie" and he almost laughed out loud. Alex wasn't surprised that his thoughts turned to Sammi. He'd been thinking about her all night and wondering how she was doing. He forced himself back to the present and concentrated on the eight women around him.

After the initial introductions were over, Alex fell into the same routine as the day before. He met with each woman one at a time and then halfway through the meetings they had brunch. Then it was back to the conversations.

After lunch, Alex first met with Courtnee.

"Hello. Courtnee, isn't it?" Alex said with a smile.

Courtnee was obviously happy that he'd remembered her name. "Yes, that's right. Hi, Al. I can't tell you how happy I am to be here and to finally get time alone with you."

Alex wondered if she knew how corny that sounded. "Where are you from again? I think you said in your video that you were from Florida?"

"Yes," Courtnee gushed. "Pensacola. I just love it there, I have the cutest little house, it's right on the beach, and…"

Alex tuned her out. Their conversation was much like the other women's. They talked on and on about themselves and didn't really once ask about him or about what he liked to do. Finally, he decided to see if she would talk about the incident yesterday.

"Uh, so, Courtnee…you must have gotten a lot of fish yesterday in order to be in the top eight, huh?" Alex asked, pretending interest.

"Yes, although I would have gotten more if Jennie hadn't pushed me out of the way of the barrel at the last second!" Courtnee exclaimed. "It really wasn't fair. I'd reached the barrel first!"

"What about Sammi?" Alex asked.

"What about her?" Courtnee responded. "She didn't have nearly as many fish as we did, so it didn't matter if she got that last fish or not. It wasn't my fault that she fell in the river. If she wasn't so clumsy she wouldn't have." It was obvious Courtnee knew exactly what he was asking about. If Alex wasn't mistaken, he could detect a hint of defensiveness in her tone.

Alex couldn't believe what he'd just heard. She honestly thought it wasn't her fault, or at least felt no remorse at knocking Sammi into the water.

"Mmmm." Alex couldn't think of anything else to respond to Courtnee that wouldn't come out as totally inappropriate.

That didn't seem to matter to her. She just kept on talking. Finally it was time for Alex to have a one-on-one with another contestant. She leaned up to Alex's ear and whispered, "I had a great time, and I think you're really hot. I know we can be red hot together…see ya later, sweetheart." With that Courtnee reached up and kissed Alex right on the lips.

As she walked away Alex ran the back of his hand across his lips. It was going to be a long afternoon.

* * *

There was a lot of speculation back at the camp. The women from the day before wanted to know what went on in the meet-and-greet and it seemed like everyone was trying to one-up everyone else in their stories about what went on in their individual meetings. Camp was actually quite boring. There wasn't a lot to do, and it was hot during the day. It was really too hot to sit in the tents, but it was too hot to sit out in the sun as well. Finally, about three o'clock, Robert and Eddie sauntered into camp.

"Gather 'round, ladies," he said pompously. "It's time to see who the next contestant going home will be." And with that, Al was brought out from behind some trees. They were told they were going to be walking a bit to get to where the competition would be. So they all trudged along after Robert and Eddie. Nikki and Kathi did their best to monopolize Al's attention. They were on either side of him and grabbed onto his arms. Sam followed along near the back of the pack. She wasn't sure that she was up to much physical movement because her side felt like it was on fire. It started to hurt more as the day went on. She figured she'd play it by ear and see what happened when they got to wherever it was they were going.

They came upon a large clearing that had been set up to look like a rodeo circle. There was a little platform on one side with chairs set up. The circle was about a hundred feet in diameter, surrounded by large boulders. The women were instructed to stand in two lines in the middle of the circle while Al was seated on the podium. *This can't be good.* Sam thought.

"Welcome to the first challenge where the loser will be saying goodbye to Al and goodbye to Australia," Robert bellowed as if they were all standing on the other side of the circle rather than right in front of him.

"Today's challenge involves your wits as well as speed and strength." With that the producers freed two large pigs into the circle. Immediately Courtnee and Missy started screeching at the top of their lungs. The pigs ran around the outside of the circle, snorting and grunting. When Sam looked closer it looked as if they were drooling too. She suppressed a smile. Finally Robert got everyone's attention again.

"There are now fifteen of you left. There will be fourteen pigs released into the circle. The object is to grab a pig and get it to the chute at the side of the circle. Once you've gotten a pig to the chute, you can't go back into the circle. The lady left without a pig will be the one who has to go home. You have ten minutes to figure out a strategy before the pigs are released."

With that, most of the women immediately started complaining. They didn't know they would be pig wrestling today. Many wore totally inappropriate clothes and shoes.

Katie was even wearing a pair of heels! Sam laughed to herself. *This ought to be good.* She wasn't altogether sure that she'd be able to hold on to one of the pigs with her side hurting like it did, but she sure wasn't going to let some of those other women make her look like a loser on national television!

Alex looked on from the platform. His thoughts were running along the same lines as Sam's. He figured it'd make for great TV to see the women running around in their heels and fancy clothes, trying to corral a pig. While the pigs didn't weigh much more than twenty pounds each, it'd be interesting to see their strategies for corralling them.

Alex looked at Sam. He once again noticed that she certainly wasn't as model pretty as the other women, but she also wasn't as "made up" as they were. She was wearing sensible shoes with jeans and a T-shirt. He watched as she stood in one place and surveyed the circle, the chute and even the two pigs that were still in the circle. She seemed stiff, but Alex knew it was because of the scrapes on her side. Not once did he see her talk to Eddie or Robert. Al knew this challenge would probably hurt her side, but he knew with one hundred percent certainty that she would suck it up and not say anything to anyone about how she was feeling. How he knew her so well when he really didn't even know her, was baffling. Her penchant to keep her thoughts to herself concerned him because he didn't want to see her lose. She was, so far, one of the main reasons this farce of a show was bearable.

Finally, Robert climbed up the short set of stairs to stand on the platform with him. There were also several camera operators on the platform as well as roaming around the circle, filming the women from all angles. The women were all placed at one side of the circle. At Robert's *"Go"* the rest of the pigs were released and the women were off and running…well, some were running. Some of the women immediately ran toward the pigs, screeching, and others just kinda stood still as if in shock and not knowing what they should do.

For a few minutes it didn't look like anyone would be able to get any of the pigs into the "end zone," but finally Jennie from Montana coaxed/pulled/pushed one into the zone. She let out a whoop of joy and was escorted to the outside of the circle. The race was on. Slowly, one by one, pigs were corralled. Ashley, Candi, Lori, and Brandi all corralled a pig. Alex's attention turned to Sam. She was slowly walking toward a pig. She'd gotten it close to the chute when Courtnee came up next to her and "tripped," shoving Sam to the ground. Courtnee then got behind the pig and pushed with all her might until the pig went running toward the chute, squealing the entire way. Courtnee had gotten her pig…at Sam's expense.

Alex surged to his feet. He'd seen the whole thing and knew that Courtnee had definitely cheated. Of course, Eddie and Robert said nothing. Alex clenched his teeth and silently cheered Sammi on. He willed her to look at him, to see that he was rooting for her. To try to give her the strength to corral another one and stay in the game. He glared at Courtnee and didn't care if she saw it.

Sam was furious. Her side hurt, she was dirty, had a horrible headache and now that bitch Courtnee had stolen her pig and was laughing, *laughing*, at her. She almost called it quits right there. This wasn't worth it. Why did she want to fight over some guy who probably was laughing at her right this minute? Sam reluctantly looked toward the podium and at Al. He was no longer sitting, but standing and it looked like he was scowling at her. Sam did a double take, why was he mad at her? What did she do? Then she looked a bit closer and it seemed like Al wasn't looking at her after all, but watching Courtnee greet the other women on the other side of the circle. Then he turned his eyes on her. Seeing that she was looking at him, he gave her a small smile and nod of his head. Sam sighed. *Shit, I guess I have to get one of these stupid pigs after all.* She wasn't going to let Courtnee win and have the satisfaction of knowing she'd gotten her kicked off the show. So, ignoring the pain in her side, Sam set out to capture another stupid pig. She had no doubt she'd succeed. She had quite a bit of motivation.

With Sam's success, finally it came down to one pig left in the circle, and two women. Kimmie and Kiki were fighting for all they were worth to try to make sure they weren't the loser. It seemed to be an even match. Finally, it seemed as if the pig was getting tired of the game. He wanted to join his buddies on the other side of the circle. He took a sharp turn and started running right for the corral. Kiki was closer to the chute and managed to grab onto the pig as it ran past her and right into the corral. Kimmie was left without a pig.

"That's not fair!" she screeched. "She didn't capture it, it ran right by her!" Kiki was grinning like a ninny while Kimmie continued to complain.

Robert told all the women to line back up in their original spots. Al came down off the podium and stood next to Robert. He spared a quick glance at Sammi and managed to give her an inconspicuous head nod.

"It looks like you're the only one without a pig, Kimmie," Robert began, "you're going to have to say goodbye to Al and the other women right here and now. Your belongings will be brought to you later. Do you have anything to say?" Darn right Kimmie had something to say…

"You're all a bunch of losers. You'd cheat and lie to your own mother if it'd serve your purpose. If you were dying of thirst I wouldn't give you a drink of water!" And with that she flounced away from the group toward the waiting car.

Sam couldn't help it. She laughed, out loud. It was too much. It was too much like the first season of *Survivor* when the one contestant said practically the same thing to the finalist. What drama, what flair…but she also knew it'd make great television.

Robert seemed to finally come out of the trance that he was in after Kimmie's departure.

"Okay, ladies, you've earned the right to stick around another day. It's time to go back to camp, and you'll meet with Al later today."

With that, Al, Eddie, and Robert left, and the women walked back to their camp. Of course, once they got there it was a free-for-all as the women all tried to fight for the shower. It seemed they didn't mind there wasn't any hot water anymore. They all wanted to get the pig smell off and get ready for their meet-and-greet with Al later on that day.

Sam was finally able to take her turn in the shower. It seemed like she'd been wet more in the last few days than she'd been in her "real" life back in Albuquerque. She didn't mind. She'd always been a good swimmer. She'd been on the water polo team in high school, so she felt comfortable in and around water, even if it was cold. When Sam walked out of the little bathroom building, she didn't see much movement around the camp. The women were mostly in the tents just hanging out, waiting for Robert or someone to come and get them.

I can't believe them. Sam thought to herself. *They're in Australia and they're sitting around in tents, waiting to hang out with some guy, whatever.* And with that Sam decided she'd take a walk back up the rise. It wasn't a long walk, and she could still see the camp from where she was. It was simply beautiful. How she'd love to explore a bit, Sam felt like she was "tied" to the camp. It wasn't fair, here she was in one of the most beautiful parts of the world and she was waiting with thirteen other women to meet the guy they were supposed to be "dating." She couldn't deny that she was attracted to him and that he was hot, but it was depressing that she was in competition for him.

Sam sighed and tried to put the whole show out of her mind, then looked behind her and saw the ever-present Kina with the camera and smirked. She'd make Kina earn her keep today. There certainly wasn't much to film back at camp. That had to be why Kina was following her. Sam noticed she wasn't filmed nearly as much as the other women were, but it didn't bother her in the least. *Let them have all the camera time.* Sam started off down the hill. She didn't know how long it would be before they were supposed to go and visit with Al, but she needed this. She needed to get away from the other women for a while. Most of them weren't bad, but they did grate on her nerves. They were just so different. For about the hundredth time Sam wondered how *she* had gotten on the show. She convinced herself that it was either a mistake or they needed some comic relief.

The sun was hot, but it really was pretty. Sam walked on, almost oblivious to Kina trudging along behind her. Every once in a while she heard Kina mumble to herself, but Kina didn't stop her or talk to her. After all, that was against the rules. Eventually, after about twenty minutes of walking, Sam stopped under a large tree, sat down, leaned against the trunk and shut her eyes, just breathing in the clean air and enjoying the fact that she was in Australia. After a few minutes Sam heard Kina sit down next to her. Sam peeked out of one eye and saw Kina had put down the camera and was looking at her.

"What?" Sam asked.

"I don't get you," Kina responded. Sam couldn't help it, she laughed.

"I know. I'm a loner, what can I say? Look around, look at how beautiful all this is. I'd choose this over sitting around talking about how much I miss the mall any day."

With that, Sam put her head back against the tree trunk and shut her eyes again, not waiting to see how Kina reacted to her bluntness.

Finally, she heard Kina say, "I like you, Sammi."

Sam smiled, but didn't say anything. *At least one person seems to like me.*

Sam and Kina sat under the tree for about thirty minutes. Sam was half asleep when she heard Kina's voice.

"You're missing it, you know," Kina finally spoke up again.

"Huh? What am I missing?" Sam asked absently.

"The meet-and-greet," Kina responded. "They left ten minutes ago."

With that Sam leaped up.

"Oh, shit, I can't believe they left without me!"

She looked at Kina again and saw she was back to her camerawoman mode. The camera was up and pointed at her again. Sam figured it wouldn't make any sense to go running back to camp, especially if the women had truly already left. They obviously knew where she was, Kina had some sort of communication with them since she knew they'd already left. *Screw it.* Sam thought. *If I've already missed the bus I might as well explore some more.* And she set off walking again. *I won't go far, just a bit more.*

Chapter Nine

The bus pulled up to the clearing where the producers had set up a sort of "living room." There were tree stumps around for seating and a few tables set up around the clearing. Alex watched as the women climbed off the bus. He was immediately surrounded by all of the women who seemed to all be talking at once again.

I can't wait until more of them are gone, Alex thought and immediately felt guilty. *It'll be much easier to talk to them and get to know everyone when there are fewer of them!* Soon enough they were sitting around and having a pretty good conversation. He was, of course, the center of attention and he allowed the talk to flow around him. The women were definitely on their best behavior today and they all looked gorgeous. He wasn't sure how they accomplished it out here in the wilds of the backcountry, but somehow they all looked like they were sitting down at a party in New York or something.

After about forty minutes of talking, Alex could identify most of the women, he could even tell most of them apart. He knew who Courtnee was, of course, and Missy was also pretty forward, so he knew her. He actually was beginning to like Amy and Jennie. They seemed a little less harsh and spoiled than the others. They weren't quite as "citified" as Katie or Kiki. Of course, he knew Sammi as well…as soon as the thought crossed his mind he realized he hadn't seen her. Before he could stop himself he found himself asking the group, "Where's Sammi?" The other women looked around and shrugged, then continued their conversations. They didn't seem to care. All they cared about was that they were here with him and trying to get his attention.

Alex started to worry. Why wasn't Sammi there? Had they kicked her off and hadn't told him? He couldn't believe it had taken him so long to realize she wasn't there. She really did stick out, not in a bad way, but she stuck out nonetheless. The next hour was the longest hour he'd spent in the Outback. He couldn't stop worrying about why Sammi wasn't at the meet and greet. Finally, the visiting time was over and the women got back on the bus to return to their camp. Upon arriving at the production site, Alex found Eddie.

"Where's Sammi?" he asked impatiently. He'd spent the last hour and a half worrying about where she might be. Was she hurt? Was she gone? If she was gone how would he be able to find her again?

Eddie looked at him and said, "She missed the bus at camp, so we left. Thought it'd be a good lesson for the other women and for her. She just can't wander off. She's here for the show, and besides, someone could get hurt." Alex couldn't believe it. Eddie was trying to teach her a lesson?

"What do you mean, wander off?" Alex asked in a low voice.

"Just what I said," Eddie said in an annoyed tone. "Look, she decided she wanted to go for a little walk. Kina is following her. Nothing is happening."

"What did she do when she realized she'd been left behind?" Alex asked.

"Don't know. They're still out there. I'm in touch with Kina. I let her know that the bus had left. I don't know if Sammi knows she missed the bus or not, but it doesn't matter. She'll come back in her own time. She can't get lost, Kina is filming her and we can watch the tapes. Calm down, Al, there are fourteen women left. You've lots of time to make your choice." And with that, Eddie was called away.

Alex wondered where the hell Sammi was and what the hell she was thinking wandering around by herself. If he was honest with himself, he was upset that he'd missed a chance to see her and get to know her.

* * *

In actuality, Sam wasn't doing much wandering. She was content to stroll around and take long breaks under the enormous trees. She was enjoying watching the different species of birds and small animals running around. The only thing she was upset about was that she didn't have a camera with her. She would've loved to be able to take pictures of what she was experiencing so she could share them with her family and friends. After a while she decided she'd better go back to the camp. She didn't know if she'd be in trouble for missing the bus and the meet-and-greet, but she figured she'd better be back at camp by the time the others got off the bus or she might really be in trouble.

After one of her breaks under a beautiful shade tree, Sam stood up and waited for Kina to get in position before she started back toward the camp. She'd learned that the best thing to do with the cameras was to let them film the way they wanted to so they'd leave her alone. Sam waited until Kina got in front of her and started walking backward so she could get a good frontal view of Sammi walking. Sam looked down at Kina's feet, impressed she could walk backwards and not trip over anything, and froze. Kina was stepping over some rocks and Sam saw a glossy black head of a snake sticking out of a crack in the rocks where it had probably been resting to get away from the sun.

Sam didn't remember all of the names of snakes found in Australia, and had no idea if this one was poisonous or not, but with the way her luck was going, it probably was.

"Kina, stop. Now." Sam's words were low and urgent.

Kina stopped in her tracks, camera still on her shoulder, pointed toward Sam. She obviously heard the panic in Sam's voice. "What?"

"A snake. Don't move, Kina," Sam said. "It's right by your foot." As Sam watched, the snake emerged from the crack in the rocks and wound itself around Kina's feet.

68

Kina froze even more if that was possible. A sad little whimper escaped from her throat. "Oh God," she moaned, "I hate snakes."

"I'm going to try to get it away from you…don't move whatever you do. Maybe it'll think you're a tree or something. I've heard they're usually more afraid of us than we are of them." Sam had no idea what she was talking about, some scientist would probably scoff at what she'd said, but she hoped Kina would believe her and feel calmer about the entire situation. Sam found a large stick. She'd watched reruns of that famous Australian guy on TV more times than she could count. She knew there was a way to pin the head to the ground and pick it up, but she sure as hell wasn't going to try that. Sam only knew she had to get that snake away from Kina's legs. She didn't know what she'd do if her actions pissed the snake off more than it already was.

The snake was huge, but to be honest, *any* snake looked huge to her. Sam estimated it to be around five feet long. It was light brown and the sun glistening off its body made it look almost pretty. Sam started to sweat. *This is all my fault.* She thought. *If I hadn't walked away from camp, Kina wouldn't be in this situation.*

Sam walked around Kina and the snake turned to follow her movements. *Good.* Sam thought. *'It's watching me and not paying attention to Kina, whose legs it's almost wrapped around.*

"Kina, it's almost wrapped around your legs, but its attention is on me. Don't put the camera down, don't move. I'm going to start backing up and hopefully it'll follow me. I have no idea if this will work or not, but I hope like hell it will. When you feel it slide away take *slow* steps in the direction you're facing. That'll put distance between you and it."

"What are you going to do?" Kina whispered. "If it follows you, how are you going to get away from it?"

"I don't know, but at least it won't be near you," Sam responded, still feeling guilty for putting Kina in this position in the first place. Then Sam said flippantly, "And besides, it'll make for great television so be sure you're filming…contestant wanders out of camp by herself and gets bitten by a killer snake…think of the ratings!" She chuckled uneasily.

While Sam had been talking to Kina she'd been slowly backing up. It seemed to be working. The snake was following her. Inch by inch it unfurled itself from around Kina. It definitely didn't look happy, and it hadn't stopped opening and closing its mouth the entire time. The thing looked like it was ready to strike. Like it *wanted* to strike. Kina took one step forward, then another…finally, she was able to turn around and face Sam and the snake. She took aim with her camera.

Sam and the snake were facing each other. Sam was armed with only a stick and the snake looked agitated. Sam started talking to the snake, not really knowing what she was saying. "Okay, Mr. Snake, we're sorry that we disturbed you. We'll be on our way, okay? You don't need to bite me. I probably don't taste very good. Now, some of the women at camp are more your style, you'd love them. How about just turning around and going home…just like I want to do. I'll just be on my way, no harm no foul. I promise not to come down this way and bother you again if you just let me go now…okay? Niiiiice snake…" Sam was backing up slowly, never taking her eyes off of the snake. Thankfully, it decided that escape was probably the better option and it slithered away into the underbrush nearby.

Sam looked up at Kina, and thus into the camera.

"Holy crap…that was a close one…are you okay, Kina?" Kina didn't respond.

"Oh, okay, we are back to the rules," Sam said with disappointment.

With that Sam turned her back on the camera and started the way they'd come. *It would've been nice for her to at least say thank you.* Suddenly, she didn't feel very good. She knew it was a reaction to the stress and fear and probably the heat as well. She started shaking and felt the sweat pop out on her forehead. She darted toward a bush and threw up what little she'd eaten that day.

"Ugh, gross," she said out loud. "That is the worst." Sam wiped a shaky hand across her mouth and trudged on toward the camp, not daring to look at Kina or the camera. She was sure there was now an up-close-and-personal shot of her losing her stomach contents that would surely be shown on TV in the not-so-distant future. Lovely.

Sam continued to shake as she walked. She thought about what had happened and what had almost happened to Kina. It was times like this that she really missed being a part of a couple. While she felt she was an independent modern woman, there was something to be said about being held safe and comfortable in a man's arms. She took a deep breath and continued on toward the camp to find out how much trouble she was in.

What had started out as a beautiful day and a peaceful walk had turned sour. She'd missed the bus and was probably in trouble for that. She'd talked to one of the camera operators, which was against the rules, so she was probably in trouble for that. Then the snake incident, which was scarier in person than she imagined it could be, *and* she humiliated herself in front of the camera and probably in front of millions of people. She *knew* the incident would show up on screen and she'd never live it down with her friends or her coworkers back in Albuquerque. She trudged on, lost in her thoughts while Kina followed behind.

Sam and Kina finally made it back to camp. She hadn't been able to arrive before the women had gotten back after all. She'd obviously been wandering around in the Outback for longer than she thought. The women were hanging around, talking about Al and his reactions to each of them and their conversations.

Missy turned to Sam and said snidely, "Where were you, Miss Tarzan? You're in big trouble, you know? You missed it. But don't worry, Al didn't miss you and neither did we. He didn't even ask about you. Right, ladies?" And with that, most of the other women laughed and giggled.

Sam was too tired to care, and was still dealing with the after effects of adrenaline that her body was producing as a result of the fear of the snake and what might have happened to Kina. She looked around and saw Kina getting into a golf cart, probably to go back to the production camp to talk about how she'd broken the rules. Sam ignored Missy and the other women, went back to the tent and lay down on her cot. What would happen now? She was worried, and was glad that she could finally lie down. She replayed the incident in her head. It'd been a close call. Kina had almost stepped directly on the snake. If she'd done that she would've been bitten for sure, and then what would Sam have done? There was no way she could've carried her all the way back to the camp. She'd put someone's life on the line for her own selfish desires. It wouldn't happen again.

Chapter Ten

Alex watched Kina get out of the golf cart and go straight to Eddie's office. He remembered the producer said that Kina was with Sammi. He followed Kina into the tent in time to hear Eddie bellow, "Where the hell were you guys?!? She missed the bus! How come you didn't tell us where you were when we asked?!?" He sounded more upset now about the situation than when Alex talked to him earlier. Then he didn't seem like it mattered or that he cared about Sammi missing the bus.

All the camera operators wore little two way microphones, that way they could communicate with production at all times.

Kina responded, "I couldn't, we were out in the middle of nowhere. If I'd started talking to you the camera would've picked it up and the footage would've been ruined."

Eddie sighed. He knew Kina was right, and there was nothing more he hated than great footage ruined by the chit chat of a camera operator.

Kina continued, "She went for a walk, I followed her. She took a nap by a tree, then we started back toward camp. On our way back, I think she might have saved my life." Eddie snapped to attention.

"What?" he yelled. "Did you get it on tape?"

"Sort of," Kina told him honestly.

Kina didn't say anything else, but held out the tape that had been in her camera that day. Eddie snatched it out of her hand faster than the snake could have bitten her today and put it into the player.

With Alex, Eddie, and Kina watching, the tape was played. They watched Sammi's face as she realized what the problem was. They heard her talking to Kina. The camera was glued to Sammi as Kina stood still above the snake. Then they saw Sammi walk out of the line of vision and continue to tell Kina what she was going to do and what Kina should do. The camera microphone had picked up Kina's frantic breathing. Finally, the camera moved and swung back around to Sammi and the snake. Alex about had a heart attack. Sammi was leaning over, waving a stick, trying to get the snake to follow her. Eventually, the snake slithered off.

"Damn, that's good footage," Eddie said, "but since the cameras aren't supposed to exist, we can't use it." Alex just looked at him incredulously.

"Sammi was talking to the camera operator, and Kina was talking back, that's not a part of the 'reality' of this show. We can't use it," Eddie defended himself as Alex glared at him.

Eddie continued, "Good job today, Kina, get some rest and you'll be back on Sammi tomorrow. Maybe she'll feel more comfortable around you and tell you juicy secrets on tape that we can use. Just don't talk to her." He grabbed the tape out of the machine and held it out to Kina. "Take this back to the production tent." And with that, he shooed Alex and Kina out of the tent.

"Kina," Alex said once they'd left, "I think that was what's known as a Fierce snake. I'm not completely sure, but I've heard my aunt talk about them enough and I've heard stories about them and how deadly their bite can be."

Kina paled. "She really *did* save my life then. Al, I was about to bolt or do something stupid and she calmed me down and led that snake away. I could feel it slithering around my legs and *knew* it was going to bite me any second." She shuddered, then continued, "That wasn't all that happened out there, you should watch the entire tape." She handed the tape they'd just watched to Alex.

"Is she really all right?" Alex asked urgently.

"She's okay, she was really quiet afterward and had a bad moment or two, but she's okay." Kina reassured him.

Alex took the tape back to his tent and watched Sammi's entire afternoon. She looked really peaceful resting against trees and he could see that she really loved being out in nature. She seemed really relaxed until Kina almost stepped on the snake. He observed again her facial expressions and watched as she tried to lead the snake away from Kina. It was just as scary the second time he saw it as it was the first time. While he was scared to death for her, he was also proud. She'd handled the situation with a sense of calm. She didn't panic, she did what she needed to do. There was nothing he wanted more than to hold her and comfort her, and that freaked him out a little bit. He wasn't like this. He never felt like this about a woman this quickly before. Hell, he really didn't know her that well, but there was something about her.

Alex watched as Sammi continued walking back toward the camp. She wasn't looking around her at the scenery like she did on the way out. He thought he could even see her shaking. Then he saw her dart to a bush and throw up. She then wiped her mouth and continued on her way without even looking at the camera.

Alex was stunned. He couldn't believe what he'd just seen. He didn't know many people that would be able to handle that kind of stress and not collapse. He was surprised it'd taken her so long to lose it. He wished he could talk to Sammi about what happened, but again, he knew no one was to know that he had access to the show's tapes. He sighed and again felt the urge to wrap Sammi up in his arms and not let go. What a predicament. He honestly admired her. Yes, she'd wandered off on her own, which wasn't that smart of a thing to do, but in a crisis she'd held herself together and not fallen apart. He couldn't image any of the other women on the show doing the same. And after she'd thrown up, she didn't throw a hissy fit, she just continued on her way. Sammi certainly was an interesting woman. One that Alex knew he'd like to get to know a lot better.

Chapter Eleven

The next day started out like any of the others at the camp. There was a mad dash for the bathroom and for the shower followed by a flurry of hairspray, makeup, and bickering. The women apparently decided that cold showers weren't that bad when the alternative was no shower. Fourteen women all intent on getting the same man was wearing thin, however. Like usual, Sam waited until most everyone was done with the bathroom before taking her turn. She'd slept in later than usual this morning, but she was so exhausted from the stress from the day before that she couldn't make herself get up. *I wonder what fun and games the producers have in store for us today.* She put her hair up in a clip and left the bathroom.

Soon the bus pulled up to the camp. Eddie and Robert got out of a golf cart following behind the bus and assembled all the women in their customary lines.

"I have good news and bad news," Robert intoned. "The good news is that no one is going home today." He paused to allow the cameras time to pan over the women who were cheering and smiling. "The bad news is that today and tomorrow you'll work harder than most of you have before in your lives." The cheering stopped as if a TV was unplugged suddenly.

"What do you mean?" Candi asked. "What kind of job could there be out here in the middle of nowhere?"

"Well," Robert continued with a smirk, as if he knew what he was about to say would ruin the women's day. "Part of Al's life is to work on his ranch back in Texas, so today and tomorrow you'll be working on a cattle ranch. Here in Australia a ranch is typically called a 'cattle station.' Your jobs will involve all the daily activities that are usually undertaken on the station. You need to pack an overnight bag with outdoor clothes and sneakers, or comfortable shoes if you brought them, and we'll leave in about half an hour."

As soon as Robert stepped off the podium and was back in his golf cart heading out, the girls started complaining.

"I can't believe this," Missy snapped. "I've never been around a *cow* in all my life, how can I work on a ranch when I don't know what I'm doing?"

"It doesn't make sense," Brandi chimed in. "What are we, slave labor? This was supposed to be fun!"

Kathi exclaimed, "I better not break a nail!"

As the women continued on with their complaining, Sam wandered back to her tent to pack her belongings. Since she shared it with some of the other contestants she couldn't get away from their mumblings, but she did her best to block them out. Courtnee nudged her in the side as she was packing.

"Are you going to run away again, Miss Bitch?" she asked nastily. "It doesn't matter to me one way or another since there's no way in hell you're going to last much longer. Why don't you just quit now?"

"Why do you say that?" Sam asked, knowing full well she wouldn't like the answer, but trying to stand up for herself nonetheless.

"Look at you," Courtnee continued, "You're short and dumpy. You have no fashion sense and you don't wear makeup." Looking around, she noticed the other women watching and it fueled the venom spewing out of her mouth. "You don't belong here. You aren't in Al's league. He needs someone who will look good by his side. Someone with his wealth needs a beautiful woman on his arm, and you certainly aren't it. I mean really, why are you even *on* this show? You don't fit in."

Sam stood there, looking at Courtnee and the other women who were watching from a small distance away.

"How would you know what he needs?" Sam fired back. "None of us know Al, we've met him what, twice? For that matter you don't know me. So what I don't look like you? I know I'm not beautiful, but that doesn't diminish my value as a person. Maybe I'm just here for the free trip to Australia." Then she glared at Courtnee. "We don't like each other, that's not big news, but Courtnee, I'll stand up for myself, so let's agree to stay away from each other and let the game unfold. I'll stay out of your way and you stay out of mine."

With that Sam turned her back on Courtnee and continued to pack. She knew she'd made an enemy, but she simply wasn't up to taking the other woman's crap like she usually would in a similar situation back home. Just because she wasn't five feet eleven inches tall and she weighed more than a seven-year-old child would, didn't mean she wasn't a good person.

Their thirty minutes to pack was up and they all piled back on the bus. The ride to the ranch was about forty-five minutes long. Sam had no idea where they were going, all she knew was that it was dusty and they seemed to be in the middle of nowhere. Finally, they saw a line of trees in the distance and buildings slowly began to take shape. They pulled into a large circle driveway in front of one of the most beautiful houses Sam had ever seen. It was huge. And was three stories high with a beautiful front porch. There were rocking chairs set out on the porch and dogs running around the yard and property. It was wonderful, beautiful, and Sam couldn't wait to get out and meet whoever was lucky enough to live in such a wonderful place.

The women filed out of the bus and were instructed to stand in their customary two lines. Robert stood in his usual spot and began talking.

"Welcome to the Choxie Station. There are over eight hundred acres on the property and you'll begin working right away. There are many different types of chores, and we'll draw from a hat to see which you'll be doing. We will choose different jobs for each of you in the morning. Are there any questions before we begin?"

Ashley raised her hand and asked, "Will Al be joining us?"

The question was one that all the women really wanted to know the answer to. They wanted to know if he'd be there to watch their supreme efforts on their chores. They wanted to know what kind of effort they'd have to put forth. If he was there, they'd try harder, if not, then they'd get by with the minimum effort they could.

"Al will be joining you later tonight. He'll spend time doing each of the chores with you tomorrow. The chores you'll be assisting with are helping in the kitchen, working with the maids, mucking out the stalls, riding the fence line, feeding the animals, and weeding the garden."

There was complete silence from the women. Sam wanted to laugh. It was too perfect. She didn't really want to do any of those jobs, but she knew she was in far better shape to do them than the other spoiled contestants. She cleaned her own house, fed her three dogs twice a day every day, cooked her own meals…she knew most of the other women probably had hired help to do all those things, or at least relied on someone else to help them. She looked around and saw the shock on their faces. She again had to stifle a giggle.

They started to draw jobs from the hat one by one. Ashley and Kathi pulled kitchen duty first. Missy, Brandi, and Katie got maid duty. Cindee, Sammi, and Amy were going to be mucking out the stalls. Nikki and Lori were going to be riding the fence lines. Kiki and Courtnee would be feeding the animals, while Jennie and Candi would be weeding the huge garden out back.

Sam figured she'd get the "poop" job…with three dogs at home it seemed as if she was constantly picking up poo at home, so why shouldn't she do it when she was on vacation too? It was actually pretty funny. She figured she could've gotten stuck with worse people than Amy and Cindee to work with as well.

The women all went off to do their respective chores. They hadn't seen Al yet, and they weren't sure when he would show up and who he would "help" first. Sammi, Cindee, and Amy were brought into a huge barn. There were stalls alongside stalls alongside stalls. No wonder there were three of them assigned to this chore. Cindee and Amy immediately scrunched up their noses at the pungent smell emanating from the stalls. *It is a bit strong.* Sam thought. But *what did I expect, it's a barn!*

They were handed long pitchforks by one of the ranch hands. He told them that in Australia, typically the male employees were called jackeroos and the females jilleroos. He gave them a quick lesson on how to shovel the horse droppings out of the stalls and into a large bin. Most of the horses were out in the pasture so they'd have the place mostly to themselves. They were given gloves—which of course were too big for them—and set to work. Sam and Amy started on one side of the barn and Cindee started on the other.

The time went by pretty fast for Sam. The job was backbreaking, but not hard. All three of the women were sweating pretty hard. The barn was insulated, but the heat of the day combined with the hard shoveling was no match for the ceiling fans lazily circling above their heads. After about three hours the girls were told they were done for the day.

"Good job, ladies, I'm impressed," a jackeroo named Henry told them. "I didn't expect you'd get as much done as you did. Thank you."

It *was* a job well done if Sam did say so herself. Together they'd mucked out all the stalls and had gotten a good start on spreading new hay as well. It wasn't perfect, they'd taken quite a few breaks to rest, but they'd done it. Henry told them they were to meet back out at the front of the house where they'd assembled when they'd first arrived. They trudged out front and saw the other women were slowly gathering. The women who were working in the house didn't look too much the worse for wear, but the women who worked outside in the sun looked very bedraggled.

Once everyone had assembled, Robert spoke, "Hopefully you enjoyed your first few hours here at Choxie Station. I think we'd all enjoy hearing about how your day went. I'd like for each group to come up and talk about how the job they did today and anything else interesting that happened. And since none of you got to work with Al today, he'd like to hear how things went as well."

Alex strode out of the house and stood next to Robert.

"This should be interesting," Sam muttered under her breath.

First up was the garden crew. Jennie and Candi walked up to join Robert and Al. Both were a bit sunburned, but not too bad considering they were pretty tan to begin with.

Jennie started discussing how their day went. "Well, the garden is huge. There are flowers as well as vegetables. We were told what we should be looking for to pull, but it was a bit difficult since neither of us has really worked in a garden before. I guess we kept pulling the wrong thing. Candi actually pulled up something that she thought was a weed, but it turned out to be a vegetable!" At that, Jennie giggled.

Candi interrupted, "Yeah, well, what about when you sat on a bunch of flowers to get a better grip on the weed that you were trying to pull?!?"

It seemed as if the light humor of the moment was gone. The competition was on. Candi and Jennie were not looking happy and were starting to glare at each other.

Alex broke the tension and said, "Did you enjoy your afternoon? Did you learn anything today?"

Jennie spoke up before Candi could. "Well, I wouldn't say it was *fun*, and I guess I learned that it's hard work and if you're going to have a big garden it'd be best to make sure you hire someone to pull weeds!" She giggled again, and Sam couldn't help but roll her eyes. She looked at Al to see what he thought about what Jennie said, but his face was blank and she couldn't tell what he was thinking.

Next up was Nikki and Lori who talked about their "fence riding" experience. It didn't sound like they got very far. Neither had even been around horses before and so they were nervous and spent a lot of time walking the horses instead of riding them because of their inexperience and fright around the horses. They watched a few jackeroos check the fences and claimed they couldn't help because the gloves didn't fit them and it might mess up their manicures.

Next it was Sam, Cindee, and Amy's turn. Cindee spoke for them all and talked about how the barn was very smelly and hot and definitely not something she wanted to do. She even complained a bit about how they didn't even get to meet the horses, only dealt with their droppings! Sam couldn't stand it anymore. It seemed like the entire session was becoming one big complaint after another.

"It wasn't too bad," Sam piped up, interrupting Cindee's complaints. "Yes, it was hot, and yes it was definitely smelly, but it felt good to be able to help the animals by making sure they'd have a clean bed when they came home for the night." Sam looked at the faces of the women in front of her. Some looked bored, others looked indifferent, but a few looked at her with daggers in their eyes. Sam didn't know why, didn't know what she said that was so bad, but then she figured that the ones who were glaring at her didn't like her anyway, so no matter what she said they'd still probably be glaring at her.

Missy, Brandi, and Katie were up next discussing the chores they had to do around the house. Missy was appalled that she had to clean toilets. She said it was degrading and "icky." It didn't sound like the things they had to do were too bad. And their description of the house was amazing. Sam wished she was able to walk around and examine the house. It was fascinating from the outside. She just knew it'd be just as beautiful inside.

Ashley and Kathi discussed the kitchen duties. They helped with the afternoon meal for the employees. Apparently Kathi dropped and broke a platter, but the head cook assured her that it was okay. They claimed to have washed "thousands" of dishes—Ashley's words—and talked about how they had to mop the floor twice.

Last to go was Kiki and Courtnee whose job it was to feed the various animals around the farm. They gushed on and on for about twenty minutes about how cute all the animals were. They made it sound like they were angels who were feeding starving animals. Sam noticed they didn't talk much about feeding the pigs. Sam had seen pigs being fed before, it wasn't a pretty sight.

Finally, they'd all told their stories and everyone got to know a bit about what each of the jobs entailed. They were tired and smelly and definitely ready to go inside and have a good meal, a shower, and hopefully visit more with Al. Robert and Eddie, as usual, had other plans for them.

"Now that you've all finished your chores today you can go and find a place to sleep in the bunkhouse." He pointed behind them toward the barn where off to the side there was a long rectangle shaped building. "There you will find your cots for the night as well as the kitchen where you'll need to fix your own food for the night. I wouldn't stay up too late, tomorrow will come soon enough."

Many of the women were flabbergasted. They weren't going to be allowed to sleep in the house tonight? What was this? How would Al get to know them and how would they get to know him better if they were stuck in the bunkhouse with each other? As it usually happens when women get together in tight spaces for too long of a time, they were starting to grate on each other's nerves. Cliques were definitely forming. It was as if the battle lines had been drawn. They were like wild dogs circling their prey—which was Al. If they didn't get first "crack" at him, then they'd fight for what they believed was "theirs."

Sam was tired of the "game" already. It wasn't the work she was doing, it was the fact that she was expected to be just as eager to discuss Al at all times and that she was expected to fight for him and to do anything to "get" him. It just wasn't her style at all. She figured if a guy was going to like her, he was going to like her as she was. She shouldn't have to *fight* for a guy. She believed if a guy was having a hard time choosing between her and another woman, then he could have the other woman.

She wanted a man who would walk into a room and the first thing he'd do would be to seek her out. Who'd walk into a room and have eyes only for her. She wanted a man who she wouldn't have to worry about where he was, if he came home from work late and who he was with. Trust. She wanted complete trust in a partner. She knew she wasn't as pretty as the women she was surrounded by. She also knew that most likely she wouldn't make it past the next few eliminations. She had high self-esteem, but it was being battered a bit constantly being around the models as she was.

Sam followed the other women to the bunkhouse where their suitcases had been dropped off earlier in the day. There were seven bunk beds set up around the small room, with a small bathroom and a kitchen. Missy immediately tried to take charge.

"Who's going to cook? It looks like we have food here," she said, looking at the other women expectantly. "Although it looks like we only have the fixings for pasta…anyone want that?" Of course, most of the women were horrified at the thought of eating all those carbs and ruining their diets. Sam was hungry. She'd spent most of the day working hard, she loved pasta, and she figured that if she was going to eat she'd better volunteer to cook. So she started getting out pots and ingredients to make the meal.

Chapter Twelve

"So what did you think of them?" Alex asked his Aunt Nancy. Nancy and her husband owned Choxie Station. Nancy had married an Australian and raised her children, Alex's cousins, there on the station. They were now all gone, the kids moved away and her husband passed away a few years ago. Eddie figured this was a great opportunity to shake up the "game" a bit. It was going to be Nancy's job to tell the producers who the next woman would be to leave. She was to get to know as many of the women as she could. She'd watch the tapes of the women doing their chores with Alex. She would also meet the women who were working in the house in person. She wouldn't get to meet them all in person, but she'd get to meet most of them.

"Where in the world did they find these women?" Nancy asked Alex. "They have no clue. They all look like Barbie dolls."

Alex agreed, "I thought the same thing. I haven't gotten to know them all very well yet, but they seem to be nice."

"Nice?" Nancy asked incredulously. "That isn't a word I'd have imagined you'd use when discussing beautiful women!" They both laughed and settled down to watch the tapes of the day.

Two hours later, the duo had enough. It was obvious that the women were out of their element. Most tried to make the best out of a bad situation, but it was clear that some of them just weren't trying. The three most obvious were Katie, Nikki, and Candi. They did everything they could do to get out of work and to let others do most of it.

"Come on Alex," Nancy said. "Let's get some chow and hit the sack. Five am is going to come up pretty fast for our city-slickers!"

At exactly five in the morning, the women were awakened by a loud clanging. It was one of the jackaroos standing outside the bunk house, banging against a metal trash can.

"Time to get up, ladies, you have twenty minutes before you need to be up in the clearing for breakfast and then for your assignments for the day."

Sam had never heard such complaining and moaning in all her life. She was pretty sore, but she couldn't believe how the others were carrying on. You'd think they'd spent yesterday being tortured or something. Sam would kill for a shower, but she knew that wasn't going to happen with all the other women also clamoring for the use of the shower. Some were showering together at the same time. There was no way Sam was going to stand next to one of the other women without any clothes on. That would be too much even for her ego.

They all trudged back to the clearing. Robert was there looking as clean cut and refreshed as ever. It was actually pretty annoying. They all sat down on benches that were put out for them as the kitchen staff brought out their breakfast. There was food piled up. It looked like they'd gone all out. There were eggs, bacon, sausage, pancakes, muffins, doughnuts, and even breakfast burritos. Sam laughed to herself, there was no way that some of those women would touch some of that food, but Sam was in heaven. She was happy she didn't have to make her own breakfast this morning. She took a bit of everything, not knowing when they'd have the chance to eat again. Besides, she knew it would give her a bit of energy for the day's activities.

When everyone finished eating, they all gathered in their respective places again and Robert began a speech about hard work and how they would be switching around jobs for the day. Al would be making the rounds and visiting each work team as they were doing their chores to see how they were getting along. Robert started pulling names out of the hat again.

Jennie and Kiki were going to work in the kitchen. Nikki, Cindee, and Candi would be working with the maids. Brandi and Ashley would be riding the fence line. Amy and Kathi would be feeding the animals. Lori and Katie would be weeding, and Courtnee, Missy, and Sam would be mucking out the stalls.

Sam couldn't believe she got the same job as she had the day before It wasn't fair, but it wasn't like any of the other jobs were really all that good either. As far as things went, she supposed it could be worse, but she wasn't happy with the fact that she'd have to work with Courtnee and Missy for the day. She knew neither of them liked her, so she figured it'd be a very long morning. No one seemed to notice or care that she'd done the same job the day before. Sam decided that if no one else was going to say anything, neither would she. It wasn't that big of a deal. As much as she wanted to get into the house and see if it was as beautiful on the inside as it was on the outside, she wasn't going to make someone switch with her. Mucking the stalls wasn't exactly a job that someone would want to switch her for anyway. She'd have loved to have spent time with the animals, but she also knew there was no way in hell that Kathi or Amy would switch with her. She couldn't blame them either.

They all left to attend to their respective jobs. As Sam, Courtnee, and Missy arrived at the barn they saw Al was already there. It looked like he'd be starting his day with them. Courtnee and Missy were beyond excited. They were glad they'd get to see him before they got all sweaty and smelly.

"Mornin', ladies," Al said with a drawl.

"Hi", "Hello", "Hey," they said in unison.

Courtnee sidled up to Al and asked, "Are you going to show us how to do this?"

Alex laughed and said, "Nope, that's Henry's Job…Henry?"

With that, Henry came over from the stall he'd been working in. Noticing Sam, he frowned at her a bit and at her small shake of the head, he looked away and started explaining the best way to handle the pitchfork and the technique for throwing poo out of the stalls. When he was done with his explanations each of them grabbed a pitchfork and started working.

"Are you going to start with me first?" Missy asked Al while fluttering her eyelashes.

"Sure," Alex replied. He really hated mucking stalls, but it was funny to think of these women doing it. He laughed at Missy's attempts to pitch the poo over the stall and into the bin. She was actually pretty fun to work in the stalls with. She was funny and entertaining and certainly easy on the eyes. Soon he moved on to Courtnee's stall and decided she was also fun to work with. Besides the over-the-top flirting, the women seemed eager to learn what to do and they were funny as well. Finally, it was Sam's turn. He moved up the barn to where Sam was working.

"Hey, looks like you got the hang of this pretty fast," Alex told her, impressed.

"Yeah well, I got lots of practice yesterday," Sam responded, deciding it didn't matter if she'd done the same thing the day before.

Alex immediately got a frown on his face. "You did this yesterday? I didn't realize—"

Sam cut him off. "It's okay, it's not a big deal. I think I'd rather be doing this than some of the other jobs." She smiled at him to try to let him know that she really was okay with it. "I've never even been near a horse, I'm sure it'd buck me off or something."

"Gosh, maybe they should hire you for a permanent job here in the barn," Alex joked. "You'd make a good jillaroo."

Sam just looked at him. Was this all he thought she would be good at?

Alex must have noticed she wasn't laughing at his feeble joke. "Hey, I was kidding," he said. When Sam turned around and continued to clean the stall, Alex touched her arm and pulled her around to look at him. "Honestly, I didn't mean anything by it."

Sam shrugged. "It's okay, really."

"Sammi," Alex said, still holding on to her arm, firmly, but not hurting her. "Don't do that."

"Do what?" Sam asked a bit peevishly.

"Don't lie and tell me what you think I want to hear rather than how you *really* feel." After a beat where Sam didn't say anything, he continued, "If you want to tell me to piss off, tell me to piss off. If I do something that hurts your feelings, tell me." His voice suddenly lowered and he took her hands in his. Sam had to lean into him to hear him over the noise of the barn.

"For the love of God, you're the only real person here. If I can't rely on you to tell me like it is, who will?" He paused. "Now, please tell me what upset you."

"It's just that…" She paused, finally continuing when Alex squeezed her hand. "I don't fit in with the other women here, and I don't want you to see me as…less…than they are. And when you said I'd be good at shoveling crap…It just hit me the wrong way."

"I don't see you as less," Alex immediately said, not even pausing to think about what he wanted to say. "We don't really know each other, but when I'm lying in my cot at night I find myself thinking about you and what *you* are thinking about." He brushed his knuckle over her reddening cheek and continued, "I'd never intentionally insult you like that. I just have to learn how I can tease you and not have you take offense."

They just stood there and looked at each other for a brief moment until they heard Courtnee laugh in the next stall over. The moment between them was broken and Alex dropped her hands and took a step back.

Searching for something to talk to him about, she asked inanely, "How're you doing? I mean, are you enjoying the experience of dating all these women?"

Alex laughed. "It's certainly interesting."

They spent the next few minutes chatting about nothing in particular while cleaning out one stall and moving to the next.

Alex rotated between talking with Courtnee, Missy, and Sam for another thirty minutes, then said he had to go and visit with the other women.

"Are you going to miss me?" Missy pouted.

"Uh, yeah, but I'll see you later," Alex responded quickly with a look in his eye, like a rabbit cornered by a hound dog.

Missy grabbed Alex and kissed him on the lips, and Courtnee, not to be outdone, also grabbed Alex and kissed her way down his face to his lips. Alex finally extricated himself from the two women and looked toward Sammi. She merely waved at Al from the stall she was cleaning, refusing to stoop to Missy's level of desperation, and then went back to work.

"Whew." Missy fanned her face. "That man is *hot*! I can't wait to have him to myself!"

"What makes you think that'll happen?" Courtnee complained. "There's no guarantee you'll get the chance."

"You idiot," Missy told Courtnee snidely. "These shows always have one-on-one time with the bachelor. I'll get my chance."

The two women continued to sit on bales of hay and discuss Al and what they'd do when they had him alone and when they won at the end. Sam tuned them out. It was obvious they were pretty much done mucking out the stalls for the day. Figured that as soon as Al left, they stopped pretending and just quit. Sam knew they wouldn't get as many stalls done as they'd done yesterday. After all, it was only her working. She'd do what she could, and Henry would just have to finish up when they were released. She didn't like to put the work back on him, but she could only do so much.

"Hey goodie-two-shoes," Sam heard Courtnee call out and decided to try to ignore her. She wasn't going to start anything with them.

"Hey, I was talking to you!" Sam heard Courtnee say from outside the stall she was currently mucking out.

"What do you want?" Sam asked peevishly, not bothering to even turn and look at the other woman.

"We're going to take a break, we've been working really hard, so you just keep shoveling and make sure you get to the other side of the barn by the time we get back. We wouldn't want anyone to think you weren't doing your work." Courtnee giggled evilly and turned and left the barn with Missy.

Sam ignored them as they walked out of the barn. It wouldn't do any good to argue, they would do what they wanted to anyway. She'd continue with her work and she'd *not* do theirs as well. It was ridiculous. They were grown women acting like they were in middle school! Sam certainly didn't want to re-live middle or high school. It wasn't terrible, but she certainly wasn't one of the popular kids. As a result, she occasionally got picked on and teased, but she had a feeling that Courtnee was a pro at making others feel small.

Sam worked hard for the next hour. She'd finished her side of the barn and had even laid down fresh hay. She'd really gotten the hang of the mucking the stalls thing. Since she was finished with her portion of the task, and she was really thirsty, she decided to go around the back of the house where she'd seen a water pump. Perhaps she'd get herself some water. She was hot and tired and she knew she probably smelled horrible.

She walked around the barn to the pump at the back of the house. She didn't see anyone around. Sam pumped some water into her hands and slurped it up. Man, was it good. The water must be coming from deep within the ground because it was ice cold. By the time Sam was finished refreshing herself, she was wet from almost head to toe. She'd splashed water onto her face and it had dripped down onto the front of her shirt. She felt much better and could even manage a smile. The water felt so good evaporating from her skin. She turned around to go back to the barn and almost collided with a woman that was standing behind her.

"Oh, excuse me, I didn't see you there," Sam said breathlessly.

"Who are you?" the woman asked with hardly any inflection in her tone.

Sam couldn't tell if she was mad or irritated or some other emotion. She decided it'd be best not to antagonize her.

"I'm Sammi," she responded, remembering her "new" name for while she was on the show. "Uh, I was working in the barn and finished up and thought I would come and get a drink…um…I'm sorry if I'm not supposed to be here, I didn't know."

Nancy looked the woman over. She'd noticed her the day before, but didn't really pay much attention. The woman hadn't done anything to garner any attention. In fact, she couldn't remember what chore she'd been assigned the day before. Nancy noticed her shirt was about soaked through from the water she'd splashed on her face. Her face was rosy red from the heat and effort she'd been putting forth in the barn. She wasn't as tall as some of the other women, and definitely not as slender, but she wasn't really overweight either. Nancy wasn't even one hundred percent convinced this woman was even a contestant on the show. She certainly didn't fit the "mold" of the other contestants. Nancy knew she needed to get to know as many of the women as possible if she was going to be able to make an informed choice about who would stay and who would be leaving. She went with the assumption that this woman was a contestant.

"It's okay, it *is* a hot day today. I'd rather you drink than pass out from heat exhaustion." And with that she let down the wall she'd unconsciously put up and smiled at Sam. "What are you doing in the barn today? I can only think of one thing, and I'm sure it's not pleasant. What job did you have yesterday?"

Sam smiled at her. "It's not too bad, it's nice to know that what I'm doing will help the horses have a comfortable place to sleep at night. And yesterday I did the same thing! Guess I was really lucky, huh?" she said with a grin.

Nancy couldn't believe the woman had to muck out the barn twice! The "rules" didn't say anything about having a different job on each day. It was the luck of the draw, she supposed. "Where are you from, Sammi?" Nancy asked.

"Albuquerque, New Mexico. I really like it there. It's not so much a huge city, but it's big enough to have what I want," Sam replied.

"I've never been there," Nancy responded somewhat expectedly, "but I've heard it's a nice city. If you could've done any of the other chores today, what would you have chosen?"

Sam didn't have to think about it and immediately told the woman standing there, "Help with feeding the animals," she responded.

"You sound like you've thought it over. Wouldn't you want to be in the house where it's air conditioned?" Nancy asked, trying to understand.

"That'd be nice on a day like today," Sam agreed, "but I love animals and I think it would've been interesting to see what everyone eats and how they're all fed," Sammi told her. "I'm a sucker for animals, especially dogs. I have three at home and I'm sure I'd have more if I could. I know feeding animals isn't as simple as some people would assume. My dogs all eat the same food, but I have to remember to put Duke's pills in his food, and the supplement in Albert's." Sam winced, it was a bit too much information, she was sure. She continued meekly, trying to forget that she was just babbling on to this stranger. "I would've loved to see the inside of the house, though. I bet it's just as beautiful on the inside as it is on the outside. I love to go to open houses and see all the fancy houses back in Albuquerque. "

Nancy looked at Sam thoughtfully. "Well, I might be biased since I live here, but I sure think it's a beautiful place to live."

"Oh!" Sam exclaimed. "You live here? I'm sorry, I didn't mean to take up your time. I'm sure you're busy. I didn't mean to keep you...I mean...I don't know if I'm even supposed to be talking to you...I'll just be on my way..." Sam looked around as if to see if anyone was seeing what she was going and looked down at her hands. "I'd offer to shake your hand, but I just washed them, and they're still damp and certainly cold."

Nancy smiled at her for the first time. "It's okay, I've shaken cold hands before." And with that she held out her own hand to Sam. Sam didn't really have a choice. She took the woman's hand and shook it firmly. They smiled at each other and each headed back from where they came.

When Nancy reached the house, she looked back to see Sam entering the barn. She tilted her head to the side, nodded, and continued into the house.

Sam entered the barn, and was glad for the shade, even though the smell was pungent. As soon as she shut the barn door she heard Courtnee talking.

"And we were working hard all day and she just walked out and left us to do her part. It's not fair!"

Sam walked up toward the front of the barn and saw Courtnee and Missy talking with John, one of the jackaroos who worked on the station. Sam hadn't met him face to face, but had seen him from a distance.

"Yeah," Missy joined in. They hadn't seen her standing in the barn door yet. "When we asked where she was going she just glared at us and said 'out.' We couldn't do hers and ours and still get it all done."

"That's a lie!" Sam said loudly, not able to keep quiet anymore while the women ground her reputation into the dirt at their feet. She startled the trio and they all turned in her direction. "If anyone wasn't doing their parts it was the two of you!"

Courtnee looked Sam up and down, paying attention to her wet shirt and then turned to John and somehow managed to have two tears fall from her eyes. "John, we've been here all day working really hard. Look at our hands, they're filthy!" Missy and Courtnee held out their hands and sure enough they were very dirty. "Let's see *her* hands."

Sam knew this was going to end badly. She knew her hands weren't exactly clean, but they were much cleaner than the other women's since she'd just washed them at the back of the house. She figured the other two women had run their hands through the dirt on the floor recently, just for this reason. Sam hesitated, not knowing whether to show them right away or explain where she was and what she'd been doing. John took the choice out of her hand and didn't let her say a word before saying gruffly, "Let's see 'em."

Sam held out her hands. They were pretty clean as Courtnee accused them of being, albeit covered with calluses and a fresh blister, but clean. The water she'd used to wash them had finally dried.

"Go outside," John said to Missy and Courtnee. The last thing Sam saw was the smirks on their faces as they went out the front of the barn.

"What do you have to say for yourself?" John asked Sam. Sam held up her head. She knew she wouldn't win this and if she tried, it would turn out badly. She now knew what Courtnee and Missy were capable of, and she really didn't want to make a big deal out of this. She knew she was an outsider in the group of women and if she made a misstep she would be even more on the outside.

She took a deep breath and willed the tears gathering in the back of her eyes not to fall and further humiliate her.

"Nothing I think you'd believe," she answered John defiantly.

"I think it's awful that you aren't even trying to do your part," John told her disdainfully. "Everyone else here is out of their element too, but you don't see *them* trying to get out of their work, do you? Look at them, they're all beautiful women who have everything going for them and they're doing their part. I don't know why *you* can't do yours too. You look like you should know better," John said in a scathing tone of voice. He continued, "I expect the rest of the *ladies* will be done with their chores soon, but since you decided you didn't want to do yours, you can finish up in here. It looks like there are ten stalls left. You clean those out and put down fresh straw. Once you finish that you can come back and join the others. If there's time left you can eat your lunch late, which is what everyone else will be doing while you're doing the work that you should've done earlier today. I'll inspect your work before you'll be allowed to leave, so don't think you can somehow get out of it. Everyone on this station does their part. We don't tolerate those who don't pull their own weight." And with that John left the barn.

Sam took another deep breath and couldn't keep a few tears from squeezing out of her eyes. She was exhausted. She'd already cleaned out most of the other stalls that day. She figured she'd do more in the first place since she knew Missy and Courtnee had no clue what they were doing and she figured they'd slack off. It wasn't fair to the horses to come back to a messy stall just because she didn't want to do extra. Besides, she really didn't have a choice. What the hell was she doing here? This was one more thing that made her think it was time for her to go home. No one wanted her here, so why was she still trying to participate in this stupid show? No guy was worth this. Sam picked up the pitchfork, walked to the first stall and tried to forget how good looking Al was and how she felt when he singled her out to talk to.

The women were all gathered around the buffet table that had been set out on the expansive lawn of the station. Discussions were going back and forth about the day and about the adventures the women had. Jennie and Kiki were telling everyone they'd made most of the meal. They were very proud of themselves. They acted like they made the entire meal all by themselves, when most of the women knew that certainly wasn't the case. They were all pretty tired from their chores for the day and for the most part took their seats on the long picnic tables and ate. There weren't even that many comments about how many calories they were consuming, they were just too tired to think about it.

Alex had spent the day going from chore to chore, talking with the women and trying to get to know them all a bit better. It was tough, especially when they were competing for his attention. That was something he usually laughed about and enjoyed when he was out with his buddies, but for some reason it was grating on his nerves here. He went in the house to look for Aunt Nancy so they could go over the highlights of the day on the tapes.

Alex found Nancy in the back family room. It looked like she'd gotten a head start and was watching the tapes from the chores from earlier in the day. She was taking it very seriously. She had a notepad out and was taking notes about the women and their actions. Al smiled. He'd always liked his aunt and he was sorry they didn't get to see each other that much since they lived on different continents.

"How's it goin'?" Alex asked her.

"Hummm," she responded, not really paying him any attention.

Alex laughed. "That good, huh? What do you think?"

Nancy turned her head and looked her nephew in the eye. "What I've noticed is that they were all on their best behavior when you were with them, and when you left their real personalities came out," she told him honestly.

"I expected as much," Alex replied. "Who's on the top of your list to go today?"

"I still think I'm leaning toward Candi and Katie. They seem to be the ones that do the least work and want the most attention. They wouldn't last very long at your ranch. It's too far out and there isn't enough attention there for them."

"Who do you like the most?" Alex asked his aunt. Since she knew who she thought should go first, he wanted her honest opinion on the other women. At some point he was going to have to choose one to keep at the end of the show. "Does anyone stand out?"

Nancy pressed the pause button on the television and looked at Alex. "It's hard to say. I don't really know them all that well, and it's hard to tell from meeting them on such short notice."

Alex interrupted, "That's what I've been going through. I tried to tell you."

"Don't be cheeky," Nancy replied smiling, "there are a few I do like. I met that Sammi woman today. Did you know she had to muck out the barn two days in a row? I wouldn't wish that on my worst enemy. Even the jackaroos switch out that duty."

"Yeah, I hadn't realized it until today when I was helping them. That's definitely one of the worst jobs the women had to do today. All three were doing a good job when I left, though. Where did you meet Sammi? Don't tell me you took a trip down to the barn?" Alex asked his aunt with an arch of his brow.

"Don't be absurd! Of course not. She came up to the water pump to get a drink and cool off," Nancy replied. "We had a short conversation and she went back to the barn."

"Who else do you like?" Alex asked, trying to get the conversation off of Sammi. He wasn't ready to admit to his aunt how much he was attracted to Sammi.

"Amy seems to be nice, as well as Kathi and Ashley," Nancy told him.

"That's about what I think too," Alex said, again downplaying his own thoughts about Sammi and the other women. "Let's finish watching this and let Eddie know who the pick is and we'll get out of your hair. I'm sure you'll be glad to have your house back."

The two sat and watched the rest of the tapes, laughing at the antics of the women trying to get and hold his attention. It was obvious they were all out of their element, but most were genuinely trying to do their chores. Finally, Nancy made her decision. It'd been a long day and it was time to have the ceremony so the women could go back to their camp and Alex and the producers could get back to theirs to start editing the tapes.

Chapter Thirteen

Alex and his aunt strolled out to the porch to see the women were done eating and were sitting around chatting. The food had been taken away and it seemed as if they were waiting on the camera crews and the producers to set them up for the final shot of the day. Alex saw Sammi walk over from the direction of the barn. Her shoulders were slumped and she looked dejected or exhausted. She didn't look up as she walked, but instead stared at the ground as if it was the most fascinating thing she'd ever seen. Alex couldn't understand what she was doing…did she go back to the barn after she ate? Something was going on and he didn't know what it was. He hated that. There wasn't any food left out, it had been taken away about half an hour ago. Had she taken another walk? If so, why did she look so sad and defeated? He watched her to go the end of one of the long picnic tables, sit, put her head down on her arms and go still. Alex looked at his aunt as if to ask if she had seen Sammi's actions, but her attention was on one of the jackaroos, John, who was walking toward them.

"Ma'am, if I may have a word with you, please," John asked Nancy in a grave tone.

"Of course," she said, gesturing for him to continue.

John looked at Alex as if to ask Nancy if they could go somewhere private.

"Alex is my nephew, I don't have any secrets from him, go ahead," Nancy told him firmly.

John shrugged and continued, "I was checking on the ladies who were working in the barn and it seems we had a problem, but I took care of it."

"I can't imagine what kind of problem you're talking about. The women weren't expected to be perfect at their jobs, what's the issue?" Nancy asked him with genuine bafflement.

"When I got there to check the work, there were only two women working. They told me that the third hadn't done much work that day and that they had to do more than their fair share of the stalls. While we were talking the third came in and contradicted the others' stories. I looked at their hands. The two women who were there had real dirty workin' hands and the third didn't have any dirt on her hands at all. So to make sure that everything was fair I had the third stay and finish up the barn. I just thought you should know. I checked her work and it was fine. The horses will be in clean stalls tonight, just like every night. I wanted to put your mind at ease. I also wanted to let you know what happened in case she tried to come complain to you…or to you," he said, looking at Alex.

"John, are you sure that you took the time to read the situation right? If the third person is who I think it was, I met her at the water pump and she told me she'd just finished her stalls and was taking a break, washing her hands and her face and getting a drink of water," Nancy questioned John carefully.

"Um, well, it seemed to be the right decision at the time," John stuttered, not knowing what to think.

Alex was furious. He could just imagine what had happened. Missy and Courtnee had taken advantage of the fact that Sammi wasn't there when John came in to check on their work and took credit for what she'd done. When she walked in the barn with clean hands John jumped to the obvious conclusion. They were all working when he was there with them, but he knew many of the women changed after he'd left their sight. He thought he knew Sammi pretty well, especially after watching her not complain about the treatment she'd received from some of the women in camp as well her lack of complaints when she was injured or uncomfortable.

"I'm not sure what happened, John, but I'll find out, you can go. If I find that you misjudged that woman, you *will* apologize to her *and* be on stall duty for the rest of the week," Nancy told him sternly.

John looked a little sheepish but said, "Yes, ma'am," and headed for the bunkhouse.

Nancy looked at Alex, who looked ready to explode.

"Calm down, Alex, let me handle this," Nancy told him sternly. "I don't believe that's what really happened either, but I won't take the empowerment away from my jackaroos either."

They both looked over at the tables. Sammi hadn't moved. She was in the same position as a few minutes ago…head on her arms on the table. Since the production crew was still setting up for the final scene of the day, Nancy sent one of the kitchen staff over to get Sammi and told her to bring her to the front room in the house. They watched as the girl bent over Sammi, touched her shoulder, then finally shook her gently. Sammi lifted her head at the summons, then looked at the house and nodded to the girl. She slowly got up and headed for the front door.

"What'd ya do now, Miss Bitch?" Courtnee yelled out as Sammi shuffled past. "Getting called to the principal's office because you didn't do your work?" And with that she and several other women laughed.

Sam glared at Courtnee and said, "You should know." She kept walking. It wasn't worth it to continue to try to come up with a better comeback. She was beyond tired and every muscle in her body hurt.

Sam was surprised when she was asked to come up to the house. She figured it couldn't get any worse than the jackaroo looking disdainfully at her and determining that her work in the barn was just "okay." Dammit, she'd cleaned the entire barn by herself. Well, almost the entire barn, Missy and Courtnee had worked when Al had been there. Sam laughed at herself, well, she'd wanted to get a look inside the house and she guessed she was now getting her chance.

Sam was led into the front room and stopped short. The woman she'd met earlier that day was there, along with Al. "Shit," Sam muttered to herself. She wasn't sure whether she was supposed to stay standing or sit down…but she also wasn't completely confident she'd be able to stand there without falling over, but she'd do it or die trying. She was embarrassed enough having to be there in front of the woman and Al like a naughty child. She wasn't going to fall over, no matter what…maybe.

"Sit down, Sammi," Nancy said, motioning toward a chair in front of the large desk.

Sam hesitated for half a second before deciding she'd better sit just so there was no chance she'd fall flat on her face. She gratefully sat, back ramrod straight looking only at the woman. She definitely didn't want to look at Al. This was too humiliating. Some impression she was making. Maybe they were going to tell her she was going home right this minute. Was that it? That had to be it. But she hadn't seen Eddie or Robert talking to the woman, although she'd seen the jackaroo from the barn talking to Nancy and saw Al's frown. This wasn't going to be a fun interview, she was sure of it.

"Sammi," Nancy began, "my jackaroo told me quite a story about what happened in the barn today. Would you like to me tell your side?"

Sam looked at Nancy, then dared to glance at Al. He was standing with his arms crossed in front of him with a stern look on his face. There was no way Sam was going to rat out the other women. They were already making her life miserable. There was no telling what would happen if she made them be caught in a lie.

"No, ma'am," Sam told the woman.

Nancy raised her eyebrows and said incredulously, "Nothing? So you admit you did nothing all day while the other women did all the work and you were just lounging around? You only worked when Al was there but stopped when he left? Is that right?" Nancy asked, deliberately trying to get under the young woman's skin.

"Ma'am, John made a judgment call based on the facts he received. I can't fault him for that. I willingly accepted my punishment. You'll find your horses will be able to rest peacefully tonight in clean beds. That really should be all you care about. Not who did what. The chore was completed. You'll never see me again after today," Sammi responded in a dull voice.

"Damn it, Sammi," Alex started to protest.

"No," Sammi interrupted. "Neither of you were there and you have to trust your employees." She looked Nancy in the eyes and continued, "You can't go around second guessing decisions that are made around here. It's a simple business decision. You empower your employees to make decisions and you stand behind them when they do, whether they're wrong or right. If they're wrong, you discuss what happened and talk about what might be done differently the next time. John did what he thought was right. I accepted it, end of story."

The three of them sat there, looking at each other for a long moment. Finally, Nancy broke the silence, "I'm fairly certain you weren't at fault today. I saw you at the pump, I know you were covered with dirt and who knows what else when you got there and that you cleaned yourself up. I do trust my jackaroos, but I also don't like for anyone to get blamed and/or punished for something they didn't do. Should I bring John in here to tell his side of the story again to see if we can't get to the bottom of this?" Nancy asked in a hard voice.

Sam sighed. She'd screwed up and obviously pissed off the woman in front of her. The last thing she wanted to do was get someone else in trouble for her stupidity. She should've known that Courtnee would pull something. All in all it wasn't that big of a deal. This was a stupid television show after all. Suddenly remembering Robert and the show, Sam looked around. She didn't see any cameras…which was odd. "Where are the cameras?" she asked belatedly, more to herself than actually thinking that anyone would answer.

"This is a private matter, not one for television," Nancy told her with crisp intonation. "Do you want me to get John in here?" she asked again, not letting Sammi leave the question unanswered.

"No," Sam said sharper than she intended. She tried to calm herself down and said in a gentler voice, "Look, I'll apologize to whomever you want me to. I took responsibility for what happened today. I'm sorry, it won't happen again." She laughed a bit at that and continued, "Not that I'll have the chance to do it again." She stopped laughing and looked the woman in the eyes and said earnestly, "I believe I did the best I could in that barn. John did the right thing, the only thing he could, and I probably would've done the same thing he did in the same situation. The evidence was against me and I took the punishment. Can I go? I'm sure the producers are ready to start by now." She finished lamely and desperately.

Nancy and Alex looked at each other and Alex gave his aunt a curt nod.

"Fine, you can go. But Sammi," Nancy said as Sam shakily stood up and started for the door, "not everyone is so easily fooled. Get some rest."

Sam nodded and paused at the door and turned back to Nancy with a small smile. Even with everything that was said and the position she was in she couldn't resist saying, "I was right, it *is* just as beautiful as the outside," and she walked out the door.

"What was that about?" Alex asked his aunt, baffled by Sammi's last comment.

"Never mind about that," Nancy said gruffly but with a trace of a smile. "What do you think?" she asked her nephew seriously.

"I don't know who or what she's protecting, but it's damn annoying. We both know she wouldn't have shirked her duty. Why won't she tell us what really happened?" Alex asked his aunt.

"I'm not sure, but she has nerves of steel. She was ready to fall over, but it looked like sheer stubbornness was keeping her upright," Nancy said thoughtfully, then finished, "I like her."

Alex looked at his aunt. "So do I," he said solemnly.

* * *

Sam walked back out to the yard. *All I have to do is get through this so I can go back to the camp and get some sleep.* Her hands hurt. Her back hurt. Her legs hurt. Hell, there wasn't a body part that didn't hurt, but underneath the hurt, she felt strangely good. She'd done a great job today, and no one would be able to take that away from her.

It seemed as if Eddie and the other producers and Robert were finally ready for the "vote off," as Sam started calling it. She was fairly certain she might be the one going home. There was no telling who else Missy and Courtnee had spewed their story to. If it was Eddie, he might make her go home for violating the rules of the show or something. All she could do was wait along with everyone else. At this point she almost didn't care. Almost.

Sam watched as Al took his spot next to Robert. He looked good. He looked more rugged now than he had before. Sam figured it was because he'd been outside most of the day and doing all the chores. She really couldn't see him doing the laundry or mopping the floor, but she'd heard snippets of the other women's conversations who'd claimed he'd done just that.

Robert was making his speech about what a great job they'd all done that day and how he was impressed with their work ethic. He asked if there were any comments about the day. A few women spoke, but for the most part it seemed they were just as anxious to get this over with as Sam was. Blessedly, even Missy and Courtnee kept their mouths shut. *Maybe they figured the less people they tell their lies to, the more likely they'll get away with it.* Sam thought. Finally, Robert was getting to the "vote off."

"As you know, ladies, one of you must be going home today. We know it's been a long day and you're tired. No one wants to leave this beautiful country and miss out on the company of Al, but alas, it must be done." Sam didn't think Robert sounded very remorseful.

He continued with his grand speech, "There were many factors that were taken into account on who'd be leaving today. It wasn't only one thing that sealed her fate, but a multitude of factors. To keep you on your toes, those factors will not be revealed to you. The person who will be leaving today is…" Robert paused to get the most dramatic effect out of his audience… "Katie."

Sam let out a breath she wasn't even aware she'd been holding. She'd thought for sure her time was up. Katie cried and hugged some of the other women she'd gotten to know on the show. She walked up to where Al and Robert were standing. Al led her away to the waiting car to say goodbye.

"It's time to go back to camp, ladies," Robert told them. "Please gather up your belongings and say goodbye and we'll go."

Since Al was walking back to the group most of the women walked toward him to say their *personal* goodbyes for the day. Sam went to sit at one of the tables until they had to load up the bus. As she was walking toward a table she saw Henry approaching her. Sam veered a bit to meet him. She'd liked the gruff jackaroo. He'd made the first day of mucking out the stables pretty fun. Sam put her hands in her back pockets as they approached each other.

"Hey, Sammi!" Henry said with a drawl. "You look like shit," he continued with no remorse.

Sam laughed as she was sure he meant her to. "Thanks, you sure know how to make a lady feel good."

"No, really, you look worn to the bone. What time did you finish up today?" he asked her.

"You'll never guess." Sammi grinned up at him, avoiding directly answering his question.

Henry raised his brows while waiting expectantly for her to answer.

"Let's just say I'm starving because I didn't make dinner," Sam told him with a grin, not about to go into the details about why she hadn't gotten to eat.

Henry put his head back and laughed. "Damn, that's bad luck! Why'd it take so long?"

Sam's smile dimmed a bit. Not wanting to answer him, she skirted around his question and instead shrugged and said, "I'll be glad not to see another barn for a while." She ran her hand through her hair, brushing it back off her face.

Henry suddenly reached out and grabbed her wrist.

"Wha…" Sam got out as she flinched in surprise. What did she really know about this man after all?

Alex watched Sammi out of the corner of his eye as the other women said their goodbyes. He didn't know why it bothered him to see her smile at one of the jackaroos, but he knew he was irritated. His mood only grew worse when he saw the man throw his head back and laugh at something Sammi said. He'd just finished saying the correct meaningless goodbye words to Kiki when he saw the jackaroo grab Sammi by the wrist. Without a second thought, he was striding across the yard to where Sammi stood.

"What in the hell did you do?" Henry rasped as he turned Sam's hand over to look at her palm. Sam tried to tug her hand away from him.

"Let me go," Sam said firmly. Henry gripped her wrist even more firmly.

"Not until you explain this," Henry said gruffly, trying to pull her toward him so he could get a better look at her palm.

"She said to let go of her," a deep voice said from behind them. Henry dropped her wrist and they both turned to see Alex standing a few feet from them.

"You okay?" he asked Sam, shifting forward so his body was between her and the other man. Alex didn't know what was going on, but he wasn't going to allow anyone to touch her without her permission. Alex didn't even take the time to think about why he felt that way, he just did. He'd never been the possessive, alpha type, but Sammi somehow brought it out in him.

Sam tucked her hand back in her jeans pocket and said, "Yup, I've got to get on the bus…"

"You won't until I find out what the hell just happened here," Alex told her with a glare. He turned his eyes to Henry. "If you want to keep your job you'd better start explaining."

Henry answered immediately and calmly, "She's hurt, I was trying to look at her hand." He'd seen Alex around a bit and knew his bark was worse than his bite. Suppressing a smile, knowing the hardworking and genuine woman standing in front of them seemed to have gotten under his skin, he nodded toward Sam and said, "Look for yourself."

Both men turned to see Sam backing away from them, hands still out of sight. "They're all waiting for me…I have to go," she stammered, almost tripping over herself trying to get away. "It was nice to meet you, Henry," Sam said, still backing away.

Alex came toward her as if he was a predator stalking his prey. "Give me your hand," he ordered, holding out his own.

"It's not a big deal, Al," Sam tried to explain, "it's just a blister from working today, I'm sure that all the others have them too…"

Alex stepped close enough to take her by the upper arm and stop her retreat.

"It's a bit more than that, hon," Henry said. "I'll leave you to deal with her," he told Al as he turned around to go back to the barn.

"Damn," Sam muttered under her breath, not believing how Henry had thrown her under the proverbial bus when it came to Alex.

"You know you're going to make my life miserable by giving me this attention, don't you?" Sam tried to reason with Alex. "They're okay, it's not life threatening. Just let me go…please?"

"I can't let you go knowing you might be hurt," Alex told her honestly. "What kind of man would I be if I just let you walk away right now knowing you were in pain and I didn't do anything about it? It's bad enough I couldn't do anything the other day when you were cold." Alex stared into Sammi's eyes, trying desperately to make her understand that he wanted to help her, that he *needed* to help her.

Sam somehow knew Al would stand there all night waiting if she didn't just get it over with and show him. She pulled out her left hand, knowing it wasn't as bad as the right one. "Fine, you want to see it, here," and she shoved it under his face.

"Holy shit, Sammi," Alex muttered, rubbing his thumb over the back of her hand while holding her palm up. It didn't look good. There were blisters on the palm under each finger. She had what looked like a blister on top of a blister at the base of her thumb and one large blister right in the center of her palm.

"What the hell happened? Why didn't you use gloves?" Alex practically yelled at her, not able to hold back his concern about how she was hurt. While he sounded mad, the hand that was holding hers was gentle.

Sam tried to yank her hand away from him, but he held firm.

"I couldn't find them this afternoon and I had to get the job done, so I did it. It's not a big deal, Al. Really. *Please*, let me get on the bus, they're all looking at us," Sam said desperately. As much as she loved the feel of Al's hands on hers she knew she'd pay for it. If she thought Courtnee and the others were playing the game before, they would really start on her now. She was enemy number one in every way.

"Let me see the other one," Alex said remorselessly, not giving into her pleas until he'd seen for himself how badly she was hurt.

Sam sighed. She knew he wouldn't let her go until he'd seen the other hand as well. Reluctantly, she pulled it out of her pocket and held it out.

Alex didn't say a word, just took a hold of her right hand and leaned over to see it closer to get a better look. It was a bit worse than the other one since she was right handed. Some of the blisters were really oozing and looked like they needed to be cleaned.

"Let's go," Alex told her abruptly, trying to tow her toward the big house.

"Where?" Sam asked, trying to pull back in the direction of the bus.

"To the house where we can have these looked at by a doctor," Alex answered determinately.

"No way!" Sam said, yanking her hand out of his grasp and taking a large step backward and away from him. "I'm going back to the bus and leaving right now. I'll clean it back at camp," she promised somewhat desperately.

Alex looked at her, then back to the bus. "Okay, I can understand you wouldn't want the other women to think you were getting unfair attention from me, but you have to have this taken care of. It won't wait."

Sam sighed and asked, "Can we compromise? Can Eddie have one of his people look at it back at camp?"

Alex pondered her statement, not liking the entire situation at all. *He* wanted to be the one to take care of her. *He* wanted to be the one who made her feel better. He really wanted her to lean on him and to see him as able to take care of her. This situation was so messed up. There was no way in the "real world" he'd let her just go off into the night knowing she needed care. He sighed and finally said, "Okay, but the next time we get together I want to see for myself that they're healing. And know that if we weren't on this show I'd take you in and make sure you were cared for. I'd probably draw you a hot bubble bath, cook you a comforting dinner and make sure you took care of yourself. I have a feeling you take care of others more than you take care of yourself."

Sam couldn't say anything at first. She allowed her eyes to say what her heart felt. She'd never had someone take care of her like that and there was nothing she wanted more than to let Al do what he just said he'd do if he could. But she knew she couldn't, and for her own self-preservation, she had to get on that bus right now and get away from the most handsome and caring man she'd ever met. She gave him a wistful, but honest, smile and softly said, "Deal." Then she turned her back on Al and walked toward the bus.

Alex watched her go. He was pleased at the smile she'd bestowed on him. It lit up her face and was definitely not the kind of smile he was used to seeing on women. He was used to seeing a small fake curling of the lips, seldom did the women he was around show any teeth when they smiled. It was refreshing to see an unfettered smile, and even better that it had been aimed at him. Alex turned away to talk to Eddie before he left the station. He wanted to see the tapes from the doctor looking at her hands later that night. He just couldn't let it go. He had to see for himself that Sammi was taken care of. It was a compulsion of sorts, a confusing one at that.

The bus was quiet on the way back to the camp. Sam fell asleep in the front seat as soon as they left the cattle station. When they pulled up to the camp it almost seemed as if they were back home, as much of a "home" as it could be. Eddie had obviously sent one of the camp doctors to meet the bus as there was a man in a white coat waiting when the bus pulled up. He called Sam over and had her sit on the truck bed he'd driven to the camp while he doctored her hands. It hurt, but Sam was so tired it wasn't as bad as it could've been. The doctor bandaged up her hands and was on his way. He didn't say much to her. Sam figured it was back to the "show" rules, but he did tell her to keep her hands dry that night and that they should be bandaged each night and covered with the salve to keep them moist and to help them heal.

Sam went into the tent to lie down. She figured a shower could wait. Even though she was filthy, she couldn't imagine being able to stand up for the amount of time it'd take. Besides, the doctor told her to keep her hands dry. The other women slowly filed into the tent after visiting the bathroom and shower.

Kathi came to stand near Sam's cot and said nastily, "So, did you plan that little interlude or what? You think you can outsmart us to get to spend more time with Al? Ain't gonna happen, bitch. You don't have a shot in hell at that man. Look at you, you're pathetic. Your games aren't going to work."

Sam looked up at Kathi and said quietly and honestly, "That wasn't what I was trying to do. All I wanted was to leave. He was the one who insisted that he look at my hands. I don't figure I'm going to win this game either."

"Damn straight," piped up Cindee. By now most of the women who were living in the tent had wandered over.

"It seems to me that Al is the kind of man who'd care about anyone that was hurt," Sam continued. "It wasn't as if he was showing me any extra affection or consideration. He'd have done the same thing if it'd been one of you that was hurt." Sam looked at each woman. "Look at it this way, now that my hands aren't in top shape, that leaves me more vulnerable to not being able to succeed in the future challenges."

The girls laughed.

"That's true," said Brandi.

They slowly all went back to their beds. It'd been a long two days and most of them were ready to get some sleep. Kathi was the last one standing near Sam's bed.

"You might have fooled them," she said in a low furious voice, cocking her head toward the other women settling down into their beds for the night, "but Missy and Courtnee told me what you did today. You like to make others think you're a saint, but you and I both know better. If you think he likes to help women that are hurt feel better, you'd better not egg him on."

Sam sighed and looked at Kathi. "Go to bed Kathi, I'm not going to fight with you. Did you see me cozying up to him? Did you see me go to him first? No. I wasn't even going to tell him, so there's fault in your logic. Remember too that this whole thing is Courtnee and Missy's fault. If they hadn't lied, I wouldn't have been hurt in the first place and Al wouldn't have had to be concerned about me. I don't *need* him or any man to help me feel better, or to take care of me…I can do it myself. Don't mess with me, Kathi. I'll stay out of your way and you stay out of mine. We only have to be around each other for another week or two and then we won't ever have to see each other again."

"I can't wait," Kathi hissed and walked away.

Sam sighed. This wasn't going well. She sure hoped the next week or two passed quickly, or that she was taken out of the show before things got really ugly.

* * *

Alex didn't go straight back to the camp. He stayed back at the station to visit with his Aunt Nancy for a bit. He wasn't sure when he'd get to see her again and he missed her. They talked a little about what had happened that day. Neither could understand what was going through Sammi's head, and while they had a good idea about what went on in the barn, neither knew for sure. When Alex asked the producer about tapes from the barn, he'd told them the cameras had taped them while he was helping them out and stayed for a bit afterward, but hadn't been back. That wasn't going to help them figure out what happened.

"You said her hands had blisters all over them?" Nancy asked her nephew with concern in her voice.

"Yes, and they were bad. I don't know how she was able to muck the barn out with them like that," Alex told her, still concerned if she'd gotten help when she got back to her camp.

"I'm sure they were fine when she was up at the water pump," Nancy told him. "We shook hands and I didn't see her flinch or feel anything out of the ordinary. In fact, I was impressed she actually shook my hand and didn't give me a "limp fish" handshake. She couldn't have done that if she'd been hurt then."

Alex agreed with his aunt. "She must not have used gloves when she went back to the barn. We could ask John about it," Alex told her, getting ready to stand up to go and find John right that second. Anything to help get to the bottom of what happened to Sammi. He was having a hard time letting it go.

"Let's just forget about it. We don't know what happened, but it doesn't really matter now. Sammi was right, John made a judgment call. We might not like it, but we weren't there either. She seems to be okay, tired but fine and she'll get her hands looked at by a doctor back at camp." Trying to change the subject, Nancy said, "Let's talk about what they have planned for you for the upcoming week." She settled in to speculate with Alex about what was going to happen next on the show.

Alex and Nancy spent the next couple of hours catching up and talking about the show and the ladies. Before long, it was time for Alex to get back to the camp. He was anxious to see the tapes and see how Sammi's hands were.

After saying good-bye to his aunt and going back to the producer's camping area, Alex sat in his tent with the tapes from that night. He was told all the women were sound asleep or at least in their tents for the night. He watched as the doctor cleaned and bandaged Sammi's hands. Neither said much. Alex could tell the cleansing process was hurting Sammi. He could see her biting her bottom lip, but she didn't say a word. He watched as she walked back to her tent. Eddie had also given him another tape. It was one from the inside of one of the women's tents. The women knew the tent cameras were there, it was all a part of the show.

Alex watched as the women settled down and got ready for bed. This camera was more of a "wide angle" lens, so he didn't have any close up shots of anyone, but he saw Kathi walk up to Sammi's bed as she was lying on it. He heard bits and pieces of the conversation, enough to know that Kathi was giving Sammi a hard time about the attention he'd given her.

That's what she was talking about, Alex thought to himself. *No wonder she just wanted me to leave her alone.*

Alex watched as the other women gathered around to hear the conversation. Alex was amazed to hear Sammi peg him when she was defending his gallant tendencies and explain how he didn't like to see women hurt. He was surprised she knew that about him already. They really hadn't spent that much time together, but he'd hoped that perhaps she had some feelings toward him. Hearing her defend him made him realize the attraction wasn't just on his side. It made him smile.

Alex watched the conversation and saw the women drift off toward their own beds until it was only Kathi and Sammi left talking. He saw Kathi lean in toward Sammi. He couldn't hear what she was saying, the camera only picked up bits and pieces of the conversation.

I'll have to tell Eddie to turn up the microphone. Alex thought as he strained to hear what was being said. He heard Kathi say something like, "saint, help women, and egg." Alex wasn't sure what to make of that. He couldn't hear what Sammi said in response, but as she spoke her words got louder and he was able to hear the end of the conversation.

"I don't *need* him or any man to help me feel better, or to take care of me…I can do it myself." He chuckled to himself. Alex never thought he could be attracted to an *independent* woman, but he found he liked the thought of Sammi not needing him, but perhaps wanting him instead. Lord knew he wanted her. He was attracted to her. More than attracted. He was thrilled there was at least some reciprocation on Sammi's behalf.

Alex watched as Kathi stormed back to her bed. He was definitely glad for the opportunity to watch the tapes from camp. He was learning a lot about the personalities of the women, and what he was learning made him more and more cynical. He was amazed at how different the ladies were around him than they were around each other. He shuddered to think about having to make a decision without knowing the true personalities of the women. Thank God he was able to see the tapes. It was bad enough to feel like a piece of meat that dogs were fighting over.

He felt as if with the tapes at least he could have a fighting chance of making the right decision at the end of the show. He might not like Eddie very much as a person, but as a producer, he certainly knew how to make a show exciting.

Chapter Fourteen

The next week went by fairly quickly for Sam. Her hands healed quickly, enough so that it no longer hurt to use them. Al was true to his word and checked them himself the first time they saw each other after the incident. It should've been awkward since they were still basically strangers, but instead it was awkward for Sam because of how she felt when Al had taken her hands in his and run his fingertips over her quickly healing palms.

Sam wanted to grab him and never let go. She imagined his hands running over the rest of her body and it was all she could do to not fall in a puddle at his feet.

The days at camp were lazy ones. Sam no longer took walks away from the camp, not because she didn't want to, but because she didn't want to put any of the camera operators in danger again. She still blamed herself for Kina almost being bitten and didn't want to have a repeat.

The women went through challenges and won "prizes" such as small group dates with Al and even a visit to a hot spring to soak in the soothing waters. There were four more women who'd been "voted off"—Candi, Nikki, Brandi, and Jennie. The women came back to camp after Jennie left to find that one of the bunkhouses had disappeared and they'd all be staying in one. That was a tough adjustment for most of the women because they'd gotten used to the space and only having four or five of them in each bunkhouse.

Sam was surprised she was still around. For the most part she avoided Kathi, Courtnee, and Missy. They certainly weren't friends, but at least they weren't enemies either. Apparently the last run-in with Kathi and the threats that hung in the air between them was enough to chill Kathi out.

Sam hung out mostly with Amy and Lori. They didn't have much in common, but when a person is put in a situation where there isn't much to do, comradeship is forced.

The women who were left were Ashley from Toledo, Cindee from Albany, Lori from Colorado Springs, Kiki from Miami, Courtnee from Pensacola, Missy from LA, Amy from El Paso, Kathi from Knoxville, and Sammi. It was an interesting mix of women. There were definitely cliques that had formed. Kathi, Courtnee, Missy, and Kiki had banded together. They acted like they were the "popular" girls in high school. They sat together, got ready in the mornings together, and probably most importantly, they helped each other in the challenges. That wasn't exactly illegal, but it reminded Sam of the Alliances that were formed in the game of Survivor.

Today was a big day because the prize for being in the top three of today's challenge was a one-on-one date with Al. So far in the show there hadn't been any of those types of dates. They'd all either been the entire group together or four or five of them at a time. They were all hoping to win one of the personal one-on-one dates, but Sam knew the "clique" would do everything in their power to win. Sam hoped, however, that since there were four of them and only three slots for the individual dates, it would work against them and their so-called friendship might not be able to handle that type of competition.

The nine women were told to wear their bathing suits and to be on the bus by nine in the morning. Obviously this was going to be a water competition. Sam was nervous, while she had a pretty healthy body image, there was no way she'd be able to compete with the other women. She was heavier than them, and she knew if she had to stand next to them while they were all wearing their skimpy swimsuits that she'd definitely be at a disadvantage.

The bus pulled out at precisely nine in the morning. The bus ride turned out to be one of the longest they'd been on to get to a challenge so far. Sam suspected it was because they had to drive quite a ways to get to a body of water.

Finally they pulled up to the most beautiful lake Sam had ever seen. It was crystal clear and huge. The production staff had obviously gotten there earlier because they had all the cameras set up and there was what looked like an obstacle course set up in the water. Sam smiled to herself. If this was a water swimming challenge, she was set.

They piled out of the bus and went to stand in front of Robert, who of course, looked immaculate. Courtnee and Missy had already taken off their tops and were wearing shorts and a bikini top. Al looked gorgeous as usual. He was wearing his usual blue jeans, but had substituted his button up shirt for a white T-shirt.

Sam tried to covertly look at Al. Over the last week she'd gotten to know him a little better. She hadn't had any time alone with him, but she honestly thought they were clicking. Of course, every time she thought it, she'd then see one of the other women plastered all over him. She gave herself a mental smack in the head. Sam thought they were clicking…but that was what he was supposed to do with every contestant. They were *all* supposed to feel like they were the "one" for him.

Sam, Beth, and Christina had a long conversation about this very thing before she left for the Outback. Every time they'd watched a reality show, they'd laughed at how emotional the women were and wondered how in the world anyone could say they were in love with someone who their whole relationship with was in front of a camera and therefore probably fake. But she got it now. It was a very intense atmosphere. There were no other distractions. The only focus was on the other person. It made for an intimate setting, manufactured, but intimate nonetheless. Sam was brought out of her musings when she heard Robert start talking.

"Welcome, ladies!" Robert boomed once everyone was in place and the cameras were rolling. "Today, you'll be competing against each other for a one-on-one date with Al. The three women who finish the course the fastest will each get to spend half a day with Al on a date of his choice. Here are the rules. Each of you will be going through the course individually. You'll enter the lake here, swim to the first buoy...attached to the buoy at the end of a rope is a small weight. You'll need to swim down to the end of the rope and untie the weight and let it fall. Then you are to swim to the next buoy and untie the weight at the end of the rope that's hanging from that rope. You will continue around the buoys until you have untied all the weights. The weight on each rope gets heavier and heavier as well as deeper and deeper as you swim around. You will then swim back to the starting point and once you cross the finish line your time will stop. The three women who either finish the course the fastest or go the furthest in the shortest amount of time will win the one-on-one dates with Al. Are there any questions?"

The contestants were given time to examine the course from the shore. On TV it always seemed as if the people just went right onto the game, but in reality that wasn't the case. There was an obnoxious amount of time spent on safety talks and explaining over and over how it was done. One of the producers even demonstrated the entire course so they would understand what they needed to do and wouldn't screw it up once they were on camera. It was exhausting and exasperating. Sam just wanted to get started already.

Once they were ready to start, Cindee asked what order they'd be competing in and Robert told her that Al would be pulling their names out of a hat to see the order they would go in. Sam almost laughed out loud. This competition had her name written all over it. She knew she could easily beat most, if not all, of the women. She hadn't been on her state champion winning water polo for nothing! Al pulled the names out of the hat and as luck would have it, Sam's name was chosen eighth. Kathi's was chosen to go last.

Sam felt way too giddy about being able to spend some time with Al alone. She again tried to warn herself that what she was feeling toward Al was manufactured and in no way could be real, but she couldn't help herself. Al was hot, and she had a major crush on him. Every time she felt his eyes on her she daydreamed that maybe, just maybe, he was feeling the same way about her.

First up was Courtnee. Since she already had her top off, she slowly shimmied out of her shorts, leaving her standing in nothing but a skimpy black bikini. Sam groaned softly. It didn't look like there was an ounce of fat on her. Her legs were long and lean, her boobs big, but not too big. Basically, she was perfect. The camera operators were getting close up shots of her body as she sauntered to the starting line. Hell, even her ass didn't jiggle! Al was standing by the lake to wish each of them good luck before they started. Sam and the other women couldn't hear what was being said, but by Courtnee's body language, they could tell that whatever he was saying to her was quite intimate.

The producers put up a set of bleachers for the women to sit on while they were waiting their turns. They watched as Courtnee went into the water and started paddling toward the first buoy. The distances weren't that far, maybe fifty yards, but it looked like Courtnee was struggling before she even got to the first buoy. She was doing a kind of dogpaddle mixed with breaststroke. Finally she made it and grasped the floating buoy as if it was a lifeline. Slowly, she started to haul the rope up to the buoy.

Sheesh. Sam thought to herself. *She'd go a lot faster if she'd just swim down to the weight rather than pull it up to her!* The women and the cameras on the bank watched as Courtnee slowly went from buoy to buoy. They could see that as Courtnee got to the buoys further on in the course, it got harder and harder to pull them up to the surface because the weights got heavier and heavier. Finally, after resting a few minutes on one of the last buoys, Courtnee motioned that she was done and wasn't going to attempt to finish the course.

"Five buoys in 23:34," Robert announced. That was the time to beat.

Again, this was another non glamorous part of a reality show. The course had to be reset after each woman went through. That meant that one of the production team had to swim out to each buoy, dive down to get the weight and reattach it. It seemed to take forever to reset. This challenge was going to last all day.

Time passed as each of the other women took their turn in the lake. Some used the same technique as Courtnee, trying to pull the weights up to the buoy, while others tried to swim down to the weight and let it free. The top times with two women left to go were Ashley finishing the course in 26:12 minutes, Kiki finishing the course with a time of 26:30 and Missy making it through six of the seven buoys and weights in 25:42. Finally, it was Sam's turn.

Sam slowly walked down to the bank where Al was waiting. She'd dreaded this part most of all. Al had gotten a good look at the other women, who were mostly all wearing string bikinis of some sort. Lori was the only other woman who'd been wearing a one piece suit. Sam took off her shorts and then whipped off her T-shirt. It was better to treat this like a Band-Aid, get it over with quickly rather than slow and painfully. She stood before Al in her one piece black suit. It was one of her practice suits. Back home, she tried to get to the pool at least once a week, and this was her most comfortable suit. It was cut high in the legs, but had a keyhole back. She and Al stood there, looking at each other for a few seconds before Al broke the silence.

"You ready?" he asked with a smile. "Do you think you can beat those times?" He sounded hopeful and was looking at her with a pleading look.

Sam *knew* she could, but the question was did she really want to? She knew beating Missy probably wasn't the smartest thing she could do, it wouldn't help the others like her, but at the same time, Sam was a competitive person and she knew she wouldn't be able to not compete and try to win. Besides, she'd really have to make herself look like she couldn't swim in order to pull it off. She tried to ignore the little voice in her head telling her that the real reason she wasn't willing to throw the competition was Al himself. She *wanted* the one-on-one time with him. For once in her life she was going to be selfish. Even if whatever was between her and Al didn't work out in the real world, she'd take this gift that was given to her and enjoy it while she could.

Realizing Al was waiting for her response, she said cheekily, "I know it, Al, just start thinking about where you want to go on our date!" With that she winked at him and ran toward the water.

Alex laughed and stared after her. Her one piece was definitely more modest than the suits the other women were wearing, but it was no less sexy. In some ways it was sexier. Al watched as the material clung to Sammi's body as she ran. She filled out her suit and then some, and it was sexy as hell. Al had thought her ass was perfect in a pair of soaking wet jeans…well, it was nothing compared to her ass in the black suit as she ran toward the water. She was muscular, but he'd noticed that she still had a small bump on her stomach. Somehow that imperfection was real. *She* was real. She wasn't perfect, but her imperfections made her seem more real. The other women were so model perfect they were almost untouchable. Alex knew if he touched Sammi she'd feel like a real woman. He was also surprised at her show of almost defiance and playfulness. This was a side he hadn't really seen before and he was eager to see more of it. He hoped she could back up her cockiness with action. He wanted her to be in the top three. He *wanted* the one-on-one time with Sammi.

This was one of the hardest challenges Eddie and the other producers had set up so far. They figured for the first one-on-one dates they wanted to make the women work a bit harder. Alex and the other women watched as Sam gracefully made her way to the first buoy. She disappeared and Alex was surprised to see her head pop up about a third of the way to the next buoy.

"Not fair!" Missy cried. "Did she even release the weight?"

While Sam was swimming to the next buoy, the producer reassured the women there were cameras attached to the weights and she'd definitely released it. They all watched as Sam glided through the water toward the other buoys. She made it look effortless. She swam a graceful freestyle stroke. It was obvious to all of the spectators that Sam was comfortable in the water and had possibly swum competitively. Finally, she reached the bank and walked up to the finish line. She'd completed the course in fifteen minutes and four seconds. Sam quickly wrapped a towel around herself and smiled at Al as if to say "told ya so." Alex smiled hugely in return. She'd done it, it felt good to win.

Kathi was the last woman to have her shot at winning the one-on-one date with Al. She'd watched Sammi swimming through the course with growing anger. It wasn't fair that *she* would get one of the coveted spots. There was no way Al would choose her in the long run. She was short and dumpy. Kathi recalled their conversation in the tent a week or so ago and knew this was her chance. She knew she wasn't going to complete the stupid course. She wasn't that fast or strong of a swimmer. Her idea of "swimming" was to hang out in a hot tub for half an hour. She *could* hold her breath for a long time, however, but she couldn't swim through the water that quickly. She thought fast and came up with a plan. If what Sammi said was true, she'd come out the true winner in this challenge.

Kathi peeled off her clothes and sauntered toward the starting line and Al. She put an extra swing in her step and swayed her butt with her walk. She knew she looked good in her slightly too small red bikini. She put on her best "come hither" smile and walked up to Alex, put her arms around his neck and kissed him. Alex was surprised. Kathi had always been pretty aggressive, but this was different. She was licking along the seam of his lips, seeking entry. There was no way Alex was going to kiss her in front of the other women. It wasn't right, seeing how he hadn't chosen his winner yet. He refused to open his mouth to Kathi's questing and hopeful tongue and peeled Kathi off of his chest.

"Are you ready?" he asked a bit peevishly.

"I was born ready," Kathi responded. She jogged off toward the water.

They all watched as Kathi reached the first buoy. Like Courtnee, she pulled the rope up rather than swimming down to it. When Kathi reached the second buoy she swam down to the weight. It was quite some time before she resurfaced next to the buoy. She went down again. Obviously she wasn't able to unhook the weight on the first try. Finally, she came up again and swam for the third buoy. She dove down again to untie the rope. Everyone waited for her to come up again. And they waited, and waited some more. Finally, when everyone started to get nervous, they saw Kathi's head break the surface. It looked like she was having some difficulties, though. She bobbed up, then went under again. She came up again and then went under again.

Sam started for the lake, but since Al was already there he was faster. He tore off his shirt and started swimming toward the place where they'd last seen Kathi. Everyone was holding their breaths. They saw Al dive down into the water and after what seemed like hours, but in reality was no more than a minute, they saw Al come up with Kathi in a classic lifesaving hold. He had a hold of her around her chest and was swimming the side stroke to shore. Sam could hear Kathi coughing, so she knew she was going to be okay. Coughing meant she was breathing. The adrenaline was flowing through Sam's body and she finally had to sink to the ground. She'd been ready to go out there and find Kathi herself. She didn't like her, but she wasn't going to let her drown!

Alex's heart was beating double time as he swam back toward the shore. For a minute he didn't think he was going to be able to find Kathi. He'd never been so scared. He was glad to hear that she was breathing, but he knew she was going to have to be looked at by a doctor. She'd been under the water for a long time. As Alex neared the shore, he turned Kathi around and held her in his arms. He carried her to shore. Kathi's arms were around his neck and she was still coughing sporadically. He looked at Eddie who by now was also standing lakeside.

"Get a car," Alex said gruffly to Eddie.

Alex gently put Kathi down on the ground near the lake. She curled to her side and continued to cough. Alex rubbed her back and told her to hang on, that they'd be getting her help soon. The other women stood back a bit and watched as Kathi coughed and tried to catch her breath.

She turned toward Al and said hesitantly, "Will you stay with me?" Al nodded and grasped her hand in his.

The producer finally came screaming up with the car, sand spewing everywhere as the car skidded to a halt near the duo. Alex carefully lifted Kathi in his arms again and started for the car that would take them to the hospital to have her checked out. Kathi snuggled into his arms and laid her head on his broad chest.

If Sam hadn't been looking right at Kathi she would've missed it. Since Sam was standing right next to Courtnee she saw Kathi subtly wink at Courtnee before closing her eyes and lying against Al again. Sam was confused for a second, she heard Kathi moan a bit and wrap her hand around the back of Al's neck and run her fingers up into his hair. Sam glanced at Courtnee and saw she had a small smirk on her face.

Sam suddenly realized what she'd just seen and was furious. Kathi was faking it! Sam recalled their conversation about a week ago and knew she'd inadvertently given Kathi the idea. Al was a protector. He'd do everything in his power to protect them, simply because they were women. It wouldn't matter if he liked the woman or not, he'd do whatever he could to make sure they weren't hurt, and if they *were* hurt, to nurture them. After all, that was what he'd done with her. Sam felt sick. She couldn't believe Kathi would stoop so low. But it'd been effective. She was wrapped around Al and on her way to the hospital where he could lavish some more TLC on her. She had found a way to get her one-on-one date with him without having to win the competition.

It was a subdued group that made its way back to the bus. Even Robert didn't seem inclined to put on his show airs and announce the winners of the contest. Everything was on hold until Kathi came back from the hospital. Sam already decided to keep her mouth shut. She knew she didn't belong here and there was nothing she hated more than to know that someone was faking an injury. She'd grown up with it in her water polo career. Her teammates were constantly faking some sort of injury to get out of hard practices. Their shoulder hurt, their knee hurt so they couldn't tread water, they had a migraine...the excuses never ended. Sam supposed that was why she hated to show any type of weakness today and why she was mentally stronger than a lot of people.

She couldn't tell Al, he probably wouldn't believe her anyway. She'd tried to tell a coach once that one of her teammates wasn't really hurt and she got in trouble. The coach yelled at her in front of the entire team and made her swim extra laps. The fact that she'd tried to do the right thing and got in trouble for it had already happened once on this show, with the barn incident, and Sam wasn't going to put herself in that position again. The hell with everyone. She knew, however, that she wasn't going to even try to be nice to Kathi after today. And she'd stay away from Courtnee as well. Those two were in this scam together and she wasn't going to have anything to do with it.

The women were all too keyed up to really do much when they got back to camp. They all waited around to see when Kathi was going to come back. Sam hoped they weren't going to keep her overnight. She wondered how she was going to explain to the hospital staff that she wasn't really sick after all.

Eventually, they saw a car pull up. Al got out with Kathi leaning heavily on his arm.

"Thank you, baby, for helping me. I don't know what I would've done without you here. You saved my life," she said, looking up at him with wide eyes. Sam watched cynically as Al walked Kathi to the tent with the rest of the women following along behind. He helped her into the tent, assisted her in lying down, kissed her on the forehead, and covered her with the blanket.

"Sleep, you'll feel better later, I'm sure." Alex turned to the other women who were now inside the bunkhouse with them. "She needs to sleep, make sure you don't bother her. She had a close call today, but she'll be fine. I'll see you all later." And with that he walked out of the bunkhouse, got back in the car and was driven away.

Sam looked sadly at the car driving away from the camp. A part of her wished Al had seen through Kathi's rouse. He hadn't even looked at her as he left the tent. Maybe it was a sign that the feelings she had for him were only one sided. Hell, she was sure that was it. There was no way he could think she was attractive, especially compared to the other women. Sam was disappointed in Al. She'd thought he was different. It was an awful feeling to think she was wrong. That he was like most of the other men she'd met in her life. Superficial and only concerned with his libido.

Sam sighed and came back to the present when the women gathered around Kathi.

"Are you really okay, Kathi?" asked Amy with a furrowed brow.

"Oh, yeah," Kathi responded a bit too cheerfully. "Are you kidding? Being carried and held and cosseted by a hunk of a man all afternoon? I'm great, just great." She smiled and looked at everyone. "Worked out better than if I won the competition. I wanted to win a one-on-one date, but I got one anyway and didn't have to finish the stupid course."

Courtnee stood up and shooed everyone back to their bunks and away from Kathi. "She needs to sleep, you heard Al. I'll stay right here and make sure she's all right, the rest of you just go to bed and you can see her later."

The other women grumbled a bit, but went back to their bunks.

"Okay, give!" Courtnee said to Kathi in a low voice as soon as everyone was away from their sides. "I want to know every detail!"

Kathi and Courtnee talked for over an hour. Kathi told her new friend all about how concerned Al was, how he wouldn't leave her side, and when she thought she was losing his attention all she had to do was moan a bit and he'd be looking at her with concern all over again. He held her hand just about the entire time. She told Courtnee how Alex had helped her into the hospital gown since all she'd been wearing was her bikini. Kathi told Courtnee about how she faked the coughing and the pain in her chest when the doctor was examining her. She did have to get an x-ray done to make sure there wasn't any more fluid in her lungs, though. They laughed at that since there was no chance of there being any fluid in there in the first place since she held her breath the entire time she was underwater. They laughed at how Kathi had taken the wind right out of Sammi's sails after her great performance.

"Al didn't even mention the contest or the show the entire time we were together," Kathi gushed. Kathi was pleased with herself. She knew she'd made a great impression on Al and she couldn't wait to see him again and show him she was better, but not *too* much better and that she needed some more TLC.

Chapter Fifteen

"God, what a day," Alex said out loud, even though no one was in his tent listening. This had to be one of the scariest days of his life. He'd almost seen another human being, a woman at that, die in front of his eyes. It'd taken everything he had to not break down in front of everyone when he knew Kathi was going to be okay. Kathi was really scared and she was obviously in a lot of pain on the way to the hospital. He'd held her the entire way. While he was scared for her, he was also a man and couldn't help but remember how well she fit into his arms. She was a good looking woman and he couldn't help but think about how they might fit together outside of the show.

Once they got to the hospital he stayed by her side for as much of the examination as he could. The doctor told them she wasn't any worse for wear and she could return to the show. She seemed to be better on her way back to the camp, almost back to normal, but once they pulled up and saw the other women waiting and watching for them, she seemed to get weak again. He couldn't understand it, but was certainly glad she was on the mend. She'd scared ten years off his life.

Alex gathered a clean set of clothes and headed to the communal bathroom to take a quick shower. He could hear the excitement around the camp. This would make for great television once the show aired. He was under the impression that sometimes he still didn't know what was going on, even though he was able to watch the tapes from camp each night. He really didn't think it was appropriate for Kathi's near death to be made into "must see" TV, but he knew what he thought didn't matter to Eddie. He'd do what he needed to do to make his show successful.

Later that night when he was relaxing in his tent he heard a soft "Alex?" come from outside his door. It was Kina. He remembered she was the camera operator who had shared her concerns about Sammi after the snake incident. She slid into his open tent after Alex invited her in and handed him a tape.

"I've already watched the day's tapes," he told her, shuddering as he remembered watching Kathi in the water and his rescue from earlier.

"This is the tape that Eddie didn't want you to see," she told him solemnly. "When you're done watching, put it out behind your tent and I'll grab it and put it back so he doesn't notice it's gone," and with that, Kina slipped out the door.

Alex wondered what was on the tape and why he hadn't been allowed to see it earlier. What was Eddie trying to keep from him? He got pissed just thinking about it. He'd *known* all along that Eddie was sneaky, but he'd hoped he was being honest with him. Alex glanced at the tape in his hand and prayed it wasn't of the women getting dressed or something just as offensive. He just didn't feel right watching that, although the women didn't seem to care a camera was watching them inside their bunkhouse.

He put the tape in the player and watched the scene from earlier that night as he helped Kathi to her bed. This was the tape from inside the bunkhouse at the women's camp. Alex watched as he walked out the door and Courtnee shooed everyone away from Kathi and back to their own bunks.

Alex couldn't believe what he saw on the tape. He knew the contestants on shows like this could be one person in public and another person when interacting with the other contestants, but for some reason, he never saw this coming. This was low. This was beyond low. Alex watched the tape three times, making sure he was hearing what he thought he was hearing. Kathi and Courtnee were talking about Kathi's "accident." He'd never been so furious in all of his life. She'd done it on purpose! Kathi wasn't drowning, she'd only pretended to be in trouble in the water and had used him. If he was back in his world he would've destroyed her, but he wasn't. He was here in the Outback on a ridiculous dating show with ridiculous women who thought they could manipulate him. He felt ashamed at how he'd felt earlier in the day with Kathi in his arms. He'd been holding a wolf in sheep's clothing.

At first he wanted to storm into Eddie's tent and quit, no matter what his contract said. Alex was disillusioned and couldn't believe anyone could stoop as low as Kathi had today. He thought about all the other times he was with the women and wondered how else he'd been manipulated by either the women or by Eddie. He wanted to lump them all in the same category as Kathi and Courtnee, but something wouldn't let him. He thought about Lori and Amy and Sammi. He felt relatively sure they, at least, were being honest with him. He thought about it a long time. He thought about what his next move should be. If Kathi wanted to make herself seem as if she was a completely different kind of person, he'd play it her way…for now.

Alex put the tape outside where he and Kina arranged, and lay back down on his bed. There had to be a reason why Eddie didn't want him to see the tape. He wondered again what else he hadn't seen. While the production team might have made him think he was one of "them," it was obvious now they were using him as much as they were using the girls. It was all about the ratings, and they didn't care who got hurt in the process. He was done playing by their rules. He'd tried, but they'd upped the ante. He'd play their game, but he had a few aces up his sleeve as well.

Chapter Sixteen

Sam was still pissed the next day. Since she'd placed first in the competition her time with Al would be the last one-on-one date and it wouldn't be until the next day. Kiki was going on her date this morning and Ashley would be going on hers that afternoon. It was a good day to relax, but that was something Sam was finding hard to do. She remembered Kathi's performance that morning about how she should have the first shot at the shower since she was still weak. Whatever.

Sam and the rest of the women watched as a giant hot-air balloon slowly appeared to the west of the camp. Holy Crap! Kiki's transportation had arrived. The balloon gracefully landed and Al climbed out. He first walked over to Kathi to see if she was feeling better. She told him yes, but that she was still weak.

Alex responded, "Make sure you get some rest today then," and grasped her hand in his, kissing the back of it.

Then he turned around and walked up to Kiki and took her by the hand. They strolled back toward the huge balloon and Alex assisted Kiki into the basket of the balloon. Everyone watched they rose up into the air until the balloon couldn't be seen anymore.

Kathi immediately huddled with Courtnee to compare notes about Al's attention to her and what it meant. Sam was disgusted. She knew she'd told herself she wasn't going to walk around by herself anymore, but dammit, she needed some time alone. Nothing was really going on at camp so there was only one camera around to film. Sam figured it was because most of the cameras were scheduled to film the dates, which was definitely more interesting than the rest of them just sitting around. Sam knew she could sneak away without being followed, either by the other contestants or a camera operator.

Sam climbed up the rise to the spot she'd spent quite a bit of time at in the past, and found a comfortable spot where she sat and tried to relax. She thought about the last few days and the other women on the show. She thought about Al, what she liked and didn't like about him. It was ironic that she'd be going on a one-on-one date with him because she was probably the only woman who really didn't care that much about "winning" him. Sam knew relationships formed by these reality dating shows usually didn't end up working in the end. There were a few—maybe two—that had, but those were few and far between.

She did like Al, he seemed to be a gentleman and he was polite to all of them. She was also very attracted to him. How could anyone not find him attractive? But how well did she really *know* him? How well did any of them know him? What was his favorite color? Did he have any siblings? Were his parents still alive? What kind of music did he listen to? There were about a million other things Sam wanted to know about him. If this was a normal courtship she'd probably already know some of the answers. Some of the contestants wanted to "win" so they could become famous and perhaps have an active career launched. Others wanted to win because Al was rich.

All Sam had ever wanted out of her life was to be content. She got lonely, but she wasn't about to marry someone for the sake of marrying them. Her life was just fine. She was employed, had a place to live, and was happy with her life. There were times on the weekends or when she wasn't that busy when she wished she had someone to talk to and share her thoughts with other than her three dogs and friends, but not enough to tie herself to anyone just for the sake of being married.

Sam heard a commotion back at the camp. She sat up and realized she'd fallen asleep. She strolled down to the camp in time to see Ashley and Al getting into a Hummer. Obviously, Al and Kiki made it back from their date.

Al helped Ashley into the passenger seat and leaned over her to buckle her seatbelt. It was a very gentlemanly thing to do. Sam's belly tightened. Everything she'd told herself while sitting on the rise felt like a lie watching Al take care of Ashley. She never thought she was the type of woman who would enjoy that type of pampering, but Al was quickly changing her mind. Sam could practically see the other women sighing at Al's actions as well. As they drove off, the other women gathered around Kiki to hear all about her date.

Sam wasn't really interested, but figured it might be enlightening to listen. She might get a better insight into Al's personality and she might learn more about him. Kiki talked about how they were in the balloon for a while and how Al was so protective when she got scared. He held her hand while they landed to help calm her down. They touched down at a site that overlooked a valley. There was a lunch all set up for them. She exclaimed about how much of a gentleman Al was and how romantic the entire thing was.

In Sam's eyes it sounded a bit contrived, but she wasn't there, so she had to take Kiki's word for it. That was a problem. Who knew what the truth was and what was embellished by Kiki showing off. After they ate, Kiki explained, they went and sat under a tree. Al held her to him as they talked about what they wanted out of life and what they wanted out of this reality show experience. Kiki said that the mood was just getting right when they had to leave. She didn't get to kiss him, except on the cheek, but she was damn sure not going to let the opportunity pass her by again.

Sam sighed. It sounded wonderful all right, but she now knew not to trust anyone and what they said. Again, who knew what really happened on the date. The rest of the day passed slowly. The women were anxious to hear back from Ashley and see what she did on their date. They were bored with themselves and really wanted something to do. Even Courtnee seemed to be getting irritated with Kathi after spending large amounts of time with her.

Evening fell and still Ashley and Al weren't back. A bonfire was lit around the fire ring and most of the women sat outside and watched the flames.

Suddenly, they heard Ashley's voice, "What a beautiful night!" They all turned around to see her walking back into camp and into the fire circle. Everyone started talking at once. Where was Al? How was the date? What did they do?

Ashley held up her hand. "Is everyone here? I only want to tell it once."

Finally, once they were all settled around the fire Ashley talked about her day. They'd driven to a small air strip where they'd then gotten on a small airplane. Al had flown the plane—which got lots of sighs since no one knew he was a pilot too—and after about twenty minutes they landed on a dusty airstrip. At first it didn't look like there was anything around, but Al led Ashley toward a wooded group of trees, and there was a picnic set up for them. They sat and talked and ate. Afterward, Al wanted to go for a walk, but Ashley told him she'd rather sit and talk some more. Ashley explained how they talked into the evening and it wasn't until it was getting dark that they realized what time it was and that he had to get her back.

"We stood up and Al took me into his arms. He looked into my eyes, said my name and gave me the sweetest kiss you can imagine." She enthused.

Most of the women thought it was the most romantic thing they'd ever heard, but Sam could also see that most of them were jealous as hell and resolved to do whatever they could in the future challenges to be the one in Al's arms. She shook her head. It sounded good, but again, how much was truth and how much was embellishment?

Missy suddenly turned to Sam and said, "So what do you think you'll be doing tomorrow?"

"I have no idea," Sam responded slowly. "But in keeping with the theme of the last two dates, I'm sure it'll be something extravagant."

                          * * *

The next morning, Sam made sure she was the first
one out of bed so she could use the shower first and be ready
to meet Al. She wouldn't put it past some of the girls,
especially Kathi, to try to sabotage her "getting ready" time.
She was actually looking forward to the date. For one thing it
would get her out of the camp and away from Kathi and
Courtnee, for another she really did want to get to know Al
better. She wasn't sure if she could really trust him, but she'd
try to give him the benefit of the doubt.

When Al pulled up in a dirty jeep about twenty
minutes after she'd gotten out of the shower, Sam was
doubly glad she'd awakened early that day. Half of the
women weren't even out of bed yet. Sam went over to meet
him.

"Good morning," Alex said softly.

"Good morning to yourself," Sam replied.

"You ready to go?" Alex asked with a gleam in his
eye.

"Sure, do I need to bring anything special?" Sam
inquired.

"Just yourself," Alex told her as he took her hand and
led her to the jeep.

"Not quite the exit that you had yesterday, huh?"
Sam asked with a smile, not able to hold back the question.

Alex laughed and told her, "I figured this would be
more your speed…was I right?"

Sam looked at him and told him honestly with some
surprise, "You pegged me right. I think I would've been
scared to be in the balloon, and the Humvee was a bit over
the top. But I like this jeep, let's hope it won't die on us as
we're out in the middle of the Outback." They both laughed
as Al helped her into her seat. Just as he did with Ashley, he
leaned over and snapped her seatbelt into place. It seemed to
Sammi that he stood over her for just a beat longer than was
necessary to snap the belt into place, but before she could

ask him if anything was wrong, he stood up and walked around the jeep.

Alex climbed in the driver's seat, pulled the seatbelt across his strong chest, clipped it in and started up the jeep. "Naw, Betty wouldn't let me down, not with the precious cargo she's carrying today."

Sam rolled her eyes. "Give me a break, not even five minutes into this date and you're already talking crap!"

They both laughed as Alex drove out of the camp. "I'd never talk crap to you, Sammi," he said seriously. "Anything I tell you is one hundred percent the truth."

Sam looked around and suddenly asked, "Where's the camera?"

"I have no idea," Alex answered, "but I'm not going to look a gift horse in the mouth. I'd love the chance to get to you know you without the camera in our face. "

"Should we go back and see if we have to pick someone up?" Sammi asked seriously. She didn't want to get in trouble for ditching the camera operator. It seemed like that would be an offense that could get her kicked off the show in a heartbeat.

Alex *had* wondered why he hadn't seen a camera, but he figured maybe it was going to be at their destination and told Sammi what he thought.

Sammi shrugged and asked Al as they bumped along the road, "So where are we going?"

"I thought about giving you a choice on what you wanted to do today," Alex told her, "but then I thought I'd make it a surprise for you. How come you never told me you could swim?" Alex asked her expectantly out of the blue.

Sam laughed. "You never asked," she told him with a smile.

Alex smiled back at her. She had a point. He didn't really have to ask much about the other women because they generally told him everything they could about themselves, whether he wanted to know it or not. He hadn't been alone with Sammi much since the show started. He found himself for the hundredth time wanting to know about her, her likes and dislikes. He knew a little about her personality from watching the tapes, and he knew she was different from the other women, but he remembered how the producers had tricked him, and wondered if there were more tricks up their sleeves.

"What do you think of the show so far?" he asked Sammi.

Sam thought for a minute. "It's a lot what I thought it would be, but at the same time not."

"Can you explain?" Alex responded, honestly wanting to know how she felt about the show, and indirectly about him.

Sam paused to gather her thoughts before answering. "I mean, I knew these "reality" shows weren't really "reality," and there was a lot the audience didn't see. I also thought since this was a dating show things would get pretty intense, but I guess I didn't expect the level of intensity from both the producers and the other contestants." Sam looked at Alex as he drove. "I mean, I like you, I think you're a great guy, but everyone around here is acting like you're the last man on the planet and if they don't win you then they'll end up single for the rest of their lives…I don't get that." Sam ended softly.

Alex was surprised at her insight. "I know what you mean," he told her. "I thought I'd come on the show, meet some great women, get to know them and BAM, be struck head over heels by cupid's arrow."

"Hasn't happened, huh?" Sam asked with a grin.

"I'm getting there," Alex told her mysteriously with a lift of his eyebrow. Suddenly, he got solemn again. "I know what you mean, though. It's that disillusionment. I knew there'd be some women on the show who were just doing it for the exposure and, of course, my money. I see that all the time back home, but with all the twists and turns in this show it's hard to really know what everyone wants and what they're really thinking."

Sam nodded as Alex continued, "And I'm scared to death that I'll really like someone, and then find out their whole personality was a lie. That everything they've said to me was a carefully crafted effort to "catch" me."

Sam shifted uneasily, thinking about Kathi and her schemes.

Suddenly, Alex pulled the jeep off to the side of the road and turned to Sam. He put his hand on the back of her seat and played with her hair unconsciously. Sam shivered. It felt so good to have him touching her, even if it was only her hair. She felt it down to her bones and shivered with the sensuality of his actions. She forced herself to pay attention to him as he started speaking.

"Tell me what you think of the other women," he said earnestly. Alex wanted to know what Sammi thought, but he also wanted to know what she knew about Kathi. When he'd asked Ashley and Kiki about what they thought about the other contestants, they were all too happy to tell him all sorts of negative things about everyone. He felt disappointed they were so eager to trash talk everyone else.

Sam looked at him with indecision. She'd never been the type of person to tell tales about other people, but she also really liked Al and didn't want him to make any decisions that he would regret when the show was over.

She decided to tell the truth as much as she could, "I like Amy, Ashley, and Lori. They are pretty friendly and seem to like you a lot. I think you should choose one of them," she told him with as much enthusiasm as she could muster.

"Not you?" Alex asked with a smile.

Sam laughed a little sadly. "We both know I'm not going to make it to the finals," she told him, holding up her hand to forestall his comment. "Look at me, I don't know how I even made it onto the show, but I'm definitely different from the other women. Personally, I think it was a mistake. I think somehow the producers messed up when they picked me. Television is about looking good, and while I certainly don't think I'm hideous, I can't hold a candle to the other women here. I don't know who's deciding who stays and who goes when there aren't competitions, but I bet the producers want the "pretty" people to stay the longest."

Alex looked at her in shock. "They wouldn't do that. Look at yourself. Seriously. You're beautiful." At her snort he continued a bit sternly. "Honestly, I wouldn't lie to you. Not all men want a woman who is skin and bones. While you have a soft glow about you, you also have a backbone of steel. I know I could be with you, in bed, and you wouldn't break," Alex said with a smile. He'd had the same suspicions lately about Eddie and the other producers and thought they were manipulating things as well, especially after they'd kept the tape Kina had brought to him secret.

Sam blushed a fiery red at Al's comment about them in bed. She'd also thought about it, but wasn't about to admit it to him. "Well, anyway, thank you for that, but I know my appeal, and if we were in the "real" world, I know a man like you would never look twice at me."

"And what kind of man am I?" Alex asked her, irritation sounding in his voice, knowing she was probably right about if he met her back home in Austin, in his normal environment, he might not have asked her out.

"Gorgeous and successful, the kind of man who could have any woman he wanted," Sam told him honestly.

They sat there looking at each other for a long moment.

"A couple of weeks ago I was cursing myself for agreeing to be on this show," he told her earnestly, "but now, I'm thanking my lucky stars. Do you believe in fate, Sammi?" he asked.

"No," Sam said without pause. "I think we're lucky to meet someone that we can love and get along with, but I don't necessarily believe that there is only one person out there for each of us."

Alex knew the conversation was getting pretty intense and was determined to lighten it up a bit.

"Okay, you told me who I *should* pick, so why not the others? What about Kathi or Missy? They seem very nice." Alex watched her reaction carefully. He knew what kind of person Kathi was, and honestly wasn't sure about the others. He wanted to know what Sammi thought. If he was completely honest with himself it was also a bit of a test.

"You're going to have to make up your own mind about them," Sam told him firmly. "I'm not going to get in the middle of a fight over you. And if they hear I was talking about you, that's what will happen." She tried to smile at him. She didn't want to lie to him, but she didn't want to tell him her opinions either. They were *her* opinions after all. "Are we going to get on with this mystery date or what?" she asked playfully, changing the subject, deciding the conversation had gotten way too serious for a first date.

"Okay, okay, I'll let the subject drop. But I only asked because I value your opinion, you know," Alex told her. He smiled and let the subject drop. "Let our date begin."

* * *

They drove for a while and finally arrived at a small town. It was more civilization than Sam had seen in a while now. She didn't say anything to Al, figuring he'd tell her what the plan was for their date in his own time. They pulled into a parking lot that was across the street from a small amusement park. It looked like one of the same traveling fairs that occasionally set up back home. Sam looked at Alex in confusion.

"Is this okay?" Alex asked with a bit of trepidation. "You seemed like the kind of person who would enjoy having some fun."

Sam beamed and resisted clapping her hands and jumping up and down in her seat like a lunatic. "It's perfect. I'm not sure I'd know what to do with myself if we did the "lunch by the river" thing!"

Alex smiled back and thought she was the cutest thing he'd ever seen. He loved that she wasn't afraid to show her excitement about their day. As they walked toward the entrance to the carnival he grabbed her hand. He looked at Sammi with his eyebrow raised as if to ask if it was okay.

Sam smiled, squeezed his hand reassuringly and they continued on.

They spent the better part of the morning on all of the rides, some more than once. They hadn't noticed any cameras around, which they both still thought was odd, but they were having so much fun, they didn't even care. Alex kept a hold of Sammi's hand as much as he could. When they were on the one roller coaster she held it tight. When they went on the "zipper," Sam buried her head in his shoulder. She'd always hated going upside down on rides, but Alex had dared her to ride it with him and of course she never turned down a dare! All in all it was a great morning. They laughed, a lot, and there was no more serious talk about the show or the other women.

Finally, they'd had enough of the park and decided to go to lunch.

"Where would you like to go?" Alex asked Sammi as they headed back toward the jeep.

"Anywhere is good. I don't really like seafood, but I can usually find something to eat in a seafood restaurant if you really want to go to one," she told him.

"We could get something to go and eat it in a nearby park that I saw." He suggested, rubbing his thumb over the top of her hand as they were talking.

"Okay, you pick," Sam told him, distracted by his nearness and by the goose bumps that spread over her arms at his touch.

Sam laughed when she saw his pick of restaurant. It was a popular fast-food burger place they had back in the States.

"This okay?" Alex asked nervously, knowing she might not want to eat the greasy food.

"Oh my God! It's perfect!" Sam laughed. "I've been craving their french fries!"

They ordered their lunch and set out for the park. Alex parked the jeep and held up his hand for her to wait as she was about to get it. He ran around the front of the jeep and opened the door for her. He held out his hand in a gallant gesture and helped her to the ground. They found an empty table in the middle of the park under a tree that was throwing a lot of shade. Sam sat down and was surprised when Al sat next to her rather than on the other side of the table. They ate their lunch and laughed and joked with each other. Sam asked most of the questions she'd been thinking about yesterday. She honestly felt as if she knew him a lot better after they'd eaten and talked. It was a good feeling. After they were finished, Alex swung one leg over the bench seat and encouraged Sammi to do the same.

"What are you doing?" she asked him.

"Shhhh, just swing your leg over and put your back to me." Alex soothed her, holding on to her hips and turning her as he spoke.

Sam did as he asked and he pulled her back to rest against his chest.

They sat there for a while, enjoying the feeling of being close to another human being and watching the other people in the park. Alex finally broke the silence.

"I'd like to think that if we'd met somewhere before this show, I would've been interested," he said quietly with his breath tickling Sam's ear. "I know in the past I've been somewhat of a ladies man, but this show, and you, have taught me what I really want."

"And what is it you really want?" Sam asked, turning her head around to look at him.

"I want someone I can laugh with. I want a woman who I can sit with on a park bench and not speak, but still be comfortable with. I want a woman who wants me for who I am, not for what I can give her. I want a woman who can be my friend as well as my lover. I want a woman who will stand in the rain just because it's there and not worry about her makeup or her hair. I want a woman who is strong, but who can still lean on me. I want to look forward to going home because I know she's there. I want a woman I can take care of. Who will let me pamper her just because I want to."

Alex took a deep breath and looked down at Sammi. "I want a companion. I want someone to call my own and a woman who can call me hers in return."

Alex saw a tear fall from Sammi's eye. He reached up with his finger to brush it away. "I want this," he said softly and dipped his head to her lips. Alex's hand went to the back of Sammi's neck and tightened, drawing her to him. His lips moved on hers. Sam let out a short moan.

Alex ran his tongue along the seam of her lips, tracing the opening as if asking permission. When he was about to pull away, Sam's tongue came out to meet his. Alex took the moment and plunged inside. Since Sam was bent at an odd angle, with her back still to his front, her hand snaked up and grabbed the back of Alex's neck as if to anchor him to her. Alex's other arm came around her waist and pulled her closer. Sam could feel his hard length in the small of her back.

Sam could barely think. God. It was as if her brain had turned to mush. Had she ever been this turned on with her other boyfriends? Had a kiss ever made her want to throw caution to the wind and give in? Alex's tongue ran over her teeth and dueled with her tongue. He thrust in and out of her mouth as if telling her how he'd take her if they were in bed together. Finally, Alex eased away, panting. He rested his cheek alongside her head and she turned to face forward again.

"I probably should apologize for that, but I won't," he told her in a hoarse voice. Sam could feel his heart beating against her body as well as his shaft hard against her back. "I don't know what it is between us, but I've never felt like this." Alex took her earlobe between his teeth and bit down softly.

Sam shivered. Her ears and neck had always been sensitive. It was hard to think with his arm across her body, his hand resting at her hip and his breath gliding over her neck.

"I know, I think I feel the same way," she answered breathlessly, hardly knowing what she was saying.

"You think?" Alex whispered in her ear.

"I don't know what to make of this," Sam answered honestly, determined to get this out. "I mean, I heard all about your other dates and how romantic they were. Essentially you're dating all these women at the same time. It's just hard for me to believe you aren't saying these things to the others as well."

Alex disentangled himself from her, stood up and squatted down next to the bench, looking up at Sam. He wrapped one hand behind her neck gently and palmed her cheek with the other hand. He looked into her eyes and willed her to believe him as he addressed her concerns.

"I swear, Sammi, the other dates I've been on were completely innocent compared to what I'm feeling here. I know we don't know what'll happen and how this game will turn out, but I want you to know that I'm being completely honest with you. I don't want to lie to you. I hope you feel the same about me."

Sam looked at Al. She was scared, she hadn't lied to him. He was everything she'd ever wanted in a man. She wanted all the same things that he did. When he was talking earlier about what he wanted in a woman, she could imagine herself doing all those things with him and being his woman, and it scared her to death. What did she really know about him? They were practically strangers. Was this just a result of being isolated in the Outback and him being the only available guy around? It wasn't like they could feel their way and take things slowly. She was in a competition. She could lose tomorrow. Her heart hurt when she thought about that. But Sam was also practical. She knew you couldn't have everything you wanted in life and this might not turn out the way she wanted it to. Then there was the honesty Al was pleading with her to give him. She knew she should tell him about Kathi and the stunt she'd pulled at the lake, but it wasn't her place, it really wasn't. She wouldn't stoop to Kathi's level to win. She'd just have to make sure Al wanted *her* around, and not the other women.

"I do feel the same and I'll do my best to be honest with you. I don't know if this is just our circumstances or if it'd be like this between us back in the States, but rest assured, that it's not one sided," she told him.

Alex beamed. "Awesome!" he said softly, leaning forward at the same time pulling her head toward him. He took her mouth again, not waiting for her to reciprocate, but plunging inside with enthusiasm. They finally pulled apart when a group of boys walking by yelled, "Get a room!"

Sam blushed and noticed her hands were holding on to his arms with her fingernails digging in. Alex leaned his forehead against hers and said, "Unfortunately, I think we have to head back, it's getting late. At the crestfallen look on her face, he said in a softer voice, "I know, I don't want to go either, but think about it this way, the faster we get back, the faster this game will be over!"

They packed up their trash and headed back to the jeep, hand in hand. All too soon they were nearing the camp. Sam sighed.

"What was that sigh for?" Alex asked, looking at her with concern.

"It's just hitting me that it's really over," Sam said, smiling at Al. "I'm just preparing myself for the third degree."

"What are you going to tell them?" Alex asked.

"The truth." Sam paused until Al looked at her with a furrow between his brows. "That we spent the day at a carnival, atc lunch, then came back. What happens between us is between us." She finished.

Alex smiled at her. "God, thank you for that. Trust me to keep our time together private as well."

Sam smiled at him. As they pulled up into the camp the other women were walking toward the jeep to meet them. She reluctantly let go of Al's hand and felt his thumb rub over the back of her hand one last time before he let go. Sam knew the women weren't coming over to see her, they just wanted another chance to talk to Al. Alex helped her out of the jeep and leaned down to place a chaste kiss on her cheek while giving her a short squeeze on her waist. Sam blushed, remembering their passionate kiss from earlier.

Alex smiled at her and said, "Until next time." He nodded hello to the other women in general, got back in the jeep and drove away. As soon as the jeep was gone, the others wanted to know what happened on their date. Sam told them only enough to appease their curiosity and escaped to the bunkhouse to dream about Al.

Chapter Seventeen

The "vote out" was supposed to be the same day as Sam's date, but since they got back later than they were supposed to, Eddie decided the light wasn't good and they'd have to wait until the next day. When Alex got back to his camp he sought Eddie out.

"I've decided who I want to go next," he told him without preamble. "After careful consideration I don't think that Kathi and I have much in common."

The producer looked surprised. "Sorry, we need to keep her around for a bit longer," he told Alex without remorse.

"What?!? Why?" asked Alex, although he had a feeling he knew why.

"She was just hurt the other day, it makes for great TV. Viewers are going to want to see how she's doing and how she's healing. And since you played Sir Galahad, we're going to play that up a bit," the producer answered.

Alex was pissed. He knew it. He *knew* he was being played. He couldn't tell Eddie he knew Kathi faked her accident. He wasn't supposed to have seen the tape in the first place. On the other hand, he knew he'd be hard pressed to act civil around her.

The producer continued, "I think it's time Sammi goes home."

"No way!" Alex responded immediately with heat. "I thought I was the one who decided who'd stay and who'd go!"

"Look," Eddie reasoned, "We're here to make money. Sammi doesn't fit in. We honestly don't even know how she got on the show. We think there was a mix up between her and another woman named Sammi. Somehow someone invited the wrong woman, and by the time we realized it, she'd already signed the contract so we couldn't make her leave. We let her stay on for a while because she was entertaining, but it's time she goes home. America doesn't want to watch overweight women on TV. That's their everyday reality. We need to give them the glamorous side of people, make them want to tune in every week to see which babe you'll end up with."

Alex was so furious he was shaking. Sammi had been right all along.

"First of all she isn't overweight. She's completely normal and viewers will probably connect with her more than the other women because of it. Second, am I or am I not choosing the final contestants?"

"Well," Eddie hedged, "you have a say...to a point. If we don't think you're making the right choice, we'll make it for you. It's not like you have to stay with this woman forever, just until the end of the show and the publicity tours on the talk shows after its aired. We tout this show as a man finding his soul mate. Everyone knows that probably won't happen, so we just want to have good TV along the way. And if that means us telling you who'll stay and who'll go, then so-be-it."

Between clenched teeth, Alex asked, "Who will the final two contestants be then?"

"We're not sure, but we have a general idea, and Sammi sure isn't one of them," the producer answered and pretend gagged, not realizing how on the edge Alex was.

Alex was beyond pissed. Eddie was a horrible person. He didn't care who he hurt as he clawed his way upward. If there was a way to get off the show he'd do it, but he knew he'd signed an iron clad contract, and there was no way they'd let him go now with the show halfway over.

"At least let her stay through one more round," Alex practically begged. He couldn't imagine what she'd think if after their date and that kiss, she left now. He especially didn't want her to think that *he* voted her off. Besides all that, he desperately wanted her to stay. He *liked* her. She was perhaps the only woman on the show that he *did* like.

The producer looked at Alex for a long time and finally bit out, "Fine. We'll get rid of Cindee tomorrow."

"Fine," parroted Alex. He gave Eddie a hard look and said, "you'd better not be lying to me."

"Cindee will go home tomorrow," Eddie promised. Alex knew he couldn't trust him, but had no choice. He finally nodded and walked away.

Shit. Alex thought as he walked back to his tent. That hadn't gone well. He knew these reality shows probably weren't true "reality," but this was ridiculous. He didn't want to see Sammi go, and he certainly didn't want to have to pretend to actually like Kathi or some of the others that were left. He had to talk to Sammi. He knew he wasn't supposed to, but she already had some idea that she was going to be kicked off soon, but he wanted her to know it wasn't him who wanted her gone.

* * *

The next morning Alex met Robert and the women at their camp for the "vote off." The nine women looked nervous, but composed as usual. Alex had purposely gotten to the camp right before the cameras would start rolling so he wouldn't have to talk to any of them. He wasn't up to pretending he was glad to see them, when all he wanted to do was talk to Sammi alone and let her know what was going on. The only drawback of arriving late was that he couldn't talk to Sammi at all before the stupid ceremony. He consoled himself with the fact that he'd talk to her after it was over and let her know what Eddie had said about the mix up in the invitation to the show. He didn't want to hurt her feelings, but she had to know. He'd promised to be honest with her.

As the ceremony began, Robert went into a speech about how it had been an interesting couple of days and he recounted the adventures at the lake and the three one-on-one dates. He asked the women to go around and tell Alex why they felt they should get to stay on the show. He asked a few pointed questions to some of the women about how they were feeling about Al and the other women. The women were on their best behavior, very aware of the television cameras and kept their answers pretty civil. Finally, Robert got to the point.

"The eighth person who will be leaving Australia will be…Cindee." Cindee gasped and immediately started crying.

It was a bit awkward around the circle as Cindee stood in place and cried but no one told her which way to walk away to leave the show.

Finally Robert said, "Cindee, unfortunately you have to leave Australia, and Al, but there is a twist today." He paused dramatically. The women looked at him expectantly. Alex looked at him with trepidation. He had a bad feeling about this.

"Throughout the show the women who've gone home have left either because they were unlucky enough to have their name chosen at random, or they lost a challenge. Today, Cindee, you get to change the game." Cindee and the others just stared at Robert, perplexed. Alex felt his teeth clench. He knew he wasn't going to like how Cindee would get to change the game. Damn Eddie.

"I wouldn't call today your lucky day, since you're going home, but you aren't the only unlucky woman here today. Someone else will also be leaving." Everyone gasped.

"Cindee, you get to choose one of the remaining women that will be leaving today as well."

Alex covered his indignation with a cough. He thought back to his conversation with Eddie the night before. He hadn't said that Cindee would be the *only* woman going home. He only promised that she'd be going home. Alex looked across the distance at Sammi in despair, and found she was looking at him. She had a grim look on her face, almost resigned. It was as if she knew what the outcome of today would be. They both ultimately knew who Cindee would choose to leave with her. He wanted to mouth 'I'm sorry' to Sammi, but was afraid the cameras would pick it up. He tried to convey his angst to her from afar. He held her eyes until she broke their eye contact and looked at the ground.

Cindee took a deep breath. Her tear ravaged face took in the women standing around, all staring at her, wondering who her choice would be.

"Wow," Cindee started rather dramatically, "I never expected this. This is going to be a tough decision. I've had a great time with everyone, and I can't imagine being the one to make someone have to leave." She paused to let her insincere speech sink in. Cindee knew she was in the spotlight and it was her time to shine. She continued on with her speech. Rambling on about the good times she'd had while on the show and how much she was going to miss everyone. She talked about how she wasn't sure how she was going to choose someone and how it wasn't fair, but someone had to go.

Sam looked up at Al again. She wondered why he looked so mad. She somehow knew this was going to be her last day at the camp and on the show. She knew she didn't fit in and there certainly wasn't any love lost between her and Cindee. After her date yesterday she'd sure miss Al, she honestly thought that maybe the two of them could've possibly made it. For a brief moment the night before, she dreamed about winning the show and having Al choose *her* at the end. But she'd never find out now. She caught Al looking at her again. She gave him a sad smile and shook her head slightly.

"I suppose since I have to choose someone, it would have to be…Sammi," Cindee finally said. Sam walked forward to where Robert and Cindee were standing. Cindee had a smug look on her face.

"Sammi, Cindee has made her choice," Robert droned, "Please say your goodbyes and Al will walk you to the car."

Cindee and the other women spent a bit of time crying and saying goodbye. Sam heard some of them thanking Cindee, not very quietly. She shrugged. Sam didn't bother going over to the other women. She knew what they thought of her and the thought of them pretending they were sad she was leaving was just too much. She walked toward Al.

Alex held his hand out toward Sammi as she walked toward him. She put her hand in his. They walked to the car.

"This wasn't my decision," he started desperately, knowing their time together was short, but stopped when Sammi put her fingers on his lips.

"I know, it was inevitable." Sam looked at Al, she had to say it. She leaned toward him and hugged him. At the same time she put her lips at his ear and said, "If you're given the choice to pick someone, you need to choose either Lori or Amy."

Alex looked at her earnest face. "Can you tell me why?" he asked softly.

"I can't, I wish I could, but I can't. Just please trust me," Sam practically begged him.

Alex squeezed Sammi desperately. He turned his head so now his mouth was by her ear and told her, "I trust you. God, I trust you. This isn't over, Sammi. I don't think I can let you go. You *will* hear from me again." He nipped her earlobe lightly and stepped back. He leaned forward, gave her a hard kiss on the lips, and turned back toward the other women without another word.

Sam climbed into the waiting car. She refused to look back as the car drove off. A lone tear tracked down her face. It wasn't fair, but she expected it, she just didn't know how much it would hurt. She wasn't TV material and she knew it. She wasn't skinny enough and her boobs weren't big enough. Sam recalled Alex's last words. She wasn't sure what he meant, but she knew it was going to be a long time between now and when the show aired.

The car dropped Sam off at a small airstrip. She was taken back to the city she'd spent the first night in Australia in, and checked into a hotel. The phone was removed from the room so she couldn't call anyone back home and was told she'd have to stay at the hotel until the end of the show.

There weren't any other contestants staying at this particular hotel so they wouldn't be able to "trade" stories from the show. Sam was given a coupon book for several local tours she could take to fill up her time until the show ended. Sam sighed. All she wanted to do was go home to her job, her friends and her dogs. The show had taken a lot out of her.

She knew she and Al had pretty good chemistry, but it looked like it wasn't meant to be. Sam hoped he took her advice about who to choose if he could. Amy and Lori really were the least of all the evils. They weren't perfect, but they were much nicer than the other women. Sam knew she'd get practically no more communication from the producers about the show or what was going on. She'd have to watch it on TC like the rest of America to see the outcome of the show and to see who Al ended up with. As she lay down to sleep in the luxurious bed that night, she couldn't stop the tears that fell and were absorbed by the pillow.

Chapter Eighteen

Five months later...

Sam, Beth, and Christina were gathered in Beth's apartment, ready for the season premiere of *Love in the Outback*. Sam chuckled. They hadn't changed the name after all. It seemed like everyone in Albuquerque knew Sam had been on the show. She'd interviewed with the local news stations as well as radio stations. She'd done her best to talk up the show, but not reveal anything either. She figured if she refused to be interviewed that would keep the interest of the media even longer so she just gave in and did the interviews. Even though the interviewers wanted to know the outcome of the show and if she was a finalist, Sam was prohibited from saying anything by the contract she'd signed. Eddie and the other producers made it very clear from the start if she let any information leak out about the outcome of the show, she'd be sued for millions of dollars.

The three friends decided they'd rotate whose place they watched the show at each week. Beth and Christina were beyond excited, Sam was definitely not. She knew that watching the show would bring back memories, mostly bad, but bittersweet too. She wasn't sure she wanted to watch the "behind the scene" shots of Al's dates. She didn't want to see what went on that she didn't know about. She was interested to see how the producers edited the show, though. She knew many people who were on so-called reality shows complained about the editing. She couldn't think of anything she'd done that would embarrass her or make the editing difficult, but who knew what the editing would make her look like.

Even though several months had passed since she'd seen Al, she missed him. It seemed like every night she lay in bed thinking about him. Where was he? Did he miss her? Did he think about her? She was embarrassed to admit she thought about him while pleasuring herself as well. She remembered everything about their date and the kiss they shared. That one kiss was better than any sex she'd ever had with anyone else. That was almost embarrassing because she had no idea if Al felt the same way.

The show had a cutesy opening, complete with music and pictures of all the women. Sam's head shot was toward the beginning of the montage, and it was only on for a few seconds, but none of the women had theirs up for long. The show started at the hotel with the women frantically searching through their bags, trying to pack what was needed. It continued with the video introductions for Al. The camera kept panning from the bus driver to the women. Sam laughed out loud.

"What?" asked Christina.

"The bus driver is Al!!" Sam exclaimed with a laugh, realizing now that it was clever on the part of the producers and that Al must've had quite the laugh over all the videos that had been shot on the bus while he'd been sitting there.

The three women burst out laughing. "Wait, shhhh," scolded Beth as she tried to hear the show.

The show continued on. It showed the women settling into the bunkhouses. Sam thought that overall the show was actually pretty boring. It ended with Wendi's name being pulled out of the cheesy cowboy hat. The cameras milked it for all they were worth and had close up shots of Wendi crying and carrying on and sobbing in her interview in the car.

Hey. Sam thought to herself. *I wonder why they didn't talk to me when I was leaving.*

The three friends laughed at the show and discussed the contestants. Of course, Beth and Christina didn't like any of the women, except for Sam. They laughed at how Sam had to be called "Sammi" and rolled their eyes at how everyone's names ended in the sound of "ie."

Beth commented at the end of the first show, "Sam, where were you? I didn't see much of you at all! Weren't you there?" She said it jokingly, but Sam had noticed the same thing. Granted she didn't socialize much with the other women, but there really were only a few shots with her in them.

"I was there," Sam insisted, trying to laugh about it. "I'm sure you'll see my fat butt next week!" They all laughed.

Finally, it got late enough that Christina and Sam had to get back home because they had to work the next day. They made plans for the next week to watch the second installment of the show.

Sam arrived at her house to a noisy greeting from her dogs. Blue, Albert, and Duke were always very excited to see her. Most of the time they just slept, but it was always nice to have an audience to listen to her ramblings. It made her feel less lonely. They were especially glad to see her when she got back from Australia. Her mom had watched them for her, but it was obvious they'd missed her.

Sam thought about Al. He looked just as good as she remembered. She wished she'd taped the show so she could watch it again and see Al. He was just so good looking, and now that she knew what a good person he was, he was even better looking in her eyes. She sighed and wished things were different.

The next day at work was pretty crazy. Everyone wanted to talk to her about the show and let her know they'd watched it. They had a ton of questions about what Sam thought about the other women, and of course they all wanted to know who "won." Sam, of course, couldn't tell them anything, so she politely fended off the questions. She had two calls from local reporters who wanted to interview her and she made appointments for the next day. Around three in the afternoon, Sam looked up from her desk to see a giant bouquet of flowers making its way toward her desk. Okay, it was actually the receptionist carrying them, but it almost looked like they were floating on their own.

The receptionist placed them on her desk and said, "Delivery for you."

Sam couldn't imagine who they could be from. She wasn't dating anyone, it wasn't her birthday, and it wasn't any kind of special day. Sam leaned over to smell the beautiful blooms. They were a mix of several different kinds of flowers. There was a lily, a carnation, a rose, some baby's breath and some other flowers that Sam didn't recognize.

The receptionist hadn't left and nosily asked, "Who're they from?" Sam looked for a card. There wasn't one.

She shrugged and said, "I have no idea, I can't find a card."

"Who sends flowers without a card?" the receptionist asked almost rhetorically. "Maybe it fell off, I'll look for it. Maybe it's a secret admirer who saw you on TV last night, or maybe it's Al!" she said animatedly. Sam could tell she really liked that idea.

"I doubt it," Sam told her. "I wasn't on the show enough last night for anyone to notice me, and we're strictly forbidden to have any contact with anyone that was on the show. It was in the contract. So even if I *did* win," she paused and winked at the receptionist, playing it up, "I can't have any contact with him until the show is over." Sam smiled to herself. Let her think about that one a bit!

After work, Sam carefully put the flowers on the front seat next to her and strapped them in using the seat belt. It wasn't often that she received flowers and she wanted to savor them in private at home. She had no idea who'd sent them. It wasn't as if she saw many people other than the ones she worked with, and there were only a few men at work anyway, and she certainly knew none of them would send her flowers. She considered throwing them out, but at the last minute couldn't make herself to do it. Hopefully her "fame" hadn't garnered her a stalker.

When Sam arrived home she put the flowers on her kitchen table. She then fed her dogs and popped a microwave meal in to cook. She sat down at her table to eat her solitary dinner. She sighed. She was lonely. She had lots of friends, and her dogs to keep her company, but it wasn't the same as having someone at home to talk to and to share the day with.

Chapter Nineteen

The next week arrived quickly. Beth and Christina came over to Sam's house this time to watch *Love in the Outback*. Sam knew this was the week when they'd have the fish competition and meet Al. It was interesting watching the show from an outside different perspective. She was there, she knew what happened, but it was weird to watch the editing and see what the producers pulled out of the show.

The three friends got their popcorn and sodas and sank onto the couches to watch the show. Albert was sleeping on his favorite pillow, Blue was on the couch next to Sam, and Duke was curled up on a pillow in the corner.

The theme song came on and the montage of pictures was on again. The teaser this week had many shots of the women looking bedraggled. Finally, the show was on. They saw some background on Al to start with. First of all his name wasn't Al, it was Alex. Sam thought Alex fit him so much better than Al did. She supposed it wasn't too far of a stretch to believe Eddie had made him change him name as well. After all, they'd changed hers. Sam briefly wondered how many of the other women had their names changed too, but her attention quickly turned back to the show. She was surprised to learn that Alex wasn't "just" a rancher that the show led them all to believe. It turned out he was the CEO of his own business in Austin. He did live on a ranch, part of the time. He owned both a house in Austin as well as the ranch. The guy was loaded, that hadn't been an exaggeration.

Beth sighed. "Wow, Sam," she said, "he's gorgeous and rich to boot!" Sam hadn't told her friends the outcome of the show. She wasn't allowed to, and besides, they said they'd rather wait and watch the show like everyone else. They said it heightened the suspense. Sam suddenly felt relieved she hadn't won the show. There was no way she'd fit into Alex's world. She might have been able to fit in on a ranch, but be the girlfriend of a CEO? No way!

The editing of the competition left much to be desired in Sam's opinion. There were, of course, lots of shots of the women soaked with water. Lots of shots of the women bending over head first in the bucket, trying to get the fish out. There were a few shots of Sam, but mostly of the other women. The friends watched as the twist came, the winners had to meet Alex right then and there or wait until the next day. Sam laughed, remembering how mad they all were, especially Missy.

She watched as the "winners" were bussed off and the rest of them stayed. It was interesting that there was no mention of her falling into the water or her being wet. She thought for sure her fall into the water would have been played up just to embarrass her, but it wasn't even mentioned. She watched the conversations Alex had with some of the women. They didn't show all of the conversations, she supposed they just showed the "interesting" ones, and of course hers wasn't included.

The show continued with the other women the next day getting to meet Alex. Sam and her friends laughed at the conversation Al had with Courtnee. They then watched as the competition with the pigs came up to see who'd be going home. It was pretty funny to watch them all running around trying to capture the pigs. Sam was absolutely dumbfounded when, through the magic of editing, *she* was left without a pig instead of Kimmie. They must've spliced together frames of her standing around empty-handed.

Sam couldn't say anything as the "elimination" took place. She watched as she walked towards a car and was driven away. She knew the shot was taken out of sequence, but she was still amazed. The teaser scenes for the next week's show came on talking about the days spent on the cattle station doing the chores. Beth and Christina hung around for a bit longer, commiserating with Sam about how she had to leave so early in the show and they told her that it wasn't fair. Sam barely heard any of it.

After her friends left, Sam sat on her couch, hugging one of the throw pillows. She now understood what all the other reality stars had been talking about when they complained about editing. They'd edited her out of the show even though she'd been there much longer. She wondered how that was going to work. How were they going to get rid of Kimmie since she wasn't at the station? She guessed they just weren't going to deal with the shoveling of the barns much since she did most of the work. It must've taken a long time for them to edit her out of all the subsequent shots.

Sam felt betrayed, but she honestly wasn't that surprised. She knew when the cameras didn't follow her on her one and only individual date with Al that something was up, but she tried to brush it off with a flimsy excuse. She knew she wasn't like the others, but she honestly didn't think they'd just erase her from the show.

Finally, after an hour or so of feeling sorry for herself, Sam decided that what happened had happened. Since she couldn't change anything about it, there was no use getting worked up and pissed off. She hadn't won, they didn't change the outcome of the show, just the order that people left. She also decided she wasn't going to watch the rest of the show. As much as she loved looking at Alex and remembering how hot he was and how he made her feel, there was no telling how much other stuff they'd manipulated with their editing. Besides, Sam didn't know if she could stand watching Alex make out with the other women. She still wanted to think of him as hers.

The next day at work was one of the longest in Sam's life. Everyone wanted to know all about the show, and they wanted to tell her how sorry they were that she wasn't able to stay longer. She was even teased by some coworkers for not being able to catch a pig. Sam laughed along with them, while inside she cringed. She'd never ever as long as she lived, agree to be on any kind of "reality" anything. It wasn't worth it. Later that day the receptionist came into her office to deliver another package. It'd been a week since she'd received the flowers. It was a flat envelope. Sam opened it and was surprised to see a gift certificate to a National pet store chain. There was a note this time, however.

Sam opened it and read, *"Hopefully you can put this to good use."* That was it. Sam turned it over to look on the back. There was no name or anything. Sam thought it was very weird. She certainly *could* use the gift certificate. Her basset hounds were constantly going through stuffed toys. They liked to "kill" them by taking out the squeaker. It was an odd gift to send to someone anonymously, but appreciated nonetheless.

The week continued and Sam constantly had to deal with the aftereffects of being on a national reality show. She participated in interviews for the local newspaper and even participated in an interview on one of the national morning news shows. She couldn't say much about the show. She wasn't allowed to say anything about who might win, and since Eddie and the other producers edited her out of the part of the show that she actually did participate in, she couldn't say anything about that either. Sam told Beth and Christina that she wasn't going to watch any more of the episodes. She explained to them since she'd been kicked out so early it didn't matter to her who won, and she didn't care to see the rest of the show. They tried to convince her to watch "just for fun," but Sam refused. If she was honest with herself, it was just too painful.

Her feelings were really hurt by the whole experience. First, she was made to feel as if she was somehow less of a person than the other contestants. Second, no one cared about her at all on the show. Not when she was hurt, not when she's saved Kina's life, and definitely not when they edited her out of the show almost altogether. Then she thought about Al…no, Alex. She stupidly thought they'd connected on their date. They had explosive chemistry even before that, but everything he did for her and to her on their date just cemented her feelings. She didn't think he had anything to do with getting her kicked off, but now that it was so much later, and her feelings were so raw, she wasn't sure of anything anymore. Sam wouldn't put herself through watching him interact with the other women on the show and having it proven to her that she was just another contestant to him and he was going and saying the same things to everyone.

The next few weeks went by and Sam received regular updates from her friends about what was happening on the show. She heard all about the ranch episode. Beth laughed herself silly at some of the girls trying to do their chores. They were both appalled at Kathi's fake drowning. It seemed like Eddie and the other producers knew all along she'd faked her accident and decided it made good television. Sam felt sick when Christina had told her how the camera zoomed in on Kathi winking to Courtnee and played it in slow motion over and over again. It sickened her and made her want to hunt Eddie down and beat the crap out of him because she knew Alex must be watching the show and seeing he'd been made a fool out of on national television. She wouldn't wish that betrayal on anyone. What she went through seemed like nothing compared to this.

Occasionally she'd see blurbs from the morning news shows about the show and she caught a few interviews with some of the contestants.

Throughout the weeks the show was on, Sam continued to get little gifts. After each show she received something. She'd received gift certificates to restaurants, another bouquet of flowers, the deluxe edition of the movie *Speed*, a pass to the local zoo…it was mostly all unusual stuff. There was never a name on who'd sent any of it. One week Sam actually called the flower place that delivered the flowers to try to see who'd ordered them, but the customer paid cash and didn't leave his name, so that was a dead end on trying to figure out who was sending the gifts.

Sam wished she knew who it was so she could thank him or her. They really made her feel good, especially after hearing the rundown of the show each week. It seemed like the show was a huge hit and everyone was talking about it.

But another part of her was completely freaked out. Not knowing who was sending the gifts was a little freaky. She thought maybe Beth or Christina were sending the gifts, but when she asked them they both denied it. Sam knew them well enough to know they weren't lying. So who knew her well enough to send such personalized gifts? She hoped the next reality show she'd be on wouldn't be one where women talked about a stalker.

* * *

Soon, enough weeks went by that the season finale was to be aired. It was down to two women for Alex to choose from. Beth and Christina begged her to come and watch the last show with them. Finally, Sam agreed, just to get them off her back. She might as well. Nine months had gone by since she'd left the show. It wasn't as if Alex was knocking down her door, and he couldn't even if he wanted to because of the contracts they'd all signed. Sam knew the final two women were Amy and Kathi. She couldn't believe that Kathi was still there. She hoped for Alex's sake that he took the advice she'd whispered to him that last day she was there.

The show started with the montage of pictures like usual. It then recapped the last week's episode where Missy left the show. The women were now staying by themselves in their own camp sites. The producers had separated them, of course, for dramatic effect. The women had one last individual date with Alex before he'd make the final decision. Kathi and Alex were flown to a nearby town where they had a romantic dinner, complete with candlelight. After dinner they took a carriage ride around the town. They then went back to a hotel where they were given the option of staying in one room together. Of course Kathi was all for that. She and Alex spent some time snuggling and kissing on the couch in front of the television in the room and then the last shot was of the two of them walking into the bedroom hand in hand.

Sam felt sick. She knew she shouldn't have watched the show. She just knew something awful like this was going to happen. Of course, the editors left enough doubt as to what was going on in the room for the audience to make their own conclusions. And the truth was, no one had any idea of what happened. God, it hurt. She wanted to tear Kathi's hair out at the same time she wanted to crawl into bed, put the covers over her head and not come out for weeks.

The final date with Amy was much the same. She and Al went out to eat, then spent some "quality" time together and were then given the option of staying the night together. After some heavy kissing on the couch, the two of them went into the bedroom together.

Beth and Christina were loving every minute of the show. They debated whether or not Alex had slept with either of the women and they were trying to decide which he should pick at the final ceremony. They knew he'd felt really sorry for Kathi after her "near drowning" and it looked like he felt responsible for her. On the other hand, Amy was a strong woman and, in Beth's and Christina's eyes, she was the prettier of the two. The added twist to the show was that the audience knew Kathi lied about the incident at the lake, but Alex didn't. It made for a suspenseful ending.

Sam got up to refill their soda glasses as Alex was debating on which woman he should choose. He was lying on his back on a sofa in a hotel room, talking out loud to himself. He talked about how he thought Amy was beautiful and since she was from El Paso they lived closer to each other. She was an outdoorsy kind of girl and they got along really well. Kathi, on the other hand, was very fragile in Al's eyes and he loved feeling like he could take care of her. She was from Knoxville, which wasn't that far away really, and besides, since he was a pilot it wouldn't make that much difference.

As much as Sam didn't want to admit it, she was as sucked into what was happening on the show as Beth and Christina were. The show changed venues to a beautiful set with the Australian sun setting in the background. Alex was wearing a tuxedo and looked so good. Goose bumps rose all over Sam's arms as she watched the show. He was so good looking and she regretted not being able to be his.

Finally, Robert came onto the set and began to talk to Alex. He asked Alex if he'd made his decision.

Al responded, "Yes, Robert, I believe I have, I think I knew what my decision was from the first week."

Sam thought that was really odd, and a huge blow to her ego. If he knew he wanted either Amy or Kathi from the first week what was he doing with her? Was what he'd told her that last day they were together a lie? She tuned back into the show.

"It was a tough decision, all the women were wonderful and I feel lucky that I've been able to get to know them throughout the past weeks. Tonight I'll make the only decision I can. I was once told I had to trust in my decision, and so tonight I will."

Sam wrinkled her brow…did that mean that he was going to trust *her*? She'd told him to trust her that last day. She was so confused. He had to pick Amy, he just *had* to.

Kathi and Amy were brought out to where Robert and Al stood. They both were beautiful. They had their hair done in dramatic upsweeps and their dresses were worthy of any runway in Hollywood. They were very striking standing next to each other. They were both tall and very slender. Finally, Alex made his speech.

He talked about how this was the hardest decision he ever had to make. Sam laughed, all contestants on reality shows said that in situations like this. Alex continued to talk about how he thought he'd made the best decision he could. He looked at the women.

"Please know that whichever one of you I don't choose, it wasn't because you aren't a good person. You're both beautiful and I know you'll have no problem finding someone back home. The woman I choose is…" he paused dramatically, "Kathi."

Sam nearly choked on the soda she was drinking.

"No way!" Beth exclaimed, "Why did he pick that bitch!?!?"

It was a great ending to the show, Sam had to admit, even though she was crushed. Kathi rushed forward and grabbed Alex around the neck. She squealed with delight. She had tears coming down her face, but Sam noticed that somehow she managed to still look beautiful. The camera panned back to Amy, she looked forlorn standing by herself. As part of the show, Alex walked her to the car.

The cameras showed Amy looking up at Alex and asking, "Why?" as if her world had ended. Alex gave Amy a big hug. It looked like he was whispering in her ear, but the microphones couldn't pick up his words since they were too low. Sam couldn't help but remember the way he'd done that to her too and how his mouth felt on her ear that day on their picnic. Her stomach lurched a bit.

Finally, he let Amy go, kissed her on the cheek and helped her into the car. It looked like he took a big breath and made his way back to Kathi and Robert. Kathi rushed into his arms again, while Robert made a speech about true love and how Alex had made his choice. As the picture faded out, Alex and Kathi were dancing to a romantic ballad. Kathi was looking up into Alex's face and running her hand through the hair at the back of his neck.

"Ugh," Christina grunted, "that was disgusting. Why did he pick *her*? She wasn't nearly as nice as Amy was. What a disappointment. I thought your Alex had better taste," she finished.

"First of all," Sam started, "he isn't *my* Alex. Secondly, he didn't see all the footage that we did here at home. He had no idea what she was really like, she was completely different around him. And I guess he's just the kind of man who doesn't like a strong independent woman. He'd rather have someone to take care of," she finished glumly. That was what was really bothering her. She simply couldn't believe Al would rather have someone like Kathi, than Amy. She'd tried to tell him, maybe he thought she was jealous or something. She should have told him about

Kathi's fake accident when she was there. If Sam couldn't have him, she didn't want Kathi to manipulate him and make him miserable either.

Beth shrugged. "No matter what the reason, it'll be a great interview on the morning news show in the morning. Now that he's seen the show and the footage about her, I wonder if that will change anything."

"Probably not," Christina said. "He seems like a forgiving kind of guy. I bet it won't matter to him. I always wonder if they've had any contact since the filming ended. I mean, isn't it in the contract that you can't have contact with the winner in case it leaks out, Sam?" she asked.

Sam nodded. "Yup, I had to sign a contract specifically saying that if I was the last woman I wouldn't contact him by phone, letter or in person until the final show aired." Secretly, she wondered if the feelings on any reality show winner's part could stand nine months apart or if they snuck around and talked anyway. She thought she'd heard about other couples from other reality shows that had met in secret before the show finished airing.

Chapter Twenty

The next morning, Sam was running late. She'd forgotten to turn on her alarm the night before because she'd cried herself to sleep. She wasn't able to get the picture of Kathi and Alex dancing cheek to cheek out of her head. Besides that, Beth and Christina hadn't left until late and she'd already been exhausted, physically and emotionally. So she was late getting up and had to take the quickest shower of her life in order to have time to feed and walk her dogs before she had to leave for work. Because she had no time, she wasn't able to watch the morning news channel that was going to have Alex and Kathi on.

Sam rushed into work only a few minutes late. Because she didn't want to irritate her boss she went right to work rather than talking to her co-workers first. As she was in the middle of answering an email to a client, she received a notification on her computer that she'd just received an email. She opened it up and didn't recognize the address it came from. The email said only:

Did you enjoy the gifts?

Sam looked around quickly…could it really be from the person who'd been sending her all the gifts? She was a bit leery, but responded immediately.

Who are you? She typed, not answering the original question and hit send.

You really don't know? Came the response.

Sam looked closely at the email address…Xander546@yahoo.com…it could be anyone.

I wouldn't have asked if I knew. Sam quickly typed and hit send again. It was actually sort of fun to have an anonymous pen-pal…fun as long as it wasn't a stalker.

You didn't answer my question, did you enjoy the gifts? The sender asked again.

Of course I did, who wouldn't? Sam typed back, not sure what else to say to this stranger.

The next email popped up immediately. *Did you watch the news this morning?*

What a strange thing to ask. Sam thought. *Nope, didn't have time, I was running late, what did I miss?* Sam asked, wondering for a moment if there'd been some terrorist attack she'd missed or something else just as big.

It took a while for a response to come back, but when it did Sam read, "*Watch the news, then we'll talk.*"

"What the hell?" Sam said a little too loud. How could she watch the news when she didn't record it on her DVR? Sam figured Xander546@yahoo.com was male, but she supposed it could be anyone. She decided maybe she'd go to a National News web site and see if anything struck her as odd. She was about to type it in when her phone rang. *Oh well, maybe later.* Sam thought as she got back to work.

It turned out there was a crisis at work that day. Sam didn't get to leave her desk to talk with her coworkers at all. Her boss asked her to take care of a nasty situation with a client and Sam spent her entire day talking to HR, the client and then to her boss as well. They had to come to some sort of compromise so the attorneys wouldn't get involved. As she was leaving work, her cell phone rang. It was Beth.

"Where are you?" Beth said as soon as Sam answered.

"I'm leaving work, where are you?" Sam asked.

"I'm at your place, hurry up and get here…did you see the news this morning?" Beth asked.

"Why is everyone asking me that today?" Sam responded grumpily. "No, I was running late. Why? What was on it?"

"I taped it for Christina because she called this morning and said she couldn't watch it. She's coming over to meet us at your house. Hurry up and get here, I think your neighbors are getting ready to call the cops on me!" Beth told her.

Sam laughed. She did have some pretty nosy neighbors. "I'll be there in ten minutes," she told Beth, starting her engine. She and Christina had constantly made fun of Beth because she still used her *very* old VCR to tape shows instead of using the DVR that most cable companies had now.

When Sam got home Christina had already arrived and both she and Beth were impatiently waiting.

"I heard all about it at work," Christina said, "I can't wait to see it for myself."

Sam was now really curious. First the email, now her best friends.

"What the hell is the big deal?" Sam asked as they entered the house.

"I can't believe you have no idea!" Christina told her. "It's the interview with Alex and Kathi! I heard it was great!"

Now Sam was confused. Was that what the email sender was talking about?

"What else was on the news this morning?" Sam asked, thinking that maybe there was something else going on in the Nation that she should know about and that pertained to the morning's emails.

"Who cares!" Beth practically shouted. "You *have* to see this!"

After letting the dogs outside, Sam sat down on the couch while Beth fiddled with the tape, shoving it into Sam's ancient VCR. Finally, she got it going. The three friends sat back to watch. The news anchors, David and Jenny, were doing their bit about the upcoming segment. They discussed Alex and Kathi and how they would be coming right up.

When Beth taped the show, she obviously edited out the commercials, because the next scene was Alex walking onto the set with Kathi. She was grinning from ear to ear. She still looked beautiful. She had on a short black dress and her hair was down around her shoulders. She was hanging onto Alex's arm like she'd fall over if she didn't have him to hold her upright. Sam thought she was even skinnier than when she was on the show. And Alex, holy crap, he looked great. He wasn't wearing jeans like he did for the show. He was wearing a business suit. It looked different, but still wonderful.

The couple walked in and sat down on the couch in front of the news anchorwoman, Jenny.

"Welcome, Alex and Kathi," she said enthusiastically. "It's great to see you. How are you both doing? Is it true that you haven't seen each other since the show ended?"

Kathi immediately answered, "It's true. But it's as if no time has gone by for us." She looked up at Alex and continued. "I'm just so thrilled to be able to be with him in public now." She gushed.

"Jenny," Alex interrupted Kathi, "I agreed to come here today because my contract says that I had to." With that, gasps were heard from the studio audience, even Jenny, a seasoned reporter looked like she didn't know what to say. Alex's tone of voice left no doubt he wasn't a happy man. When Kathi was about to interrupt, Alex continued.

"I've watched the show along with the rest of America and have seen things I didn't know were going on while the show was being taped. Because I feel as if I was deceived, I don't think like I need to continue on with this farce of a relationship. I could never be with someone who wasn't honest with me. I hope that everyone can understand and hopefully they support me in my decision. I'm sure that Kathi…" and with that he turned to look at the woman sitting next to him, who was staring at him in shock, "will find a man out there who'll be perfect for her in every way. I honestly don't believe I'm that man."

Jenny asked him quickly, sensing he was about to stand up and leave, "Is there someone else?"

Alex looked at her, then looked at the camera. "I hope so, if she'll have me."

With that Alex stood up, kissed Jenny on the cheek, and walked off the set. Jenny then, apparently still in shock, wrapped up the segment without giving Kathi a chance to defend herself or protest and the program cut to a commercial.

"Holy Cow!" Christina said. "That was better than a soap opera! I'm so glad he left her skanky butt! But I'm sure the network executives are having a cow!"

"I don't know," Beth responded slowly. "This is great publicity. They probably didn't expect that their final woman and Alex would stay together anyway, and they'll get more leverage out of this than if they'd stayed together."

Sam couldn't say anything, she was in shock. Alex had sounded so calm and confident in his little speech. He didn't sound heartbroken at all. She couldn't understand it. Wasn't he embarrassed? He chose Kathi over Amy, wasn't he upset about it at all? She thought about it for a bit while Beth and Christina continued to speculate about Alex and Kathi. Suddenly, a small smile came over her face.

"What?" Beth demanded. "You have the weirdest look on your face."

"He played them," Sam said, "Just as they played him. It was brilliant. No wonder he owns his own company!"

The three women just laughed. Finally, Beth and Christina left. Sam asked Beth if she could keep the tape. She watched it three more times. The look on Kathi's face was priceless. Alex didn't look brokenhearted, he looked triumphant. Sam was a bit crestfallen about the fact that he already had another girlfriend, but at least he didn't end up with Kathi. She didn't think she'd be able to stomach that. The last thing Sam thought before she went to sleep was if she'd hear from her mysterious email pen-pal the next day. Was the interview what she was supposed to watch?

Chapter Twenty-One

Sam arrived at work early the next day. She eagerly opened her email. As she'd hoped, she had an email from Xander546@yahoo.com.

It was an invitation to talk over an instant messaging program. Sam already had the program on her computer since the company used it to talk to each other. She quickly added Xander's email. As soon as it was added she heard a "ping." She'd received a message from Xander.

Did you watch it? Was all it said.

Sam responded, *Yes. What part are you referring to?*

The Love in the Outback Section.

I saw it.

What did you think? Xander replied.

I thought it was a smart thing to do, Sam responded, not knowing who she was really talking to. It could be a reporter looking for more information, or it could be a producer trying to get her to break her contract somehow.

Why? Xander asked.

Look... Sam typed, *I don't know who you are or what you want. How did you get my email anyway? Why are you sending me things? This is getting a little creepy.* She was getting a little freaked out by the whole thing. She wasn't sure what Xander wanted and how he'd gotten her information.

I'm sorry. Xander typed, *I mean you no harm, I was just curious as to what you thought about the situation. Would you feel more comfortable if we met in person?*

Sam paused. She was interested, but she was also a bit scared. She must have paused too long.

I don't mean to scare you. Xander typed. *We can meet wherever and whenever you want. It can be at a fast food restaurant for all I care, but I'd like to meet with you. I think it'll clear up a lot of confusion on your part. I know it's not fair of me, but I ask you to trust me.*

Sam thought she must be crazy because she typed back. *Okay, this weekend? I'm not sure where…*

Xander quickly typed back. *Great! You won't regret it, I promise. How about the tram?*

The tram? Sam asked.

Yeah, why don't we say Friday night, at the top of the tram off of Tramway Blvd, 8pm. Then once you hear what I have to say, we can either have dinner or you can leave.

Sam had always loved the tram. She didn't like the trip to the top in the tram car much, but it was so beautiful at the top of Sandia Peak. Looking over the city it almost made up for the scary ride up there. *Okay, how will I know who you are?* she asked.

You'll know, Xander responded. *Until then.*

With that Xander logged off of the messaging program. Sam immediately called Beth to tell her what she'd done. Now that she'd agreed to meet whoever this Xander was, she was scared to death. Beth, however, was thrilled. She was sure it had to be a man, someone who'd seen her on the show and was in love with her and finally got up the guts to ask her out. Sam wasn't sure. The entire situation was odd, and she wasn't sure she wanted to get into a relationship with anyone. It was hard enough getting over Alex, and they didn't even really have a relationship in the first place!

Later that day Sam received another package. This one was from one of the local department stores. When she opened it, it was a pair of princess cut solitaire diamond earrings. They weren't that big, maybe half a carat, but Sam was still shocked. Like usual there was a note, but it didn't say who it was from.

Please wear these this weekend. It would please me to no end.

Sam had never received anything so beautiful in all her life. She wasn't sure she should accept them, but she didn't know who to return them to. She'd always wanted a pair of diamond earrings, but figured it was too big of an expense to splurge on for herself. Figuring she'd be meeting a man that weekend rather than a female was now almost a certainty.

Friday night came pretty fast. Sam had made a plan with Christina to call her about eight-thirty on her cell. It was a typical ploy that they came up with when going on a blind date. Christina would pretend to be a neighbor and say that one of her dogs had gotten out and that she had her at her house and would Sam please come and get her. That would give Sam a chance to leave if she wanted to.

Sam looked around the parking lot at the tram station. She didn't recognize any of the other cars. She didn't like coming alone, but there were plenty of other people around. She bought her ticket, then hung out in the small gift shop until her tram arrived. She got on with the other passengers. As the car started its slow ascent, Sam wondered for the hundredth time what she was doing. She had worn the earrings. They were beautiful and she couldn't imagine not wearing them. In fact, she'd been wearing them all week. They'd most likely become her new "everyday" pair. Sam had taken great pains to dress up tonight. She wanted to look nice, but not *too* nice considering she wasn't sure about Xander's motives. She wore a black pair of pants and a lime green turtleneck sweater.

After about twenty minutes the tram finally docked at the top of Sandia Peak. Sam let the other passengers push their way out of the car while she tried to look around to see if she recognized anyone. She slowly made her way out of the car and toward the small building. She didn't see anyone who looked like they were looking for her, so she entered the building. Most of the other passengers obviously had reservations at the restaurant and were making their way toward it. Sam stepped in and looked around. There were two children with their mother and some other people waiting for the return trip down to the tram station. Sam walked further into the building. Around the corner, she saw a man standing by the windows on the north side, looking out. Sam looked around. She didn't see anyone else around. When she turned back toward the man he'd turned so he was facing her.

Sam couldn't believe her eyes. It was Alex! What was he doing here? All she could do was stare at him in confusion as he walked toward her.

Alex approached Sammi. She looked beautiful. He couldn't believe it'd been so long since he'd seen and talked to her. It was almost as if it was the same as the day they parted. Alex thought the confused look on her face was cute. He reached out to take her hands.

"Sit with me?" he asked with some trepidation.

Sam could only nod. Alex led her over to one of the benches alongside the windows. Sam sat down and Alex took the seat next to her.

"What are you doing here?" Sam asked with her brow furrowed.

"Sammi," Alex started "I—"

Sam interrupted him. "Actually, my name is Sam," she told him, blushing lightly.

Alex smiled. "I'd wondered about that. I knew your email said that was your name, but I thought maybe you went by Sammi. I should've known. My name isn't Al either. It's Alexander David Sanders the third."

Sam finally smiled. "I heard that when the show aired. That fits you much better than Al. Do you go by Alexander? I feel like I don't know you at all."

Alex smiled. "You know me, Sam. We weren't together very long, but I think we got to know each other pretty well. I go by Alex."

"Alex, okay," Sam told him. Suddenly, a thought struck her. "Xander in your email…short for Alexander, huh?" She smiled at him.

"I wondered when you'd figure that one out," he told her.

"I don't understand, Alex." Sam's voice trailed off.

"I know, and I'm sorry. I wanted to explain to you," Alex said. "And I did promise you'd hear from me again, remember?"

Sam nodded, but didn't say anything. Her head was reeling. She couldn't believe Alex was here, apparently for her. It blew her mind.

"You know about the contract I was under because you were under the same rules. I wasn't allowed to contact anyone from the show until after it was over. It said I couldn't write, call or see anyone, it didn't say anything about sending things." Alex smiled. "I'm sorry about the show, Sam. It wasn't fair what they did in the editing to you. I called and cussed out Eddie after that second show. I don't think he really cared since the show was doing so well, though. Frankly, I was surprised they were able to do it so well. But I'll tell you one thing, I'm not sorry for—" He paused.

"For what?" Sam asked him, leaning toward him and putting her hand on his arm. She sighed. It felt so good being able to touch him again.

"I'm not sorry our date wasn't shown on National TV. That kiss we shared would've melted televisions around the country." He smiled at her.

Sam looked at him sadly. "I felt the same way, Alex, but after seeing you on the finale…" Her voice trailed off. How could she explain to him what it did to her to see him being intimate with Amy and especially Kathi?

Alex looked her straight in the eye. "Sam, if I could, I'd take it back. I was getting a lot of pressure from Eddie to step it up a notch. What you saw was for the cameras. After we went through that bedroom door we went our separate ways. I swear to you what you saw was all we did." He waited anxiously for her response.

Sam looked at Alex. He looked very earnest. "I believe you. I know how they edited me out of the show, and I'm sure it was easy to make the audience think you did something you didn't. But honestly? I don't know why you're here and what you want from me."

Alex stood up and took her hand. "Please, I'd like the opportunity to talk to you more. Will you have dinner with me?"

He looked so sincere, Sam stood up and squeezed his hand. "Of course, Alex, I'd love that."

They walked hand in hand down to the restaurant at the top of the mountain. Alex had already made reservations in the hopes that Sam would agree to stay there with him. As they were waiting to be taken to their table, Sam's cell phone rang. Knowing exactly who it was, Sam blushed as she answered it.

"Hello? Oh, hi. Uh huh. Yup, no problem. Okay, see you later." She hung up and looked at Alex, who was smiling from ear to ear.

"Problem?" he asked, laughing. Sam had an idea he knew exactly what had just happened.

"Uh, no, everything's fine," she said, trying to act nonchalantly.

Alex threw his head back and laughed some more. "I'm glad you want to stay, and I don't blame you for coming up with a contingency plan."

Sam blushed some more. Luckily, right then the hostess came back and led them to their table. It was located right by the windows overlooking the city. Alex held Sam's chair for her, then unexpectedly sat down next to her rather than across from her.

"Is this okay?" he asked.

"It's great," Sam told him earnestly.

The waitress came by and they ordered drinks. Alex turned toward Sam and took her hand in his again. "I don't know where to start," he said honestly.

"I know," Sam began, "it seems as if we just met yesterday, but we know each other better than a usual blind date couple would. I know things were pretty intense in Australia."

"They were," Alex agreed, "but there are things you don't know about our time over there that I feel like I have to tell you."

Sam started to look and feel nervous.

"Nothing bad, I promise, but I told myself if you agreed to meet with me I'd be honest with you and I want to do that. I feel like there's something between us. If I'm wrong, please tell me now before I get too far involved in this."

Now Alex looked nervous. His thumb was smoothing over the back of Sam's hand absently, sending shivers down her spine, only making her want him more.

"I feel the same, Alex," Sam told him quietly. "There are things that happened in Australia that I'd like to share with you too."

"I get to go first." Alex insisted with a smile.

The waitress came back and they ordered their meals. Sam knew the restaurant was expensive, but Alex didn't seem to care about the prices. After some more small talk their meals arrived. They took their time eating. Sam seemed to enjoy the meal more than she ever had before eating at the top of the mountain. Perhaps it was the little brushes of her arm against Alex's, or maybe it was the small talk they engaged in. Whatever it was, it made the meal almost magical.

Finally, after they both finished their meals, Alex said, "I don't really know where to start, but I did want to tell you that I had nothing to do with you going home or the editing of the show."

"I know," Sam reassured him for a second time. "I never thought you did. I figured you were as much in the dark as the rest of us were."

"The fact is, though," Alex continued nervously, "I *was* consulted and asked on many occasions who I wanted to leave. I chose the first five or six women who went home. Including the very first one, it wasn't a random thing."

"How is that possible?" Sam asked. "We hadn't even met you yet!"

"I'm assuming you watched the show, right?"

"Some of it. I really only watched the first couple shows and the last one," Sam admitted reluctantly.

Alex would have teased her, but he was too intent on telling her everything about the show. "Remember, I was the bus driver, I made the decision based on first impressions."

"That's right, you saw all of our video introductions live and in person." Sam blushed, remembering her video. "Man, I was a dork!"

"On the contrary, I thought you were very refreshing. After listening to the other women talk about where they liked to shop and go out at night your story about the bus was precious." Alex reassured her. "Eddie asked me who I wanted to go home, I told him and they rigged the outcome. On the day you went home, Eddie told me you were going to go. I begged him to let you stay. He tricked me. He promised me Cindee would be going home that night, but he didn't say for certain that you *wouldn't* be."

"It's okay, Alex." Sam soothed him. "I knew that given the choice, any of the other women would choose me to leave. I simply didn't fit in with them. And I know I didn't fit in on the show."

Alex leaned over and kissed her gently, cupping the side of her face with his palm and keeping her face close to his. "The other reason I knew who I wanted to go home was because I was allowed to see all the tapes from the camp and from the competitions and stuff when I went home at night." Alex explained.

Sam stared at him. What was he saying? That he'd seen everything they'd done at the camp? "What do you mean?" Sam asked confused.

"Just what I said, Sam, I saw you fall in the river and not complain one bit. I saw the scrapes on your side from that fall. I saw you save Kina's life with that snake. I saw the conversations that everyone had back at the camp, I saw everything..."

Sam could only stare at him. "W-w-what do you mean?" She stuttered, feeling stupid.

Alex pulled her close again and rested his forehead against hers. "I mean just what I said. I think I fell in love with you after that first night. You were freezing, but you never complained, never brought attention to yourself, never told anyone you were hurt. Beauty in a woman I can take or leave, but true courage, pure unselfishness gets me every time. When you saved Kina's life and didn't bring it to the attention of anyone else, not a lot of women would have done that. And let's not even start to talk about the barn incident. Why didn't you tell my aunt and I what really happened?" he asked her firmly, leaning back and mock glaring at her.

"Your aunt?" Was all Sam could manage. She was dumbfounded with all that Alex was telling her. She couldn't wrap her mind around it all.

Alex chuckled. "Yeah, Nancy is my aunt. We watched all the tapes together and she helped me decide who was leaving. You impressed the hell out of her, you know. We didn't know what really happened in the barn, but we could make an educated guess. But without you telling us for sure, we couldn't say or do anything."

"I did it for selfish reasons, Alex," she told him honestly. "If I'd said anything they would've made my life a living hell. I was able to do it, it wasn't a big deal. I felt pretty darn proud of myself."

"Ah, honey," Alex murmured, bringing her palm up to his mouth and kissing it tenderly before continuing. "That's not selfish, it's self-preservation. I just wish you didn't have to get hurt in the process."

"So you saw all the tapes every day?" Sam asked, trying to take his mind off of the barn.

"Not all of them. Eddie got pretty sneaky and started leaving out the most interesting ones…"

"How did you know they were leaving some out?" Sam asked.

"Kina would bring them to me. I think you made quite an impression on her," he told her. "She'd bring me the ones that Eddie was leaving out on purpose."

Sam stared at him. "I had no idea. I was afraid she didn't like me since I almost got her killed with that snake.

Then when they weren't filming me much anymore I figured that was why."

"No, Sam," Alex continued, "you were her favorite from day one. I think she was as mad as I was when you left."

Sam could only stare at him, overwhelmed.

"I saw the tapes from that day at the lake as well. I had no idea Kathi was faking it until Kina brought me the tape. I saw the wink that night, Sam. I knew Kathi was lying. I knew she didn't almost drown. I about lost it. I wanted to quit the show, but I was under a contractual obligation. Besides, Eddie wouldn't let me kick her off. I tried. God, how I tried. He said it made for good television…and ultimately he was right."

"But, I don't really understand why you chose her at the end then," Sam said with confusion. "If you knew the whole time, didn't it matter to you?"

"Of course it mattered. It was hard for me to even be civil to her. You said you didn't watch much of the show, but did you see any of it after the lake competition?"

"Honestly? No. After the second episode when they twisted everything around I had no desire to watch. My girlfriends made me watch the last episode with them. I didn't see anything in between."

"I don't know whether to be pleased or irritated," Alex told her with a grin. "While Eddie told me that I had to keep Kathi around, I did my best to not have her win individual dates, and I certainly didn't help her that much while she was 'recovering'," Alex told her. "As to why I chose her at the end? I heard what you told me while we were on our date, and I honestly liked Amy. But if I'd picked Amy I'd have no reason after the show ended to dump her. I didn't want to hurt her. By choosing Kathi I had a perfect excuse to break up with her on National Television and use the information the show provided as my reasoning."

"I don't understand, Alex," Sam said, "If you'd chosen Amy you could've made that work. She was pretty nice, and I know you got along, and she's from Texas, you could've seen her all the time. You have a lot in common."

"Sam," Alex said quietly and intensely, "I didn't *want* it to work. I knew the day you left that *you* were the one I wanted to make it work with. Do you remember what I said the other day on that morning news show?"

Sam could only shake her head in confusion. Had he really just said he wanted to be with *her*?

"I was asked if there was someone else, and I said I thought there was. That someone else is *you* Sam. I want to make *us* work. I know we have some obstacles in front of us, but I haven't stopped thinking about you since you left the show. I go to sleep wondering what you're doing. I dream about meeting your dogs. I can see us mucking out my barn together." He smiled. Then said, "Please say something..." he trailed off.

"I'm not really sure *what* to say," Sam told him honestly. "I like you too. I guess that's part of the reason why I didn't watch any more of the episodes after they edited me out. I know how I felt that day on our date, but I figured there was no way I'd fit into your world anyway." Sam saw the irritated glint in Alex's eyes and quickly continued. "Don't get mad, Alex. I know as CEO of your company you have to project a certain image, just as I know I'm not that image."

"Don't sell yourself short, Sam," he told her. "I'm a person just like you and just like everyone who works for my company. Are you telling me you think they'd rather have me be with a person like Kathi who would lie her way through life?"

"No, that's not what I'm saying," Sam said with exasperation. "I meant that you should have someone by your side that is beautiful and thin and—"

Alex cut her off and grasped her arms, looking into her eyes. "*You* are beautiful. Why won't you believe me? I've never liked bony women. There's nothing to hold on to." He smiled at her. "You're beautiful, Sam. You're beautiful in part because of who you are. You make me happy to be around you. I love your long legs, your eyes sparkle with life…there isn't anything about you I don't think is beautiful. I'd rather have you by my side than any of those women on that show. I thank my lucky stars every day you were in Australia, I'm not sure we ever would've met otherwise. Please tell me there's a chance for us. I want to date you, Sam. I want to get to know you here in our own little corner of the world. I want to take you out to eat, to the zoo, I want to hang out with you and your dogs and watch movies on the weekends. I want to hear about your day when you get home and be able to tell you about mine. I want to spend all day in bed with you, exploring your body and making you come apart under me. Do you think we can try that?"

Blushing because she'd thought about having Alex in her bed as well, she managed to say, "But we live so far apart," Sam hesitantly told him.

"Did you forget I'm a pilot?" Alex grinned at her. "You think I'm going to let a few miles stand between us?" He got serious and stared into her eyes. "I'm not saying it'll be easy, Sam. All I'm saying is that I want a chance. I want the chance to make you happy. If, down the line, we decide together we should make our home here in Albuquerque, we will. If we decide Austin is where we should live, we will."

At Sam's surprised look, he continued. "I'm in this for the long haul, Sam. I want us to end up together, married, together for the rest of our lives. This isn't a short-term fling for me. I want us to go into this expecting that we'll make it permanent. I'm not promising anything, things might not work out, but I want you to know I'm serious here. I've had nine months to think about this, about us, and even though we weren't physically together very long, I've watched those tapes from the show over and over and I've missed you terribly…please let me know what you're thinking behind those beautiful eyes."

Sam looked at Alex. He looked so earnest, so worried. She lifted her hand and smoothed it over his brow.

"I want those things too, Alex. I never expected to find someone like you. I'd like to try."

Alex leaned in and caught Sam's lips with his own. He couldn't be gentle. He slanted his head to the side and ravaged her mouth. God, she tasted so good and all he could think of was laying her down and spending all night exploring her body. They spent the next few minutes lost in each other's kiss and only came up for air when they heard the waitress clearing her throat next to the table.

"Did you need anything else?" she asked with a grin.

"No, I have everything I need right here," Alex replied, never taking his eyes off of Sam. "I'm the luckiest man alive."

"No," Sam replied. "*We* are the luckiest people alive."

Sam and Alex were lying on the couch, watching a movie. Sam was lying with her head in Alex's lap and his hands were idly brushing through her hair. The last year was like a dream. After Alex had come to Albuquerque to get her, the media frenzy was unbelievable. The newspapers and entertainment shows had gone crazy over the story of the reality show hunk who ended up with one of the rejected contestants.

They'd dated for a few months, but Sam quickly realized there wasn't anything keeping her in Albuquerque, except for Beth and Christina. They wouldn't let her stay for them. They wanted her to be happy and they loved Alex. Alex made it a point to include them in something every time he visited. Sometimes they all went out to dinner and other times they just hung out at Sam's house and watched movies. As a result of his efforts to include them in their relationship, they were the first to tell Sam to move to Austin.

They sat down with her and had a long talk. The three talked about Sam's relationship, they talked about what would happen with Sam's career, and they talked about sex. Anytime the three of them got together, the talk most often turned to sex.

Sam wasn't one to talk much about what she and Alex did in the bedroom, but she'd admitted to her friends that Alex was incredible. She hadn't been a virgin when they'd gotten together, but he made her feel inexperienced. He was patient and the two of them together were explosive.

The night Sam told Alex she was thinking about moving to Austin was amazing. Alex showed her his appreciation for hours in her bedroom. It hadn't taken him long to arrange to have her belongings moved into his ranch outside of Austin. Albert, Duke, and Blue were happy to move to a bigger house as well. They quickly acclimated, but then again, they were happy anywhere Sam went.

Blue was currently lying at Sam's feet on the couch, while Duke and Albert were napping on one of the many dog beds strewn about the room.

Alex's cell phone rang and Sam looked up as he leaned over to answer it. She only heard his side of the conversation.

"This is Alex. Hello, Eddie. Good. Really? Congratulations. What? Uh, I'm not sure. It's not about the money, Eddie. Hell, you know we don't need it. All right, I'll talk to her and we'll think about it. Yeah. You too. Bye."

Sam watched as Alex ended the call and put the phone back on the table next to the couch. His hand returned to stroking her hair. Sam waited, knowing he'd tell her what the call was about when he was ready. There was no telling what Eddie wanted now. Sam really couldn't hate the man. After all, he *was* one of the reasons she was with Alex now, but she also knew how the man operated. He never did anything out of the kindness of his heart.

Finally, Alex took a deep breath.

"That was Eddie."

Sam nodded and sat up, snuggling into Alex's side.

"He wanted to let me know he's starting a new reality show based in Arizona." Alex shook his head and chuckled. "He wanted us to come to the set one day to meet the contestants and encourage them with our story."

Sam laughed. "He *does* remember that I was kicked off and he arranged to edit me out of the entire show, right? What kind of encouragement will our showing up offer anyone?"

"Maybe that they too can make it out alive?" Alex said sarcastically.

Sam laughed. "You decide," she told Alex. "I don't care what we do. I've got you, you've got me and he can't do anything to break us up."

"Damn straight," Alex said.

"I do feel sorry for whoever is on that show, though," Sam said. She squealed as Alex suddenly stood up, cradling her against his chest.

"Those poor bastards," he agreed, nuzzling against Sam's neck, breathing in her scent. He carried her up the stairs to their bedroom. "I suppose we should make an appearance to keep Eddie off our backs. You know he won't give up if he wants us there."

Sam barely managed a nod as Alex leaned over and placed her on their bed. She had much better things to think about than some new reality show that Eddie was planning. She had to think about how she'd please her man.

Flaming Hearts

Beyond Reality
Book 2

by Susan Stoker

Chapter One

Rebecca was excited. She couldn't believe it was finally time for her reality show to start! Becky was a reality show junkie. She'd started watching reality shows when she was a little girl and couldn't believe she was finally going to be on one.

Becky used to watch with her mom when she was sick. It was a great way to get away from the reality of the disease that was taking her mom's life away one day at a time. Her mom refused to go into hospice care and wanted to die at home. So Becky did as she wished. She had no siblings, and her dad had died a long time ago. It was just her and her mom.

They'd laughed at the contestants, at their scheming and conniving ways, but loved every minute of the shows. They weren't particular as to what kind of reality shows they'd watch. Love matches, cop shows, extreme survival shows, teenagers getting pregnant…it didn't matter. What mattered was the time they spent together.

Becky applied to every show she could with her mom's help. They had a blast printing off the forms and finding the best way to market Becky. Neither figured she'd ever get chosen. After all, millions of people probably applied to be on the shows, but it was fun nevertheless.

They'd also had a long conversation about the kinds of women who were typically chosen to be on reality shows. Actresses, models, former beauty pageant queens…it was really quite nauseating. Very rarely did they see any women on the shows who were considered "normal."

Becky's mom died before knowing she'd been chosen to be on a show. It was bittersweet. She admitted to herself that she was excited to be chosen, but was also sad because Becky knew her mom would never see her on TV.

The show she'd been chosen to be on was a bachelorette type of show. She wasn't too fond of most of the reality shows that were currently running, but Becky figured it might be worth giving it a try. Thank goodness she wasn't chosen for one of the survivalist-type shows. She shuddered. She knew she'd never make it even one day on one of those, not that she'd ever even apply for one. She hated bugs, hated to be cold, or hot, and wasn't an outdoorsy type of person, except for the occasional hike. She knew the show she'd be on would be different from what was airing now, but she had no idea how.

All she knew was that she'd get to choose from a posse of men! Now *that* was exciting. Her love life had suffered over the last few months because of taking care of her mom, but she wouldn't have had it any other way.

The last reality love-type show she'd watched was one that had been filmed in Australia. The man on that show had been very good looking. Becky had applied for that show, but obviously wasn't chosen. The producer of that show was also producing the one she'd be on. Becky loved the twists and turns of the Australian production, and hoped some fun things were going to happen in her show as well. Of course, watching people run after pigs and shovel manure was probably a lot more fun to watch than it was to actually do in person. Oh well. She was excited anyway.

Becky wasn't exactly sure how she'd gotten chosen for this show. She knew she wasn't a typical bachelorette. She was a bit older than a lot of the women she'd seen on TV. She wasn't over the hill yet, hell she was only 32, but she also wasn't in her early twenties either. She wasn't an actress or a model. She'd never been on television before. She was just…Becky.

She had a normal job. She wasn't an executive and she didn't own her own business. She worked for an insurance company as an underwriter. Her job was to accept applications as they came in and look them over to make sure that whatever the person wanted insured was eligible. Houses had to be in good condition, Becky had to check the claim history to make sure it wasn't excessive and other things related to the application. She also took phone calls from agents and policyholders to discuss the policies and answered any questions they had. The worst was when the policy was cancelled. No one was happy and they usually took it out on her, which wasn't fun at all. All in all, her job was perfectly normal and actually quite boring. But it paid the bills.

Becky was flattered Eddie and the other producers had chosen *her* to be the bachelorette on their show. She'd never known any of the other women on the dating shows she'd watched to have a normal job as she had.

Apparently the producers had noticed her application for the Australian show and decided she'd be a perfect bachelorette for their new reality show. Becky knew she was heavier than the women that had been showcased before. However, she'd read that Alex, the bachelor in Australia, in the end had chosen a woman—she couldn't remember her name—that wasn't model thin either. Maybe there was hope for her yet! Becky knew she wasn't obese by any stretch, but she also wasn't bikini material either. She'd rather go hiking than clubbing, but on the other hand she'd rather hang out watching TV than go shopping. And she'd rather do just about anything other than put on a fancy dress and makeup! But Becky had put her best face forward in the application and through subsequent interviews, and apparently she'd passed the psychological tests. Now she was on her way to Arizona to participate on the show.

She had no idea what would come out of the experience. Would she fall in love and get married? Would she become famous? Would she hate the entire experience and become a bitter old woman? There was no telling what would happen. That was part of the excitement.

She'd been given the five star treatment throughout her travel to Arizona. They flew her first class and she'd been driven to the huge mansion she'd be staying at by a limousine, complete with a stern faced driver. She met the host of the show and he seemed nice enough. She was a bit giddy because the host was the same as the Australian show, Robert. It was like meeting a movie star!

She'd be at the house for two months while they filmed. Eight weeks didn't seem long enough to be able to meet a man and fall in love, but she knew being on these shows really accelerated the dating process because it was so intense. She wasn't allowed to talk to anyone from her "real world," of course, unless there was an emergency, and she wasn't allowed to watch television at all. There wasn't really anyone who she'd miss. Oh, she had friends, but they were mostly work acquaintances. She had some people from the animal shelter she volunteered at that she might miss, but again, they were more work acquaintances than true friends.

Becky knew she'd miss her mom, though. They'd both talked about what would happen if she was ever chosen to be on a show and she'd miss being able to talk and gossip with her mom when she got home in eight weeks. The thought of actually sitting down and watching the show when it aired without her mom was also very hard to imagine.

Becky was able to take a leave of absence from the insurance company and luckily she had a good boss who'd let her come back after the show was over. She didn't have leave time saved up to cover the entire eight weeks, but Human Resources was allowing her to take leave-without-pay to cover the rest of the time that she didn't have the time for. It was very generous of them actually.

Her coworkers had thrown a huge party for her on her last day of work. They'd all teased her about becoming rich and famous and forgetting all about them. Becky had laughed. It wasn't as if being an underwriter was anyone's dream job. She knew they'd all leave in a heartbeat if they could. But she was touched that everyone wished her well, especially considering they'd have to take up her slack on the job since she wouldn't be there.

Overall, she was ready. She couldn't wait to meet the men on the show. She figured if she fell in love great, but if not, at least it'd be an experience to remember!

* * *

Jonathan stood with the other camera operators listening to instructions given to them by Eddie, the producer of the reality show. Jonathan had sort of fallen into the whole camera operator gig and was finding that it really wasn't his thing, but he'd agreed to work on two last jobs, this one and one last show in Alaska. He was thrilled this show was filming in Arizona because he'd been working in Los Angeles for the past four years and he missed his brother and the rest of his close-knit family. They were a bit crazy, but he wouldn't change anything about them.

When he was done with his camera operator contract, his brother, Dean, said he could come home and work with him. Jonathan was thrilled. Dean had worked his butt off and finally had a job he loved. He was a security expert and got called to consult all over the country on both big and small cases. He'd visit a business or home and recommend what security was needed based on the client's needs. He'd consulted for huge corporations down to small seven hundred square foot homes.

Jonathan was also not surprised when he'd heard Dean would take cases pro-bono for women who were trying to protect themselves from stalkers or violent ex's. Jonathan couldn't wait to make a difference in someone's life as he knew Dean was. Filming people trying to become famous, if only for their five minutes of fame, wasn't how he wanted to be remembered. He couldn't wait to work with his brother professionally.

Jonathan was in his mid-thirties and wasn't ashamed about wanting to be closer to home. His family had always been close. He missed Dean. Jonathan smiled when he thought about his older brother. Neither of them had ever been married. Jonathan had come close once, but it didn't work out. Dean was a strong man. Someone who knew what he wanted and didn't put up with any crap from anyone, male or female. Jonathan knew most people thought Dean was way too intense. He was an alpha male to the nth degree. Jonathan loved that about his brother. When he was little, Dean not only protected Jonathan from bullies who thought he should be into sports rather than art and photography, but Dean also protected everyone else too.

There was one day Jonathan remembered when their mom had gotten a call from the local police chief and demanded they bring Dean into the station. The whole family went down to the station with Dean and heard the police chief lambast him for beating up the local high school football hero.

Their dad requested Dean explain what was going on. Jonathan would never forget his brother standing in the small interrogation room, defiant even at fifteen years old, and calmly explaining how he'd walked around the corner of the high school and seen the boy hitting his girlfriend. He'd stepped in and beat the crap out of the boy in retaliation. He'd seen someone in need and stepped in and did what was necessary. He hadn't cared who the boy was. It didn't matter he was a football hero and one of the most popular guys at the school…and older than him to boot. He did what was right. Period.

Jonathan knew Dean would do anything for him too. Family meant a lot to them. He'd missed that. He missed the feeling of belonging. While he still belonged to his family, it was hard to connect with them when he was in Los Angeles and they were all back in Arizona.

Jonathan turned his attention back to Eddie as he spelled out the duties of the camera operators for the shoot. They'd rotate jobs throughout the day and throughout the show. Eddie felt it wasn't good for one camera operator to get too close to any of the contestants, and vice versa. When Jonathan tried to bring up the fact that sometimes if the contestants were more comfortable with the camera operator they seemed to open up more and be more themselves, Eddie didn't want to listen.

Jonathan knew this was going be a tough shoot. Eddie seemed to have an agenda and he was acting pretty sneaky. He knew Eddie had been in charge of the reality show that had just ended in Australia and apparently made a ton of money for the network. He couldn't remember all the details, but thought he remembered reading something about a ton of twists and turns throughout the show. Why anyone would want to be on a reality show was beyond his comprehension. Jonathan mentally shrugged and told himself it was a job and it was money, and he really didn't care what went on with the spoiled contestants…as long as he was paid, he didn't care.

* * *

Becky took a deep breath and tried to calm herself. She'd just come from a meeting with the producer and couldn't believe what she'd gotten herself into. She was so excited to have been chosen for the show and to meet some great guys, but she understood now *why* she'd been chosen. Apparently she was going to have to compete for the attentions of the men on the show…she was going to have to compete with a woman that looked like a walking, talking Barbie doll. Marissa was beautiful. She was polished, skinny, and had a set of boobs that even Becky had a hard time looking away from.

Becky knew she didn't have a chance of getting any of the men on the show to look at her. She also knew the whole experience was going to be a let-down, but now she didn't have a choice. She'd signed the contract, she was here and she had to go on with it. She sat in a chair in her room, hands folded in her lap, and watched as a tear landed on the back of her hand. She'd never felt so alone in her life.

Chapter Two

Becky watched as the men were introduced at the first cocktail hour. She'd felt sorry for herself for about ten minutes, then got herself under control. She was here, she might as well make the best of the situation. Maybe, just maybe some of the guys would look deeper than the surface and see *her*.

She'd been instructed to dress as though she was going on a first date, so she'd chosen a pair of khaki pants and a nice pink blouse. When she walked into the room and saw Marissa, she wanted to sink through the floor. She'd screwed up. Marissa was wearing a slinky black dress that left most of her back bare, and four inch heels. Her hair was in an up-do with small tendrils hanging down, framing her face. Becky knew she was out of her element. She looked positively frumpy standing next to Marissa. She'd been pleased with what she'd seen when she looked in the mirror before coming down the stairs, but now she felt very much like the ugly stepsister.

When the men were introduced, Becky was glad to note that they weren't half "hunks" and the other half "nerds" as she feared and once seen on a reality show, but every one of them was very handsome.

Becky walked around the room, talking to each of the men in the room. She made a point to make eye contact with each and to try to get to know them. Even if she knew she was at a disadvantage next to Marissa, she still wanted to make the effort.

There was certainly a mix of men and professions. Becky had a hard time keeping them all straight. David and Derek were the easiest to remember because they were identical twins. She had no idea who was who, but at least she could remember their names. Becky wasn't sure what they did for a living, as they didn't stick around to talk to her for very long, they only had eyes for Marissa. There was also Ryan, Alex, Jose, Patrick and James. Again, she couldn't remember what they did for jobs, but Becky knew she'd figure it out as the show went on.

After meeting so many people, she had no idea what the other men's names were. She'd always been bad at remembering names. Someone could introduce themselves to her and two minutes later she'd have no idea how they'd introduced themselves. It was embarrassing and she was trying to work on it, but there was no way she'd remember everyone's name here tonight. She sighed.

Becky kept her eye on Marissa and saw her sitting on a couch with a circle of men around her. She seemed at ease and flirtatiously talked to each one. Occasionally, she'd touch them on the knee or the arm or hand. She had the art of flirting down to a science. The longer the evening went on, the more uncomfortable Becky felt. What was the point of this? She knew which woman the men would prefer…maybe that was it! Maybe this *would* be the end of this torture! Maybe the men would get to choose who they'd vie for and she could go home with a nice consolation prize. A girl could dream, right?

Finally their host, Robert, brought Marissa and Becky into a back room and told them they'd each be choosing seven men to stay, and the other four men not chosen would be going home. It was a lot like the singles shows she'd watched with her mom in the past, but it was weird that there were two girls this time. She guessed it was an interesting twist on the premise of the bachelor/bachelorette concept. Darn it, Becky was really hoping Robert would've told them the guys were choosing which woman they wanted to compete for and the other woman had to go home right then.

Robert asked each of them if they knew who they'd ask to stay and Marissa asked him slyly, "What if I want more than seven to stay? Can I ask Becky to use one of her slots to add one of the men I want?" After a pause she added,

"And vice versa, of course." Marissa giggled, thinking her words were the funniest thing ever.

"Of course," Robert told her, "Any way you want to split up the decision you can. It's up to the two of you."

Marissa turned to Becky and said, "I think Derek and David are soooo hot. They both have to stay. I love Trevon's name. Jose is rich as hell, so he has to stay as well. I also want to keep Samuel, Ryan, Joel, Dexter, and Conner, John, and Alex because they paid the most attention to me. I don't want Ned and Carter to stay. You can choose the other three that you want to stay and two that you want to go." She shrugged as if she didn't just take over the show entirely.

At this point Becky didn't really care as she didn't know any of the men, but she also didn't want Marissa to think she could walk all over her for the entire show.

"So who does that leave?" Becky asked Marissa sarcastically.

"Duh," Marissa said with disdain. "Patrick, James, Chris, Oliver, and Tommy."

Becky didn't like Marissa all that much, but she couldn't help but be impressed with her memory of all the men's names.

Becky didn't want to make someone go home solely based on what they looked like, as that wasn't the type of person she was, but Marissa seemed to know who she wanted, and since none of the men really stood out in her eyes, she'd agree, but with conditions.

"You know you just chose eleven guys to stay when really you only get to choose seven, right?" She waited for Marissa to nod and then continued. "But since I don't know any of them that well, I'll let you have more than your fair share this time. But if in the future I want to negotiate, you'll let me."

Happy that she'd gotten her way Marissa beamed at Becky and agreed immediately. They walked back out into the main room to let the men know who would stay and who would go.

Robert lined all the men up in the typical way these things were done on reality shows, into two lines with nine men in each line. They had a platform set up so the men in back were standing taller than the men in front. Becky and Marissa stood across from the men with Robert between them.

"Welcome to *Arizona Reality*!" Robert boomed, arms spread wide. Becky inwardly cringed. Who the hell came up with the names of these shows? It sounded like they were selling a house or something.

Robert continued dramatically, "Hopefully you had a good time tonight getting to know each other. Becky, Marissa, you will each get the chance to have seven men stay to compete for your affections. Unfortunately, four of you men will be leaving tonight. Marissa, we'll start with you. Who do you want to stay tonight and get to know you better?"

Marissa, in her glory, beamed and dramatically stepped forward to give her speech. "I had such a good time tonight," she gushed, "I'm so happy to meet all of you. This is *such* a hard decision! If it was up to me I'd have *all* of you stay so I could get to know you better, but unfortunately that's impossible." Marissa pouted prettily. She named seven of the men she wanted to stay, pausing dramatically between each name.

When it was Becky's turn she felt her stomach turn. There were eleven men looking intensely at her. She really didn't want to have to disappoint any of them. She tried hard to remember who the men were that Becky wanted to keep and didn't mention. It was easier to remember the names of the men who weren't staying.

"Uh, Like Marissa said, this choice was really hard. I enjoyed meeting all of you and I wasn't sure how to decide who I wanted to stay and who I wanted to go as I don't really *know* any of you." Seeing the impatient looks on the remaining men's faces she decided to hurry and get this over with. This part of the show definitely sucked. She didn't like it when people were mad at her, and she was definitely going to make four of these men unhappy. Becky turned toward the men and rushed through the seven names, hoping she had them right, but knowing even if she didn't, it wouldn't make much difference to her. Marissa might care, but she didn't. "John, Conner, Dexter, Joel, James, Patrick and Samuel."

Becky and Marissa both jumped as Robert boomed as soon as Becky finished saying Samuel's name. "The choice has been made!"

"What the hell?" Becky heard Carter say unbelievably. "This show sucks." He snarled the words and stepped off the platform toward the front door of the huge house. He wrenched the door open and actually slammed it behind him like he was three years old.

Robert continued, even though Carter had stormed out of the house and ruined his planned dramatic delivery of his speech. "I'm so sorry Ned, Tommy, Carter, and Oliver, but you've not been invited to stay by our lovely ladies. It's time to say goodbye."

The three men who were still there came over and kissed Marissa on the cheek, shook Becky's hand and walked out. Becky felt awkward as hell as the men displayed the favoritism so blatantly. This left the other fourteen men standing in their two lines, all with goofy smiles on their faces. Becky sighed. This was going to be a *long* eight weeks.

Chapter Three

Jonathan watched in disbelief at the spectacle in front of him. He'd been working for about three weeks on the reality show and was beyond disgusted. It wasn't the basic premise of the show, single guys trying to get the attention of a single lady, but more the way Eddie and the other producers were making one of the women look.

Jonathan knew when the producers chose the single women the men would be competing for, they picked two women who were complete opposites on purpose. Of course, it would make for good television, but it certainly didn't mean the women were treated the same way. It wasn't as if Becky wasn't attractive, because she was, but when put side by side with Marissa, Jonathan knew most people would think Marissa was the pretty one, and Becky was the "lesser" one.

It wasn't just their looks either. It was obvious Becky was uncomfortable in most of the settings they'd put her in thus far. One week the group went to a local disco club. The music was loud, and it was hard to hear anything, even with the microphones the contestants were wearing. Jonathan's job was to follow Becky around and all he heard all night was her answering questions about Marissa and who she thought Marissa liked best. He'd been watching Becky over the last few weeks and had seen her grow less and less animated.

When he'd first seen her at the introductory meeting of the show and to let the contestants meet the camera operators, she'd seemed at ease with herself and she smiled a lot. She was certainly excited to be on the show and for it to start. She was very friendly with all of the camera operators and joked around with them. At that point she hadn't realized they weren't allowed to really talk to her much, and she'd spoken freely about how glad she was to meet them all and how happy she was to be there.

Now her smile was forced and Jonathan knew she gritted her teeth a lot. She had bags under her eyes and it was obvious she wasn't sleeping well. She no longer tried to engage with the camera operators and any time she met their eyes, she'd look away in consternation.

He could sense her frustration, embarrassment, and sadness. It went against Jonathan's nature to allow any woman to be disgraced like Becky was, but there was nothing he could do but watch through his lens. He thought he'd been jaded by Hollywood before starting this job, but this was the last straw. He was so thankful he only had one more show to get through after this one before he could start working with his brother. He wanted out of show business for good.

That night after going off duty on the set, Jonathan was sitting at Dean's dining room table, talking with his brother. He'd be working for the next three nights, so all he wanted to do was sit around and talk to his brother tonight.

"I can't believe what they're doing to her," Jonathan told Dean. "Seriously, they're making a fool out of this woman and she knows it. There's nothing she can do, but try to pretend everything is okay."

Dean looked at Jonathan carefully. "Why do you care, bro'?" he asked seriously. "It's not like she's actually being harmed, if she's experiencing a little embarrassment, she probably deserves it for agreeing to be on the show in the first place."

Jonathan looked at Dean and answered as honestly as possible. "I know. Intellectually, I know she brought it on herself by signing the contract, but you taught me to watch out for people, Dean, and I'm watching and she's hurting. I can't do anything for her and it's awful. It's like she's on an island surrounded by water and dying of thirst. I don't know." He paused, then continued, "There's something about her. She almost feels like…" His voice faded off.

"Feels like what?" Dean asked, honestly perplexed. He'd never seen his brother like this. *He* was the one in their family who usually had the need to protect others, not Jonathan. "There had to have been situations like this in California that you've seen before in the industry. Women who are being taken advantage of, who are making bad choices. Why is this so different? Do you think she's your *One*?" Dean asked seriously, sitting up in his chair with an expectant look on his face. "It'd explain the feeling…"

Every man in their family had been quick to fall in love. It was as if there was only one person in the world for them, and as soon as they saw that woman, they knew it immediately. This was the case as far back as any of them could remember. Their parents were cases in point. Both Jonathan and Dean had been told over and over the story of how they met and how their dad knew instantly their mom would be his. Of course, the women usually didn't feel the same way at first and required some wooing and courting. It was a tough thing to believe and while Dean wanted to believe he'd find his *One* just like all of his ancestors did, it was a farfetched idea. But the hope that he'd really meet someone and know on the spot she was the one for him was why he'd never been married yet. He was holding out for the fairytale, even though anyone who knew him would scoff at the very idea.

"No, no, no." Jonathan was quick to reassure him. "Believe me, she's not my *One*. It's just…I connect with her somehow, but not in a 'you're mine' kind of way. There's just something about her that makes me want to bash all the other contestants and that stupid producer upside the head for the way they're treating her." Jonathan continued trying to explain to his brother.

"You should've seen her the other day. Eddie put together a pool party for the contestants. I think it was mostly so the audience could ogle everyone in their swimsuits. Everyone in the industry knows sex sells. Marissa was in her element. She wore a skimpy white bikini and strutted her stuff all afternoon. Becky wore a one piece black suit with some sarong thing and sat at a table next to the pool all afternoon. Not one of the men asked if she wanted something to drink. Oh, some came over and talked to her, but mainly to try to pump her for information about Marissa. She had to watch as man after man brought Marissa something to drink, or a snack, or offered to rub lotion on her back, or helped her from the water when she went swimming.

"Over and over it was rubbed in Becky's face that she wasn't desirable, wasn't worth their notice, wasn't as pretty as Marissa. She had to sit there and take it all afternoon. She had a fake smile on her face the entire time the party went on. As soon as Eddie proclaimed the party over she stood up and walked back into the house and never looked back. She didn't say anything to anyone, just went straight up the stairs into her room. I'm telling you, bro', she's miserable and knows what's going on around her, but she just doesn't know how to stop it and in fact *can't* stop it."

Dean listened to his brother speak with a deep passion about this woman. It was the first time he'd ever heard him be protective about a woman in his life. Oh, he respected them, but Jonathan was more a "love 'em and leave 'em" type of man. He generally didn't concern himself about finding his *One* and settling down or about what emotions a woman might be feeling. The fact he was this concerned about this woman was curious and out of character, and made Dean want to meet her.

"You've got me interested, bro'," Dean told Jonathan honestly. "Any chance I could come to the set and visit?"

Jonathan beamed. "I was hoping you'd say that!" He pulled a guest pass to the set out of his back pocket. "You'll have to sign a confidentiality agreement before you're allowed into the production house, but I've already got it arranged!" Jonathan paused for a moment and told Dean, "Tomorrow the two ladies are going on a double date. Last week Marissa got to choose where they'd go, and this week Becky got to choose. I heard she wanted to go on a hike. I think she chose it just to irritate Marissa. I've seen her subtly do it before. She purposely chooses activities she knows Marissa will hate. She isn't obvious about it, but I know she's aware of exactly what she's doing."

"Where are they going?" Dean asked, knowing there weren't too many places around that would be appropriate.

"I think she chose Devil's Canyon," Jonathan said with a smile.

Dean smiled too. He knew the hike started out pretty tame, but quickly became quite strenuous. It was only two miles to the canyon, but after the first three fourths of a mile there was a pretty intense elevation gain.

"Maybe I'll take a rain check on that set visit," he told his brother, and when he saw him frown, quickly continued, "I think I'll visit Devil's Canyon tomorrow and check things out. I've got a hankering to take a hike."

Jonathan smiled. "Perfect! Just be sure to let them get there first. You can then meet them on the trail and watch what happens. I'm not assigned to film them tomorrow. I'll be back at the house with the other men and filming them while the ladies are on their double date. Don't be surprised at anything you might see out there. Eddie is slick and knows how to throw a curve ball at everyone. Marissa is just as bad."

Dean smiled. "Don't worry, bro', I'll be discrete. You've got me curious to meet both Marissa and Becky now. I'll call when I get back."

The two brothers sat for a while longer, enjoying each other's company and simply shooting the shit before heading up to bed. Tomorrow would be a long day for both of them.

Chapter Four

Becky sighed. This so-called date was going to suck. She'd chosen the hike option, not only because she wanted to see Devil's Canyon, but because she was annoyed at Marissa and wanted to piss her off. She should've known somehow it would end up backfiring on her. She couldn't catch a break. For the thousandth time she regretted agreeing to be on the show. It was the worst reality show in the history of reality shows, and that was saying something since there were so many bad ones on nowadays. Thank God her mom hadn't lived long enough to watch it. That was Becky's only consolation right about now, even if it made her feel like crap to actually think it.

The five of them arrived at the trailhead around ten in the morning. Marissa, Becky, the cameraman, Jose, and Alex all piled out of the van in the parking area. Jose was nice enough, at least he talked to her like she was a real person, but Alex was like all the popular kids she knew back in high school…ignoring those around him who he thought were beneath him. Becky knew he thought she was beneath him.

They'd started off on the hike and everyone was happy and acting like they couldn't imagine being anywhere else, but soon Marissa started complaining. It was too hot. It was too rocky. Her backpack was itching…anything and everything had her complaining. Becky tried to ignore her and enjoy the beautiful day. It was a perfect day for hiking and she was determined to have a good time. Right when the trail started ascending, Marissa suddenly collapsed on the ground and grabbed her ankle.

"Owwwwwww, I think I twisted it…bad!"

Jose and Alex were right there, patting her shoulder and asking what they could do to help. Becky looked at the cameraman. He had his camera pointed at the trio and the drama. She rolled her eyes, knowing they wouldn't catch it on film. She didn't really know the camera operators that well. When she met them for the first time she thought she'd be able to be friends with them, but she soon found out they weren't allowed to talk to the contestants. It bummed her out at first, but now that the show was continuing she was glad she hadn't gotten to know them. It was just too embarrassing. She'd seen some of them looking at her with pity. Becky hated that. She knew she was being made out to look pathetic on national television, but there was nothing she could do about it. She didn't know the cameraman who was with them today very well. Eddie kept moving them around so she and Marissa couldn't get to know them. Even if she wanted to talk to them, she couldn't. It was against the "rules." Eddie was a stickler for the "rules."

Becky watched Marissa bitch and moan a bit more and finally couldn't help herself, she said sternly, "Come on, Marissa, it can't hurt that badly, let's keep going."

Marissa glared up at Becky. "What do you know? It's not *your* ankle that's hurt! I can't possibly go on!"

Becky sighed. "Fine, you want to sit here and wait while we continue on?" She gestured toward Jose and Alex. "We'll pick you up on the way back." Becky couldn't believe she'd actually said it, but she was sick of sitting around letting everyone else make all the decisions for her.

"I can't possibly wait here by myself!" Marissa moaned, not surprisingly, and grabbed both Alex and Jose by an arm. "You guys'll stay here with me, right? I mean, it's not like you really *wanted* to walk around in the heat, right?"

What could the men say to that…of course they agreed.

"Fine!" Becky said, pissed off. "You guys stay here. I really want to see Devil's Canyon. It sounds fascinating and I've wanted to see it since I got here. It's not that much farther. I'll just go on up the trail, and then I'll come back and meet you here. Then we can go back to the house."

She watched as Marissa's eyes lit up with satisfaction and Alex and Jose both nodded. She looked up at the camera operator, knowing he'd be torn between following her and staying with the trio.

She said in a gentler voice to him, "You stay with them. It's not good TV to just film me walking." She winked at him, not surprised when he nodded, and she set off up the trail without looking back. It was great to get some time to herself. The only time she'd been by herself was when she'd been sleeping, and she hadn't been sleeping all that great lately anyway. The air was nice and fresh and there wasn't anyone else on the trail. It was a good day to forget all about the stupid show and what an idiot she was for agreeing to be on it in the first place. She could enjoy seeing a part of the country she'd never seen before.

Almost as soon as Becky was out of sight, Marissa started manipulating Alex and Jose into leaving. She wanted to teach Becky a lesson and having her come back and not finding them there would be a great way! She moaned that her ankle was probably really hurt and she couldn't wait for Becky to come back before seeing a doctor. She finally convinced them they needed to take her to the emergency room and they could come back for Becky. After all, it wouldn't take too long to see a doctor and Becky would be gone for such a loooong time. So the foursome, including the camera operator, walked/hobbled back to the parking area and headed for the hospital. Leaving no note for Becky and no sign they'd even been there.

* * *

Becky reached the top of the trail and sat down harshly on the bench. Holy crap, that was a tough hike. She knew there was no way Marissa would've made it. She would've been too concerned about her makeup and not huffing and puffing in front of the guys. It was probably good she'd been hurt before attempting the steep part of the trail. Becky didn't realize how tough it was going to be, but it was beautiful.

She gazed out at the canyon. It wasn't as big as the Grand Canyon, obviously, but it was a good size. There was a small waterfall off to the left and the color of the rocks was amazing. Becky scooted her butt forward, put her head on the back of the bench and closed her eyes, letting the warmth of the sun soak into her skin. She knew she couldn't stay there too long, Marissa would get restless and she'd have to get back, but ah, the peacefulness was a blessing.

Becky sat up when she heard a noise in the brush off to her right. She turned toward the noise, expecting to see a deer or a fox or another small animal. She couldn't believe her eyes when she noticed a huge coyote. The animal was lying in the brush, not moving, but staring at her. Becky stood up slowly and climbed up on the bench. It wasn't any protection at all, but it made her feel a bit better. The coyote was beautiful. It was black with white paws and white on its chest and the tip of its tail. It just lay there on the ground, staring at her. Becky was a bit nervous as she'd always heard coyotes were aggressive animals and the fact it was just sitting there was downright eerie. She hoped it didn't have rabies or anything. Becky stared right back at the animal. She couldn't believe she was this close to it, but it made no sudden moves and didn't even seem to be threatened by her.

She whispered, "Hello, coyote," expecting it to leap up and race away. All that happened was its tail started wagging. The coyote's eyes never left her face.

"You really aren't so big and bad, are you?" she asked nervously, not expecting an answer. "You know you probably shouldn't be here. There are way too many people that come around here, you could be in danger," Becky continued on, a little unnerved by the way the coyote kept staring at her. *Was* it rabid? Animals did odd things when they were sick. "You should go home to your mate and pups." She didn't know what gender the coyote was, but she imagined it was a male. It was large, therefore, she reasoned, it must be male. She had no basis for thinking that, but there it was anyway.

"She must be wondering where you are…go on…you go and I'll just be on my way." Still the coyote just lay there in an unnatural way…finally Becky knew she had to get going down the trail. She couldn't stand there any longer and have a one way conversation with the animal.

"Okay, here's the deal. I have to get going…so I'm going to step down…if you promise not to eat me, I promise not to tell anyone you were here…deal?" She waited, not expecting any response, but waiting as if she'd get one anyway. She was totally shocked when the coyote backed up a bit…really it was more of a shuffle as it never really stood up, but it scooted back as if to agree with her.

Becky slowly put one foot on the ground, wishing she had her camera with her. Darn Eddie and his rules. They weren't allowed to have their cell phones or cameras while filming, which she thought was ridiculous. No one was without their camera phone nowadays. No one would ever believe this encounter with the coyote and this animal was so beautiful Becky wished she could immortalize him on film. Besides, if it attacked her, she thought morbidly, she could've always taken pictures of her mangled body to show her coworkers back home.

She put her second foot on the ground and slowly backed away from the bench, never taking her eyes off of the coyote, noticing it never took its eyes off her either. Finally Becky knew she had to turn around and watch where she was going. It was a steep trail and she couldn't walk down it backward. She took a deep breath and turned her back on the coyote…waiting. When nothing happened she looked over her shoulder as she started down the trail and saw that the coyote was gone. She knew she hadn't dreamed it, but it was uncanny how quickly and quietly the animal disappeared.

* * *

Dean called Jonathan to let him know he'd arrived at the parking lot for Devil's Canyon. "Yo, bro', I'm here at the parking area but there's no one around. Are you sure they were coming here today?"

"Yes, I know that's where they were hiking today because Eddie kept talking about how the name of the canyon was great for drama on the show," Jonathan told him emphatically. "Maybe you missed them?" he said skeptically.

Before Dean had a chance to answer they both heard a commotion on the set. "Hold on," Jonathan told him unnecessarily. "I think they're back…"

Dean waited while Jonathan listened to the pandemonium nearby. He couldn't hear what was going on, but knew his brother would let him know. Jonathan quickly came back on the phone and asked urgently and in a low voice, "Are you still at the parking lot at Devil's Canyon?" Dean didn't understand the urgency in his brother's voice but unconsciously and automatically kicked into protector mode.

"Yeah, I'm sitting here, looking at the trail head. What's up?"

Jonathan told him quietly, "I'm going to put my cell on speaker, so you can hear, but don't say anything. Becky might need your help…"

Dean's whole body clenched. Hearing that a woman needed help did that to him every time. He hadn't even met Becky, but he'd heard Jonathan talk about her so much he *felt* as if he knew her anyway. Dean suddenly heard a woman's voice in the middle of a conversation with at least one other man.

"…and I hurt my ankle really badly…so Jose and Alex volunteered to take me to the hospital…"

"Are you all right?" asked a male voice with fake sincerity.

"I am now. Luckily Alex and Jose were there! I can't imagine what I would've done out there all alone with no one to help me." Dean could just imagine the look the woman was giving the two men. She sounded whiny and manipulative to him. There weren't many things a woman could do that would turn him off, but being manipulative was one of them.

"Where's Becky?" Dean heard Jonathan ask the woman, most likely Marissa, gruffly.

"Oh, she left us. She wanted to continue on the hike. She didn't *care* that I was hurt," the woman said in a nasally voice that grated on Dean's nerves even more than it had before.

Dean heard Jonathan ask a man standing near him, presumably a camera operator, "You left her out there? By herself? At Devil's Canyon?"

"Hey, she seemed perfectly willing to go…she didn't seem to mind…." His voice trailed off and Dean could hear that he finally felt guilty for leaving Becky. The sad thing was that it had taken this long for him to feel that guilt.

"We had to get Marissa to the hospital." Alex defended their actions. "She was hurt. We knew that we'd get back here and someone could go and get Becky. I'm sure she's fine. She can take care of herself." Alex's tone was nonchalant and almost disgusted, as if a woman taking care of herself was a bad thing.

Dean had heard enough. He disconnected the call. He knew what Jonathan wanted him to do, and he didn't even have to ask. Jonathan would know he was on it. If Becky was alone out on the trail he'd be sure she made it back to the production house all right. Chances were that the woman *was* fine and there was no need to worry. He knew Jonathan had a soft spot for Becky from hearing him talk about her. He figured he'd head out on the trail, find Becky and accompany her back to the production house. He'd get to meet the woman who had Jonathan so tied up in knots as well as make sure she got back to the set with no issues.

Dean got out of his truck, grabbed his backpack, and headed over to the trail head. He'd start out on the trail and hopefully he'd run into her as she made her way back down from the canyon.

Chapter Five

Becky lay on the ground and tried to orient herself. She remembered walking down the steep trail, thinking about the strange behavior of the coyote at the top…then nothing. She was at the bottom of a small ravine, obviously having slipped down the slope. She looked up and winced. Her head hurt. She saw the slide mark her body had made as it came down the side of the hill. She looked at her hands. They were pretty scraped up too. She didn't remember the fall, but obviously she'd tried to slow herself down as she tumbled.

She reached up to feel the back of her head where it hurt the most and her hand came away with blood on it. Crap and double crap. She figured she'd probably hit her head on a rock or something as she tumbled down the steep hill.

She forced herself to a sitting position and took stock. It didn't feel like anything was broken, thank God. She could move her legs and her arms with no blinding pain. She was able to move her head back and forth, although it felt like someone was pounding on her skull from the inside. She slowly turned over and got on her hands and knees. There was no use sitting there. It wasn't as if she could wait until Marissa and the guys would come looking for her.

She thought back to the coyote she'd seen earlier. If there was one, there'd probably be others and she didn't want the smell of her blood to attract other wild animals. She was lucky with the coyote at the top of the trail. She didn't want to push it. Becky knew some time had passed and Marissa would be furious for having to wait for her. She dreaded having to deal with her and her attitude with her head hurting as it was, but it would be kind of nice to at least be back with other people. They'd help her, no matter if they weren't attracted to her. She'd procrastinated enough, it was time to make her way back up the hill.

Slowly but surely, Becky crawled up the steep slippery slope. Many times she slid back down, negating her progress, but she held on to whatever she could and finally made it back to the trail. She was sweating profusely and was covered in dirt. Her hands were filthy and her clothes were also covered in smears of dirt. As far as she could tell, her head wasn't bleeding anymore, but it still hurt like nothing she'd ever experienced before. She'd tied her hair back in a messy bun at the back of her head before starting her hike. That would prevent her from feeling the stickiness of her hair where the blood had seeped through, and maybe at the same time put a bit of pressure on the wound, stopping any more bleeding. Becky glanced at her watch. Crap. Three hours had gone by from the time she'd left the group. Marissa was going to be beyond pissed, and Becky couldn't really blame her. She'd be ticked too.

Once she'd reached the trail at the top of the hill, Becky stood up slowly and felt the world tilt. She quickly knelt on the ground right there in the middle of the trail. She had to get it together. She had to get down the trail, and staying here wasn't an option. She crawled over to a nearby rock, wincing as her scraped and bruised hands landed on the rocks on the trail. She pulled herself up and sat upright. See? She could do this. She *had* to do this. She couldn't very well crawl all the way back down the trail.

Becky straightened her backpack that had miraculously stayed put throughout her mishap, and slowly brought herself upright once more. There! She was vertical. She took baby steps as she walked down the trail, keeping her head down, watching where her feet were landing, counting her steps to keep the pain of her head out of her mind. The last thing she needed was to fall over a root or rock in the path and hurt herself even more.

Becky finally got to the place where Marissa and the others had said they'd wait for her. Becky sat on the rock with a sigh. There was no sign of them. It was eerily quiet in fact. Other than the birds chipping merrily in the trees she couldn't hear signs of anyone else. What did she expect?

That spoiled Marissa would calmly just sit in the wilderness bored out of her mind waiting for her? Hell no. She should've known better.

Becky eased her backpack off and leaned it against a rock, then eased herself down onto the same rock. She closed her eyes for a moment before taking her water bottle out of a side pocket of her backpack. She took a drink and tried to figure out what to do next. She couldn't quite concentrate; figuring she probably had a concussion.

Where would Marissa go? She knew she'd been gone a long time, but would they really leave her out here? No way…okay, maybe…yeah, probably. Becky sighed. She had to get to the start of the trail to the parking area. It was a long shot, but maybe they'd be there waiting for her to get back. The cameraman wouldn't leave her. There was no way. But if for some reason they weren't there maybe she could find someone to give her a ride. If no one was there *somebody* back at the show had to realize she was gone and come and get her. She was on a reality show, for God's sake. She was one of the damn *stars* of the reality show, they'd come back to get her. She just had to make it to the parking lot. She put her head in her hands and sighed. She'd get up in just a minute.

Dean walked quickly up the trail toward Devil's Canyon. He wasn't sure where along the path the woman might be, but he'd find her. It wasn't as if she could walk back to the set. She had to be out here somewhere. He had his first aid supplies in his backpack, just in case. He'd learned a long time ago to be prepared for anything.

He rounded a corner in the path about half a mile from the start of the steep incline and saw a woman sitting on a rock with her head in her hands. Dean stopped dead in his tracks. Was that Becky? She looked hurt, and his heart almost stopped. There was nothing worse than a woman who was hurt. He could handle pissed, he could handle sad, he could even handle tears, but a woman who'd been hurt made his heart ache and made his protective instincts hard to control.

He had to calm down before he scared the woman to death. He slowly made his way toward her, trying to make enough noise so she'd hear him coming and not be startled by her presence.

Becky heard someone on the trail and forced herself to look up. She was tired and not feeling well, but knew this person might be her chance to get out of there. She hadn't seen anyone else on the trail the entire time she'd been there, so if this person had a car, then she'd ask, or beg, for a ride. It wasn't the safest thing to do, but what choice did she have really? She'd have to take the chance that this person wasn't a homicidal killer.

She looked up…and up…and up at the man coming toward her. He wasn't handsome in the classical sense, but he carried himself with a sense of purpose and strength as if he wasn't scared of anything. He was wearing a pair of jeans and a plain gray T-shirt with a backpack. He was dressed for hiking. Her gaze continued upward until she met his eyes. They were dark, probably brown, but they were looking at her with an intensity she'd not been looked at before. She couldn't tear her gaze away as he came nearer. Crap, if he was a serial killer she was in big trouble, but damn, he was easy on the eyes.

Dean looked at the woman sitting on the rock on the side of the trail. She looked tired, a little scared, and a bit pissed, all at the same time. Other than her emotional state, she looked okay, until he got closer and could see blood on her hands and the collar of her shirt. Her clothes were streaked with dirt. It was obvious she'd taken a fall at some point. The blood worried him, he hoped it was nothing serious.

When she finally looked up at him he stumbled a bit as he continued toward her. Her eyes were a pale blue, almost gray in color. She was dressed plainly in a pair of jeans and a T-shirt. Her face was pale, but had swaths of red in both cheeks, probably from exertion as well as some sunburn. Since she was sitting down he couldn't see how tall she was, but she looked tiny to him. Hell, most people looked tiny to him.

But the one thing Dean thought most of all, was that she was beautiful. Sitting on the rock, looking up at him, trying not to look like she needed help. Damn. It hit him. Holy crap. She was his. His *One*.

He took a deep breath. Holy shit. It was true. All it took was one look and he wanted her more than he'd ever wanted anything. He hadn't completely believed the stories he'd heard his entire life, but it was true. A part of him still thought it was ridiculous. He didn't know anything about her. She could be a raving bitch. She could be married. She could be so many things, including *not* Becky, but it didn't seem to matter to his heart. She was his. *His.*

Dean stopped in front of the woman and watched as she tilted her head back and winced as she looked up at him. He squatted down in the middle of the trail to talk to her, not getting too close to her so she'd feel more comfortable.

"Hi," he said quietly. "Are you okay?" He wanted nothing more than to reach for her, fold her in his arms and keep her safe. She'd probably deck him if he tried it, though. He was a stranger to her after all. He might know she was his, but she had no idea. Throughout his family's history the men always had a hard time convincing their *One* that she *was* their *One*. It seemed it would be the same in his case as well.

Becky tried to smile at the gorgeous man in front of her. She furiously blushed, knowing she looked like crap. Why couldn't she meet someone like him when she was all dressed up and looking her best? Figured. "Hi, of course, just resting for a bit. It's a long hike." She mentally smacked herself in the head. She was such a dork. Just resting for a bit? Jesus, she sounded stupid even to her own ears.

She wasn't quite sure how to go about asking for help, as she didn't have to do it very often but she didn't have a choice.

"Have you seen a woman and two—no…three men back that way?" she asked, gesturing toward the direction the parking lot was in.

Dean shook his head. "No, I haven't seen anyone and my truck is the only vehicle in the lot."

Becky sighed. She figured they would've left, but it still hurt to hear her suspicions were correct. She really was nobody important on the stupid show. She tried not to let it depress her any more than she already was. After all, she knew it by the way everyone acted around her, but she couldn't help it when her shoulders sagged. Shit. Could this day get any worse?

"Can I help?" Dean asked quietly. Every bone in his body was screaming at him to pick her up, hold her close and never let her go. To tell her nothing would ever hurt her again, that he wouldn't allow it. But he knew he couldn't do it. He was a stranger. She didn't recognize him as her *One*. He had to be careful not to alienate her. He just wanted to help her.

"Can you call someone for me? I don't have a cell phone on me," Becky asked quietly, and when Dean took out his cell phone, she shook her head. "Crap…uh…never mind…sorry…I don't know the number at my friend's house," she said awkwardly. She must sound like the biggest flake.

Dean simply put the phone back in his pocket, relieved he had a reason to prolong his contact with her, and held out his hand.

"My name is Dean," he said simply. "Dean Baker."

Becky looked at the hand the man reached toward her. It was calloused and big and she wanted to grab a hold of it and never let go. She could even imagine him laying it on her cheek and brushing his thumb over her cheek. Jesus. She shook her head and figured she was feeling needy because of the last couple of weeks of not having anyone look at her like she was someone.

She reached toward his hand. "Becky Reynolds," she told him. She followed his eyes to her hand she was holding out and at the last minute took it back and hugged it to her chest. It was scraped and bleeding…there was no way she could shake his hand without it hurting. She met his eyes and shrugged apologetically.

Dean saw her hand and held his breath. It was killing him that she was hurt. It was physically hurting him as much as she probably hurt herself. He was in a pickle. This was his *One* and she was on a reality show to find a husband. How the hell was he going to get around *that*?

Dean moved slowly toward the rock that Becky was sitting on and gestured toward it as if asking permission to sit next to her. Becky scooted over and gave him some room.

Dean asked again, "Are you okay? What happened? You look a little worse for the wear," he said with a smile, hoping she'd trust him just a little. He *needed* her to trust him. He held his hand out toward her again, palm up. "Can I see your hand? I promise to be gentle."

Becky grimaced at herself. Not answering his question about letting him see her hand, she kept it close to her chest and said, "Yeah, I slipped on the trail on my way down…but I'm okay. Thanks for asking."

Dean slipped his backpack off and told her calmly, trying to sound nonchalant, "I have some basic first aid things in my bag, let me help." He kept his voice low and calm, trying once again to help her.

"I really just need to get a ride back to my friend's house," Becky said again, trying desperately not to break down. Why was he being so nice? "I'm not hurt that badly, I can get cleaned up there," she said with a quaver in her voice.

Dean continued to hold his hand out toward her. He didn't understand why she was downplaying her injuries. By the way she was squinting he knew she had to have a headache, and there was the blood he could see on her palms and on the collar of her shirt.

"Please," he told her quietly. "Let me help you. I can at least help you wash your hands so they don't get infected.

Then can you please let me take a look at your head where you hit it? I'm worried about you."

Becky cocked her head and looked at him, ignoring his comment about worrying about her, even though it sent tingles throughout her body. She asked after a moment, "How do you know I hit my head?"

Dean took a deep breath. This was killing him. Why wouldn't she just give in and let him help her? He usually admired women who were tough in the face of adversity, but he'd give anything for Becky to want to lean on him and let him take care of her. He answered honestly, "You're squinting like your head hurts, and I can see a bit of blood on the collar of your shirt. You also have some dried blood under your fingertips. I figured it had to have come from your head somewhere. If you aren't going to let me do it, please take this wet wipe and clean your hands so they don't get infected. I really want to at least check out your head to make sure it's not worse than you think it is. I'm sure you know head wounds can be dangerous."

"It's not bleeding anymore," Becky told him quietly. "It'll hold until I get back to the house."

"What can it hurt for me to take a look to be sure?" Dean insisted, about ready to be done with the back and forth between them and just take her hands into his own and take care of her whether she wanted him to or not.

Becky sighed. She really did just want to get back the house and not have to deal with this anymore. But it didn't look like this man was going anywhere anytime soon and he genuinely sounded like he wanted to help her.

"You aren't an escaped murderer, are you?" she asked him, only half kidding.

Dean shook his head and tried to look as non-threatening as he could. "Would a crazed escaped killer take the time to try to wash your hands before he killed you?" he asked with a chuckle.

Becky giggled and shook her head, wincing when the movement made her head ache again. She reached up to take the scrunchie out of her hair when Dean stopped her.

"Let me," he said as he reached for her hair.

Becky flinched as he reached toward her and she made a conscious effort not to back away from him.

Dean noticed the flinch and paused in mid reach and asked, "May I? I promise I'll be gentle and will do what I can not to hurt you further."

At Becky's reluctant nod he reached over slowly and unwound the hairband and loosened her hair, careful not to pull on it or otherwise cause her any unnecessary pain.

Becky closed her eyes. Man, it felt good to have his hands in her hair. Even though the pain of her injury persisted; she could enjoy his hands on her. She'd never really been touched that much after her mom died, maybe hugs by some friends every now and then, and his hands were so gentle. It was pathetic that this was turning her on. She really needed to get out more. Dean removed her hair from its bindings.

She took a deep breath and smelled…him. Holy crap, he smelled good. She didn't think he was wearing cologne, because he didn't seem like the kind of man who would drown himself in a manufactured scent, but whatever soap he used must be slightly scented. He smelled like the ocean and…man. She didn't know how to describe it, but it was delicious.

Dean was trying to control himself. He couldn't believe she was here. That he'd finally found his *One*. The fact it was because she was injured was making it not quite what he'd envisioned, but it didn't matter. He'd take care of her, then figure out what came next. He'd not lose her now.

Her hair was smooth and when he ran his fingers through it, loosening it up and making sure it was all out of the scrunchie, it slid through his fingers easily.

Dean immediately felt the wound on the back of her head. It seemed pretty big and he could tell that it had bled somewhat profusely. It was still oozing just a little bit of blood, but for the most part it'd stopped and didn't look life threatening.

He took a washcloth from his pack and wet it with his water bottle. He looked at Becky. She had her eyes closed and her hands in her lap. She didn't flinch when he started cleaning her wound, but he saw her hands clench into tight fists. He knew he was hurting her, but he also knew he didn't have a choice.

"You really hit your head hard, Becky," he told her. "Are you sure you're feeling okay?"

Becky gave him a small nod.

"Will you let me take you to the hospital?" He tried again and as soon as he said the word 'hospital,' Becky jerked away from him and stood up with a wobble.

"No, I told you, I'm fine! I don't need to go to the hospital!"

"Okay, okay," Dean said soothingly. "I'm sorry. I'm just worried about that bump."

Becky sighed. Crap. She was screwing this up royally. "Really, I'm fine. I'm sorry I snapped at you. I just want to get back to my friend's house. I've had a concussion before, this isn't one. Yes, it hurts, and yes I have a headache, but nothing is rattling around in there, I promise."

She tried to smile at him. Dean couldn't smile back. He was reaching the end of his limit of letting her stand alone and not allow him to help her. He reached back into his pack and came up with a small bottle.

"How about a couple of aspirin then?" he said with a small smile. "Will you at least take these?" Becky gratefully held out her hand and took the peace offering. If he was a killer and was offering her cyanide pills or something, so be it. She'd take the chance. She *needed* those aspirin.

"Thank you, Dean. Seriously. I'm sorry I'm being such a bitch. This hasn't been the best day for me. Will you help me wash the rest of the blood out of my hair before we go? I'd rather not go back to the house with the blood in my hair." She had no idea why she was trusting this stranger, this man, like she was. It was unlike her. It was especially unlike her to want to lay her head on his broad chest and have him hold her.

"Of course, Becky, I'll do anything you want me to," Dean answered honestly. "And you're not being a bitch. As you said, you're having a bad day. Give me your hands, let's start there."

She sat back down beside him and held her hands out to him with her palms facing up.

Dean took her right hand in his and used the wet wipe to clean her palm. Because of the fall, and the subsequent climb up the hill, they were filthy. After wiping the dirt away he could see the scrapes underneath. When he was finished with that hand, he brought it up to his mouth and kissed her palm. He held his lips to her skin for as long as he thought he could get away with before placing it back in her lap and taking her left hand into his and beginning to clean it as well.

Becky curled her right hand into a fist as if she could hold the feel of his lips on her skin a little longer by the action. She'd never, in her entire life, felt the way she had when Dean had kissed her. She felt...special. Wanted. Desired. So much feeling by one simple touch of his lips. It took her breath away.

Dean finished wiping her left hand clean and kissed it the same way he did the right. He placed that hand back into her lap, took her by the shoulders and turned her away from him.

Everything he did was no nonsense and done with a purpose. Becky thought it was sexy as hell.

"Turn this way so I can get to your head easier," he told her softly as he spun her around. "Tip your head back and look at the sky. I don't want to get your shirt wet. I'm going to pour some of my water on your hair to rinse the blood out."

Becky did as he asked and closed her eyes as she looked upward. He carefully cleaned the back of her head and got as much blood out of her hair as he could. She opened her eyes when he started drying her hair with something. Oh man, if he'd taken his shirt off she didn't know what she'd do. She looked and sighed with relief, at least she tried to convince herself it was relief. He'd taken an extra shirt from his backpack and used that to dry her hair as best he could. He'd been so gentle with her. He'd done just as he said he would, and hadn't hurt her.

Dean's hands on her shoulders were gentle. Becky opened her eyes and found herself looking into his eyes. He'd knelt on the ground in front of her and was staring at her intently.

Dean looked at this amazing woman, who, thank God was his, and said seriously, "I'm worried about you. I'm not sure I can just drop you off and forget about it. Will you let me contact you? Will you let me know you're okay after today?"

Becky swallowed. Why couldn't *this* man be on the show? Then again, she figured as soon as he saw Marissa he'd probably forget all about her.

"Dean," she said hesitantly. "I'm not sure I'll be able to."

Dean cut her off. "Please, I *need* to know you're all right, Becky," he said urgently.

Becky looked at the man in front of her. He sounded sincere and she wasn't sure what to tell him. She really, *really* didn't want to lie to him, and she was conscious of the confidentiality contract that she'd signed. But she also liked him. Here she was, covered in blood and dirt. It was irrational as hell, not to mention that she wasn't at her best at the moment, but something about him drew her in.

"I don't have a phone, and um…I'm not allowed to receive any phone calls…I'm kinda on vacation right now…but it's also kind of a job…" Her voice trailed off, realizing how dumb and flighty she sounded. She didn't want Dean to think that she didn't *want* to talk to him. "Oh, shit…here's the deal…I'm on a reality show being filmed here in Arizona," she blurted out suddenly. The hell with it, she wasn't going to find anyone to spend her life with among the choices on the show, so why not? She didn't know what she expected Dean to say but it wasn't what came out of his mouth.

"Really? Are you serious? Cool! My brother is a camera operator on that show!" Dean tried to sound as convincing as possible. It wasn't that he wanted to lie to her, he just figured it would be better if she thought he didn't know who she was.

Becky just looked at him in disbelief. A camera operator? What were the odds? "He is?" was all she could get out.

"Yes, ma'am, and that means I'll be able to have a guest pass to come to the set! That is…" He paused and suddenly looked nervous, "if you *want* me to come and see you."

Becky looked down. "Um, Dean, I don't think I'll be able to talk to you when I go back. It's, um…a dating show…and I'm only supposed to talk to the other people on the show…" She didn't want to discourage him, but she had no idea how this could work. There was no way Eddie was going to allow her to have 'visitors,' especially if it was a man.

Dean smiled at her. "You know what? Where there's a will there's a way. Now that I know where you'll be, we'll figure it out. Just know that I *want* to figure it out. Come on, let's get you back to the house so you can shower and rest. You'll feel better once you can take a nice long shower and get into clean clothes."

He carefully took her hand and helped her stand up. He kept his hand on her waist until he was sure she was steady on her feet. Then he helped her shrug on her backpack and started back down the trail toward the parking lot. He reached out and gently took her hand in his as they walked, smiling at her when she didn't protest or pull it out of his grasp.

Becky smiled back at him as she walked. Even though her head hurt and she didn't know what would be waiting for her back at the house, she felt content holding Dean's hand and just being with him. It was the oddest feeling, and she wouldn't have believed it if she hadn't been experiencing it for herself. It freaked her out on one hand, but on the other she was so tired of being treated like crap and feeling like she was nothing. She'd gladly soak up every ounce of attention she could get from this man. And it wasn't as if Dean was hard on the eyes. He was gorgeous and she got goosebumps remembering the feel of his lips on her palm.

Suddenly, she thought of something else. She was on a dating show and his brother probably knew everything that was going on since he was a camera operator. She was instantly mortified. What had his brother told him about the show already…about her? Maybe he'd known she was going to be here today and wanted to see the reality show reject. She stopped walking suddenly and pulled her hand out of his.

"Did you know I was going to be here today?" she asked Dean abruptly.

Dean looked down at Becky calmly. She was definitely riled up. "No, sweetheart, I didn't," he easily bent the truth a bit, the endearment coming out of his mouth without any thought, "I had no idea I'd meet such a beautiful woman today, or that I'd get to play a knight in shining armor," he told her honestly. "Am I happy that I met you? Definitely. Am I happy that we can't be together right now? No way, but I can wait. I know you have obligations, and believe it or not, so do I. But I feel better knowing my brother will be around in case you need him and just to keep watch over you."

Becky's forehead furrowed and she awkwardly stood in the middle of the trail. "I don't understand this. You. I don't understand you. Why would you care? I mean, you just met me, you don't know me. Unless your brother has told you about me?" she asked in a small voice, dreading his answer.

Dean wanted to beat the crap out of all the men on the show. He could tell from her demeanor and the way she asked the question she was embarrassed.

"Jonathan didn't tell me quite how pretty you are or how tough you are," he answered honestly. He didn't want to lie and tell her he didn't know anything about her, she wouldn't believe it anyway, but he certainly was telling the truth about how beautiful she was.

"Tell me, though," Dean asked, trying to slightly change the subject. "How did you end up out here alone if you're on a reality show?" He wanted to hear what she'd say.

Becky sighed and started walking again. How much should she tell him? She thought about how nice it felt to be taken care of and how wonderful his hand felt holding her tenderly as they walked along the trail. She decided to be honest with him. If he really did want to see her again she wanted to start this, whatever *this* was, off on the right foot.

"It's stupid really. I was on a double date with the other woman on the show..."

"Whoa, other woman?" Dean interrupted. "What kind of dating show *is* this?"

Becky laughed and said under her breath, "A terrible one."

She sighed again and told Dean the premise of the show, that there were two bachelorettes the men were competing for.

"So how will it end?" Dean asked seriously. "Will you both end up with a man or what?"

Becky was embarrassed she hadn't even thought about that. Was that what Eddie had in mind for the show? That they'd each end up with a perfect match? She knew *that* wasn't going to happen. The men didn't want her, they wanted Marissa. But how else could it end? Crap, she should've asked more questions of Eddie when they met and he explained how the show would go. Would it get down to one guy and *he* would pick which woman he wanted? That would just cap off her humiliation. There were just too many awful scenarios to imagine. She mentally shrugged, it was too late now.

"I have no idea," she told Dean honestly, "but you wanted to know what happened today right?" She wanted to change the subject back to his original question.

Dean nodded and Becky told him about how she and Marissa were on a double date and it was her turn to choose what they'd do on the date. She didn't feel like going into the past dates and how disastrous they were for her, it was too embarrassing. She explained how Marissa had hurt herself and how she herself had been selfish and wanted to continue on to see Devil's Canyon.

Dean told her as they walked, "It doesn't seem to me that you were the selfish one, Becky."

Becky sighed. "Well, if I'd just gone back like she wanted to when she twisted her ankle, I wouldn't have gotten hurt and stranded here today."

"Yeah, but you wouldn't have met me either," Dean said with a cocky grin, reaching out to hold her hand again.

Becky smiled hugely, at both his words and his actions. "True, very true."

After a small silence, Becky decided she'd tell Dean about her meeting with the coyote at the top of the trail. She didn't know why she wanted to share it with him, other than the fact she needed something to talk about until they reached the parking lot, and besides, she thought he might appreciate it as much as she did.

"Something did happen to me on the trail, though," she started, looking up at Dean while they walked.

"Are you okay?" he immediately asked, concerned.

She laughed and squeezed his hand lightly. "Nothing like that, I saw the most beautiful coyote while I was up there."

Dean stopped and looked at Becky with surprise. "You did?"

"Yes, it was at the top of the trail. It's beautiful there and everything was quiet and I heard something and looked over and there he was. Just sitting in the grass."

"Were you scared?" Dean asked her quietly. Most women would have freaked out and screamed or something. Not his Becky. He smiled, he liked that. *His* Becky.

"Not really. Well, I was at first, but he just lay there, looking at me. He didn't make any moves toward me. It was really peaceful, actually."

Dean continued to smile at her. She was amazing. She was sensitive, and beautiful and tough, as he'd told her earlier.

"That sounds like it was a very fortunate meeting, Becky. You do have to be careful though, as you can't trust all wild animals." He felt compelled to say something about her trusting that coyote, even if it didn't do anything threatening.

"I know," Becky told him. "I'm not an idiot, but he wasn't scary in any way. It was as if he fit into the atmosphere and I didn't get any wild vibes from him! I was afraid for a moment it was rabid, but it wasn't drooling or doing anything other than just lying in the grass, watching me. He was beautiful. I feel fortunate for being able to have had the experience. It's hard for me to even think about how some people never will get to experience anything like this because they live in cities."

"I knew I liked you for a reason," Dean said mysteriously as they continued walking.

Becky heard the teasing note in his voice and laughed, not knowing exactly why. "And why is that, good sir?" She teased right back.

"My parents live near here and operate a wild animal refuge. They have a huge area just for coyotes that have been hurt or need relocating because they won't stop harassing the local ranchers. They aren't pets, but they're given a place to roam and run and be free, but still be protected at the same time."

Becky just looked at Dean in amazement. "Are you kidding?" she asked quietly, coming to a stop.

Dean stopped too, since they were holding hands and he didn't want to let her go. "No. I'm not kidding," he told her, wondering why she seemed so shocked.

"All my life, from the time I was a little girl," Becky started, looking into his eyes as she spoke, "I've wanted to help animals. I had this grand idea that I'd buy a piece of property and start taking in dogs and horses and pigs and cats and llamas and hamsters and whatever other animals were in need of help. My mom was constantly trying to take care of mice and birds and any other small animal I brought home that needed saving. I saw so many homeless and abused animals growing up, it broke my heart. I've never been able to get anywhere near accomplishing that goal. But to hear that your family..." Her voice broke and she couldn't go on.

Dean didn't hesitate but gathered Becky in his arms to comfort her. Finally. She was in his arms. She was the perfect height. Her head fit right under his chin and she felt so good against his chest, against his heart.

"My family does what they can," he told her, murmuring into her hair at the top of her head. "They take in all the animals they can and have a whole staff to help them. I'd love for you to meet them and to meet all the animals someday." He realized suddenly there was nothing more he wanted to do than bundle her up and take her home to meet his folks. They'd love her.

"Really?" Becky said skeptically, leaning back to look up at the man holding her in his arms. God, it felt good there. She was feeling emotionally shaky and his arms holding her close were just what she needed. For whatever reason it didn't even feel weird. With other men she'd dated it had taken quite a few dates before she'd let them get this close. Why Dean was different she had no idea, but she really liked being in his arms.

"Really," Dean said. "When you're done with your show I'll take you to meet them."

Becky didn't know what to say. It'd be a dream come true for her to be able to visit the animal sanctuary, but she didn't understand why Dean would even offer it. It wasn't as if they actually knew each other. It'd been what, only about an hour since they'd met? But deep down Becky knew why he'd made the offer. There was some connection between them. She could feel it and she assumed he could too. What truly sucked was that she couldn't do anything about it right now. She had obligations…but God she wished Dean was on the show. Although, if he was, with her luck, Marissa would kick him off just for showing any attention to her.

They started walking again and it wasn't too much longer before they'd made it back to the parking lot. Dean helped Becky into his truck and walked around to the driver's side. Before he started the engine he looked at Becky.

"Seriously, Becky," he said, getting back to something he'd said earlier and she'd blown off. "If you need a friend or anything else, please let my brother know and he'll get in touch with me and I'll get it for you. I'll point him out when we get back so you'll know who he is. It'll make me feel better. I've never been on a reality show, but I can imagine it can be a lonely experience."

Becky looked down at her hands. Man, he was intense, but she liked it. It seemed as if he honestly wanted to take care of her. "Thank you, Dean," she told him with emotion in her voice. "Trust me, you don't ever want to be on a reality show. It *does* get lonely, but I'm not sure I'll need anything. I appreciate the sentiment though."

She wasn't sure what was in store for her on the show, but she also wasn't sure she'd actually be able to contact anyone about anything when she was back on the set. Unfortunately, Becky also wasn't sure about the connection she seemed to have with Dean. She figured once he talked to his brother, *really* talked to him about the show and about her, and once he saw Marissa, his attention would most likely wane.

Soon enough they were pulling up near the house and the set. There was a lot of activity, as usual, but nothing out of the ordinary. Becky guessed that perhaps no one had missed her yet…or cared she was gone. She sighed, trying not to get sucked back into the doldrums just seeing the house tried to push her into.

"Go ahead and stop here," she told Dean as they got close to the gate.

"I'll bring you all the way to the door," Dean told her, not liking the thought of dropping her off and letting her go back to the set on her own. Not because he thought she couldn't do it on her own, but because he wanted to lend her moral support for what waited her inside.

"Please don't," Becky said. "Seriously, I'm not supposed to talk to anyone off the set, especially someone like you." Her voice trailed off.

"Someone like me?" Dean asked, seriously wondering what she'd meant.

Becky blushed. "Yeah, someone as good looking as you." She smiled in his direction.

Dean laughed. "I'm just a regular guy doing a good deed," he told her.

Becky got serious again. "No, really, you aren't just a regular guy. Most regular guys I know wouldn't have done what you did for me today, or at least they wouldn't have been as gentle and patient. Besides, I don't want you to get in trouble, and it'll just be easier if you let me out here and let me go up by myself. I'll tell them I took a taxi home and they'll believe it."

"Most regular guys *would* have done what I did for you today, sweetheart," Dean said earnestly. "You've just been hanging around the wrong kind of men."

"Obviously," Becky agreed softly, not looking away from him. When Dean looked inclined to continue trying to persuade her to let him bring her up to the house, she simply looked him in the eyes and said, "You need to stay here. Please." She tried to sound firm, when she really felt anything but. "You can tell me what your brother looks like so I'll know it's him." *So I can try to avoid him.* Becky thought to herself.

Dean sighed, pulled over to the curb and shut off the engine. He told her to stay put, got out and walked around the truck to her door and opened it. He didn't step away when she turned sideways to slide out of the seat, but instead put both arms above his head on the door jam and leaned against the truck toward his woman. He would've rather put his hands on her body, but knew it was too soon for that intimate of a gesture. He tried to put into words what he felt, how serious he was about her.

"This isn't the end for us, Becky. You might as well know this now, you might be on a reality show, but I aim to be an unofficial contestant. I've never felt about someone the way I feel about you, even though we've only just met. I want to spend more time with you and I want to get to know you. I want you to get to know me. Just please tell me you won't forget about me while this damn show is being taped. I want a chance with you."

Becky just looked at Dean. She thought his little speech was the most romantic thing anyone had ever said to her. She cleared her throat twice before she could answer him.

"Dean, I'm not sure what to say. I…I want to get to know you too, but I'm only here for this show…I don't live here…I—"

Dean stopped her simply by putting his finger to her lips.

"Just tell me I'm not alone in this," he begged. Him, begging. He knew if his brother or friends could see him now they'd laugh their asses off. This moment meant more to him than anything ever had in his life. If she rejected him he wasn't sure what he'd do.

"You're not alone," Becky whispered shyly.

Dean leaned down and kissed her. Softly, lightly, on the lips. For a first kiss it left a lot to be desired, but he'd take what he could get and he didn't want to rush or scare her.

As soon as Dean's lips touched hers, Becky wanted to sink into the kiss and never come up for air. Unfortunately, it was a short, sweet kiss, definitely not the type of kiss Becky longed for from this man. Damn. She had it bad.

Dean ran the back of his fingers down her cheek and then slowly backed up and held out his hand for her. She gripped his hand and he helped her out of the truck.

"Be careful, sweetheart," he whispered. "Remember, if you need anything find my brother, Jonathan. He's about my height, has dark hair, long, down to the middle of his back, you can't miss him. He'll get in touch with me and we'll help you with whatever you need." At her skeptical look he put his hand at the back of her neck and pulled her toward him gently. "Seriously, Becky. Anytime. For any reason."

He watched her nod, gave the back of her neck a quick squeeze and backed away toward the front of his truck. He watched as Becky backed toward the house…both of them reluctant to break eye contact. Finally, she turned and let herself in through the gate, then disappeared. Dean got in his truck and drove off toward his house. He'd wait for his brother to get home, and they'd make a plan.

Chapter Six

When Becky arrived back at the production house she'd explained to Eddie that she'd been hiking and when she got back to the parking lot she had to wait for someone to show up so she could call a taxi. Eddie didn't seem to care, only saying absently, "Next time don't leave the group. That's not the way this show works. You don't get to go off on your own."

What an asshole. Becky thought to herself while nodding at Eddie. She went up the stairs to her room to shower and get ready for dinner.

Jonathan stood off to the side and listened as Becky explained what happened to Eddie and knew there had to be more to the story, but he didn't say a word as the attention in the house quickly turned back to Marissa and her "hurt" ankle. Jonathan knew Becky was hurt as well because he could see blood on the collar of her shirt and that her hands were scraped up. He watched as she went up the stairs. There was no rule that said that the women had to stay in the common area with the men at all times, and he figured she was going to take a shower.

That night at the mixed dinner—with both the women and the men eating together—Marissa ruled the table with her story about what happened to her and the men ate it up. Jose sat next to Becky at the table and seemed to be feeling guilty about leaving her behind. Out of all the men at least he seemed to feel bad about what happened, although he *did* still leave her stranded on the trail while he tried to play rescuer to Marissa.

Watching through his camera lens, Johnathan heard Jose apologize to Becky about leaving her behind. He didn't know if Jose *really* felt bad or if he wanted to butter up

Becky for the ceremony that would be held later that night. He shrugged and turned back to his camera, concentrating on getting the best shot of the contestants eating and scheming during dinner.

Marissa and Becky met in the conference room before the ceremony that night to discuss their choices for which men would be staying and which would be leaving. There were going to be two men leaving and Marissa wanted Jose to leave. She'd decided he wasn't as attentive to her as the others and she wanted him gone.

Becky wasn't surprised. Jose hadn't fawned all over her at dinner and since he'd showed *her* some attention, of course Marissa wanted him to leave. Becky almost rolled her eyes. The whole show was a farce and ridiculous. The fact that Eddie was making her and Marissa work "together" to decide who'd be leaving was creating more and more friction between them. Becky didn't think Marissa was a bad person. She was just caught up in the competitive nature of the show. Marissa could vote off whoever she wanted, Becky would do what she wanted and the hell with what Marissa wanted her to do.

Becky decided enough was enough, she was done letting Marissa make all the choices on the show. None of the men there might be attracted to her, nor she to them, but she'd be damned if she let the one man who'd actually shown some speck of thoughtfulness to her leave just because Marissa was acting like a small spoiled child. How she wished Dean could've been there. Although, she thought for what seemed like the hundredth time, that if he was, he'd probably be just as gaga over Marissa as the others.

Robert did his typically dramatic entrance for the ceremony. He asked Marissa and Becky some questions about their day and then turned to get some thoughts from the men who were left as well. Marissa once again went first and named the men she wanted to stay on the show. Then it was up to Becky to choose who she wanted to say. She voted to keep Jose and because Alex wasn't listed in her group of who was staying, he had to leave. Becky did it purposely just to piss Marissa off.

"The choice has been made." Robert boomed his line right after Becky named her last guy, once again with great dramatic affect. Even though they knew it was coming, it still startled both Becky and Marissa. Dammit. Becky hated when he did that.

Marissa stormed up to Becky after the ceremony. "What the hell was that?!?" she shrieked. "You *knew* I liked Alex, and you *knew* I wanted Jose to go! You bitch!"

"Look, Marissa." Becky tried to say calmly and rationally. "You don't get to make all the decisions on this show. I liked Jose, and I want him to stay. It's as easy as that. We only get to pick who we want to stay, not who goes. Since you didn't pick Jose, I had just as much right to ask him to stay as you did. I'm not going to go with whatever you want. I warned you before."

"You'll pay for that, you heifer!" Marissa said ominously, obviously trying to be threatening.

Becky ignored her, turned her back and went up to her room. She didn't care anymore. She couldn't even think about the stupid men on the show, about how ridiculous Marissa was being, or about the ceremony. Her head still throbbed from her fall, and all she wanted to do was sleep.

As she lay in bed the last thing she thought about before she fell asleep was Dean and the way he'd looked at her so intently when he said he wanted to see her again. It was the type of look she'd always dreamed she'd get from a man, but never figured she would.

* * *

Jonathan knew Dean would be waiting for him when he got back to Dean's house. It was around ten at night and he wanted to hear what Dean had to say about what happened at Devil's Canyon. He knew Dean was probably the one who gave Becky a ride home, but he'd kept his mouth shut. For one thing, no one ever asked a camera operator for his or her opinion. He'd noticed another operator paying close attention to Becky and her conversation with Eddie, but he wasn't sure of her name. He knew she was attractive, but he hadn't had any time to get to know her. They'd always been put on different assignments so far on the show. He forgot all about the woman when he walked into the house and saw Dean sitting on the couch, staring off into space, not even watching the television that was on low in front of him.

He turned and looked at Jonathan when he'd walked in and simply said, "It's her."

Jonathan knew exactly what his brother meant. "Wow. What are you going to do about it?" he asked curiously.

Finding their *One* was a huge deal in their family, but Dean and Becky had more than the usual amount of obstacles in their way. She didn't live in the area and was on a reality show. Jonathan wasn't even sure where else to start with the issues they had.

"I was hoping you'd help me, bro'," Dean told Jonathan.

Without hesitating, Jonathan returned, "Of course, you don't even have to ask. At least now I know why I was drawn to her earlier. Not because she's mine, but because she's family."

Dean nodded. He knew what he meant. While Jonathan might not be sexually attracted to Becky, somehow he knew she belonged in their family.

If Becky was in trouble, once she and Dean got married, Dean knew Jonathan would lay down his life for her. It was the way it was. He'd do the same once Jonathan found his *One*.

"Tell me what really happened out there," Jonathan asked, settling down on the easy chair across from his brother.

Dean recounted the story of how he'd found Becky sitting alone on the trail and her wounds.

"She's amazing, Jonathan," Dean said, unable to hold back his praise. "I've rarely met another person, let alone a woman, with that kind of fortitude and courage. She didn't cry once, she glossed over her injuries as if they weren't hurting her. She's not one to complain. I'll have to watch her carefully in the future so she doesn't hurt herself further by ignoring something that really could be wrong."

Jonathan nodded. "I've noticed that about her while watching her on the show. It's as if the more those around her complain, the less she does. It's confounding. She'd prefer to fade into the background than bring any attention to herself."

Jonathan proceeded to tell Dean about the night on the set and the most recent ceremony. "You would've been so proud of her, Dean. She finally stood up to Marissa, and boy was Marissa pissed. It took everything I had not to laugh at the look on her face when Becky said she wanted Jose to stay."

Dean had a hard time finding any enjoyment in the fact that not only was Marissa apparently pissed at his woman, but hearing about Becky choosing another man, even in the context of defying Marissa, made him crazy. She was *his*, dammit. This was torture.

"How did she look? Did she get a shower? Was she able to see a doctor at all?"

Johnathan said that while Becky looked tired, she was holding her own and seemed to be okay. The shower she'd obviously taken when she got back to the set did her a lot of good. She never said anything about needing medical attention and Eddie apparently didn't even notice the scrapes on her hands.

"I told Becky she could get in touch with you if she needed anything and you'd tell me, but I'm not sure she will. She's independent and has a lot of honor. She knows she signed the confidentiality agreement and I'm not sure she'll break it. She's not one to ask for help, but I need to see her, to talk to her." Dean looked at his brother expectantly.

"I know, I'll see if I can't get to her tomorrow and talk to her. What if we take her one of those disposable cell phones? You know the contestants have no access to phones or computers, but if I can get her a cell, then you can call her or she can at least get in touch with you directly if she needs you, or wants to talk to you." Jonathan suggested.

"That's a great idea." Dean enthused. "I'll go out in the morning and pick up a phone for her." The two brothers sat in a companionable silence for a while.

Dean broke the silence. "I appreciate your help, Jonathan. I have a bad feeling about the show, and I have no idea why. I don't know if it's because I can't be near her, or if it's because of all that you've told me about what's happening on the set, or what. I don't want any of the men near her, especially if they're only using her to get near Marissa."

"She's tough," Jonathan told his brother seriously. "I'm sure she'll be fine. We'll work out a plan so you can talk to her throughout the show. That should make you feel better."

Dean nodded and Jonathan suddenly sat up and said excitably, "I have another idea…what do you think?" He proceeded to outline his plan to Dean.

"I love it!" Dean exclaimed, thrilled that he'd be able to be closer to Becky over the next few weeks. They'd put the plan into action the next day. He'd get to see Becky sooner rather than later. He couldn't wait to see the look on her face when he strolled onto the set. She'd be surprised all right!

Chapter Seven

The next morning Jonathan went into work earlier than normal and requested to meet with Eddie to put their plan in action.

"Hey, Eddie," he started, trying to look serious and trustworthy. "I heard about this wealthy local guy who's interested in the reality show business and wants to take a look at this show. I heard he was interested in backing your next show in the future."

It was like waving a red flag in front of a bull. Eddie's nose flared and Jonathan swore he could even see his eyes dilating.

"Who is it? Do I know him? Do you know how to get in touch with him?" Eddie was asking his questions so fast he wasn't giving Jonathan time to answer any of them. He was conceited, rightly so, since his last reality show, *Love in the Outback*, was a huge hit.

"I don't know him directly," Jonathan lied easily, "but I was able to get his name and number for you." He handed over a piece of paper with Dean's name and phone number written on it. He was sure Eddie wouldn't take the time to actually investigate Dean and would take him at his word. Jonathan had no idea how he'd made it as far in show business as he had. Oh, well. As long as it would insure Dean unlimited access to the set and the house and Becky, all was good.

Jonathan watched as Eddie quickly stepped out of the room and headed off to make the call, visions of dollar signs dancing in his head.

* * *

Becky was sitting in the house's common area, reading a book when a commotion caught her eye. She looked over and saw Eddie talking to a man at the door. She looked back at her book. She wasn't interested in the comings and goings of people from the house. She was actually bored and only half interested in her book, but Marissa wasn't out of bed yet and there wasn't anything planned for the day, as far as she knew, so she tried to entertain herself. Lord knew the guys who were hanging around weren't entertaining her. They'd barely said two words to her this morning. She would've loved to have taken a walk, but that wasn't allowed. She wasn't allowed out of the house without an escort…i.e. a camera operator and an agenda.

She was so engrossed in her book and so used to ignoring the production staff around her that she was startled to hear Eddie addressing her while standing next to the couch. She looked up and almost choked. What the hell? What was Dean doing there? Was he getting her in trouble? Was *he* in trouble? Had Eddie found out about yesterday?

Dean watched as Becky tried to process his presence on the set. He wished Eddie would hurry up and get on with it so she could relax. He could feel her tension, her worry and dismay, and he wanted to reassure her that everything was okay, but he had to wait until he was introduced as he wasn't supposed to know her yet.

"This is Dean," Eddie said importantly.

Becky put her book down and stood up uncertainly, waiting for Eddie to continue speaking. God, Dean was just as hot today as he was yesterday. She nervously smoothed her hair behind one of her ears. God, did she look okay? Why hadn't she spent more time on getting dressed today? Crap, Eddie was talking, she had to pay attention rather than continue to stare at Dean and imagine what he looked like without his shirt on.

"He's an investor and is interested in funding my next show. He'll be hanging out watching the production of the show. Dean, this is Becky, she's one of the stars."

Dean held out his hand to Becky. He couldn't wait to touch her again, to feel her skin on his. Her skin looked so soft today. She looked healthy and full of life. He thought she looked good on the trail, sweaty and hurt, but now? Wearing comfortable clothes and relaxing on the sofa? Whoa. God, he had to get it together. If he wasn't careful he'd embarrass himself, and Becky, by getting hard in front of Eddie. He shifted a little, telling himself to cool it and waited for Becky to grasp his hand.

Becky took Dean's hand and almost jolted at the feeling of his hand against hers. Again, she marveled at how it just felt right. How she felt safe with his hand wrapped around hers. Why did she feel that way? It wasn't normal, but damn it felt good.

"N-nice to meet you, Dean," she said softly, trying to sound as if she was meeting him for the first time and she hadn't had his lips on hers not too long ago.

"The pleasure's all mine," Dean told her with a smile and secretly squeezed her hand before reluctantly letting go.

Eddie continued to beam at Dean as if he was his new best friend. "Come on, I'll show you around. Marissa will be down in a bit and you can meet her too."

As Eddie pulled him away, Dean looked back and mouthed, "Later" at Becky. She sat down with a plop on the couch. She was glad to see him, but shocked at the knowledge that he was an investor…or was he? She wasn't sure she wanted him hanging around the set. She was already embarrassed at most of the things that went on, she didn't think she could stand for Dean to witness her humiliation as well as everyone else.

And then there was Marissa. Dean was good looking—okay, he was hot as hell, and even though he wasn't a part of the show, she knew Marissa would set her sights on him too. She tried not to think about it, she'd already thought about it more than was healthy, but she couldn't help herself. She thought he'd probably forget all about her once he met Marissa. Most men did. Overall she didn't think this was a good idea at all.

A bit later as Becky was going upstairs to change out of her "lounging" clothes and into her "show" clothes she was stopped by a camera operator. It was Dean's brother. She could tell by his long hair and his resemblance to Dean, and he matched the description Dean had given her the night before to a tee. She hadn't ever gotten a good look at him in the past because the camera was always in front of his face.

"Becky, my brother wanted me to give you this," and he slipped a disposable cell phone into her hand. "In case you need him, or me, our numbers have been programmed in. Be sure to keep it to yourself so Eddie, the director and the other contestants don't find out about it. It's also been set on vibrate so you don't have to worry about the noise alerting anyone to the fact that you have it."

Becky looked at the phone in her hand and then back up at Jonathan in confusion. What was going on? Why would she need a phone? She was already confused about why they thought she'd need to contact them in the first place. It was all very confusing. She slipped the phone into her pocket.

The baffled look on her face must have been telling because Jonathan said softly and urgently, "Look, my brother really likes you, and he wants to keep in touch with you, that's why he's on the set. He's definitely *not* investing in any reality shows. It's just an excuse to be here with you. He just wants to get to know you. He's also a bit protective. He wants to be sure you have a way of getting a hold of someone outside this silly show..." He paused a bit to clear his throat. "...in case you need anything. And Becky..." He hesitated again, not really knowing how to say this next part, but wanting to say something to let her know she wasn't alone. "Not every man is as shallow and dense as the men on this show are...give Dean a chance..." He didn't give her time to respond as he turned and went the other way.

Neither Jonathan nor Becky saw the camera woman quietly standing at the end of the hall. She smiled and then disappeared into a nearby room as soon as Jonathan turned and walked away.

Becky clenched the phone in her pocket tightly. Wow, Jonathan and Dean were intense, but they were straightforward and didn't seem to hold back what they were thinking. That felt so good right now because it seemed like everyone else she'd been around over the last few weeks never said what they really meant and they were all out for themselves. She wanted to feel embarrassed all over again about the show and what had been going on, but she couldn't really.

Jonathan's words meant a lot to her. It was hard to live in a "reality bubble" and not get sucked into what was happening around her all the time. It'd be great to have a link to the outside world just in case she needed it. She tried to imagine herself calling Dean just to chat and just couldn't quite make it work in her head. She knew she'd never call him out of the blue. It just wasn't in her nature to make the first move toward a guy. It did make her feel better to think Dean thought enough about her to want to give her a way to contact him or his brother. It lifted her spirits. She'd try to hold onto that feeling throughout the outing that was planned for the day. It was gonna suck. She knew it.

* * *

Dean sat and watched the dynamics of the people on the show. He was expecting Marissa to be horrible after what Jonathan had told him about the show, but it was hard to truly explain to someone who hadn't met her and hadn't seen how she acted, how bad she really was. He was sure she was a nice person, well, relatively sure, but on the show she presented a catty possessive side. She wanted all the men on the show to pay attention to her and she made sure to put Becky in a bad light whenever she could.

Dean knew Becky was embarrassed to have him there, but he wanted to be sure to let her know that she had an ally. It didn't seem like anyone else, especially not the director or Eddie or Robert, cared about her feelings. And the men on the show seemed to be just as bad. He honestly didn't understand how they could not look past Marissa's mechanisms and see that she was poison. How could they not see the beautiful person Becky was? Yes, she was his *One* and he was biased, but he'd always preferred a woman who was confident and beautiful on the inside to someone who was only beautiful on the outside.

* * *

Becky was beyond embarrassed. It was bad enough she had to endure the social events on the show, but now that Dean was there, it was worse. Holy crap. She went over in her head what she'd rather be doing at this very moment other than being on this show and having the man she wanted to like her, with every fiber of her being, watching her being humiliated. Gynecologist exam, dentist, having a broken arm set…geez, the list could go on and on.

She was sure at any time he'd walk out never to come back. Hell, she wouldn't blame him. Recently she'd been dreaming about walking out almost every day.

She'd watched Marissa meet Dean with dismay. Just as she thought she would, Marissa simpered and fawned all over him. To be fair, Dean hadn't seemed to give her any outward encouraging behavior. He was only polite, but Becky had learned the hard way that just because a man was nice to you didn't mean he meant it. She'd seen it happen over and over on the show. The men seemed to want to get to know her, but inevitably conversation would always turn to Marissa and what she thought of the other men.

This afternoon she and Marissa and their "dates" would be going to the spa. This was one of Marissa's choices of activities for the day, no big surprise there, and Becky knew she'd be miserable. There wasn't anything about a spa that she enjoyed. She didn't like having gobs of makeup put on, she knew her hair didn't hold a style very well because it was thin, and she'd never enjoyed getting a massage. On top of that her nails were short and her feet were so ticklish that pedicures were pure torture. The only good thing about the day would be that Dean wouldn't be there. Becky sighed. Since they were going off-set only the Director, Eddie and the camera operators would be accompanying them.

As Becky and Marissa and their dates were leaving the house, Becky couldn't help but look back toward Dean and found him looking right at her. The intensity in his eyes startled her for a moment, but also warmed her from her head to her toes. He gave her a small secret smile as she walked out the door.

God, that smile could keep her going for hours. Becky smiled to herself and turned to get into the van to travel to the spa only to meet Marissa's scowling face.

"You really don't think *he* is interested in *you*, do you?" she said snidely. She didn't say anything else as the men from the show were getting into the van. She knew when to keep her cattiness to herself and when to act like Becky's best friend.

Becky knew she wasn't done with the conversation. Marissa would never let the fact she saw a man pay attention to Becky, and not herself, go without making a big deal about it. Becky knew she'd probably come up with all sorts of reasons why the look Dean sent her wasn't what it looked like. Becky didn't care. The promise and heat in Dean's eyes when he looked at her was honest and hot as hell.

Becky blocked out the inane conversation going on between the other contestants on the way to the spa and daydreamed about Dean. She imagined them on a real date, just the two of them. He'd hold her hand and kiss her throughout the date as if he couldn't help himself. At the end of the night he'd walk her to her door, back her up against it and start kissing her. His hands would roam her body and when things would start to get inappropriate he'd pull away and ask if he could come up for coffee. Just as Becky was imaging what would happen when they went inside, Eddie announced that they'd arrived. Darn.

Once they exited the van and went inside the high-end spa, Becky and Marissa were whisked away, with their camera operator in tow, toward the ladies room where they'd change into their robes and be ready to be pampered for the afternoon. Becky saw the camera operator following them into the dressing room was a woman. She wasn't very tall, but Becky could see she was extremely muscular. She figured she'd have to be in order to hold a camera on her shoulder all day.

Becky and Marissa had been signed up for the "couples" spa day, which meant they'd spend the day side by side with their dates, and each other, while being pampered. Becky wondered if the men were as reluctant for the day as she was. Probably not. Becky figured they were probably scheming to get Marissa alone at some point, preferably when she didn't have many clothes on, and wondering if they could ditch her. Derek and James didn't really seem to be the "spa" type of people, but in order to "win" Marissa she knew they'd do whatever they had to do.

As soon as they were alone in the dressing room Marissa lit into Becky, finally able to let her true self show through since there weren't any men around to see her actions.

"Seriously? You think he likes *you*?" she snarled. Repeating what she'd said earlier. "From what I've heard he's as rich as hell and there's *no* way your mousey fat ass could attract him. Just give it up. Besides, if you so much as *try* anything with him I'll report you to Eddie so fast it'll make your head spin. You're under contract, just like me, and if you screw this show up for me I'll sue your ugly ass so fast you won't know what hit you." Marissa wound down with a glare.

Becky just looked at her. Wow, that was harsh, even for Marissa. She wasn't sure what bug had gotten up her butt but she was sick of being stomped on by her and the other men on the show. It wasn't as if she and Dean had lay down on the ground and started going at it—okay, that *was* a great image, but seriously. If one look from a man toward her and not toward Marissa could make her turn into this bee-otch from hell, she had no idea what Marissa would think if any of the men actually dared to actually kiss her.

She'd had enough of Marissa's attitude. "Just because I don't have boobs out to here," Becky said, gesturing about a foot in front of her chest, "and just because I don't simper over every single thing everyone here says, doesn't mean I can't attract a man. I'd rather someone like me for who I am rather than what I look like or what I wear. And if you think for a *minute* that the men on this show like you for who you are, you're crazy. They're after the money and fame, just as you are. I guaran-damn-tee you won't have a happy-ever-after ending with anyone here. Oh, you'll both play the same game and pretend you're madly in love, but your relationship will end, just like all the others have."

Becky took a breath, interrupting Marissa when she was about to snap back at her.

"So you just keep on pretending you're little Miss Perfect and that you'd happily end up with any of those men. I'll keep playing my part and you can "win" this stupid reality show, but if you *ever* get in my face again you'll wish you hadn't. Just leave me alone, Marissa. You play the game your way, I'll play it mine and we'll go our separate ways. If you can't handle another man even *looking* at me without losing your shit, I feel sorry for you."

And with that parting shot Becky tightened the belt on her robe and slammed out of the locker room, leaving Marissa standing there with her mouth open. She hadn't expected Becky to push back.

It had felt *good*. She wasn't one to speak her mind like that, but Marissa had pushed her too far. Some of what Marissa had said hurt, but she tried to forget about it. She was a bitch, she just had to keep reminding herself of that. What really pissed her off was Marissa belittling what she'd started to feel for Dean and to insinuate there was no way she could ever keep his attention. That hit a bit too close to what she was feeling for herself and had tried to push to the back of her mind. She knew she couldn't compare to Marissa in the looks department, but damn it, she was a good person and she certainly wasn't a troll. So what if she didn't cake on makeup or wear designer clothes, or weigh under a hundred and twenty pounds. Not everyone in the world did, and *they* still ended up happily married. She'd tolerate the day and get through it, get through the show and go back to her boring life, the way she liked it. Even if it killed her.

Becky took a deep breath and was about to head out to where Derek and James were waiting with Robert and Eddie and who knows who else from the show, when she noticed the camera woman come out of the dressing room. The camera was hanging at her side for once, and she looked Becky directly in the eyes.

"Good for you, Becky!" she said unexpectedly. "That bitch has had that coming for a long time now."

Becky could only stare at her. Finally, she managed, "Uh…thanks?"

The camera operator laughed and took a step toward Becky. She didn't hold out her hand in greeting, probably because she was worried someone would see them, but she came closer so they could talk quietly. "My name is Kina. Me and most of the other camera operators have been rooting for you from day one. Most of us were together in Australia and couldn't believe the crap that went on behind the scenes with the women on the show. Marissa would've fit in perfectly with that bunch. But thank God Alex and Sam were able to work through all that crap and find each other in spite of the way all the others acted."

Becky again could only stand there and nod. She'd watched *Love in the Outback* and didn't really understand how Alex and Sam even ended up together, since Sam was kicked off the first week.

Kina seemed to understand Becky's confusion because she continued speaking. "Becky, Sam wasn't really kicked off the first week. She made it at least half way through the show. Eddie and the other producers only edited the show to make it *seem* as if she left that early. Alex and Sam had plenty of time to get to know each other. Sam even saved my life on the set one day."

"What?" Becky exclaimed fascinated. Crap, she didn't have time to listen to the story, but God how she wanted to. It sounded like it was an amazing story. She looked behind her at where the others would be gathering and heard Kina speak again.

"I know, this is a bad time to even have brought it up, sorry. But I wanted you to know that we're all rooting for you. Don't let Marissa get you down. You have a friend in each one of us. When she's acting all bitchy look into the camera and see us standing behind the lens and know that we're cheering you on."

Becky had no idea what to say to the woman, but she didn't have to say anything. Kina hefted the camera back up to her shoulder and was obviously back in work mode. Becky had a lot to think about. It felt good to have another woman on her side. Hell, it felt good to know the other camera operators were on her side and didn't think she was pathetic. She took a deep breath and headed toward the group. It was going to be a long day, but deep down inside Becky felt a spark of her old self returning. It was time to stop letting Marissa and the guys on the show make her feel bad.

* * *

When the group got back to the house it was time for another ceremony. Becky had been massaged and made up and poked within an inch of her life. She was tired and cranky and didn't feel like herself at all. They'd stuffed her into a designer dress with two inch heels. They'd wanted to put her in four inch heels, but Becky flat-out refused. There was no way she'd be able to walk in anything higher than the two inches she was currently wearing. Not only did her feet *already* hurt, but she just knew she'd fall on her face on national television if they made her wear the higher heels.

They'd teased her hair and put it up in a fancy upsweep and had caked makeup on her face. She'd never had so much on before in her life and she knew she probably looked ridiculous. She only wanted to go and take a shower,

257

put on her stretchy pants and a T-shirt and get back to her normal self.

That night at the casual meet and greet time before the ceremony, the men all seemed to take extra notice of her. Becky knew it was a result of the spa treatment and not because they suddenly wanted to get to know her. All this crap she was wearing wasn't her. It was ridiculous that all of a sudden the men were paying more attention to her. She knew Dean hadn't been there when they'd gotten back. At least she hadn't seen him, but all of a sudden she felt a tingle up the back of her neck and knew he'd arrived.

She refused to turn around. She didn't want to see the same look in his eyes as in the men all around her. Well, she *did* want to see him looking at her admiringly, but she was scared he'd only look at her that way because of what they'd done to her, not because of who she was inside. She was afraid what he'd think about the new-and-improved her. Afraid that he'd like it too much, and afraid that he wouldn't like it at all. Gah! She was so confused and so stressed out.

Finally, after a long day and night, it was her turn to stand in front of the men and make her choices. Robert had done his normal speech and asked the women to choose who they wanted to stay. She still really didn't care who stayed and who left. For the first time Marissa hadn't tried to come to her before the show and tell her who to have stay. The touchy-feely, working together times were over.

Becky knew Marissa had already chosen her favorites, and asked that Trevon leave, so she chose the best of the bunch that was remaining. She actually felt bad she had to tell someone to leave, because she didn't really even know the men that were left. In another spurt of defiance toward Marissa she'd deliberately not chosen Conner, so he'd have to leave the show. She'd overheard Marissa telling him how much she liked him and couldn't wait to go on an individual date with him. Well, as much individual as you could get when you were essentially on a double date, date with him.

"The choice has been made!" Robert boomed once again. Becky felt good about the fact that she hadn't flinched that time. She'd finally been expecting the cheesy line.

When it was over and the cameras were shut down she turned to leave to go and shower when Eddie called her name and gestured for her to come and talk to him. She reluctantly went over to where he and Dean were standing. She'd almost forgotten Dean was there, almost.

"Becky, since you're one of the stars of the show I'd like for you to take some time and talk to Dean about your role in the show and your favorite parts," he told her gravely.

She knew what he was really saying. He wanted her to talk up the show and try to influence Dean to finance his next reality venture. He knew how she really felt, at least he *should* know how she really felt. With Eddie there was no telling. He was good at ignoring everyone around him and plowing ahead with whatever he wanted to do, damn the consequences. Eddie stood there expectantly, waiting for her to start talking. Awkward!!

"If you don't mind, Eddie, I'd like to talk to Becky alone. I think she'll be more honest if she doesn't have to worry about pleasing you." Dean put his hand on Becky's elbow and led her toward a set of chairs just off the set.

Eddie had no choice but to let them go. He was sucking up big time and he didn't want to do anything his future investor wouldn't like. He didn't go far, but at least he was out of earshot.

"How are you doing, sweetheart?" Dean asked in a low voice, helping her to sit but never letting go of her arm.

Becky looked at Dean, thrilled they were getting a chance to talk, but also nervous as she wasn't sure where they stood now. She shivered as his fingers caressed her elbow covertly.

"I-I'm fine." She stumbled over her words, then continued, "Are you really going to invest in another reality show?" She couldn't help it, that just blurted out. Even with Jonathan telling her he wasn't really going to invest she had a hard time believing he'd go to the lengths he had just so he could see her. She didn't *really* believe he'd want to invest in something as silly as a reality show, but she didn't know him all that well. She wanted to hear the confirmation from his lips directly.

"Of course not!" Dean exclaimed. "Why would I invest in something as ridiculous as this kind of show? But it was the only way I could think of to be able to be close to you for the next few weeks." He winked as he said it.

Becky was flattered, but the day had taken a toll on her and her confidence, even with the pep talk she'd gotten from Kina and from herself.

"Why, Dean? I mean, it's not like you're hurting for women. Why work so hard for me? I'm nobody special," she finished honestly, looking him in the eye.

Dean turned his chair around so they were face to face instead of side by side and leaned in close. Not too close so it'd be inappropriate to anyone who might be watching, but close enough he was looking her in the eyes and somehow talking straight to her heart.

"Becky, I told you last night, it's *you* I want to get to know. There's something about you, something true, something that speaks to me. I've never felt this way before and I want to see where it goes. And you're the most beautiful woman in this room and the most beautiful woman I've honestly ever seen."

Becky snorted. "Yeah right, Dean, give me a break! I've never been called beautiful by anyone before, and no matter how much makeup I'm wearing right now I know it's still not the case!" She was embarrassed at her outburst and dropped her eyes to the ground between them.

"Becky," Dean said urgently. "Please look at me." When she didn't look up, he continued, "I want to put my hand under your chin and raise your head so you have to look at me, but I know that would look strange to Eddie and other people. Please. Please look at me."

Becky raised her head and managed to meet his eyes. God, she was so courageous and beautiful to him. "It's not what you're wearing, or what you look like on the outside, although you *are* beautiful on the outside…it's who you are inside. You'd never tell anyone they were stupid, or not be a friend to someone based on the way they look. You appreciate animals and would do anything to help them. You'd rather wear sweats and be comfortable than put on heels and a fancy dress and hobnob with the most important people in the world. *That* is what I find beautiful about you. In fact…" he continued earnestly, "I much prefer you in your jeans and T-shirt than that dress and your hair done up and your face covered in gunk."

Becky giggled. He sure knew how to make her feel better. She saw he wasn't smiling back at her. He was serious as he could be. God, what she'd give to not be here, to be able to snuggle down into his arms and rest her head on his chest. To feel safe.

Dean tried to relax. God, he wanted to haul her over his lap and hold her close to his chest. He wanted to kiss the hell out of her so everyone around would know she was his. He wanted to mark her as his. He could just imagine how a hickey would look on her neck. Juvenile, but he couldn't help it. He couldn't stand it when the men on the show were ogling her before the ceremony. He was surprised at her looks when she got back from the spa, but he was being honest with her when he'd told her he preferred her other look. Done up the way she was now she just looked fake. She looked stiff and uncomfortable. He much preferred her in her natural state.

"Did Jonathan give you the phone?" he asked Becky, scooting his chair back a bit and leaning back. If he didn't change the subject and put some space between them she'd end up in his lap no matter who was watching. He didn't want to give Eddie any reason to suspect he was anything other than an investor.

Becky nodded. "I'm not sure exactly why you gave it to me, though…especially if you're going to be around the set."

"I was hoping we could talk when you went up to your room at night. God, Becky," his voice got huskier, "I'd love to imagine you lying in your bed, wearing some sexy silky thing talking to me…" He cleared his throat and continued, "I also wanted you to know you had an ally, and a way to get in touch with the outside world if you needed it."

"Thank you," Becky said. "I'd enjoy talking to you and getting to know you as well." He might want to think about her lying in her bed, and she could almost picture it in her mind. Both of them lying on their backs lazily, talking about their day…crap, she had to concentrate. She couldn't go there right now, as much as she wanted to think about him naked in bed.

She tried to be funny. "First of all, I don't sleep in anything silky and sexy. Typically I sleep in boy shorts and a tank top."

Dean gulped. "Jesus, hon. You're going to give me a heart attack. Before I could only imagine what you'd look like in bed, but you've just given me a perfect picture that I won't be able to get out of my head."

Becky smiled shyly at him, enjoying knowing he'd be thinking about her in bed. Changing the subject, she said, "I don't think they'd kick me off the show if I got caught with the phone, but you never know, so we'd have to be careful." She watched as he nodded in agreement and then continued. "I'm not sure why I'd need to get in touch with the outside world as you called it, but thank you just the same. I appreciate it more than you know that someone is trying to look out for me."

"You're killing me, sweetheart," Dean said, compassion shining in his eyes. "I'll always look out for you."

The two smiled at each other, communicating without words. Dean knew his time was up for the night. He didn't want it to end, but he saw Eddie walking toward them.

"I'll see you tomorrow, Becky," he said softly. "I'll let you sleep tonight, but I'll call tomorrow night. You can tell me how your day went and all the things you'd tell a friend about this experience that you can't tell anyone else."

Becky could only nod and watch as he shook Eddie's hand and expressed delight in talking to her.

"When you come by next I'll let you spend some time with Marissa," Eddie told him excitedly. Becky frowned. It couldn't be helped, but she hoped Dean was telling the truth about all the things he'd said to her today. Becky knew Marissa would really lay on the charm just to prove she was more attractive to Dean than she was.

Chapter Eight

The next night, Becky went up to bed exhausted. Marissa was going out of her way to be snide and rude and to try to make her look bad. Becky supposed it was a direct result of the way she'd stuck up for herself at the spa yesterday. It was hard to keep up a pretense of being happy and enjoying herself when all she had to deal with every day was fake people who were doing their best to make her miserable.

After her shower, Becky lay down on her bed and just stared at the ceiling. Seriously, why had she thought this would be a good idea? She'd probably lose whatever friends she did have when the show finally aired. She knew it wasn't going to show her in a good light and she was totally depressed. How could it? She couldn't hide from the cameras, they were everywhere. And while she remembered Kina had said all the camera people liked her, they still had to film her, it was their job.

She also remembered what Kina had said about that Australian show, how Sam was edited out after the first episode when in reality she didn't leave until at least half way through the show. If she was lucky, Eddie would do that to her as well. She could be edited out first thing and no one would have to see her be humiliated day in and day out. Becky sighed. She didn't think it would be possible, however, since the entire premise of the show was all the men "fighting over" two women bachelorettes.

Then today there was Dean. Specifically, watching Marissa suck up to him and put her hands all over him. Dean had come back to the show on Eddie's request and he'd introduced them, just as he had with Becky yesterday. Marissa had taken every chance she could to touch him. She patted his arm, she stood very close to him, and at one point she leaned in while laughing and put her hand on his chest. Becky wanted to march over to them and tear Marissa's hair out. It frankly surprised her as she generally wasn't a jealous woman, but there was just something about Dean that made her want to claim him as her own in front of the world. She sighed. She wasn't sure she was going to make it the last few weeks.

She could tell Dean was trying to put distance between him and Marissa as they spoke, but it just wasn't working. He looked at her a few times, but when Marissa realized what he was doing, she manipulated them so his back was to her and he couldn't see her anymore. Becky remembered Marissa's smirk at her when she did it too. What a bitch.

Becky lay there on her bed, enjoying the quiet. All she could hear was the tick-tock of the wall clock in her room. Suddenly she felt her pillow vibrating…what the heck? Then she remembered she'd put the phone under her pillow to hide it, and so it was close at hand…just in case, and it was ringing. She reached under her head and pulled it out and answered hesitantly…just in case it wasn't Dean.

"Hi, Becky," Dean said in a low smooth voice. "How are you?"

Becky was thrilled to hear from him. He called! Just like he said he would. She felt like she was back in the seventh grade and was giddy to be hearing from a boy. Becky was instantly awake. She scooted up the bed and rested her back against the headboard.

"Tired," Becky told him honestly. "It's getting harder and harder to stay up each night and pretend to like what I'm doing."

"I could tell," Dean told her. "I'm worried about you. You didn't eat much tonight."

Becky flushed, even though she knew he couldn't see her.

"Believe me, Dean, I eat enough…too much probably." She gave a short laugh.

"Please don't," Dean told her. "As I've already told you, you're beautiful and perfect. I like you exactly the way you are. Don't let those people make you feel like you can't eat a normal meal. *They* are the ones who aren't normal!" he said urgently.

Becky sighed. She knew he was right. She *knew* it. "I know, but…" Her voice trailed off. "It's just hard." That was a lame explanation, and sort of like calling the ocean "big." She didn't really know how to explain it, but she tried. "I feel like I'm in this bubble. I'm floating around, watching what's going on around me. I can see the dangerous sharp things around that will pop my bubble and since I'm not steering, all I can do is hope I don't run into them. I'm always aware of the cameras and I can't help but think of when this show finally airs what it's going to make me look like. I know that sounds vain and selfish, but I'm trying to watch everything I say and everything I do and everywhere I look, but I know I'm still making a fool out of myself." Becky's voice trailed off once more.

Dean was furious, not at Becky, but at Eddie and the director. They were shredding this woman's self-esteem in front of his eyes, and he couldn't say or do anything to stop it. He felt as helpless as she just described being inside a floating bubble.

"Listen, Becky," he told her with urgency lacing his tone. "Please. This is what *I* saw today watching you…will you listen to me?"

Becky nodded, then realizing he couldn't see her, mumbled, "Uh-huh."

Dean took a deep breath. He knew this moment was very important and what he said to her now would hopefully lighten her load.

"During lunch today, when Marissa was complaining about the temperature of the soup, you touched the server's hand and thanked her for her efforts. You probably didn't know this, but she smiled all the way back to the kitchen simply because you took the time to compliment her. Out by the pool when everyone else was swimming and playing, you were sitting in the lounge chair. When everyone went in, you gathered up all of the used towels and put them on a chair so someone else didn't have to do it. You smiled at one of the camera operators for no special reason as you went into the house. I even saw you tell one of the assistant producers happy birthday, when no one else on the show seemed to care. Hell, I have no idea how you even knew it *was* his birthday! Even when the clueless men on the show are ignoring you and simpering all over Marissa, when they aren't able to get near her, you still talk to them and try to get to know them. You answer all their questions about Marissa and try to give them hope she just might choose them. I even saw you open a damn window today because a fly was buzzing on the pane and couldn't get outside. You're a good person, Becky. To the core. No matter what these people throw at you, no matter what they say, you remember this...I see you. I see the real you. Not only do I see you, I like what I see. And I know America will see it too."

His voice tapered off. He waited. He heard Becky sniff once. Oh God, he'd made her cry. He hadn't meant to make her cry. "Sweetheart?" he asked softly. "I didn't say all that to make you cry." When she didn't immediately say anything, he said with frustration, "Damn, I should've kept my mouth shut. I want to be there to hold you, Becky, and it's pissing me off I can't be. Are you okay?"

"I know, I'm okay, Dean. Really. I just..." She paused and sniffed again. "I've just had a bad day and that was possibly the nicest thing anyone has ever said to me in my entire life."

Dean laughed and tried to lighten the mood. He wanted her to stop crying, he couldn't stand it. "If that was the nicest, then I'd better get to work trying to beat it!"

Becky laughed, as she was supposed to. "Tell me more about yourself, Dean," Becky asked. "I don't know that much about you, only that we have this crazy chemistry." She laughed some more.

Dean smiled. She didn't know the half of it. He was so glad she wasn't crying anymore, he'd tell her anything she wanted to know. He proceeded to tell her about his family and about his job, how he was in the security field. He talked about what he liked and what he disliked and as much other information as he could. He answered all of her questions.

Becky also told Dean about herself in return. About how she didn't like to cook, how she liked her job, but didn't love it. She confessed while she had a lot of people that she knew, she didn't have a lot of close friends. She admitted she loved Arizona. It was a big and open land. And so far, away from the set at least, people had been very friendly.

Becky realized they'd been talking for over two hours. Ugh, she knew it'd be hard to get up tomorrow, well, today. It was well past midnight. Talking with Dean was soothing and she'd practically forgotten about the stupid show she was on and the tension she was feeling a few short hours ago.

"Dean, it's late, and while I've loved talking to you, I have to get going."

"I know, sweetheart," Dean told her regretfully, "I need to go as well."

Becky tried to ignore how much she loved hearing him call her sweetheart in his low rumbly voice. She felt it deep in her heart and it felt so good. Becky hesitated and then said quietly, "I have a question for you, though…" She didn't know how he'd take it. Then she mentally shrugged and just asked, "I need some ideas for my dates."

She waited and hearing nothing but silence on the other end of the line said, "I didn't mean that like it sounded." She laughed nervously. "I mean I need help on what to do here on the show. Marissa and I take turns choosing the dates and it's my turn coming up and I don't know what we should do. I'm not from around here…and…" Her voice trailed off.

Dean laughed. "I understand, hon. For a second there I thought you wanted my help in a different area about your 'dates'." They both laughed.

"I have an idea and I think after what you told me when we were at Devil's Canyon you'll think it's a good one. As I told you before, my family operates a refuge center for animals, including coyotes."

He heard Becky's indrawn breath and continued, "It's more a rescue center for the coyotes that have gotten too close to people's homes and are in danger of being killed as a result. I thought maybe you might like to go there and see not only the coyotes, but meet some of my family as well," Dean finished. He couldn't believe how nervous he was. He'd never cared enough about a woman to bring her home to meet his entire family and friends. He knew they'd talked about it when they were on the trail at Devil's Canyon, but that was "someday." Someday was now here. Would Becky want to do that with him? In her typical style, she didn't keep him waiting for her answer.

"Are you kidding?" Becky exclaimed. "I'd *love* that! Oh, Dean, I can't wait to see the animals." Her voice trailed off when she thought about the coyote she saw while hiking. "Does that mean you'll have to hunt and find the coyote I saw at the Canyon for your refuge?" she asked, worriedly thinking about how odd the animal's behavior had been.

"I doubt it," Dean answering honestly. "As long as there aren't any reports of attacks on people or anyone's pets, that coyote is probably safe."

Dean made sure Becky knew what the refuge was called so she could pass the information along to Eddie in the morning.

While he would have gladly talked to her all night, he could hear she was fading fast.

"I'm going to let you go, sweetheart," he told her softly. "I've loved talking to you and getting to know you better. One of these nights we'll have to do a different kind of talking while we're both in bed." He paused. When he heard her indrawn breath he continued, "I'm looking forward to my family meeting you. They'll love you. Sleep well, love."

"Good night." He heard Becky say breathlessly.

"Good night," he answered back and clicked off the phone.

Becky was more than half asleep. She clicked off her phone and leaned down to grab the phone charger. She plugged it in and shoved it under her bed so it was out of sight. She only dared charge the thing at night when there was no chance of anyone seeing it. She snuggled down into the covers. She felt good. She'd gone to bed feeling depressed, but talking with Dean raised her spirits and she was looking forward to seeing his family's sanctuary, even though she had to "officially" spend the day with a man other than Dean. The last thing she thought of as she drifted off to sleep was his low voice calling her "love" as he'd ended their call.

Chapter Nine

The next day, Dean went to the refuge to meet with his parents and he explained he'd met his *One*. His parents, Steve and Bethany, were beyond pleased. Dean knew his parents' story by heart. When his dad explained to him and Jonathan how they'd probably meet a woman one day and know immediately she was the one for them, he'd told them how he met their mom.

Steve was a firefighter and he'd been called to the scene of a bad car wreck. Upon arriving he found out Bethany was the person who'd witnessed the accident and had called for help. He took one look at her standing on the side of the road, arms wrapped around her waist, waiting for help to arrive, and knew she'd be his.

Dean knew his dad was lucky. He'd really only half believed him about the knowing when he met a woman that she'd be the *One* for him, but there was no mistaking his feelings when he first laid eyes on Becky sitting on that rock on the trail at Devil's Canyon.

He explained to his parents a bit about how Becky was on a reality dating show and the role of wealthy investor he'd taken on so he could keep an eye on her. He also had to explain he'd invited her, and the production crew, to their family refuge. He supposed he should've asked permission first, but he knew his dad would understand and would not only want to meet Becky, but would think it was a great idea as well.

Their animal refuge was a safe place for all types of animals, but they had a lot of coyotes on the property. It allowed them a safe place to run and live without worrying about humans. Having the reality show filming on the property would be annoying, but it'd certainly be good to get some publicity and hopefully be able to raise some money to help with its continued upkeep.

Steve agreed to talk to all of the employees at the refuge and explain what was going on. Dean wanted to make sure everyone knew Becky was his *One* and wanted his dad to explain the circumstances. He didn't want anyone to look down on Becky because she was on the show and "dating" someone else when she was supposed to be his. He was looking forward to seeing her interact with the coyotes and his family and friends.

* * *

Becky explained what she wanted to do to Eddie and really had to push him to accept. It seemed the producers wanted her to choose to take the group ice skating at a nearby mall. Becky had never been ice skating before and knew it'd be just another chance to make her look bad, so she stuck to her guns and told them she chose the animal refuge and if they denied her she'd walk off the show. She wasn't sure she really had the guts or legal leg to do it, but everyone knew at this point if she did, it would ruin the entire show. Ultimately, Becky knew it wasn't her threats that made Eddie cave, but more the fact he'd found out his potential investor's family owned the refuge. That made him agree to allowing the dates to be filmed there.

Later that day, after the selection process to find out which of the remaining men would be going on the dates with them, they headed over to the refuge. The twins Derek and David were going, as were Dexter and John. Becky didn't really care anymore who won the dates. It wasn't like any of the men really wanted to hang out with her. She really didn't care for Derek and David, though. They were a bit creepy to her, but of course Marissa thought they were, in her words, dreamy, and was thrilled they'd be on their outing.

Becky hadn't seen Dean on the set that day, but knew he'd be at the refuge when they arrived. He'd said that his family owned it, so she figured he'd be there as well. She looked around to see if Jonathan was one of the camera operators assigned to the outing and when she didn't see him, she assumed he'd be staying back at the production house. She was a little disappointed. She didn't really know Jonathan, but she liked what she knew about him. She had time to watch people in the house each day, partly because it was boring as hell just sitting around all the time, but also because no one cared much about what she did, especially if Marissa was around.

She'd watched as Jonathan would help the other camera operators move equipment around. He always did his part and never let anyone struggle with anything on their own. He volunteered for the shifts she knew others didn't like. She'd even noticed him watching Kina with an interested look in his eye, but she never saw them actually talking.

Becky turned her attention back to the refuge they were approaching. As they neared the gate, Becky could see a ten foot high fence stretching as far as her eye could see. It lined the road and disappeared off into the distance. The property was huge and it looked like a wonderful place for coyotes and other animals to spend out their lives. She didn't know a lot about coyotes, but what she did know, fascinated her.

They pulled up to a huge house with a large white porch that surrounded the entire front of the building. There was a big red barn off to the side and a series of gates leading into the enclosure. Becky saw a man and a woman standing on the porch, obviously waiting for them. As they all stumbled out of the vans and the camera operators started setting up their equipment, she saw Eddie and the director walk over to the couple on the porch.

It wasn't long before they all came over to where she and Marissa were standing with their dates. Eddie introduced the couple as Steve and Bethany. Marissa shook their hands, but was obviously not interested much in them, she was too engrossed in her dates and Becky's dates and trying to keep hold of all of their interests.

In direct opposition to the way Marissa had acted when meeting the couple, Becky shook both Steve and Bethany's hands and expressed delight they'd allowed them to come to their refuge.

"It's our pleasure, Becky," Bethany said, holding on to Becky's hand a bit longer than was socially acceptable. Becky dropped her eyes at the intense gaze of the woman. It wasn't disrespectful, but Becky thought it best she didn't hold her eyes. She wasn't sure why, but it felt like the right thing to do. Bethany nodded, beamed, and dropped Becky's hand.

She squeezed her husband's hand in approval.

"We need to discuss a bit more with Eddie about the plans for the shoot today and what exactly we'll be doing. Please," Steve said, gesturing to the property, "look around, but don't go inside the gates, for obvious reasons, or the barn. We'll give you an official tour later."

They all nodded their heads. Marissa and her dates walked toward the production truck, intending to sit inside until shooting was ready to begin. Becky turned to Dexter and John, her dates for the day, and asked if they'd like to walk around. They looked back at Marissa, engrossed in conversation with David and Derek, shrugged their shoulders and agreed. The three of them, with a camera following, wandered over to the fence line near the barn. She didn't really want to spend time with the two men, but she figured since it was expected of her, she'd better at least try to look like she was enjoying the show. Better ratings and all that.

"I wonder if we'll see any of the coyotes today," Becky mused, straining her eyes to see any movement on the other side of the fence. There was a large pasture around the house, then a line of trees and a wood line. The coyotes were probably off in the woods doing whatever it was that coyotes did, but she sure hoped they'd get to see some of them.

The men finally got bored with her inane conversation and wandered off to the production truck where

Marissa was holding court with the other men. Becky didn't care. She'd stay right where she was in the hopes of a glimpse of a coyote. She resisted the urge to look around for Dean. If he was there, he was there, but she didn't want to seem desperate to see him.

Dean found her about ten minutes later. She was sitting on the ground, legs crossed, with her elbows resting on her knees, her chin in her hands, scanning the countryside. He smiled. He was so in love with her. Hell, he had no idea why or how he'd fallen so fast, but there it was. Just looking at her made his heart beat faster and made him want to protect her from any and all threats. He never wanted her to be hurt. Ever.

He'd never understood how his dad and granddad fell in love so fast when they found their *One*, but now he knew. It was just there. That feeling of rightness and contentedness, and yes, love.

Dean walked over to Becky with his dad following close behind. He knew he wanted his father to approve of his woman. This was a big moment for him. He'd never wanted anything so badly in all of his life than for his dad to meet and like Becky. He didn't think it'd be a problem, but there was always that doubt. If they didn't like or approve of her it'd make coming home awkward. He loved his family and hoped they'd love Becky and vice versa.

Becky stood up when she saw the men coming toward her. She wiped her hands on her jeans and tried to knock off any stray grass or dirt she'd picked up by sitting on the ground. She hoped she wasn't doing anything wrong. She hadn't gone near the barn, but she couldn't read the expression on either one of their faces.

At seeing the nervous look Becky had on her face there was nothing more that Dean wanted to do than to sweep his woman up in a huge reassuring hug, but he knew he had to show some decorum, especially with all the production crew hanging around, not to mention the director and Eddie as well.

"Hi, Dean," Becky said shyly as they walked up to her.

Dean reached over, took her hand and squeezed it tightly in his.

"I know you met my parents earlier, but I wanted to introduce you myself." He turned to Steve and dipped in a formal little bow. "Steve, this is Becky." Then he turned toward Becky. "Becky, this is Steve."

Becky didn't know why Dean was being so formal in introducing her to his dad, but she unconsciously mirrored Dean's motions and bowed a bit when she took his dad's hand. She knew somehow this was an important moment, but she wasn't sure why or how. All she knew was that she hoped Steve liked her since he was Dean's father and it seemed so important to him.

"It's very nice to meet you, Mr. Baker, and I'm so thankful you let us all come out today. I know it's terribly intrusive for all the cameras and such, and I'm sure you'll be bored to tears once they actually do start filming. Your place is beautiful and the animals are so lucky to be able to call this home and be safe here."

She looked up at Dean's dad and watched him smile at her.

"You're right, Becky, they're lucky, but we're lucky too. We get to watch them get healthy and know they're safe for the rest of their lives. And please know that as Dean's girlfriend you're welcome here anytime. You come back with Dean after the show is over and we'll have dinner...okay? But I only have one condition." He paused for dramatic affect and continued quickly when he saw Dean frown. "You have to call me Steve, not Mr. Baker."

They all laughed and Becky readily agreed.

Dean smiled as his dad slapped him good naturedly on the back.

"Thank you, Dad...just...thank you," he told him sincerely, not quite able to hold back the emotion in his voice. His dad seemed to like Becky. All would be right in their world as soon as the damn reality show was over.

As the tension seemed to be over, Becky couldn't hold her excitement back anymore and blurted out, "Where are all the animals? Will we get to see them today?"

Dean and his dad chuckled together.

"Patience, little one," Steve told her. "They'll come. You'll see lots of animals today."

Just then they heard Eddie call for attention over a bullhorn and proclaim they'd start shooting in twenty minutes.

"I'd better go," Becky said, looking over her shoulder at the group gathering near the production truck. "Seriously…" she said nervously, "this is going to be really boring…you don't want to watch, do you?"

She hoped he wouldn't, that no one else would have to watch her in this stupid show and see her be humiliated.

"It's okay, sweetheart," Dean told her soothingly. "Remember what I told you yesterday."

Becky sighed. "Okay, well…thanks again, Steve. It was so nice to meet you. You've undertaken something of great importance here and I'll try to make sure it gets across on the show." She turned around and walked toward the others.

Steve looked at his son. "I like her, Dean, I like her a lot."

Dean grinned. "So do I, Dad, so do I!"

* * *

The show got started about forty minutes later. They were supposed to walk around the fence toward the barn. Then once they got in the barn, they were supposed to be shown how the food was prepared. Once that was wrapped up they'd be given a chance to feed some of the animals, including the coyotes. They were reassured that the coyotes knew the sound of the dinner bell, for lack of a better term for it, and would show up for the food.

From the moment the cameras started Marissa became lively and energetic…and claimed the spotlight. She exclaimed how beautiful the refuge was and wondered if the coyotes would be scary…and Becky knew what was to come. When they did finally see them she'd play the damsel in distress and get all the men to reassure her that she was safe.

For once Becky didn't care what Marissa did, she was just so happy to be here at all. This really was a chance of a lifetime. She hadn't lied when she'd told Dean it was her dream to own a place like this. She'd always loved animals and it'd be such a privilege to be able to help them when they needed it.

Becky listened as their guide, Sarah, took them around and explained the process of how the various animals came to be at the refuge and what they did once they were here. She talked about the horses that were abused and neglected, she told stories about some of the dogs and cats and how they ended up with them. She even explained how coyotes don't necessarily mate for life like wolves do, but that the mated pair would usually stay together for a number of years before they went their separate ways.

The refuge even had some cubs born on the property in the past as well. Sarah explained how they prepared the food and how they even had some live food out in the boundary as well. They didn't want the coyotes to be bored or get too used to people, which could happen if they were always fed prepared slabs of meat. There were plenty of squirrels, mice, birds, snakes and other live animals they could feed on.

"Are you ever scared of the coyotes or other animals?" Marissa interrupted, not being able to stand not being the center of attention.

"Not really," answered Sarah. "We learn to read them pretty well and know the signs if they are feeling aggressive and when we should avoid them."

"Do you go into the pen?" asked Becky, unable to keep her questions to herself anymore.

Sarah smiled at Becky. She knew all about Becky and how she was Dean's woman, even if Becky herself didn't know it yet. It was good she was showing interest and asking questions since she'd be in the family soon.

"We do," she answered. "You have to understand, these are wild coyotes, but some have been here a while and do recognize us. They are *not* domestic dogs, as some people like to think, but they're also not aggressive killing machines as others believe either."

Becky smiled and the little group continued walking around, observing some of the other animals and generally getting a tour of the property. As soon as they walked into the barn Marissa couldn't stop complaining about the smell. She'd pretended to gag and covered her nose and mouth with her hand.

David happened to have a handkerchief with him and gave it to her. Becky thought it was extremely rude. The barn smelled like…well, a barn. Becky thought to herself that Marissa was born to be melodramatic.

Sarah rang the bell that hung outside the back of the barn and soon Becky saw shapes running toward them from the tree line.

"Oh my gosh," she said quietly, "they're beautiful."

Ten coyotes came running to the fence. They were different shapes and sizes and even ages. They did look a lot like dogs. Becky couldn't take her eyes off of them. She stepped up to the fence and grasped the chain link and just stared. She didn't notice the crowd of people off to the side. Many of the employees at the refuge wanted to meet the woman Dean had claimed, and even more so because she was on a television show.

They weren't sure what to think, especially after seeing how Marissa acted with the men and her attitude toward all of them. The employees all hoped Becky was good enough for their employer's son. They were all relieved to hear Steve approved of her, but they also wanted to see for themselves.

"Would you like to feed them?" Sarah asked the group.

"Ick!" Marissa immediately said disgustingly. "No way!"

The men agreed, which was no surprise, they wouldn't disagree with anything Marissa said.

Sarah looked expectantly at Becky.

"I'd love to," Becky said quietly. "Will they let me? I mean, they don't know me."

Sarah nodded. "I'll be right next to you, it'll be fine."

Marissa and her dates, at least that was how Becky thought of the men at this point, sat on a set of bleachers nearby. They were set up for demonstrations such as this one when groups came to the refuge. Marissa was between her dates and not paying any attention to the coyotes or anything Becky was doing. She'd turn from one man to another, flirting with all of them, trying to hold all of their attentions.

Becky followed Sarah into the pen, oblivious to the crowd of people. She'd gotten so used to so many people being around the shoot that she tended to just ignore them all. Dean stood with his mom and dad along with some of the other employees and watched the interaction between Sarah, his woman, and the coyotes.

Becky watched carefully how Sarah threw the meat toward the group of coyotes, then stepped back. When it was time, Sarah told her to go ahead and throw the meat toward the coyotes. Becky threw it exactly where Sarah told her to aim.

The coyotes basically ignored the humans and feasted on their meal. Becky noticed a small coyote slinking toward the others. She hadn't noticed it before. It was smaller than the others and hesitant. Becky asked Sarah about it.

"Oh, that's our newest arrival," Sarah told her. "We don't know her story yet, but we think she was a part of a traveling zoo. She was kept in a small box and beaten by the humans who kept her locked up. Eventually the zoo was raided by the humane society and the cops and she was freed. We were contacted and she came here to live. She doesn't trust us, and she doesn't trust the other coyotes in the sanctuary yet either. We aren't sure what to do about her. If she's not accepted by the other coyotes then we can't leave her here. They'll turn against her and she'll be worse off than she was before."

Becky thought that was the saddest thing she'd ever heard. For an animal to live through all that abuse and then not be accepted into the group of coyotes here at the refuge was just so awful.

"How long has she been here?" Becky asked, not taking her eyes off the coyote.

"For about two weeks," Sarah told her.

Becky gasped. "Has she eaten at all since she's arrived?" It certainly didn't look like it as the coyote was very skinny.

"I'm not sure," Sarah answered honestly. "She might be catching some of the small rodents and animals that are around their penned in area, but we have no way of knowing for sure."

Sarah knew she and the other employees at the refuge had tried everything they could to get the coyote to trust them. They'd tried to approach her, but the animal was so scared that she wouldn't let them anywhere near her. They'd even thrown the food so it would land right in front of her, but she always ignored it and another one of the coyotes ended up eating it instead. Sarah had told Becky the truth. They weren't sure what to do with the little coyote. It was breaking their hearts, but if she couldn't bond with them or the other coyotes, she'd have to go elsewhere for her own safety.

Becky continued to look at the little coyote. She could see she was scared to death, and had only come near the other animals and the fence because she was probably starving. Becky couldn't stand it anymore.

"Do you think I could try to feed her?" she asked Sarah. Sarah looked at Dean's woman. The match couldn't have been more perfect. Sarah knew Dean liked to protect people and even made a career out of it. Becky was trying to protect the little coyote as best she knew how. Sarah thought she'd do Steve's family proud. She didn't think she'd be successful with the little coyote, but it wouldn't hurt for her to try.

"Of course you can, Becky, just don't feel bad if she won't come near you or if she won't eat."

Sarah went over with her again about the proper way to feed a coyote and what to do. She didn't think Becky was really listening to her, though, and finally just told her to go ahead.

Becky didn't know what she was doing. She only knew that if she didn't try to help this little coyote she'd regret it forever. The animal didn't deserve to be in a traveling zoo. She didn't deserve to go through her life rejected and not trusting. Becky watched the coyote flinch when Marissa's shrill laugh suddenly sounded loud in the clearing. She took her eyes off the enclosure long enough to glare at the woman, only to see Steve striding over to the woman and her dates. Thank God. Steve would take care of her and make her shut up.

After entering the fenced-in area Becky walked about forty feet away from the feeding area. Far enough away that she'd be in big trouble if the coyotes decided they wanted to eat *her*, but she didn't care. She was focused on the little scared coyote. She thought it'd be best to get it away from the humans, the barn, and the other animals. She sat down cross-legged with her back to the barn and the people. Becky knew they were all still there, watching her, but she didn't care, she was solely focused on the sad little animal in front of her.

She sat very still, with her head down but had her eyes up, watching the little coyote. She held the small piece of meat in her hand, outstretched on the ground in front of her. And she waited. For ten minutes the coyote didn't move. She didn't move toward her, but she also didn't run away either. Becky decided to be encouraged by that rather than discouraged. The other coyotes finished eating and, taking a wide berth around her, headed back toward the wood line, and still she and the coyote sat still, waiting each other out.

Becky sat very still. Her legs were asleep, but she didn't move. Finally, after what seemed an eternity, the small coyote took one step toward her and then sat again. That one step lifted Becky's spirits immensely. She'd sit out there all day if that was what it took. Becky decided to start talking to the coyote. She spoke low and quietly. She crooned nonsense to her. She told her how pretty she was and how she didn't blame her for not trusting people. She told the little coyote that it wasn't her fault. That if she trusted these people they'd help her. That this was a safe place, one where she could heal and grow big and strong. She continued to murmur nonsense to the coyote in the hopes the animal would hear the lack of anger and encouragement in her voice.

Dean's family and friends watched silently from nearby. They were standing close enough that they could hear everything Becky was murmuring to the little coyote. They held their breaths. They wanted Becky to succeed just as much as she herself did. When the little coyote took another step toward her they were amazed.

One employee whispered, "She's gonna do it." Everyone else just nodded in agreement and held their breaths. They all felt humbled watching Becky charm the little coyote and get her to trust again.

Becky held her breath as well. This was it. The little coyote was only about four feet from her. Sweat ran down the side of Becky's face, but she ignored it.

"Okay, little one. I'm going to throw this meat toward you...don't be scared, okay? Here it comes." Becky gave the meat a light toss and it landed right in front of the coyote. At first the animal backed up, but suddenly she shot forward, snatched up the meat, and backed up about ten feet and stared at Becky.

"Go ahead, it's okay," Becky soothed, her voice quivering with excitement. "It's all yours. You just go ahead and eat it. These people are here to help you. They won't hurt you. You have to trust them. They only want you to get better."

She watched as the little coyote gulped down the meat. Then instead of running off, the coyote sat there and stared at Becky expectantly.

"I'm sorry, I don't have any more," Becky told the coyote sadly, holding her empty hands out.

She held out her hand toward the coyote. "Come here," she coaxed, not knowing what she was doing. Was she even supposed to be touching a wild coyote? Should she be trying to touch a wild animal that was abused? She figured probably not, but this coyote needed some sort of comforting touch. She'd probably never experienced such a thing before, not even from another of her kind.

"Come on," she said again, wiggling her fingers, half wondering if she'd lose them. Becky didn't hear Sarah or anyone else complaining or freaking out, so she continued to try to coax the coyote toward her. As slowly as before, the coyote made her way toward Becky. Finally, when she was about two feet from her, she dropped to her haunches and crawled toward her outstretched hand.

The first time her hand touched the top of the little coyote's head, Becky fell in love. Her coat was rough and coarse. It was also matted and dirty, but the head under the fur was so tiny and delicate. Becky knew this coyote would be gorgeous once cleaned up and given some love.

"Come on, come here," she continued to coax. Slowly, ever so slowly, the little coyote crawled closer to Becky until her head was in Becky's lap. Becky stroked her head and shoulders, murmuring the whole time what a good girl she was and how pretty she was.

Dean looked over at his mom and saw tears streaming down her face.

Bethany turned toward her son and said, "Do you know how many of us have tried to do what your woman has just done? We tried everything, but that little coyote wouldn't come near us. We're so fortunate she came by today and we're so happy for you."

Dean beamed, but said with caution, "She doesn't know she's mine yet, mom. She has no idea how I feel or about our family history with the *One* and all that."

Bethany scolded him with her eyes. "Look at her, Dean, does that look like a woman who'll freak out when you tell her?"

Dean chuckled. "No, but I also don't want to scare her away just yet."

"Take your time, son. She's yours and you have plenty of time to get her used to the idea. Just don't wait too long. It's obvious this place needs her."

They looked back toward Becky just in time to see the little coyote stand up and push Becky over. Dean was about to burst into the pen and save Becky from a mauling when they heard her laugh. The little coyote was actually playing with her!

Becky giggled as the coyote pushed her over. She was so happy she thought she'd bust. This moment would be forever etched in her memory as one of the best experiences of her life. She looked over toward the crowd of people standing by the barn and caught Dean's eye. He was beaming at her and she felt tingles go down to the tips of her toes.

"Ewwww…look! She rolled in crap!" Marissa screeched, pointing at Becky.

Sure enough Becky had fallen backward when she'd been tackled by the coyote and had gotten some manure in her hair. She heard the men laughing along with Marissa. She couldn't hear what they were saying, but she immediately felt embarrassed and humiliated.

The little coyote had immediately jumped off of Becky at Marissa's loud words and was walking backward, growling. The moment was broken. Once again Marissa had brought all the attention back to her and made Becky look like a fool.

Becky watched sadly as the little coyote turned and bounded away toward the woods without looking back. She slowly stood up, painfully aware, now, of what she looked like. Her jeans were dirty, her hands and shirt smelled like something rotten from coming in contact with the filthy coyote, and she had poop in her hair. Great, just great. She could just imagine the camera angles on this one.

Becky walked back toward Sarah and the barn with a fake smile on her face. Of course her humiliation had to be witnessed by not only Dean, but his friends, family, and the cameras—and thus the world. She ducked her head. If only she could get away for a moment to compose herself. She wanted to cry.

As soon as she got back to the gate where Sarah was waiting to let her out of the pen, the cameras were right there. Eddie had decided while she was in the pen with the little coyote that this would make a great backdrop for the next ceremony. He was also probably trying to show off to Dean and impress him so he'd decide to invest in him. He'd ordered the cameras to capture Becky in all her gloriousness while ordering another producer to head back to the house and gather the other contestants and Robert so they could join them at the refuge for a ceremony.

Becky was horrified. Was he serious? As if it wasn't bad enough she'd just been humiliated by Marissa on national television, now he wanted to bring all the other men here to witness it? Jesus. Eddie must hate her. Becky felt her face heat up. She held her head up and took a deep breath. Fine. So be it.

She tried to ignore the camera as she went through the gate to the yard. She thought she saw Kina, if she remembered the camera operator's name right, in an argument with Eddie off to the side, but turned away, knowing she had to watch where she was walking or else she'd fall on her face.

She knew by Eddie deciding to have the ceremony immediately she wouldn't be able to do anything about her appearance. He wanted her to look like she was, the jerk. She looked around and grabbed a piece of twine off the ground that was used to bale hay and tied her hair up with it. She might have crap in her hair, but at least she could tie it up so it wasn't as obvious.

Becky refused to look at Dean or his family again. Sarah came over and touched her arm.

"Hey Becky," she said, "You did good, *really* good. I couldn't believe it when she came over to you! That was amazing."

Becky smiled at the woman. It *was* amazing, and she was proud of herself, but she knew she'd have to get through the next hour or so before she could let herself think about it again. She'd have to be on her guard against the snide comments she was sure she'd receive.

"Thanks Sarah," she said in a tight voice and walked away, not looking back.

Sarah growled under her breath and took a step toward Becky's retreating back. Dean suddenly appeared at Sarah's side, grabbing her elbow before she could take off after Becky.

"Let her be," he said intensely.

Sarah shook her head. "Let me go, Dean, I'm going to go shove that other woman's head in the dirt."

Dean gripped her arm harder, but not hurtfully, knowing the longtime employee and friend would do just that given half a chance.

"That will humiliate Becky even more," he said simply, somehow knowing it was true.

It was the right thing to say. Dean could feel Sarah's body relax.

"Bitch!" she said about Marissa to no one in particular.

Then she turned toward Dean again, "Oh my God, Dean, did you see that? She…was…awesome…*that* was awesome."

Dean smiled and nodded, gazing toward Becky. "She *is* awesome, Sarah. Awesome."

* * *

Becky gritted her teeth throughout the next hour. She had to endure the comments and joking from the rest of the men once they'd arrived at the refuge. They hadn't seen the miracle of the little coyote, they only saw her covered in dirt and smelling like shit, literally. She didn't need them making sarcastic comments about the 'smell in the air.' Becky knew she smelled, she could smell herself.

Marissa, of course, took the opportunity to tell everyone how Becky had rolled in crap in the yard and how funny she'd looked. She, of course, didn't mention anything about the coyote and what had happened. Becky tried to tell one group of the men, but their attention was quickly diverted by Marissa's wild laughter nearby. Their heads turned and Becky lost their attention. Becky gave up. She didn't have an ally on the show. She figured at least Steve and Bethany were happy, but since they weren't on the show it didn't help her at the moment.

The ceremony was the same as usual. Marissa and Becky had to choose the men who they wanted to stay and who they wanted to leave. Becky barely cared about any of them. They were all out to get fame and fortune by winning Marissa's hand…and hers too if that was what they had to do. It wasn't like they actually wanted to be picked by *her*, but they'd take it if it was the only option. They put on a good show during the ceremony, but generally she knew, as did everyone, that Marissa was the grand prize.

Marissa chose the men she wanted to stay and Becky did the same. When it was all over, Ryan and Samuel were going home.

"The choice has been made!" Becky couldn't even smile at Robert's theatrical antics anymore.

There were only seven men left. The twins, Derek and David, Jose, Patrick, James, Dexter, and John. They were all good looking, but also extremely shallow and fake.

Chapter Ten

After watching Ryan and Samuel get into the limo that would take them away from the show for good, the day was finally over. Becky stood off to the side near the pen, looking out at the land, wondering if the coyotes were out there watching. She heard Marissa and some of the men complaining to Eddie about how she smelled and how they refused to ride in the same vehicle as her. She supposed she couldn't blame them, she did smell gross. She gripped the fence tighter, wishing she was at home, wishing…oh she didn't know anymore. She went from feeling great being around Dean, to feeling totally depressed after filming. She knew it wasn't healthy, but wasn't sure what do to about it either. A lone tear escaped before she could will it away. God, would this torture ever end? She'd never complain about her boring insurance job again.

Finally, after getting control of her tears and wiping her face, she turned around to go back toward the vehicles and saw Steve talking with Eddie. Eddie shook his hand, looked relieved and turned toward Marissa, Robert, and the other men and motioned for them to board the van.

Becky walked toward the group and took a deep breath, readying herself to bear the jokes and comments from the others with dignity, but was intercepted by Steve who took her firmly by the arm as she passed him.

"We're taking you home later, Becky," he told her, steering her away from the production vans and toward the house.

"But…" Becky said, craning her neck to look back at the van and the people loading themselves into it.

"I just talked to Eddie, and he agreed it'd be best if you cleaned up here and we took you back in a bit." Becky blushed a fiery red and looked down at her feet as he continued to guide them toward the house. Great. Just great. Now her humiliation was complete.

Steve suddenly stopped walking, took Becky by the shoulders and turned her toward him. He put his knuckle under her chin and forced her head up to look at him.

"Don't let that asshole get you down, Becky," he told her sternly. "Look around. Look at my friends and *your* friends now. Look how happy they are. *You've* done that. *You* have made us all very happy by doing something none of us were able to. We want to celebrate with you and we know if you go back now, you certainly won't get to celebrate. Do you want to stay? I can tell Eddie that you want to go back now…" He let his voice trail off, letting her think about what she wanted.

Becky did take a look around. The men and women that had been there today were all standing around talking to each other, smiling and laughing. They seemed happy. She was being selfish and conceited to think they were all looking at her and laughing.

She nodded shyly at Steve. "Thank you, Steve. I'd love to stay."

Steve nodded and turned toward the house with her elbow in his hand.

"Do you think, however," she started to ask hesitantly, "that I might be able to clean up before we celebrate?"

Steve laughed and nodded as he towed her toward the house.

Dean grabbed Becky as soon as she stepped into the house, away from the eyes of the production crew and the other contestants. He hugged her to him as tight as he dared.

Becky laughed and pushed frantically at Dean. "Let me go, Dean!" She laughed. "I smell horrible…you'll get it on you."

Dean released his hold on Becky enough to put a bit of room between them, but didn't let her go.

"You're amazing," he told her with a smile on his face.

"No, you mean I'm smelly." She laughed back at him, deciding once and for all to shake herself out of the doldrums. "Seriously, let me go, I'm gonna get you all gross."

"You could never get me 'all gross'," he told her with a flare of heat in his eyes.

Just as he was bending down toward her to kiss the daylights out of her, they were surrounded by many of the people that had watched the entire incident with the little coyote, all talking at once.

"How did you do that?"

"That was awesome."

"That made my day."

"What a bitch that other woman is."

The comments flowed over her and she stared into Dean's gaze which had never left hers. She shut her eyes for a moment. It felt so good to finally be with people who were as thrilled with what had happened as she was.

She opened her eyes again only to find Dean still staring at her. She broke eye contact and said to the group in general, "Wasn't that cool?"

Everyone laughed with her. "*Now*, can I *please* go and clean up?" Everyone broke into uncontrolled laugher again and Bethany had to forcefully break through the circle of people surrounding her son and his *One*.

"Come on, Becky, I'm sure I can find you something to wear while we wash your clothes."

Becky smiled shyly at Dean's mom and nodded. She glanced back at Dean before disappearing into the bowels of the house.

Dean watched Becky walk away with his mom. His heart felt so big. Not only did Becky get along with his family, but she'd made a great impression on them as well. He'd wanted, like he had so many times before, to sweep her away from the set and protect her from the humiliation they were forcing on her, but he knew he couldn't. All he could do was support her at night when they talked and give her some great experiences with his family and friends, like today. Time would have to take care of the rest. Once she was away from the show and living a normal life, things would settle down.

When Becky came back down with Bethany she was wearing a pair of sweat pants and a T-shirt, probably one of Steve's. She smelled fresh and clean as if she'd just taken a shower. Hell, of course she had. Her hair was wet and was down around her shoulders. Dean had to force himself not to rush over to her and kiss the hell out of her. This was not the time nor the place to start something they couldn't finish.

Becky smiled at Dean shyly. "I hope this is okay. It was what I was most comfortable in."

Dean smiled. "Of course, sweetheart. Whatever you want to wear is fine by me." He met his mom's eyes over Becky's shoulder and they smiled at each other.

All during dinner everyone re-hashed what happened that day. Becky learned more about what the little coyote had gone through before she'd gotten to the refuge and how indignant everyone was about it. They'd so wanted to help her and were losing hope that they could. Becky didn't understand why *she* was the one who was able to break through the little coyote's barrier, but she was so happy she had.

"Do you think she'll eat more now? That she'll trust you guys?" Becky asked worriedly.

Steve answered for the group. "I think so. We'll let Dean try to feed her next. I think maybe if you go out to the pen with him one more time tonight and she sees you with him maybe she'll learn to trust more than just you. And if your scent is on him, and vice versa, it'll give her an extra incentive."

Becky looked at Steve and then back at Dean. "My scent?"

Dean took her hand and explained. "Yeah, when I hold your hand, some of your skin cells get mixed in with mine." He rubbed his thumb back and forth over the back of her hand as he spoke. "The natural scent of your skin will mix with mine. A coyote's sense of smell is very strong and she'll be able to smell both of us, even after we're gone. It's worth a shot."

Becky nodded. "Great, let's go now!"

Everyone laughed. "In a bit, sweetheart, finish your dinner first," Dean told her, laughing at her enthusiasm while continuing to stroke her hand with his, not letting go, forcing her to finish her meal with her other hand.

Dean knew it was getting late and Becky would have to get back to the production set soon. He hated to leave her. He felt anxious when he was separated from her. He wished he knew if she was feeling the same intense feelings he was, but Dean knew he'd have to take their relationship slow at first and rely on her instincts to recognize him as her soul mate.

After eating, Dean excused himself and Becky so they could go back out to the pen to see if they could get the little coyote to come back and if she'd take food from Dean. He smiled at the knowing smile his parents gave him as he left the house. They knew he'd take advantage of the alone time with Becky to further his pursuit of her as his own.

The two went out to the edge of the yard near the pen. Nobody followed them outside, knowing if they all went outside at the same time, they'd spook the little coyote. Dean grasped Becky's hand in his and led them to the fence. Once they arrived, he turned Becky so her back was to him and he curled his arms around her waist and pulled her back against him. They both sighed in contentment. They stood like that for a bit and finally Becky broke the silence.

"How is she going to know we're here?" Becky asked quietly.

"She'll know," Dean responded, leaning down and whispering directly into her ear, "but you can call to her if you want."

Becky turned her head and looked back at him with her eyebrows scrunched up in confusion.

"Just start out with a little howl, then make a little yipping noise…it doesn't have to be loud, just choose a pitch that you're comfortable with and see if it works. Yipping is how coyotes usually 'talk' to each other," Dean explained, laughing at the look on her face.

"I'm embarrassed," Becky said, ducking her head quickly and looking straight ahead again. "It's not the kind of thing a woman would normally do around a hot guy," she finished quickly, blushing.

Dean smiled and moved one hand away from her waist to grasp her chin lightly. He gently turned it back and up so he could look her in the eyes. "Sweetheart, don't you know? Nothing you'd do around me would turn me off. I'm already yours."

Becky stared at Dean, watching as he bent down toward her slowly. Her heart hammered in her chest. This was it! He was really going to kiss her! She'd dreamed about this moment for so long and now that it was here it felt as natural as breathing. She met him halfway, coming up on her toes. Their lips met and Becky swore she could feel sparks arc between them. She felt Dean's tongue swipe along the seam of her lips and she eagerly opened for him.

Dean groaned low in his throat. He was finally kissing his *One*. For real kissing her. He'd kissed her before when he'd dropped her off at the house after bringing her home from Devil's Canyon, but this was a *kiss*. She tasted amazing, like…Becky. He'd never kiss another woman as long as he lived. This was it for him. *She* was it for him.

He turned her in his arms without breaking the kiss. He wound his arms tightly around her back and pulled her close to his chest. Becky gasped and went right on kissing Dean. He was amazing. She almost felt lightheaded. His tongue swept around her mouth like he owned it. She loved every second. She met his tongue with her own and they took turns exploring each other's mouths.

Finally, giving her bottom lip a nip, Dean pulled back to let her take a breath, but kissed his way down her neck toward her shoulder. The T-shirt she was wearing was big on her and Dean easily swept aside the collar to suck and nibble on her shoulder. Goose bumps rose on Becky's flesh. Her head dropped back. She never wanted him to stop.

Dean's hands wandered on their own volition. He'd been so patient with her, and himself, and he couldn't help it. He grazed his hands up Becky's sides until they were just under her breasts. He stopped his movement, but squeezed lightly. He felt her shiver and fought with himself to back off.

Dean didn't want to stop, but he knew he had to. First, his parents weren't more than a hundred yards away and secondly, he knew if he didn't stop now, he'd probably go further than Becky would be comfortable with. That was what ultimately made him curb his own reactions to her. He never wanted Becky to regret anything they did, and he didn't want to rush her.

He was going to have to take a long run tonight to get himself back under control. Becky finally noticed Dean had stopped nibbling on her neck. She slowly opened her eyes, only to look right into Dean's smiling face. One hand rubbed circles on her lower back while the other was still against her side and she could feel his thumb rubbing rhythmically on the soft fleshy underside of her breast.

She blushed like a virgin. "That was…er…" Her voice faded off.

Dean took up where she left off, "…amazing, wonderful, life changing," he whispered. Becky could only nod and bury her face into Dean's shoulder. She felt him rest his chin on the top of her head and was grateful he was giving her time to control herself.

Finally, she took a deep breath and looked up at him with a shy smile. "Just make a few yipping sounds and the coyote will come, huh?" she said shakily, changing to a more neutral subject. Even though she wanted nothing more than for Dean to lay her down right there in the dirt and make love to her, she knew they couldn't do it. She wanted him so badly, but felt like they needed to get to know each other better before taking their relationship to that level. She respected him even more for not even trying to go any further than they already had.

Dean turned her in his arms so her back was once again nestled against his chest and wrapped his arms around her waist once more, but this time he lifted her shirt and rested his hands on her bare skin. He wanted and needed the connection with her.

Becky could feel his hardness against the small of her back. Jesus. He felt amazing. She shook her head and tried to concentrate as he chuckled, seemingly knowing what she was thinking about.

He leaned down and said right next to her ear, tickling the hair hanging there. "Yes, just a few little yips should do it. As I said before, she knows you're here, it'll be your call to her."

Becky felt utterly ridiculous, and a little off kilter after the amazing kiss she'd shared with Dean, not to mention still feeling his amazing body as he'd cradled her against his body, but she gave it a try anyway.

She howled a bit, softly at first, trying to get the hang of it and to find the right pitch. When she did find a tone that was comfortable and didn't sound too abrasive to her own ears, she increased the volume just a bit and yipped three times.

Dean moved his hand from her waist to her stomach and felt the sounds move through her. He immediately got harder than he already was. Christ. There was no way he could hide it from Becky, seeing how her back was plastered to his front. Her howl broke a bit, but then picked back up again as she yipped some more. He felt her shift and actually push back against him. Holy mother of God...he wasn't going to make it. Sweat broke out on his forehead and the iron control he had on his body almost broke. She might be embarrassed about calling to the coyote, but it was sexy as hell to Dean.

Becky let her voice fade off and waited. She would've waited there forever in Dean's arms, but suddenly she saw a shape off in the distance. It was the little coyote! She was slowly making her way toward them.

Becky gasped and kneeled down, clutching the fence. She was really coming toward them! It'd worked. She looked up at Dean, beaming.

Dean didn't think he'd ever seen anything as beautiful as Becky at that moment.

"She's coming!" Becky said reverently to Dean. He nodded and watched as the little coyote approached them cautiously.

Just as she had earlier, Becky started talking in a low voice. Telling the little coyote that everything was okay, that she had to leave, but she'd hopefully be back. But in the meantime she should trust Dean.

Dean kneeled down next to Becky, reached forward and took her hand in his, holding it close to the fence with his.

Becky understood what he was doing and said, "You can trust him, little star," Becky told the coyote. "He's with me."

Dean could feel Becky hold her breath as the coyote slowly inched her way toward them.

"That's it," she crooned. "You have to trust him and the others, they won't hurt you, they only want to help you."

They stayed like that for a few minutes. Dean and Becky kneeling, with the coyote on the other side, sniffing their interwoven fingers as they gripped the fence. Finally, the coyote rolled over on her back as if to say, 'Rub my belly!'

Becky laughed low.

"I can't rub you today, but I'll be back," she said, hoping she wasn't lying to herself or the coyote. "Go on now, go and find the other coyotes and try to make friends. Be sure to come and get something to eat tomorrow, you're too skinny!"

As if the coyote could understand her, she stood up and ran for the trees. She stopped once, looked back at the two humans and took off again. Becky stood up awkwardly, feeling Dean brace her as she stood.

"Star?" he asked with a smile in his voice.

"She looks like a Star to me," Becky told him sheepishly. "I thought she deserved a beautiful name. She might be small, but she's a Star in my eyes."

Dean hugged Becky to him again, unable to help himself. His woman was so unassuming and unselfish. He was the luckiest man alive.

* * *

Steve insisted on driving Becky back to the production set. Becky sat between him and Dean on the front seat of the truck. She felt very protected between the two large men. She sighed, knowing her lovely night was about to end. She didn't want to go back into the house and deal with the comments and jokes she was sure to get. She also didn't want to continue with the show, but she knew she didn't have a choice. She'd signed the stupid contract and she was obliged. Thank God it was almost over. It couldn't end soon enough for her.

Steve pulled up outside the gates of the house, much as Dean had the first time he'd dropped her off. Neither man moved. Becky looked from one to the other in confusion, waiting for someone to say something.

Finally, Steve broke the silence.

"Becky, we're thrilled to have met you today and want you to know that we approve of your relationship with Dean. We hope you'll come back soon. We want to get to know you better and we want you to get to know us better."

Becky wasn't sure what to say, so she didn't say anything, but nodded her head in agreement.

Dean took her hand and she turned her attention to him.

"I've told you before, Becky, but I'll tell you again now…you're mine. I'm sorry if that comes out too macho and controlling, I don't mean it to, but when this silly show is over I want you to stay. I want you here with me and my friends and family. I know I'm asking a lot. Believe me, I know it. I get that you have a job and you'd have to move away from your home and friends, but I want to be with you. We can do the long distance thing for a while until you've worked things out back home, but eventually I want you here…with me."

Becky swallowed…hard…opened her mouth to respond, and nothing would come out. She was nervous about the whole situation, but it felt right, and that scared her more than anything else. She didn't think Dean was being macho and overpowering. At this moment, she wanted to be with him as much as he apparently wanted to be with her. Goosebumps rose on her flesh at the thought of him wanting her as much as he did to brave saying all of these things in front of his dad.

Dean squeezed her hand. "Don't answer now. Think about it for a while, sweetheart, but know, from the bottom of my heart to yours, that I want to be with you. What we have between us is real."

Becky nodded and watched as Dean scooted out of the truck, she followed behind him, turning when Steve spoke.

"Becky, if you ever need anything, please know I'm here for you and so is my wife…anything at all, even if it's just to come out and see your coyote again…we're just a phone call away. Dean will give you our number so you can get in touch with us. Okay?"

Becky nodded her head and finished sliding out of the truck. Dean leaned down and captured her lips with his in a swift, but intense kiss. He then kissed her forehead and held her for a long moment before letting go and stepping back. Becky knew he watched as she let herself through the gate and onto the grounds of the house. The truck didn't pull away until she was safely inside the house. That small act of respect and protection made her smile.

Chapter Eleven

The next night, after another day of the same old crap, Becky lay in bed, waiting for Dean to call. It seemed as if her late night talks with Dean were the only thing keeping her going. There were now only five men left on the show and the pressure was getting to all of them. James, John, Jose, Derek and David were the last contestants. Marissa was unbearable, expecting all five of them to be showering her with attention all the time. She'd even begun playing one against the other, enjoying the jealously they displayed and the lengths they'd go to keep her attention. Marissa hardly talked to Becky anymore, but that was perfectly fine with Becky. Marisa was a raving bitch and Becky didn't want anything to do with her.

The only bright spot in the last week was a visit from Sam and Alex, who were on Eddie's previous reality show in Australia. Eddie had called them and asked if they'd visit the set.

They'd arrived hand in hand and Becky could see the love they had for each other. It was unexpected, but truly awesome to witness. She didn't think anyone could find love on TV, but they seemed to have done it.

Sam and Alex met with the group that was left and they laughed about Alex's experiences while he was in Australia. Becky noticed that Sam didn't say much, but she seemed to try to be friendly for Alex's sake.

At one point Sam asked if she could talk to Becky alone. Becky jumped at the chance. She really wanted to get Sam's perspective of the whole reality show thing, especially after remembering what Kina had said about how Eddie edited the show. Sam had been where she was. Sam *knew* what she was feeling. At least Becky thought she might.

After settling on a couch on the other side of the room Sam didn't beat around the bush and jumped right into the conversation. "How are you holding up?"

"I'm okay. I'm ready for this whole thing to be over," she answered honestly.

"I bet you are," Sam told her. "Is having two women competing over all the men as bad as it sounds like it'd be?"

"You have no idea!" Becky said with a laugh. "If I had my way, I'd tell Marissa she could have them all and walk off the set today!"

Becky expected Sam to laugh, but was surprised when she not only didn't laugh, but asked, "Why don't you?"

"Uh, because I signed a contract?" Beck said with some surprise. Surely Sam had to sign the same sort of contract when she joined the Australian reality show.

Sam sighed and looked around as if to see if anyone was within earshot. Upon seeing no one, she leaned toward Becky and said softly, "In case you didn't know this, Eddie will do whatever he can to twist the show and make it good for ratings. Even if you *did* walk off at this point, Eddie wouldn't care. He'd probably think it'd be a ratings boon. And in a sick way, he'd be right." Sam laughed with Becky and then continued, "Seriously, Becky, I was on the show for weeks, and he edited me right out of the show just because I didn't fit the mold of what he wanted the women on his show to be. I'm sure he has some twist up his sleeve for this show too. Just be careful."

Becky nodded. Because the conversation had gotten pretty intense, she changed the subject. "So, did you really save Kina's life while you were in Australia?"

Sam laughed and told her the entire story of how Kina was filming her walking around in the Outback and had almost stepped on a deadly snake. She couldn't move or the snake would've bitten her. Sam explained how she'd distracted the snake so Kina could get out of the way.

"Kina wasn't allowed to talk to me on set, for obvious reasons, but after the show was over she contacted me and we've been friends ever since." Sam turned serious again. "She's told me about some of the things that have been happening on this show, Becky." At Becky's blush Sam continued quickly. "Please, don't be embarrassed. I've been in your shoes, literally, and I *know* what you're going through. Keep your chin up. Don't let them get you down. The only reason I agreed to come with Alex to this damn set was to see you. If I had my way I'd never talk to Eddie again. He hurt me. I wasn't pretty enough or good enough to be on his show and he didn't care if I knew it. I don't think I, or Alex, will ever forgive him for that. He certainly knows how to make money, but he doesn't know how to treat people decently."

Sam took Becky's hand in hers and finished, "You're beautiful, Becky. I know you probably can't see it now, but hang in there, finish up the damn show and go on with your life. Things can work out, look at me and Alex!"

Becky squeezed Sam's hand and nodded. She was right. She had to look out for herself and all she had to do was get through the next week of the show and she'd be done with show business for good.

"Thanks for coming today, Sam. It was great to meet you, and I'm so glad you're happy."

The two women hugged each other briefly. Becky watched as Alex seemed to know exactly when Sam was done talking to her because he came over and grabbed her hand. They laughed together and walked around the set saying hello to the camera operators they'd met while in Australia. Becky watched as both Sam and Alex gave Kina a big hug. Sam hadn't been lying, she and Kina *were* friends. Becky shook off the embarrassment she felt knowing Kina had told the other woman all about what was happening on the set. Oh well, the whole world would know it sooner rather than later, she had to get over it.

Lying in bed, Becky reflected on the day's visit with Sam and Alex. Sam's talk with her helped immensely. It gave her some of her self-esteem back and Becky felt stronger. While she wasn't glad Sam had gone through what she did in Australia, it was nice to know she wasn't alone. Becky was done with the crap the men were giving her and she was done with Marissa. She'd do what she wanted, what she had to do to be done with the show and see if she could work things out with Dean. She knew he wanted to be with her, he'd told her repeatedly, and Becky knew she wanted him back. When she talked to him tonight she'd tell him she'd stay here in Arizona after the show was over. She wanted to give them a chance.

After waiting what seemed to be forever, Becky finally felt the vibration of the disposable phone Dean had given her and eagerly answered it. Expecting to hear Dean, she was surprised to hear a different voice.

"Becky? This is Steve."

Becky sucked in a breath. Why was Steve calling her? It couldn't be good. "Oh my God, is Dean all right?"

Steve was quick to reassure her, "Yes, he's fine. I'm sorry. Jeez, I didn't think. I didn't mean to frighten you."

Becky breathed a sigh of relief. She knew she liked Dean, but she didn't realize how much until she thought Steve was calling to tell her he'd been hurt or worse. She tried to control her adrenaline rush and asked, "What's up?"

"Dean asked me to call. You know he works in security, right?" At Becky's affirmative response he continued, "Well he's going to be out on a job for about four days. He won't be able to contact you as he'll be going up into the mountains around Fresno and won't have any cell service. He wanted to let you know how sorry he was that he couldn't tell you himself. It was a sudden thing and he had to leave right away."

"Is everything all right?" Becky asked.

"It will be," Steve told her. "I can't give you any specific details, but there's a woman who's being stalked and her stalker found where she'd been staying and attacked her. She left town as soon as she could but she's still scared that he'll find her again. Dean was called in to make sure the house she's staying at in the mountains has adequate security and that no one can break in, or if they do get near her, she has time to call for help.”

Becky felt bad. Steve sounded almost sad for her.

“It’s okay, Steve,” she told him brightly. “I’m glad he’s going to help that woman. She has to be so frightened. Four days isn’t that long and I’ll be finishing up this show anyway. If you talk to him, tell him I’m fine and I’ll see him when he gets back.”

Steve knew Becky wasn’t as fine as she was trying to let on, but he also knew if he called her on it, her pride would be hurt.

“Becky, I’ve told you this before, but if you need anything please don’t hesitate to contact me or Jonathan. Even though Dean is out of town, we’re still here. Did Dean give you my number? You have it, right?”

“Thanks, Steve, I have it.” Becky didn’t tell him she wasn’t planning on having any need to call him. What could go wrong in four days? Yes, the show was awful, but there wasn’t anything that Steve or Jonathan or even Dean could do about it. She’d just have to hang in there, like she’d been doing, until the end of the show and then see if there was anything between her and Dean in the “real world.” She was excited about that prospect, just dreading getting through to the end of the show.

Becky thanked Steve again. “Thanks, Steve, I appreciate you calling and letting me know about Dean. I think there’s only about a week left on the show and then I’m free!”

“When you’re ‘free’,” Steve said with a laugh, “Let Dean pick you up and bring you here. We’ll have a huge party!”

Becky laughed and agreed. They said goodnight to each other and hung up. So much for her relaxing phone call from Dean. She mentally shrugged and snuggled down into the covers to try to catch some sleep so she could make it through the next few days.

Chapter Twelve

As the show was coming to an end, Marissa and the other contestants seemed to get more and more intense, if that was even possible. Becky supposed if she was really interested in any of the men, she'd probably feel the same way. She'd feel pressure at the ceremonies to choose the right guy and if she liked more than one she'd want Marissa to choose the men she liked to stay. But because she didn't care one whit about any of the men, or who Marissa wanted to continue on, it was torture.

Marissa had started coming to her again before the ceremonies to try to tell her who she should choose to stay. She wanted all of her choices to stay, even though she didn't get one hundred percent of the say. In the beginning, Becky would just do what she wanted, but some of the men that were left weren't very nice, at all. In fact, Becky knew if she met any of the men in a bar or anywhere else, they'd probably scare her. Generally they were big, and they were pretty mean. Oh, they were nice to Marissa for sure, but when Marissa wasn't looking they were downright rude, talking about how Becky was an ugly cow and most likely frigid to boot and how they couldn't wait to 'tap' Marissa.

They never did it in front of the cameras, but their comments to Becky as she walked by them were getting worse and worse and downright scary. Derek actually threatened her the other day. They'd been walking past each other in the hallway and he'd stopped her and told her that if she didn't continue to choose him, if Marissa didn't, that she'd regret it.

Becky had tried to talk to Eddie and even the other producers, but they didn't want to hear it. Eddie had practically patted her on the head and said it was all a part of the show. And the other producers wouldn't even take the time to talk to her. Eddie was more concerned that his big investor—Dean—hadn't shown up for the last few days. He'd been told he was away on business, but he didn't believe it and was scrambling to try to figure out what he'd done wrong. Every day he'd grill Jonathan about his "friend" and if he'd be coming back for the show's finale.

Becky didn't dare tell Jonathan or Dean about the threats. She figured she'd just deal with them herself and she'd be sure to never be alone with any of the men who were left on the show. Dean wouldn't be able to do anything, even if he were here for her to talk to. She knew enough about his personality to know it'd be a bad idea to tell him. He was protective of her, as was his dad and even Jonathan, and that made her want to keep this from them. If they did something or said something to any of the men they could get in real trouble. The last thing Becky wanted was to be the cause of trouble for anyone she cared for. Yes, she finally admitted she cared for Dean and his family.

On one of the last days where there were individual dates, Becky had unfortunately "won" a date with Derek. The producers were no longer having Marissa and Becky go on double dates, but letting them go out with the remaining men by themselves. Becky sat in her room before she was supposed to leave on her date with Derek and fingered the phone. Oh, how she wished she could talk to Dean. It'd been a long couple of days and she was kinda scared to go out with Derek. She knew there'd be a camera there, so it wouldn't be like they were truly alone, but she knew Derek didn't like her and she didn't like him in return. It would be very awkward, if nothing else. They had to go out to dinner, and then they were supposed to come back to the house and watch a movie in the TV room.

Becky considered calling Steve for a pre-date pep talk, but then decided that would be ridiculous. She couldn't call her sorta boyfriend's dad before she went on a date with another man. She again reminded herself there was nothing Steve could do and she returned the phone under her pillow.

She took a deep breath and walked out of the room. Ready or not, it was time for her date.

Dinner was awkward. Neither of them wanted to be there and they weren't sure what to say to each other. Derek was only interested in winning the stupid show and didn't even try to engage Becky in any meaningful conversation. The only thing he wanted to know about was Marissa and if she was going to choose him to stay at the next ceremony.

After dinner they came back to the house and sat on the couch, on opposite sides, watching a movie. Becky had seen it before and Derek didn't seem remotely interested in what was happening on the screen.

At one point Eddie walked into the room and interrupted them, asking to speak with Derek. They left the room and Derek came back in about five minutes later. He sat very close to Becky and put his arm on the back of the sofa behind her.

Becky was freaking out. What the hell? Derek hadn't shown any affection toward her the entire show, and now, after speaking with Eddie he was suddenly pretending this was a real date? What a joke. Eddie had to have put him up to it.

"What are you doing?" she asked him sharply when he actually had the nerve to put his arm around her shoulder.

"What does it look like, baby?" he asked while winking at the camera that was in the room.

Becky whipped around to see that yes, there was a camera there. The red light blinked at her mockingly, letting her know they were being filmed. She stood up and moved over to the lone chair in the room.

"I don't know you well enough for you to be touching me like that, Derek," she said, knowing she sounded prudish. But seriously? He wanted to pretend to like her now when the entire show he'd been a jerk to her and had actually threatened her the other day? No.

Derek pouted and they both continued to watch the movie. Not long after Eddie left he asked Becky if she was watching the movie. When she shook her head he suggested they call it a night. Becky was all for ending the farce of the date early and settling down, alone, in her bed. She wanted to dream about Dean and hoped that maybe he'd get home early and might call.

Derek offered to walk her to her room. She knew it was just because the cameras were following them. When they got there, she opened her door and when she turned around, Derek was standing right there. He grabbed her in a hug and forced his lips down on hers.

Becky tried to push him away, but he was too strong. He had one hand around the back of her neck, holding her lips to his and the other was like a vice around her waist. He brutally dug his fingers into her side and squeezed. It hurt. Becky tried to break his hold, but he was too strong.

He walked them backwards into her room through the open door. Becky continued to struggle, albeit futilely. Derek's mouth was wet and disgusting, and he was hurting her with the force of both his kiss and his grip on her body.

He finally lifted his head from hers to turn around and grab the door. He blocked Becky's view of the camera, but she heard him say, "I think I'll take it alone from here," in a suggestive tone and he shut the door.

Becky was furious and a little scared. He'd done that on purpose; made it look like they were going to make out in her room, or worse!

When Derek turned back around from the now-closed door she shoved him as hard as she could. Surprisingly, he let go of her, but quickly recovered and shoved her back, hard. Becky went flying and landed hard on her butt on the floor.

Derek came at her again and Becky tried to crab walk backward to keep away from him. She wasn't fast enough and he viciously grabbed her arm and hauled her upright.

Becky was shocked. Although Derek was kind of scary she'd never thought he'd turn violent with her. What the hell was he doing?

She was freaked because she was alone in her room with a man who'd just forced a kiss on her, lied to the camera, held her tight enough to leave bruises, and shoved her across the room. She had to get him out of there.

"Let go of me," Becky said through clenched teeth, trying to wrench her arm out of his grasp.

"No way," Derek hissed. "You owe me," and he threw her around so she landed on her bed.

Becky knew this was quickly getting out of hand. She had no idea what Derek thought she owed him, but she knew she had to do something, fast.

She scrambled across to the other side of the bed before Derek could get a hold of her again. She was *not* going to be raped.

"You asshole," she hissed. "You won't get away with this." Becky looked around the room for her options. She didn't see anything she could use as a weapon. She didn't have her handy baseball bat on the set. She always kept one in her room back home at her apartment. She figured the attached bathroom was her best option at this point.

She knew there was a lock on the door and if she could reach it, then she should be okay, at least theoretically. Of course, Derek could always break the door down, but she didn't *think* he'd go that far. She feigned left and when Derek fell for it and reached for her, she ran to the right and toward the bathroom.

She slammed the door behind her and locked it just as Derek reached the doorknob. He tried it and she could tell he was furious it was locked.

"Open the damn door," he hissed at her, obviously trying to be quiet so everyone else in the house didn't hear him.

Becky didn't answer him, only backed away toward the opposite wall. Like hell she was opening the door. Did he think she was stupid? There was a window in the bathroom, but it was too small for her to climb out of, and besides she was on the second floor. Not to mention she wasn't exactly a ninja and able to land on her feet if she did manage to get out of the stupid thing.

She held her breath, waiting to see what Derek would do. Her heart was beating a million miles an hour and she could feel the adrenaline coursing through her. When Becky heard nothing for ten minutes, she tried to relax. She didn't know if Derek had left or not, he could be trying to wait her out on the other side, but she wasn't leaving this room and the security it offered.

She thought longingly about the phone that was tucked away under her pillow. Damn. She'd give anything to have that phone right now so she could call someone. She knew Dean wasn't around, but Steve *had* said she could call him any time for any reason. This certainly would be a time for her to call him. But there was no way she was leaving the sanctuary of the bathroom. It was amazing what a little wooden door could do to make her feel safe, even if it was only an illusion.

She slid down the wall across from the door to the floor, her knees shaking from the adrenaline rush and reaction to her fright, and put her arms around her knees. She put her head down sideways, resting it on her knees, keeping the door in her sight, just in case. She stayed like that for the rest of the night.

* * *

When the morning came Becky almost didn't know what to do. She so badly wanted to talk to Dean, or Jonathan, or even Steve, but what would they be able to do for her now? Nothing. They weren't here. They weren't in charge of this stupid show. She was stuck, complaining to them wouldn't solve anything, and certainly telling Eddie wouldn't work. She tried to shake some sense into herself. She was an adult woman who could handle this on her own. She didn't need any help.

She thought back to the night before how it wasn't until after Eddie had talked to Derek that he'd come up with the idea to walk her to her room. It was obvious Eddie had given the suggestion to Derek. If Becky had been raped it

310

would've been as much Eddie's fault as it was Derek's. She truly felt that way.

Becky felt sick. She was outnumbered and had no allies on this show. None. She was done. She had a black and blue mark on her arm where Derek had grabbed her, her tailbone was sore after landing on it where he'd shoved her. She also had bruising around her waist from where Derek had held her to him as he pushed them through her bedroom door in front of the camera. Becky knew she'd been lucky and it was time to end this farce. Dean wasn't home from wherever he was, but she couldn't wait any longer.

She cautiously opened the bathroom door and peeked out. The bedroom was empty. Nothing seemed out of place, but Becky wasn't taking any chances. The first thing she checked was the phone, it was still there. She grabbed it and the rest of her things and put them in her suitcase. She went back into the bathroom with her bag and locked the door and took a quick shower. She had to be ready. She'd be leaving the show today, and she knew just how she'd do it. She had to do it while the cameras were rolling so no one could say or do anything. If she did it in "public," then she'd be all right, she reasoned with herself. Once she got off this show she could start her life again. Hopefully with Dean.

Chapter Thirteen

Later that afternoon was another ceremony. The five men who were left stood in their spots. Both Becky and Marissa were supposed to choose two to stay. Marissa, of course, came to her before the ceremony and informed her of who she was supposed to vote to keep.

Becky didn't say anything. She just let Marissa think she was going along with what she wanted. Whatever. Becky was so done with Marissa and the stupid show. She actually couldn't believe Marissa still had the nerve to try to tell her who she should choose to keep. After everything that had happened so far and everything that had been said between the two of them, it was completely ridiculous.

Finally, it was time. Robert had a dramatic speech about how the end was nearing and how everyone was on pins and needles to see who'd be staying this time and who'd be going home.

When Robert finally finished with his soliloquy, it was once again Marissa's turn to make her choices. She stood up in front of the men and the cameras and gave a long speech about how hard the decision was and how it was the hardest decision yet, which every reality show contestant in the history of reality television always said, and the same thing that Marissa said every damn week. She chose to keep Jose and John.

Then it was Becky's turn. There were three men left, one of which was Derek. Becky knew which two Marissa wanted her to keep. She'd gone on and on to her about how cute Derek and David were and what great TV it made that they were also twins. It'd be such a great theatrical ending if the two of them ended up as the final choices.

Everyone was staring at Becky intently. The cameras were caching the drama on film. Eddie was watching to make sure his money-train kept clacking along. Derek, David, and James were watching her, staring at her, hoping to somehow influence her telepathically to choose them so they'd have another chance at winning Marissa and becoming famous in the process. Robert and Marissa were looking at her expectantly, waiting for her to start.

Becky took a deep breath.

"This week the decision is an easy one for me," Becky said clearly, being sure to look at each camera in the room before turning back to the men. She wasn't going to make a long speech and blame people for the miserable experience. She just wanted it done.

"I choose…" She paused, dragging out the moment for dramatic effect. "No one."

No one said anything at first and it was so quiet Becky could hear the grandfather clock in the corner ticking. Had they heard her? Surely they had.

When Marissa finally gasped, Becky continued, "I don't feel compatible with any of the men that are left, and I'm sure they don't feel compatible with me. The last dates I've been on haven't gone well, and it's obvious the men who are remaining would rather be with Marissa than with me. I'm okay with that. It was never guaranteed I'd find the man of my dreams on the show."

Becky thought she was laying it on a big thick, but she continued anyway, "After last night," she couldn't help herself and glared at Derek, "it was brought home even more to me that I need to move on. I'm forfeiting my choice tonight and would like for Marissa to finish the show. She can choose two more men of her liking, or less, depending on how the producers would like to proceed. I wish her, and all of you," she nodded to the remaining men, "the best of luck."

Eddie called out, "Cut!" and stormed onto the set.

"You can't do that!" he raged at Becky. She didn't even flinch.

"I just did," she told him defiantly, wondering where her backbone had been up until now. "You set me up to be the pathetic second-choice woman from the start. Well, I'm done. I played your game long enough. It's obvious none of the men are going to choose me," she said, waving her hand in the direction of the remaining contestants. "And I think you knew that would happen from the start. You'd better just take what I've done and run with it. It's a great twist to the show and you can continue on as planned with just Marissa and the remaining men. I'm done."

Becky looked Eddie straight in the eyes as she spoke. He knew she was dead serious and for the first time in a long time was flustered and out of his element. He hadn't seen this coming. Usually *he* was the one driving the twists and turns in his shows.

"You won't get a dime, this is a breach of contract," he sputtered at her meanly, not knowing what else to do.

"I don't care," Becky retorted, "I just want out of this house and off this show."

She turned around and walked toward the door. She passed Jonathan on her way and he reached out to take her by the arm. Becky flinched, he'd managed to grab the same spot that Derek had last night and it was still painful.

Jonathan saw her flinch and his eyes narrowed. "What the hell? Are you all right? What's really going on?" he asked urgently.

Becky laughed awkwardly. "Of course, Jonathan, I just humiliated myself for the last time on National TV, why wouldn't I be okay?" She willed the tears not to fall. She had to make it through this last bit before she fell apart.

Jonathan didn't like the look in Becky's eyes, and he certainly didn't like the way she'd flinched from his touch. He knew he hadn't grabbed her that roughly. What was going on? Dean should be here, Becky needed him.

"Dammit!" He swore softly. He knew he couldn't get off the set until the shoot was over. And after Becky's bombshell he knew they wouldn't be leaving anytime soon. Eddie would have to regroup and figure out how to best use

Becky's actions to make the show a success. His hands were tied. He'd call his dad as soon as he could. Maybe he could go and see Becky or could somehow get a hold of Dean. His brother was going to be pissed he wasn't there for Becky when everything had gone down.

The cameras followed Becky as she left the house, suitcase in hand and got into the limo. Kina happened to be the camera operator on duty and sat across from Becky in the limo and filmed her as they pulled away from the house. Becky knew they were going to a local hotel. She refused to look at the camera, just stared out the window at the passing scenery. She had to stay there until the end of the show, just as all of the other men on the show who'd been dismissed had to. She hoped she wouldn't run into any of them, it could get complicated. She didn't know if they'd be mad at her or if they would even care.

Kina put down the camera and looked at Becky.

"That was the best thing I've seen on this show so far," she told Becky with a smile. "In fact, I think it was the best thing I've seen in *any* of the shows I've filmed."

Becky smiled weakly back at her, but didn't really have anything witty to say back to her. She was done. Mentally just done.

"They're all assholes, Becky, you just keep being you, you're okay."

Becky just stared at her. Okay, well, at least everyone on the show didn't see her as pathetic.

"We all think that way, you know," she reminded her. "All the camera operators, that is. We've seen all of the crap they've put you through and you've definitely come through it looking like the better person. We'll be sorry to see you go, Becky, you've been the only interesting part of this show!"

Kina leaned forward, touched her knee and looked Becky in the eye. "Seriously, Becky. Men are assholes. I've never met one I'd trust with my life. I thought I had once, but I was wrong. Way wrong. Don't be like me. My heart is frozen to the core. I'm a hard woman and don't ever see any man being able to thaw me out. But you…" She paused, and seemed to fight back some sort of emotion, then continued, "You're a good person. Please don't let this experience, and these jerks change you. There's a guy out there for you, you just have to keep looking."

Becky pondered what Kina said and nodded. "I know, I think I've already found him," she told Kina honestly.

Kina smiled at her as they arrived at the hotel. She helped her out of the seat and waved as she turned to go into the hotel. As Becky got to the door of the hotel she looked back and watched as the limo headed back to the production house. Becky was sad for Kina. She didn't know her story, but it had to have been something awful for her to believe she'd never find anyone for herself.

Becky couldn't wait to get to her room, take a shower and process all that had happened. She wanted to talk to Dean, but she didn't really know what to say yet. Besides, she had no idea if he was even back from the job he was on. She decided she'd call him later. There was no need to call Steve either. She was out of the house and off the show. It wasn't as if she was allowed out of the hotel. She had to stay until the end of the show.

It was as if a huge weight had been lifted off of her shoulders. She could be herself again. She didn't have to worry about cameras being around, or about watching what she said and what she did for fear it'd be taped and end up on television. Becky was ready to relax for a few days and then get back to her life. A life that hopefully would include Dean and his incredible family.

Chapter Fourteen

After a long, hot shower and a short nap, Becky felt a hundred percent better. It was amazing the amount of stress she felt lifted from her shoulders as a result of not being on the show or around the set anymore. She wasn't sure how long she'd have to stay in the hotel, but she figured someone would let her know the show was over. They were, after all, paying the bill. She should be thankful of that, considering how pissed Eddie was at her.

Becky decided to make her way downstairs to the restaurant. She was starving. She was looking forward to a nice big salad and a bowl of soup. She was seated in the restaurant near the front window. It was interesting to watch the comings and goings of the other guests from the lobby. Lord knew she didn't have anything else to entertain her. She ordered her food and it didn't take long for it to arrive.

Eating and not having to carry on a conversation at the same time was awesome. It was just as great to not have to worry about a camera catching her with food in her teeth or dribbling down her chin. It was awkward to eat and know you were being filmed.

Just as she was finishing up her soup she noticed a limo pull up in front of the hotel's lobby. She watched as two men got out. Holy crap! It was the twins, Derek and David! She about choked on her soup. This wasn't happening! She thought she'd gotten away from Derek by leaving the show, but somehow it looked like Marissa didn't choose to keep him *or* his brother on the show. Becky wondered how that came about. Marissa had been adamant that both men be allowed to stay. After all, she'd said, you couldn't split up a pair of twins. Becky knew she'd have to avoid them at all costs. It was better if they didn't know she was here.

That would be easier said than done. As per the contract rules, contestants weren't allowed to be seen "out and about," so they were essentially kept prisoner in the hotel. They were allowed to freely roam the grounds, but they weren't supposed to leave. In some ways it was worse than being on the actual show. She couldn't image what the men like Ned and Oliver had gone through. They left the show in the first ceremony and had been at the hotel a long time.

Later that night, Becky finally tried to call Dean. He didn't answer, which wasn't totally surprising as his dad had said he probably wouldn't have any cell service where he was going, so she left him a message. She didn't mean to be cryptic, but it was just too complicated to try to explain everything that had happened over the phone.

Hey Dean, she said softly after the beep sounded, letting her know she could leave a message. *I miss you. I hope everything is going okay with your job. Your dad told me a bit about what you're doing, I hope that's all right. I know you'll make that woman feel safe. I know I always feel safe when I'm around you. I know you won't let anything happen to me. Anyway, some stuff happened on the show today, nothing bad, but it's kinda complicated and too long to tell you in a message. I'll talk to you soon and tell you all about it. Be safe. Don't worry about me and hopefully I'll see you soon. I wanted to tell you as well, that…well…if you still want me to, I want to stay here and get to know you better…okay, well, call me when you get back. Bye.*

After sitting around her hotel room for a few hours, Becky was bored. The thought of sitting in her room watching any more boring television wasn't appealing. Even though she hadn't seen any television the entire time she'd been in the production house, it just wasn't cutting it. She supposed she'd been weaned off it.

She'd eaten a late lunch and, while she wasn't hungry enough for a full dinner, Becky figured she could get an appetizer and that would tide her over. She could've ordered room service, but she was already going stir crazy. She decided she'd just go downstairs and grab something quick and get back up here to her room.

As she made her way into the restaurant she saw Derek, his twin, and some of the other men from the show in the bar area. They'd obviously been there a while as they were loud and quite drunk.

Becky shrugged her shoulders and went into the restaurant. She'd just stay away from the bar. Soon after she ordered, Derek and his twin suddenly appeared at her table.

"Can we join you?" Derek asked snidely, pulling out the chair and sitting without giving her a chance to answer him.

Becky's heart rate doubled. Crap. This was not good. This was not good. This was not good. She hadn't talked to Derek after he'd tried to rape her and she hadn't seen him other than at the last ceremony. David also sat down and didn't say a word. That was almost creepier than if he'd said hello or even if he'd said something rude.

Derek leaned close to her and growled, "You bitch, you ruined my chance to be famous and my chance with Marissa. You also ruined his chances too," pointing toward his brother.

"But I didn't make you leave." Becky tried to explain, shrinking back into the squeaky pleather of the booth. She looked around, hoping to see someone, anyone, that might notice what was going on and help her. Of course, no one was around.

"Yeah, well, after you left, Eddie changed the game and would only allow Marissa to keep one more guy. She decided if she couldn't have both of us, she didn't want either of us. So because you decided to quit, we had to leave. It's directly your fault, cunt. You have to pay for that!"

Becky's heart almost stopped. She had no idea Eddie would do anything so drastic. She figured Marissa would be able to choose two men to stay in her place. No wonder Derek was so pissed. It was also pure Marissa to decide to ditch both Derek and David. What good was one twin to her? It wouldn't pull in nearly enough attention. Becky swallowed hard and tried to think of something to say to get herself out of the situation.

Derek dragged her out of the booth by her arm, squeezing in the same place he'd gripped her the day before. Becky opened her mouth to protest, to scream, something…after all she was in a public place.

Derek gripped her arm even harder, digging his fingernails into her skin cruelly and said, "If you say anything, you'll only make it worse for yourself. You want to make a scene? Go ahead, we'll claim that you're bipolar and having an episode. Who do you think they'll believe? You? An ugly fat hag? Or us? Gorgeous, muscular twins who are only concerned about their poor crazy sister?"

Becky shut up. She was scared to death. What were they planning? Maybe she could talk them down when they got out of the restaurant. David still hadn't said a word, but obviously was supportive of anything his brother did. He threw a twenty dollar bill on the table to cover her meal and the three of them walked out of the restaurant and to the elevators.

Becky noticed they were going to the eighth floor. Hers was on the fourth floor.

She swallowed hard and finally said, "What the hell are you doing, Derek? Let me go, seriously, get over it." She pretended to have more bravado than she actually had. "This is ridiculous, what will this do? Get you back on the show? No, it's only going to make things worse!" She tried to reason with him as well as David. "David, seriously, I had nothing to do with you getting kicked off the show. You can't be serious." When both Derek and David ignored her, she resorted to pleading with them.

"Please, guys, don't do this. Let me go. I'll go back to the set and say whatever you want. I'll tell Eddie I want back on the show and you can come back and I'll choose you both. I swear it. Please…" Her voice fell off as they dragged her down the hall to room eight twelve. Where the hell were all the guests? Why wasn't anyone around?

Derek opened the door and pushed her in the room with David following close on their heels. Becky knew once they got her in their room she was screwed. She watched as the hotel door closed behind them. David turned to the door and locked it while Derek dragged her to the bed.

* * *

Becky woke up the next morning slowly. She tried to roll over and gasped. She hurt everywhere. She looked around. She was alone in the room. She thought frantically…where were Derek and David? Did they leave her alone momentarily with plans to come back and continue where they left off? Becky painfully pulled herself to a sitting position. She was naked. She could see her clothes strewn about the room. She shakily stood up and forced herself to gather up her clothes. She wanted out of this room now. Finally, mostly dressed, she made her way to the stairwell. She didn't want to chance using the elevators in case the twins were making their way back to the room. She walked down the four flights to her floor and cautiously opened the door. The hallway was empty, thank God. She went to her room and slipped in, miraculously her room key was still in the pocket of her pants. She walked numbly to the bathroom and stared at herself in the mirror.

Even she was shocked. Her face looked like she'd gone three rounds with a boxer. She had two black eyes and her face was swollen to twice its normal size. She opened her mouth and saw that her front tooth had a chip in it. She didn't remember when that happened, but she supposed it had been when Derek had hit her…one of the times.

She sat on the toilet seat and tried to get her breath. Her chest hurt, probably because she'd been held down. David had sat on her chest at one point because she wouldn't stay still. Her arms were covered in bruises from being held as well. She'd fought them until she'd finally passed out.

She stifled a hysterical laugh at the black permanent marker all over her body. Apparently the twins had a problem with alcohol and being able to get it up. They'd tried to rape her, but the fact she wouldn't quit fighting them combined with the alcohol in their system wouldn't allow them to be able to hold an erection.

When they couldn't get their dicks to cooperate they'd gotten out the permanent marker. For some reason they thought it would be hilarious to write all over her. The words were obscene in their starkness. Whore. Bitch. Cunt. Fat. Cow. Stupid. They'd tried to get creative and couldn't really think of too many other derogatory words in their inebriated state. Most of the words were smeared. Some were illegible because again, Becky wouldn't lie still and let them have their fun.

They'd also spit on her. Over and over. Calling her names and saying she wasn't worth the ground she walked on. At one point she thought she remembered them having a contest to see who could hawk the biggest loogie and hit her in the face with it. She shuddered with revulsion.

She sobbed once and then ruthlessly choked it back. If she started crying, she didn't know if she'd be able to stop. She continued to take stock of her body. The writing on her skin wasn't physically painful, only mentally so. She was sore from being held down and fighting them. She could walk, so her legs weren't broken, but she thought she might have a broken collarbone. It hurt like hell. She'd once broken her collarbone when she was little. A cast wouldn't work. All they did was put her arm in a sling and told her to be careful.

Becky thought about what she should do next. If she took a shower she'd probably wash away any physical evidence Derek and David left on her, but would anything happen if she went to the police? She'd probably have to testify, and the last thing she wanted to do was see the twins again.

The hell with it. She slowly got up and stripped off her clothes. She was in a state of shock, she knew it, but she couldn't deal with anything right now other than taking a shower to get clean and getting the hell out of there.

The shower was longer than she'd planned, but she just couldn't get clean. She scrubbed at her face to get the feeling of their spit off of her. It hurt, bad, but she didn't stop. The marker wouldn't come off her skin no matter how hard she scrubbed. She used the washcloth and rubbed her skin until it was red and raw and she could still see the words. Cow. Bitch. Cunt.

She couldn't stop remembering the laughs and the taunts and the pain as the men took turns holding her down and writing on her. As they swore at her as they tried to get it up. They hit her when they couldn't and blamed her for being butt ugly and a cow.

Their words haunted her.

Finally, she made herself get out of the shower. Becky knew she'd ruined her best chances of the men paying for what they did, but it was hard to think. She did take the trash can liner out of the can and put the clothes she'd been wearing in it. She figured it might be better than nothing if she decided down the line to press charges, but that was as far as she could go in trying to preserve any evidence.

She got dressed again, jeans and a long sleeved shirt to cover her arms, and a sweatshirt. She couldn't get warm. She knew it was shock, but she didn't stop to think about it. She packed up the rest of her belongings and left the room. She didn't even tell the front desk she was leaving. The hell with the show, the hell with Eddie, and the hell with the hotel.

She went out a side door and walked to the nearest fast food restaurant. She asked the manager to call a cab, and as a testimony to what her face looked like, he didn't even question her other than asking if she was all right.

Ten minutes later she was in the cab. When the driver asked her where she wanted to go, Becky's mind immediately flashed to Dean and his family. She shook her head. She couldn't go there in her mind yet. But she did want to say goodbye to Star. Something pulled her toward the little coyote and Becky wanted to make sure she was okay before she left. She gave the driver directions, put her head back on the seat and closed her eyes.

* * *

Jonathan tried to call his brother a few times after his shift on the show was over, but he wasn't answering his phone. It wasn't necessarily unusual because he knew Dean was up in the mountains and most of the time there wasn't cell service up there. But Jonathan was worried about Becky. After she left in the limo, Eddie decided that Marissa had to choose two men to leave rather than only one more, as it would've been originally.

Marissa pitched a fit. Jonathan heard her yelling at Eddie behind a closed door. She was stomping her feet and wanting to change her original choices as a result of Becky leaving. Eddie refused to let her.

Jonathan knew Marissa was heartless, but he hadn't realized she didn't have a speck of honor in her body when he heard her tell Eddie without a speck of remorse, "Fine, David and Derek will have to go then because it's no good to only have one twin. They're only good if they're together."

He knew the contestants who were no longer on the show were brought to a hotel to wait out the show. Jonathan stopped by last night after filming to see if he could get a hold of Becky, but there was no answer when he was transferred to her room by the hotel operator.

They, of course, wouldn't give him her room number so he had no way of getting a hold of her and thus no choice but to leave. His instincts were telling him something wasn't right, but he had nothing to go on and he couldn't get a hold of Becky. He decided he'd keep trying to call Dean and would get a hold of Becky the next day. If he had to he'd get his dad involved and see if he could get a hold of Dean, somehow.

* * *

Becky opened her eyes when the cab stopped near the front gates of the refuge.

"Ya want me to pull in, lady?" the driver asked gruffly. He'd seen how badly she'd been beaten and felt sorry for her. He'd wanted to bring her to the hospital, but Becky refused. She wasn't ready.

She quickly answered, "No, please, just pull over here...and...if it's not too much to ask...can you wait for me? I promise I won't be long...I just...there's something I have to do."

The driver turned around and looked at the pathetic woman in his cab.

"You're not going to do something illegal, are you?" he asked sternly. "Or hurt yourself?"

"Oh, no!" Becky answered quickly. "I just have to say goodbye to someone before I leave town."

The driver gazed at the woman for several moments and once again tried to urge her to let him take her to a doctor. When she refused he finally gave in and said, "Okay, but the meter's runnin'." Becky nodded. Thank God cabs took credit cards nowadays.

She stepped out of the cab and walked a little ways down the fence line along the gravel road. She went around a small corner and sat on the ground gingerly. It hurt too much to crouch.

She very softly howled and yipped just as Dean had taught her what seemed so long ago. She really wanted to see Star. She wasn't sure why, but she just wanted to be sure she was all right and had been eating.

After a minute or so she heard movement in the trees surrounding the fence. Suddenly the coyote was there. She walked straight up to the fence with no hesitation and whined. Becky stuck her fingers through the fence. Again, maybe not the smartest thing she'd ever done, but hell, nothing could make her feel worse right now. What was a dog bite added to everything else?

"Hey, girl...you okay? I wanted to come and see you again...before I left..."

Becky felt a tear fall down her face. She sniffed. "I'm gonna miss you, girl. Have you been eating? And making friends?"

The coyote stared at Becky and tilted her head. It was as if the coyote could really see her, could really understand her. She whined again and licked Becky's fingers through the fence.

Becky's tears fell harder. "Oh God, Star…" Becky's voice trailed off. The coyote had gotten a hold of the sleeve of Becky's sweatshirt and was pulling on it…as if to say, "follow me."

Becky pulled back on the material, and heard it tear. Ignoring her torn clothing, she looked over toward the bend in the road where she hoped the cab was still waiting on her. She knew another car could come by and catch her…and she didn't want anyone in Dean's family to see her looking like she was. She wished she was braver and could go to Steve and Bethany and ask for help. But she was embarrassed and humiliated and didn't want anyone to see her, especially the awful words that she couldn't scrub off her body.

"I have to go, Star," Becky said, finally tugging her sleeve free. "I wish I could stay. I wish I could be a part of this family, but I can't…" The coyote whined. "You just don't understand, Star…I can't go to him…he can't see me…" Her voice trailed off. Through her tears she managed to say, "You be a good girl. I'll miss you." She slowly stood up, wiped the tears from her face and made her way back to the cab.

* * *

The same afternoon Becky said goodbye to the little coyote, Dean arrived back into town and went straight to the refuge. The security job hadn't been tough physically, but it'd been torture for Dean mentally. He'd seen what the stalker had done to the woman and he'd made it his mission to make her feel as safe as possible. He'd patiently gone over and over the codes to the alarms and explained how they worked, just so she'd feel okay about her safety after he left.

Satisfied he'd done all he could, Dean made his way back home and to his *One*. He'd missed her terribly and felt bad he hadn't been able to talk to her while he was gone. He never liked being out of touch with his family for long periods of time, but there was no way he was going to leave the woman alone up in the mountains until he'd set up all the security systems.

He'd listened to Becky's phone message earlier and at first couldn't think about anything else but about how she'd told him she wanted to give them a chance and wanted to stay here with him. His heart leapt with joy. It wasn't until he couldn't get a hold of her when he'd called her back that he'd started to get concerned. He wondered if whatever happened on the show had something to do with it. He didn't like not having all the details and he definitely didn't like not being able to reach her. It made him twitchy, especially coming off of the job he had.

Now, heading to the refuge he still hadn't been able to connect with Becky. It was making him more than a little uneasy. He wanted to be able to see her and hold her to be sure everything was all right. He'd gotten used to being able to talk to her every day. He wanted to hear about what happened on the show and to make sure she was all right. He knew Becky had been having issues and desperately wanted to leave the set, and it killed him that he couldn't help her. All he could do was listen and try to support her from afar.

Dean pulled up to the house at the refuge center to talk to his dad and decompress. Helping with the animals was the best therapy he'd ever found, even if helping was mucking out the barn, and he was glad to be home. He cut the engine on his truck and massaged the kinks out of his neck. He'd been traveling a long time and wanted nothing more than to see and talk to Becky and possibly go for a run, in that order. He headed toward the house. The sooner he talked to his dad the sooner he'd hopefully see his woman.

The house was in chaos when he opened the door. The hair stood up on the back of his neck. All thoughts of being tired disappeared and he quickly walked over to his father. Steve saw him when he walked in the door and went over to intercept him.

"What's going on?" Dean asked quickly as he approached.

"Becky's missing." Steve told him without beating around the bush.

"What?" Dean roared, feeling dizzy. How could she be missing? What did he mean?

Steve steered his son toward a chair and motioned for the other employees to clear the room. Dean finally noticed Jonathan standing near their mother.

"What happened?" Dean asked again firmly.

Jonathan answered, "We don't know, bro'. She took herself off the show and then she disappeared."

Dean's head spun. Was this what she'd wanted to tell him that night?

"Start from the beginning," Dean ordered tightly.

Jonathan recounted the events from the other night. How Becky had enough of the show and essentially voted herself off. He explained what went down after she left with the twins and Marissa and how he went to the hotel after he was released from the set and couldn't get a hold of her. He explained how the next day, when he finally convinced a hotel employee to check on her, her room was empty. She'd left. They'd tried to track her down, with no luck. No one had seen her leave and they didn't know where she'd gone.

* * *

Dean sat in front of his brother and parents and tried to think about what to do next. He worked in security for a living, he should know what to do, but he couldn't wrap his mind around the fact that his *One* had just left...it felt like she'd left *him*. Had she not wanted to be with him after all?

328

She said on the phone message she wanted to stay, had she changed her mind?

He thought he'd made it clear he wanted to be with her, that she was his. Had Dean come on too strong? Had Becky decided he was too protective, too controlling? Too many questions were chasing through his head at once. He shook his head as if to clear it…and realized the noise he heard wasn't coming from inside him, but from outside in the pen, it was a coyote…howling mournfully out in the yard. Howling like that was unusual for a coyote. They were much more likely to communicate by yipping. He looked out the window, then back at his dad.

"She's been doing that for a while now. We can't get her to come near us, and she won't stop howling," Steve said.

Chills ran down Dean's back. It was Star. He knew it. She knew something, she was trying to communicate with them, but he hadn't been home. He knew how hard it was for the little coyote to trust. People generally didn't give animals enough credit. They knew when something was wrong. There were so many stories of dogs predicting earthquakes and other bad weather. Had Becky come back to see "her" coyote before she'd left? She had to have. How else would the coyote know to be upset?

He stood up so fast the chair he'd been sitting in was knocked to the ground. He strode toward the door, Steve and Jonathan following close behind. He went toward the gate and let himself into the enclosure. He walked toward the sound. Steve and Jonathan stayed back at the fence to watch. They'd both tried to get close to the little coyote with no luck. Every time they'd tried, the coyote had run off into the bush, only to return and start howling again once they'd left. Perhaps Dean could get near her. It was worth a shot.

Dean knew it wasn't like he'd be able to talk to the animal, but maybe he could at least calm her down. It was breaking everyone's hearts to hear the little coyote howl so mournfully.

Dean strode through the enclosure toward the tree line. He followed the sound of the coyote's howling. He slowed down when he saw the little coyote. She was sitting staring at the fence that lined the road to their refuge. Becky had to have been here. Why else would the coyote be sitting right there?

He said softly, "Star, what is it? What's wrong? Do you know what happened to my *One*? Where is she?"

He didn't know what to expect. He didn't think the coyote would suddenly stand up and start talking, but he sure didn't expect her to come running toward him and leap at him. He automatically caught her as he fell backward. Dean hoped she wasn't attacking him. He'd hate to harm her, but he'd protect himself.

As he lay on his back the coyote just stood over him. Staring at him. Staring into his eyes. Dean repeated more urgently, not even thinking about how silly it was to be talking to an animal as if it would answer him. "You know what happened, don't you? Oh God, I wish you could talk, where is she?"

Star backed off of Dean and kept backing up until she was a distance away from him. She howled again. Another mournful howl. Dean sat up and watched the coyote as she turned toward the fence once more and trotted over to it. She picked something up from the ground with her teeth and brought it over to where Dean was still sitting on the ground.

It was a piece of fabric. A small one, but it proved to Dean that Becky had more than likely been there. This coyote was smart. Dean looked at her again, closely. It dawned on him for the first time that she was probably mixed with some sort of dog. Many times coyotes would mate with feral dogs or even neighborhood dogs that were out and running around. Maybe that was why she was more willing to play with Becky and why she had such a close bond with her.

He stood up slowly, the material clutched tightly in his hand. Something was terribly wrong. He knew it. Becky wouldn't have come to say goodbye to the little coyote if she was coming back. Something had happened. Dean's stomach got tight, if she'd been hurt…enough of this bullshit. He had to do something. Becky wasn't leaving him without a word. He'd find her and fix whatever had happened to spook her.

Dean turned and started back toward the house. Surprisingly the coyote followed him closely, as if she knew he'd take care of her new friend.

When Dean arrived at the gate to the pen, he turned around and kneeled to face the little coyote. He held out his hand and she came to him without hesitation. Dean scratched her ears and bent toward her, saying for her ears only, "Thank you, Star. I'll get her back, I promise."

He then stood up and left the enclosure, heading back to where his family was standing. He saw that his brother was talking on the phone and listening intently to whomever was on the other side. Finally, he hung up.

"I had a hunch and called around to a few taxi companies. If she did leave the hotel she had to have gotten a ride from someone. She doesn't have a car here, so I figured she'd take a taxi somewhere."

The others nodded and Dean impatiently gestured for him to continue. He wasn't usually so brusque, but this was his woman and he was beyond worried about her.

Jonathan continued, "I got lucky and the second company I called had a record of picking up a woman from a restaurant near the hotel around the general time I figured she'd left. I got even luckier and got to talk to the driver himself." He paused and looked at his brother. "You're not going to like what he said, Dean."

Dean nodded. "I don't like any of this. Go on."

"He said she looked like she'd been beaten up," Jonathan said bluntly, knowing now wasn't the time to sugarcoat anything. They had to get to the bottom of what happened to Becky and find her. "She did come to the refuge. The driver said she asked to come here and he stopped outside the gates. She asked for him to wait and she went around the corner where he couldn't see her and was gone about ten minutes. When she came back she was crying. He tried again to get her to let him take her to a doctor, but she refused."

"Where did he finally drop her off?" Dean asked impatiently, trying to come to terms with all he'd learned in the last few minutes.

"He brought her to another hotel on the other side of the city," Jonathan said.

"Why didn't she come to us?" Bethany asked.

No one said anything for a moment until Dean finally answered the question he figured everyone was thinking. "I think she was embarrassed. She didn't want to be a burden. I've talked to her on the phone almost every night she's been in that house and on the show and gotten to know her pretty well. She wanted to let her little coyote know she didn't abandon her, but whatever happened must have humiliated and embarrassed her and she wasn't ready to see anyone."

"But Dean," his mom said haltingly. "She's your *One*, doesn't she know you'd protect her and she'd never have any reason to be embarrassed with you?"

"For starters," Dean tried to explain something he wasn't sure he completely understood. "She doesn't really know you guys. She only knows you're my family. Sure, she knows me pretty well after all our conversations, but remember, I wasn't here. She'd have to deal with you guys. She had no idea when I'd be back." His voice broke on the last word. He hadn't been here for her. On one hand he knew it wasn't his fault. He was working, it wasn't like he was away on a pleasure cruise, but on the other hand, irrationally, it felt like he'd let down the most important person in his life.

Dean cleared his throat and tried to ignore the compassionate looks his family was giving him. They knew how much this was hurting him. "The first instinct anyone has, be that a person or an animal, when they're hurt is to hide. We want to get away from what's scaring or hurting us. I've seen it over and over again with the women I help set up personal security for. I'm hoping I can find Becky and let her know that this is *her* refuge as much as it is an animal's. She can always come here to hide if I can't be around to let her hide in my arms."

He looked at his family standing around him, supporting him. "I'll find her," he said resolutely. "Jonathan, give me the address of the hotel she was dropped off at. I'll start there."

"I'll go with you," Jonathan said without hesitation.

God, Dean loved his family. They'd do anything for him without asking for anything in return. That loyalty was one reason why he still lived near his folks. He was so grateful Jonathan was making his way back to Arizona as well. He loved having him back in his life.

Steve's phone rang shrilly, startling everyone. He pulled it out of his pocket and saw it was an unknown number.

"Hello?"

"Hi. Uh, Steve?"

Steve frantically motioned to Dean as he answered. "Yes, Becky, it's me. Where are you? Are you okay? We've been worried sick about you." There was so much more he wanted to say, but first things first. They had to find her. Dean had to find her.

Becky answered softly, "I'm going to be fine. I'm so sorry I didn't call you right away. I know you said I could, I just…" Her voice faded off.

Dean was reaching for the phone at the same time Steve was holding it out toward him. Steve knew Dean had to talk to her.

"Sweetheart?" he said softly but urgently. "Tell me where you are and I'll come and get you. Whatever happened we'll get through together, okay?"

He heard her sniff and it about killed him.

Becky had to get the tough apology out of the way first. She knew with Dean's sense of family loyalty she was going to have to answer to that first of all. She repeated what she'd said to his dad. "I'm sorry I didn't call your dad or brother before."

"You're calling now, sweetheart, it's all that matters. Where are you?" Dean asked again. He didn't want to break the connection until he found that out.

He heard her take a deep breath. "I'm in town, I'm at the hospital." At his sharp inhalation she continued on quickly, "But I'm all right, Dean, I promise."

"We're on our way," he said to her, already walking toward his truck. His family immediately mobilized as well. There was no way they were letting Dean go without them. They figured both he and Becky would need their unwavering support to get through whatever happened.

"No, wait, don't hang up," Becky pleaded frantically, not wanting him to hang up. Now that she'd made the decision to call and now that she was actually talking to Dean, she didn't want to let him go.

"I'm not going anywhere, sweetheart," Dean said soothingly. "I'm not hanging up."

Becky sniffed again, frantically trying to hold her tears back. God, she couldn't lose it now. "I know you want to know what happened," she started hesitantly.

"Actually, no," Dean said surprisingly. "I want to wait for you to tell me where you've been and what happened while I have you safe in my arms."

There was dead silence on the other end of the line for a moment, then Dean heard her sobbing.

"Oh, Becky, God, please don't. Please don't cry when I'm not there with you. Hang on, I'll be there as soon as I can."

Becky tried to get it together. God, he never stopped surprising her with the sweet things he said. She figured most people would be clamoring to get the entire story immediately. She didn't want to tell him about the whole humiliating experience, but she didn't have a choice. One part of her wanted to tell him on the phone so she wouldn't have to face him, but that obviously wasn't going to happen. She had to warn him, though.

"Uh, Dean," she said, knowing he wasn't going to like what she said next.

"Yes, sweetheart?"

Becky could hear the truck start up and hear Jonathan in the background talking to someone. It looked like Dean's entire family was on their way as well. Lovely.

"I, uh, my face…" Hell, she had no idea how to tell him what she looked like.

"I know, Becky. We talked to the cab driver and he said you'd been beaten up. It's okay. It'll all be okay."

Becky nodded, knowing Dean couldn't see her. Thank goodness he already knew about her face. She figured he knew on one hand, but seeing it would be another story. Oh, well. Nothing she could do about that now.

Becky and Dean continued to talk about nothing in particular until Dean finally told her they were pulling up into the hospital parking lot and he'd be with her soon. They finally hung up. Becky sat on the edge of the bed nervously. They hadn't admitted her. She was beaten up, but as she'd told Steve, she was essentially all right. They'd put her right arm into a sling to keep her immobile so her collarbone could heal.

She was sitting on the edge of the bed, wearing the stupid hospital gown that was way too short when Dean, his parents and Jonathan came through the curtain. She looked up nervously. She had no time to say anything before Dean had caught her up in his arms and was holding her tightly.

Becky's face was nestled up against his throat. Her one good arm went around his waist without thought, while the other was smushed again his chest, secure in its sling. She felt one of his hands at the back of her head, holding her head to him gently, and the other was against her back, holding her close. She lost it. She couldn't stop the tears to save her life. Dean was here. He'd make everything better.

Dean turned them around and sat on the edge of the bed, holding Becky to him. God. He'd only gotten a glimpse of her face but that one glimpse was bad enough. He'd seen women who'd been beaten up before, but not someone who belonged to him. Not someone in *his* family. Not someone he loved. He suddenly knew how the relatives of the women he'd helped felt. Helpless. Like riding in a train car with no breaks. There was nothing you could do to make the hurt go away. The only thing he could do was hold her and let her cry. He was shaking. Him. The rock. Shaking. His *One* was hurt and he'd never let her go again.

Dean didn't know how long he'd been sitting on the bed holding Becky, but when he finally lifted his head and looked around he saw that his family was no longer in the room. They'd given him the privacy he needed with his woman.

Becky had stopped crying a bit ago and was now just sniffling. He could feel the wetness on his neck from her tears. He looked down at Becky and said, trying to lighten the moment, "You aren't wiping your snot on me, are you?"

Becky laughed lightly as he wanted her to. He took the hand that had been on her head and put a finger under her chin, raising her head until he could see her face fully for the first time. He held back his gasp and tried to look at her objectively.

She had two black eyes, and dark circles under them. Her lip was cut and had obviously been stitched, probably just that morning. He ran his thumb lightly over her lips while continuing to run his gaze over her face. God, what had she been through? And by who? He needed to hear the story, but he'd wait until she was ready. It was enough, for now, she was here in his arms and in one piece.

"Can you tell me what happened now, sweetheart? If not, that's okay, I'll wait, but please know you can trust me. I'm here for you. Nothing you say will change the feelings I have for you."

He watched as Becky nodded and quietly gathered her thoughts.

"I've watched TV, I've seen movies, I've read stories…" she began softly, "but I never thought I'd be in the position to be scared for my life and wonder if I'd live to see the next day."

Dean's arms tightened, and he consciously had to tell himself to loosen his hold. This was going to be torture for him, but he knew Becky had to get it out. Hell, he had to hear it. He wanted to know everything she went through so he could best figure out how to help her.

Becky continued, understanding that Dean had himself under control and he'd let her tell the story her way.

"I never figured anyone would hate me enough to want to hurt me. I couldn't understand that kind of hate. But I get it now. It's irrational. I tried to stop it, but eventually I figured out that they weren't going to stop no matter what I said."

"They?" Dean interrupted, barely holding on to his anger.

Becky nodded, and ignoring Dean's interruption continued. She told Dean everything that had happened after he'd left for the mountains. How she'd had enough after Derek had tried to attack her after their date.

Afraid Dean would lose control she was surprised when he simply said, "Good for you, Becky. You knew it was time to get out and you did."

"I wasn't scared at all when I left the house. All I could think of was you, and how I'd finally get to be with you out in public. It was such a relief." She sighed. She told Dean about seeing Derek and David getting out of the limo and having a bad feeling about it. She told him about how stupid she'd been by deciding to eat in the restaurant when she should've been staying in her room avoiding all the former contestants. She explained how the twins intercepted her while she was eating and about how drunk they were. She even told him about the attempted rapes and when they couldn't get hard how they'd started taunting her and hitting her. It wasn't until she started telling him about them writing on her that she broke down again.

"You know, as I lay on the floor of that hotel room I convinced myself it was better for them to hit me than to rape me. They hadn't broken me. I could take that. It wasn't until they got out the markers and started writing on me that I lost it."

Becky started to shake uncontrollably and Dean had to lean down so his ear was right next to her mouth to hear her next words. "I couldn't stand it that others would see what they did. It was one thing for them to try to rape me, no one could see that, no one would know, but to write all over me was different. Everyone would see. I couldn't go to your dad, Dean," she said miserably, "he'd *see* what they did."

"Ah Jesus, sweetheart," Dean crooned to the devastated woman in his arms. How did he make her understand what Derek and David did to her wasn't what people would see?

"My family sees *you*, Becky. What they did to you, isn't *you*. *You* are the woman their son is in love with. *You* are the woman who came to that refuge center and sat down on the ground and did whatever you could to make a small defenseless animal feel comfortable. *You* are mine, Becky. Mine. That's what they would've seen."

He let her cry against him again. God. If only her tears could wash away the feeling of those men touching her. If only they could wash away the feelings of helplessness and humiliation she was feeling.

Finally, Becky pulled back again and shyly looked up at Dean.

"You're in love with me?"

"God, yes. I know we have a long road ahead of us. You have to get some help too, so you can deal with what happened. We need to get you moved down here. We need to spend time together, just the two of us, and really get to know each other. But ultimately, I know deep in my heart, you're mine. You belong to me and I belong to you. I hope to Christ you'll learn to feel the same way, but I want you to know up front where I'm coming from. I'm not leaving you. I'll be at your side as we deal with this together."

"I want that too," she said, looking into his eyes.

She leaned forward and placed her lips lightly on his. Dean didn't want to hurt her and he gently ran his tongue along the seam of her lips, avoiding her stiches, and then pulled back.

"What did the doctor say? Are you allowed to leave?"

"I think she wants to come back in and talk to me some more. I already talked to the police…they took pictures," her voice cracked, but she bravely continued, "and said they'd be in touch."

Dean nodded. "Okay, we'll deal with them when they get back in touch with you. Are you allowed to get dressed?"

Becky nodded. "Are you going to help me?"

Dean shook his head. At seeing the shock and hurt in Becky's eyes at his negative answer, he quickly said, "The marker and the words don't matter one whit to me, sweetheart. Don't get me wrong, I want to literally kill them for hurting you, for doing that to you. But don't think for one second I don't want to look at your gorgeous body. I want to spend hours examining you and making sure you're all right. I want to take my time and check out all the nooks and crannies of what makes you, you. I want to lay you down and make love to you for hours and worship your body, *but* I want it to be at a time that *we* decide. In our bed. I want the first time I see you to be special for us both. I don't want it to be in a hospital room wondering if someone is going to walk in. I'll see what those assholes did to you Becky, make no mistake, but now isn't the time. Okay?"

Becky could only nod. God, every time he opened his mouth he slayed her with his sincerity and emotion.

"I'll just go and get my family while you get dressed. I'll send in a nurse to help you navigate around that sling. We'll meet you back here to talk with the doctor and I'll take you home."

Becky slowly got dressed with the nurse's help, thinking about all that had happened to her in the last couple of days. She'd had such extreme highs and lows she was amazed she was still standing upright. One thing was clear, however, Dean wanted her. She smiled and waited for him to return for her.

Dean returned and Steve, Bethany and Jonathan crowded into the small room behind him. Each of them gave her a huge gentle hug and didn't demand answers, she was thankful they were tactful enough to give her some time.

Finally, the doctor came in to talk to all of them.

"You're Rebecca's family?" she asked with a raised eyebrow.

Dean answered for all of them, "Yes, I'm her fiancé, and these are her future father and mother-in-law and brother-in-law."

The doctor looked to Becky for confirmation and she could only nod. She shouldn't have been shocked by Dean's words, but deep down she still was. She hadn't been a hundred percent sure he was serious about the entire being together thing, but obviously he was.

Dr. Sumner ran down the list of injuries Becky had. When she was done, Becky could see Dean and his family were looking a bit queasy.

"Honestly, guys," she said, trying to make them feel better. "It sounds a lot worse than it is."

"No, Becky," Jonathan disagreed, "it sounds just as bad as it looks. You're coming home with us, aren't you? You'll let us take care of you while you heal?"

Dean answered for her, "Yes, she's coming with me."

The others just nodded their heads as if it was a foregone conclusion all along.

Dr. Sumner wrote out a couple of prescriptions. One for pain and one for antibiotics. She encouraged Becky to go to her own physician for a follow-up in a few days. Becky was about to explain that she wasn't from around here and didn't have a doctor when Bethany piped up.

"Becky, I have a great physician. I'll make you an appointment. If you like her, then you can set up further visits with her."

It was settled. Becky was on her way home with Dean and his family. There was no place she'd rather be.

Chapter Fifteen

Becky knew the time had arrived to talk to Dean's family. They'd been so great to her. Very patient, and they didn't ask her why she hadn't come to them or anything. She owed them an explanation, but she only wanted to do it once. She didn't think she had the strength to go over it more than one time.

When they arrived back at the refuge center, which was also Steve and Bethany's home, they settled her on the couch and ran around trying to get her everything they thought she needed to be comfortable. Bethany brought her a pillow and a soft fleece blanket. Steve brought her a large class of water and Jonathan hovered nearby as if waiting for her to ask about needing something. Dean sat next to her on the couch and held her hand, not saying a word, but providing some much needed support just by being there.

"I wanted to talk to you all if you'd let me," Becky told them with only a hint of emotion making her voice crack. "I want to explain what I was thinking and why I didn't immediately come to you."

"Oh, honey," Bethany said immediately. "We understand."

"No," Becky said quickly. "You don't, but I'm hoping you will after I'm done."

Understanding this was apparently important to her, they all sat down around the couch to hear what she had to say.

"After I left the hotel I didn't know what to do. All sorts of thoughts were racing through my head. I thought I could just leave and pretend that nothing had happened. As time went on I started to hurt more and more. Everything hurt."

She could feel Dean tense beside her, but she tried to ignore it and continue.

"I got mad, at myself and at Derek and David. Who were they to do this to me and get away with it? If they'd done it to me, how many others would they do it to as well? Would they succeed in actually raping someone else? Had they done it in the past? I knew I had to stop them. But I was also mad at myself. I'm usually not so pathetic. I should've come to you guys right away. I know you would've helped me and not made me feel bad. I did know it. But I was embarrassed. I'm still embarrassed that you know what happened. I didn't want you guys to look at me with guilt or pity."

She took a deep breath. This next part was hard.

"I'm afraid you'll look at me differently now. Not just because of what my face looks like or because you know what happened to me, but because I let you all down. For all my talk about getting that little coyote to trust, at the first sign of trouble, *I* didn't trust you. I really am sorry I didn't contact you right away, Steve. I mean, I know I should have, but I was a coward."

Steve got up from his seat and came toward the vulnerable young woman sitting next to his son. He put his finger up to her lips gently to keep her from saying anything until he said his peace.

"You could never be a coward, Becky. You just needed some time to process what happened to you. In the end you *did* contact me. You called me to help you and we came. What I feel for you, what we all feel for you, isn't pity. We're sorry this happened. We're so sorry you're hurt and you had to go through that awful experience. We're pissed for you. We're pissed at those men. But there's no pity. The only thing we feel when we look at you is joy that you're here with us, with Dean, and that you'll be okay."

Becky sniffed and nodded. She leaned toward Steve hesitantly and put her one good arm around his neck. "Thank you, Steve. Thank you."

Steve hugged his son's woman gently, knowing she was still in pain. "I hope at some point you'll feel comfortable enough to call me Dad."

Becky leaned back to feel Dean's hand against her lower back. "I'd be honored…Dad," she said softly and grinned lopsidedly at him.

Becky turned when Dean said, "I'm just so sorry I wasn't there to protect you, sweetheart. That this had to happen to you…"

Becky shook her head. "It's not your fault, Dean. It would've happened if you'd been in town or not."

Dean shook his head, knowing that wasn't true. "We're going to have to disagree on that one, sweetheart. If I was in town, the second you left that damn show I would've picked up you and brought you home."

"But the contract…" Becky started to say.

"The hell with the contract. I would've brought you to my home, where you would've been safe," he told her, running his hand over her head and cupping her cheek again.

Becky closed her eyes and leaned against his hand.

She didn't want to admit to what she'd done, but she had to get it all out now. "I screwed up," she baldly told the group around her.

At the shake of Dean's head and the frown on Steve's face, she nodded her head. "Yes, I did. I knew I waited too long to come to the hospital after it happened and I took a shower." She bowed her head. "I knew I'd be destroying evidence, but I had to…I just had to." Her voice got really soft. "I did keep my clothes separate and they took samples when I did come in…I just hope it's enough."

Bethany was the one who came over toward Becky next and she put her hand on Becky's leg. "It's okay, Becky, believe me when I say we don't blame you and I know I would've done the same thing."

Becky didn't know how she'd gotten so lucky to have met this family, but she knew she'd be thanking her lucky stars for the rest of her life. They'd been so supportive and she knew she'd be a mess if it wasn't for them.

"Okay, guys," Bethany said a bit more cheerily, trying to lighten the mood a bit. "Let's go. Becky needs her rest. Dean, you stay."

Dean managed a smile. He loved his mom. She always seemed to know what someone needed, and right now Becky needed some time to process all his family had said and done for her.

Bethany and Steve left the room, but before Jonathan left, he came up to the couch and touched Becky on the shoulder.

"I'll take care of this for you," he said quietly. "I'm so sorry I wasn't there for you. I knew something was wrong and I came to the hotel that night, but when I couldn't find you I left. I shouldn't have, and for that I'll never forgive myself."

He turned to leave, but Becky reached up and grabbed his hand.

"Jonathan…please…this isn't your fault. Please, look at me," Becky pleaded with him.

Jonathan looked into her eyes and Becky could see how much he was torturing himself over her. She reached up and placed her hand on the side of his face, amazed at how right it felt and how she wasn't scared, even though this was the first time she'd ever touched this man. She was half afraid she'd never be normal again and never be able to touch another man without having flashbacks.

"Thank you for looking for me," she told him quietly. "I know you would've done everything you could to help me if you could have, and I'll forever be grateful for that." And amazingly she *did* know it. She wasn't sure if it was because of the odd connection she had with Dean or what, but she knew Jonathan would've done anything he could have for her.

Jonathan nodded. "Thanks, Becky. I'm going to go to the police station and talk to them about what I know about those two. I've watched them for the last month or so through the camera lens and I think I could probably help with some more information. I'm also going to talk to the other camera operators to see if they'd also help."

At seeing Becky's face drain of color, he quickly reassured her. "They don't know all that happened, Becky. All they know is that Derek and David beat you up. They don't know about…anything else."

Becky nodded and tried to remind herself she didn't do anything wrong. "Okay, any help they can give to get those two off the streets is good. I appreciate your help, Jonathan."

He leaned down and kissed her on the cheek, squeezed her hand and left the room.

Becky leaned back carefully so her back was to Dean's chest. He turned them so they were reclining on the couch. Dean put his arm around Becky's waist and held her to him. He couldn't believe he could've lost her. If Derek and David had been a bit more sober, or even had gotten their hands on some sort of weapon, they easily could've killed her. He'd seen it happen too many times in his line of work to take for granted the close call his *One* had.

He kissed the top of her head. "Relax, sweetheart. I've got you. We'll get this all figured out…later. For now, just relax and know you're safe. I'll always keep you safe."

Becky nodded off to sleep, secure in the knowledge that she was safe in Dean's arms.

Epilogue

The last couple of months had gone by in a blur for Becky. She'd stayed with Dean's family until she'd been able to move without pain and Dean had quickly moved her into his home. It was, of course, gorgeous. She ended up quitting her underwriting job because Dean's parents had offered her the chance to work at the refuge center with them. They'd sworn it wasn't a pity job, and Becky eventually believed them. She worked her butt off and loved every minute.

Dean agreed to move Star into their home. It was a bit of a risk, since she wasn't a full blooded domestic dog, but Star had proven to be very loyal to Becky and hardly ever left her side. She was allowed to come to the refuge center every day with Becky and seemed to know when it was appropriate to laze around on the porch at the house when she was working with skittish abused animals, and when it was okay to tag along aside her as she did chores. Even when it looked like Star was sound asleep on the porch, she always knew where Becky was. It was as if the two of them had some telepathic connection with each other. The second Becky would finish working with an animal Star couldn't be around, the little coyote-mix would bound off the porch and find her beloved Becky.

Dean told Becky about how Star had kept the scrap of fabric she'd torn off her sleeve when Becky came to say goodbye. Becky was amazed. All she could do was hug the little coyote-mix and thank her for her unconditional love.

Derek and David had been found. Incredibly, they hadn't even been hiding. Jonathan had kept his word and gone to the police, along with Kina and a few other camera operators and they'd told the cops everything they knew about the brothers. It turned out they'd actually been arrested in the past for attempted rape, but because the woman was scared to testify, they hadn't been convicted of the crime.

Derek had tried to claim the night was consensual, and David had tried to blame everything on his brother. So much for brotherly love. They were eventually sentenced to five years in jail for kidnapping and attempted rape, among other things. They were convicted mostly based on the testimony from Becky. She knew they probably wouldn't spend that much time in jail and would make probation, but she was glad at least they'd pay for what they did to her. She didn't worry about them coming after her, she had Dean, and Jonathan, and their parents and all of the employees who worked at the refuge looking out for her. She felt safe.

Becky hadn't wanted to testify. It scared her to death to face the two men in the courtroom, but she knew she had to. She knew they'd do it to someone else eventually if she chickened out. With the help of her therapist, and her new family, she was able to get through the trial.

Dean and his family had been amazing. She knew her own family had loved her, but the no strings attached love Steve and Bethany had shown her was amazing. They joked with her, and even sometimes cried with her when she needed it. Amazingly, it didn't even feel awkward.

Becky couldn't believe how much she loved Dean. When he'd taken her home after she got out of the hospital he'd done exactly what he said he would. He undressed her slowly and lovingly caressed every inch of her body. The words Derek and David had written on her body in the permanent marker were still faintly visible and he'd kissed every single one and replaced the memory of them being etched on her body with the memory of his lips kissing and nipping at her skin. He never took his own clothes off that first night, not wanting her to feel any pressure or remember how *their* naked bodies felt against her own. After trying to wipe out all the negative emotions she'd received at their hands, he simply wrapped her up in his arms and held her all night long.

Dean never told her he hadn't slept at all that night, but she'd overheard him telling Jonathan. Apparently, he'd watched her sleep and cried. He was just so overcome with emotions. He'd finally gotten to see firsthand what those two creeps had done to her body. It was such a bittersweet moment. He told Jonathan he'd been overwhelmed with joy at being able to touch her for the first time, but also furious at how she'd been violated. She never told him she'd overheard him having the emotional conversation with his brother, but hearing his words helped her heal. He hadn't been disgusted at seeing her. Rather more awestruck at how strong she'd been to get through it.

It took some time for Becky to convince herself she'd done all she could to get away and to let go of the negative feelings that had lingered. The weekly visits to the therapist helped immensely. Every now and then when she felt overwhelmed she'd make an appointment to go back and see her. Every time, she felt lighter. She knew eventually she wouldn't need to see her anymore, but for now she was content.

One night while they were eating dinner at the refuge, Steve told Becky the story about the men in their family and their *One*. She was amazed.

"Was that how it happened with you?" she'd asked Dean incredulously. He'd only nodded and said calmly, "Yes, I knew you belonged to me from the moment I saw you look up from that rock at Devil's Canyon and your eyes met mine."

Becky knew she was the luckiest woman alive. And to think if it hadn't been for the stupid reality show she never would've met Dean.

Jonathan was currently in Alaska on his last assignment as a camera operator. He hadn't wanted to go, but Becky convinced him she was fine. She knew he still felt guilty about not searching harder for her when he'd gone to the hotel that night, but she'd tried to reassure him that there wasn't anything else he could've done.

Jonathan was excited to move back to Arizona to be with his family and start working with Dean. He'd seen firsthand how abusive people could be and he wanted to be a part of protecting those who needed it.

Eddie and his production crew got off relatively easily after the fiasco with Derek and David. The lawyers tried to convince Becky to press charges against Eddie on the grounds he should've done a more extensive background check on the applicants for the show. They argued if he had, then Derek and David's past allegations against them would've come to light and Becky never would've been hurt. Becky declined. She honestly just didn't want to think about it anymore and wanted to put the entire nightmare behind her.

Dean gave her the best advice, though. Becky still grinned every time she thought about it. He suggested the lawyers get in writing as a part of the condition of her not suing Eddie and the production company in the future, that the reality show never be aired. Becky didn't think Eddie would go for it, especially considering how much money had already been spent on the production of the show, but surprisingly he did. She supposed he probably had some pressure put on him from the executives, but whatever the reason, she was thrilled.

Becky didn't have to worry about what she'd look like to millions of people and she *never* had to worry about seeing re-runs of Derek and David haunting her forever. She thought about Marissa and how all her dreams of becoming famous went down the drain and had to laugh. Becky figured she deserved it. She felt bad for about ten minutes, but Dean distracted her by picking her up and carrying her to their bedroom, and all thoughts of Marissa and what she thought disappeared in an instant.

* * *

Jonathan stood in the wind and shivered. God, he couldn't wait to be done with this stupid show and get back

349

to Arizona where it was warm. He looked out of the corner of his eye at Kina. Kina. His *One*. She was standing next to him, also filming. He'd been blown away when he'd gone to talk to her after they'd found Becky and realized in an instant that Kina was his. Damn. He hadn't ever really talked to her much or even seen her very often on the set in Arizona. It was only when he needed her help he'd actually realized that not only was she incredibly beautiful, but she was the one woman made especially for him.

He never really believed the *One* nonsense his dad had always talked about growing up, until he'd seen it happen to his brother. Dean had taken one look at Becky and known he wanted to spend the rest of his life with her. It'd taken a while, but eventually Becky fell for him too and now, even after everything Becky had gone through, they were together and happy.

Jonathan knew Kina would be a different story. She was hard. He didn't know how he knew that, but he did. She didn't smile much and he'd overheard her talking with another camera operator about how she didn't believe in love anymore. Something had happened to her to make her think that way. He was trying to figure out a way to get closer to her, but it was difficult. She stayed to herself and didn't encourage the other camera operators to get close to her. He'd find a way, though, he had to. She was his. Even if she didn't know it. She'd figure it out in the long run.

Frozen Hearts

Beyond Reality
Book 3

by Susan Stoker

Chapter One

Alaska was cold. That was the first thing Jonathan Baker thought after walking out of the airport in Anchorage. Hell, it was September, it theoretically wasn't *that* cold yet, but apparently his Arizona blood wasn't used to it. He knew it was going to be a long shoot.

This was Jonathan's last job before he could go home to Arizona and start work with his brother Dean. Dean was an independent consultant and set up security for businesses and others who requested his services. He also did some pro-bono work for women who'd been stalked or who had an ex-husband or boyfriend who wouldn't leave them alone.

Jonathan couldn't wait. He loved his brother and his family. He was thrilled Dean and Becky had finally ended up together after the fiasco of a reality show Jonathan had just filmed. The producer, Eddie, was good at his job, but he tended to only see money signs when dreaming up different ways to put 'normal' people on television. It had backfired on him in Arizona because he hadn't done his homework when choosing the contestants. Two of the men who'd been voted off the show had hurt Becky in retaliation.

Luckily, they were too drunk to do any lasting harm, although they'd beaten the crap out of her. As a result of the entire thing, after the lawyers got involved, it was determined that Eddie wasn't allowed to air the reality show Becky had been on. Jonathan knew both his sister-in-law and brother were relieved not to have to deal with the publicity and any mental issues that might be triggered in Becky by watching the show and re-living the events.

Jonathan was just thrilled his brother had found his One in Becky. Throughout their family history, the men in their family found they had one woman in the world who was meant for them. Finding her was never easy, but as soon as they met her, they knew. No one understood it, but they'd heard story after story of it happening. Becky was Dean's One. He'd taken one look at her and known. Of course she was on a reality show to find love and Dean wasn't a contestant, so it took a bit of time, but eventually everything had worked out.

They'd gotten married in a small but very emotional ceremony at the family's animal refuge. Becky had wanted to elope to Vegas and do it there, but Dean wanted to give her a proper wedding, even if it was small and low-key.

Jonathan loved Becky and was thrilled to have her as a part of their family. She was great for Dean and she loved the family and the animal refuge his parents owned and operated in Arizona. Jonathan was still trying to get over what he perceived as his role in her ordeal, but thank goodness she'd put the incident mostly behind her. He only wished he could put it behind him as easily.

It was only a matter of time before Jonathan could get back to the warm weather of Arizona and his new career, but he had this one last job to complete as a camera operator on the reality show to finish first. Since Eddie's last production hadn't worked out, he'd completely changed the theme of his current reality show. He'd apparently had enough of trying to hook people up and decided to go with a "tough man" theme. This show in Alaska was about men trying to compete with each other to be crowned the one and only 'Extreme Alaskan.'

It was quite a change from the man's previous shows and Jonathan wasn't sure Eddie could pull it off. It seemed to Jonathan that there were a lot of additional safety factors that would have to be taken into account and he wasn't sure Eddie had even thought about them. If the men on the show were going to have to survive extreme Alaskan conditions, he hoped Eddie had made all of the contestants sign a liability waiver. Maybe he'd learned his lesson after the Arizona show.

Jonathan was one of a handful of camera operators. The number of crew had been reduced drastically for this show. Eddie said this was because it wasn't necessary to film the contestants back at the house they'd rented as men typically didn't have as much drama as women when they were cooped up together. Besides, Eddie had said he didn't really care if they did have drama, he was going to concentrate on filming their extreme challenges and not their antics back at the house. Jonathan figured Eddie was also probably trying to save money. He'd lost a ton of it since he hadn't been able to air his last show, so fewer camera operators equaled less money spent here in Alaska. Cheapskate.

Jonathan was looking forward to this job more than ever, because it was his last one behind the camera. This wasn't what he wanted to do with the rest of his life, and thanks to Dean, he was going to get a chance to do something different. He was also excited about this job because he'd be spending time with Kina, another camera operator. Kina was his One. She'd been filming on the last show in Arizona. Jonathan hadn't truly met her until the end of the show, when he'd gone to the other camera operators for help when Becky had been hurt. Kina was standoffish and somewhat rude to most everyone, but the first time Jonathan spoke to her, he knew. She was his. Somehow, some way, he'd have to make her see it.

* * *

Kina Venable shook her head. Eddie was an idiot. She had no idea why they had to film this stupid show in the wilds of Alaska, but once Eddie got something in his head, no one could change his mind. She'd been working with Eddie for a while now, as part of his crew in Australia and on the show they'd just finished in Arizona. She'd pretty much decided this would be the last time she worked for him, though. He wasn't very savvy when it came to people. Oh, he was a great producer and knew how to generate great dramatic TV, but he had no clue when it came to treating people with respect.

357

Kina had become good friends with Sam, one of the female contestants on the show in Australia. After the show was over, Kina had kept in touch with her. That was uncharacteristic for Kina, as she was standoffish with most people, but Sam had saved her life, and honestly, Kina liked her and wanted to get to know her better. She had spent some time visiting Sam after the last show wrapped up, needing the down-time. Seeing what'd happened to Becky had shaken her up.

She loved seeing how happy Alex and Sam were now. Eddie had tried to make sure they didn't end up together in Australia, but even editing Sam out of the reality show altogether hadn't kept the two apart.

Spending time on their ranch in Texas was always so peaceful. Sam was down-to-earth and always wanted to please everyone. Kina didn't trust many people in her life, but Sam was now one of the few people she'd trust with any secret. Something about the other woman made Kina want to open up and share her thoughts and feelings.

While she'd visited, she and Sam spent a lot of time talking about what had happened to Becky in Arizona. Kina was horrified the men she'd gotten to know through the camera could have it in them to do something so hideous to another human being. Kina would never understand how people could do such awful things to someone else. Murderers, stalkers, rapists, pedophiles…the list went on and on. Both Kina and Sam agreed the world could be a scary place. Thank goodness Becky was all right and had Dean to lean on, now.

Kina wasn't jealous—exactly, she was happy for her friend Sam, and for Becky, but even as tough as she always acted, she wanted what they had. She hadn't had good luck finding a man who would let her be who she was, though. Because of her experiences she knew she'd become cynical and had a reputation for being a man-hater.

But for now, Kina was stuck in Alaska. As luck would have it, she was the only female camera operator on the show. Eddie had pared down the number of operators to only five. He was being really tight with money. Because of all the crap that went down in Arizona, he'd completely changed the premise of the show from another *'find your soul mate'* type of show, to a more extreme, *'see how macho you can be'* format. Just the sort of thing Kina hated.

She'd had enough of men acting like they were God's gift to women and behaving as if they were superior in all ways to everyone around them, especially women. Lately, she didn't like many of the guys she met. She wasn't a lesbian, although at times she thought it was a pity that she didn't swing that way. She was tired of having to have to deal with a man's crap in order to get laid. She just wanted to find a man who'd let her be who she was, but at the same time would be there for her. Her last relationship was such a disaster it almost turned her off to dating altogether. Matt had been a complete jerk. She couldn't even remember what it was that she'd liked about him in the first place.

It was ridiculous. She knew she was being unreasonable. She wanted a guy who'd let her do whatever it was she wanted to do, but yet would be as sweet to her as Alex was with Sam. Gah. She was totally messed up in the head. A man like that likely didn't exist.

Kina thought about the guys who also operated the cameras on the show. She'd worked with all of the men who were contracted for this show at one time or another. Carl and Taylor, she knew from the Australian show, Jonathan, she knew from Arizona, and Jeff, she'd worked with on a past show, with a different producer.

Jeff was a jerk; she'd learned that from working with him in the past. Carl and Taylor were good men. They were both married and pulled out pictures of their kids all the time to show off, whenever they could. Carl's kids were Celeste and Catherine. And Taylor also happened to have two daughters, Phyllis and Beth. Kina loved listening to them try to outdo each other when telling stories about how cute their daughters were. Their stories were always hilarious, and of course, their kids were adorable.

Jonathan was altogether different. He made her nervous. She couldn't put her finger on why, he just did. Not nervous as in she was scared he'd hurt her, just nervous as in jittery. He was single, always polite, and she liked the way he went out of his way to help Becky when the assholes on the last show had hurt her, but there was just something about him that threw her for a loop.

He was way too good-looking, for one thing. Not many men could pull off long hair and not look like a seventies biker dude, but he managed it. His black hair was thick and went down to about the middle of his back. He usually wore it pulled back in a ponytail so it didn't get in his way while he was working. His main outfit of choice was faded jeans and a tight shirt. They were mostly short-sleeved when they had filmed in Arizona, but up here in Alaska, they were long-sleeved.

Kina never saw him lose his cool. Ever. He was the most even-keeled person she'd ever met, besides herself, and that freaked her out. It was her experience that people, especially men, were hot-headed and impulsive. Even Taylor and Carl got upset at Eddie, the contestants, each other, her…but not Jonathan.

Kina always tried to be honest with herself, but it was hard to admit that she admired Jonathan and might even like him. She typically didn't like men. But somehow, something, wouldn't let her dismiss Jonathan as easily as she had other men in the past. She admired him. That was what made him different from the other men she'd known. He was tenacious and had made sure he'd gotten all of the camera operators to talk to the police in Arizona to help Becky, and he wasn't even in love with her. That kind of loyalty and compassion was rare in Kina's life and watching it made her crave it for herself. What would it feel like to have someone feel that way about her? To have that loyalty to her? It was something she'd never had, but now that she'd seen it firsthand, she wanted it to the bottom of her soul.

There was no way she'd do anything about it however, she'd just have to make it through the next six weeks until the show was over. Unless Eddie changed drastically, she'd find another production company to join up with and be on her way.

Chapter Two

Eddie gathered his camera operators around him for their first production meeting before the contestants were to arrive later that day.

"Hello again, everyone. Welcome to Alaska. I wanted to make sure you knew what I expected of you for this shoot and what the general plan is for the show. As you know, this is not a dating show. I'm bringing in twelve men to compete in typical Alaskan challenges each week. At the end of the six weeks, there will be two men left and they will have to go out in the wild and survive over a three day period. The person who completes all of the tasks the best will be named the ultimate *Extreme Alaskan*.

"The plan for the first few weeks is to travel only a short distance away from Anchorage to compete in mini-challenges. While those challenges are going on, you'll all have to be on hand for filming. When we aren't filming challenges, your time will mostly be your own, as will the contestants'. They won't be allowed to leave the production house, but neither will we be filming them all day, every day, either.

"Generally, you'll all be working at the same time. You won't be assigned to work all day every day, but it'll vary with what is going, as to how long you'll work. I've procured a different hotel than where you stayed last night. This one is closer to the production house. You'll stay there for the rest of the shoot. I expect you to arrive at the set on time and to work your entire shift. There's a rental SUV that you'll have to share. You pay for your own gas if you decide to go anywhere other than the set and the hotel. It's up to the five of you to figure out who's driving when and where. I don't have time to deal with that crap. Also, I've had enough drama to last me a lifetime, so keep it to yourselves. I don't want to hear about it. Nothing can go wrong on this show, and I mean nothing. The rest of my career depends on this show going off without a hitch. Does anyone have any issues with anything I've said so far?"

Nobody said a word. Even Jeff, who was usually a complete smartass, kept his mouth shut. It was obvious Eddie was dead serious and that his past legal troubles had changed the type of producer he was.

"Great," Eddie said, continuing with his rules for the show. "When we get down to the last few challenges they'll most likely be overnight wilderness trips. You'll be split up and will be paired together to watch and film the men competing in and completing the challenges. The contestants will be sent out either in pairs or in a trio and there will be two cameras on them the entire time. I expect you to work together amicably and to get the money shots while they're out there. If you don't think you can hack the temperatures or the kind of terrain we'll be sending the contestants out in, let me know now and I'll replace you."

Kina scowled at Eddie, as he stared right at her. She glared back. Just because she was female didn't mean she couldn't handle the cold temperatures. What a jerk. When she didn't say anything, Eddie finally nodded his head and continued.

"All the contestants have signed waivers of liability so if anything happens to them on the set, anything at all, no one can come back and sue us. You're all covered as well because of the contract you signed. If you get hurt, you're covered by the company's insurance." Left unsaid, was the implication that the show would be aired no matter what might happen to a contestant or one of the camera operators as well.

"Great. Well, if you have no questions, I'll meet you all back at the production house at three this afternoon where you'll meet the men and we can get this show started."

At no point did Eddie thank them for their time or for their service. They were employees, no more and no less.

Kina watched as Eddie threw a set of keys to Taylor. He caught them midair and turned to the rest of them with a smirk. "Who's driving?" he asked unnecessarily.

They all agreed that Taylor could be the designated driver for now. He was the oldest and no one had any issues with him driving them around.

They all checked into the hotel and found their rooms were on the same floor, clustered together at the end of a hallway. It wasn't the fanciest place to stay in Anchorage, but it wasn't a dump either. Kina was actually a bit surprised. With the money problems Eddie and the production company had, she figured they'd be put up in a 'rent by the hour' kind of place. Kina noticed her room was right next to Jonathan's. She tried to ignore the tingles in her stomach at the thought of him being that close, but deep down, she was pleased.

* * *

Jonathan had listened to Eddie's words with only half an ear. He was standing by Kina and trying not to watch her as they all listened to the producer. She was beautiful. Not very tall, but all muscle. The top of her head came up to about his shoulder. She might be small, but he knew she was strong as hell. He'd watched her lug her camera equipment all over the set in Arizona and knew firsthand how heavy it was. She was no-nonsense and he admired the hell out of her for agreeing to film here. Alaska in September and October wasn't a walk in the park. After learning they'd all have to be trekking along with the contestants and roughing it just as they were, he was even more impressed. He didn't think she'd back out of the challenge and he was right.

He did have to tamp down his desire to speak up and tell her she shouldn't do it. He knew it wouldn't be safe. He saw how she'd glared at Eddie, when the man had dared to look at her when he was telling them to let him know if anyone didn't think they could handle the filming schedule and atmosphere. She wouldn't hesitate to put him in his place if Jonathan piped up and said anything to her.

Eddie had a lot to prove, so he knew the challenges and situations the contestants would be put in would be extreme. And if the men were doing extreme things, the camera operators would have to be as well, because they had to get it all on film. It wasn't as if he didn't think Kina could do the things they'd be asked to do, he just didn't want her to get hurt or even be uncomfortable. He was smart enough to keep his mouth shut, though. Kina would hate him for sure, if he even for a second, insinuated she shouldn't do it.

He was thrilled beyond words, to be right next door to her in the hotel, even though their rooms didn't have connecting doors. Just being close to her made him feel more relaxed. It was silly, she was a grown woman and had been taking care of herself for her entire life, but he felt reassured just the same. Of course the other camera operators were also nearby. That didn't sit as well with him, but Jonathan tried to reassure himself that Carl and Taylor were happily married. He didn't know Jeff at all, but would give him the benefit of the doubt, for now.

In about three hours, it'd be time to get to the set and start setting up for their first shoot. This was always an exciting time for the contestants and camera operators alike. The time for planning was over. The show was about to start.

Chapter Three

Because this program wasn't a dating show, Eddie had ditched his previous host, Robert. But since he knew he had to market the show to both men and women, he'd hired a woman named Shannel to be the host of this new reality show. Shannel was tall, slender, and of course, beautiful. She had an innate grace about her. Kina wanted to hate her at first glance, both because of the woman's looks and her own experiences with the previous beautiful women on Eddie's shows, but unfortunately she couldn't. Shannel was a riot. She swore like a sailor and had a wicked sense of humor. It was really hard to dislike her when the first words out of her mouth when she met all the camera operators were, "Thank you for all the hard work you do."

Jonathan, Kina, and the other camera operators got to work setting up their equipment so they'd be ready when Eddie started the show. Jonathan watched Jeff sidle up to Kina and start flirting with her. He really wasn't surprised when she ignored him and continued getting her camera ready to go. Jonathan heard Jeff mumble, "Dyke" as he walked away toward his own camera. Jonathan just shook his head. Why did guys do that? If they couldn't score with a woman they automatically accused her of being a lesbian. Ridiculous.

When the time came to set up their places for filming, Jonathan made sure he was between Kina and Jeff. There was no use even pretending he wanted Jeff anywhere near her. He mentally shrugged as Eddie introduced the contestants.

Most of the men were tall and all were muscular. Jonathan thought they'd all have some outdoor experience, or at least some sort of survivalist job, but Eddie was smarter than that. He knew there were already shows on television about extreme survivalists competing against one another.

Eddie had chosen strong muscular men, but ones with regular jobs.

Jonathan knew he'd never keep them straight, but then again, he didn't really have to. His job was to film them, regardless of who they were. As long as he had good camera angles and got all their actions on film, nothing else mattered.

Kina was fascinated with the group of men Eddie had picked for his show. The men were all good-looking and from all walks of life. Slade was a lawyer, Julio designed websites, Trent was a nurse, Zach worked in IT, Ian owned his own restaurant, Benedict was a licensed sex therapist, Drew was a probation officer, Nash wrote articles for a newspaper, Cole was a security officer, Grant was a radiologist, Roger a teacher and last, was Darius, a chemist.

It was an eclectic mix of people and jobs, and most likely, personalities. Eddie might claim to not want drama and to believe there wouldn't be any at the production house, but Kina knew he was wrong. Sometimes men could provide more drama than their female counterparts, they were usually more subtle about it, though. At the very least, the competition itself would cause the men to have some disagreements.

Kina worked in tandem with the other camera operators to get close-ups of the contestants and to get good angles of Shannel meeting each man and introducing the premise of the show. Everyone seemed eager to get started. The first challenge would be the next morning. Two men would be sent home then. Eddie's general plan was to send two men home each time they had a competition. Kina could tell the contestants were nervous, but excited at the same time.

The ride back to the hotel was filled with good humor. Everyone on the crew was in good spirits and was excited to get the show started. When they arrived back at the hotel, everyone piled out and headed toward their rooms. Jonathan watched as Kina unlocked her door and stepped inside. He made sure the door shut securely behind her and turned to glare at Jeff, who'd been watching Kina from his door as well. The other man gave Jonathan a chin lift and closed his door.

Jonathan took a deep breath. Should he or shouldn't he? It was killing him to let Kina be, knowing she was his, but he didn't have a choice. He couldn't very well invite himself into her room and settle in, no matter if he really wanted to do so. He'd barely spoken with her and he knew she was very closed-off. He didn't want to do anything to turn her against him before she really got to know him. He'd just have to wait. It wasn't what he wanted to do, but for now he'd do it.

The camera crew had arranged to meet at the car early the next morning so they could get to the set on time and be ready to go when Eddie assembled the contestants. Jonathan subtly arranged to sit next to Kina in the far back seat.

"Good morning, Kina."

"Good morning, Jonathan."

"Did you sleep well?"

"Yes, you?"

"Not really."

Kina looked directly at him for the first time that morning, her eyebrows raised. Jonathan answered her unasked question.

"I never sleep well the first night in a strange place." He debated what he wanted to say next and decided to go ahead and tell her something personal about himself in the hope she'd want to get to know him better. "I also sometimes have nightmares, so I generally don't sleep well anywhere."

Wow. Kina wasn't sure what to say to that. She desperately wanted to know more about the handsome man sitting next to her, but she didn't want to be nosey. She knew she had a reputation of being standoffish, but she didn't want to be with this man. Aw, the hell with it. He'd brought it up in the first place.

"Nightmares?"

"Yeah, nothing I want to go into here and now, but if you get to know me better, I'll share."

Kina blushed. Shit. She hadn't meant to lead him on in any way. She never did with any man, but he took her words the wrong way. She tried to backpedal. "I didn't mean…"

Jonathan interrupted her. "It's okay. I want to get to know you better and I want you to get to know me better. I probably shouldn't have thrown that out there, knowing we didn't have the time, or the privacy, to talk." He looked her in the eyes and lowered his voice, knowing the others in the car were probably listening. "I like you, Kina." He laid it on the line.

Kina blushed again. Double shit. She liked what she knew of him too, but didn't want to encourage him. Things with guys never worked out with her. Ever. Even if she wanted them to. She had to protect herself.

"Well, I don't think I like you." She turned away from him and focused on the scenery.

Jonathan laughed. Kina fumed. How dare he laugh! He was supposed to get pissed at her, any other normal man would. She didn't understand him at all.

Neither of them said anything else all the way to the set. When they arrived, Kina immediately got busy with her equipment and tried to ignore Jonathan altogether. She didn't miss it when he stepped in front of Jeff and blocked him from setting his gear down next to hers. Interesting. She appreciated that more than she could say, but she'd never tell him. Jeff was a pain in her butt. She was constantly rebuffing him, but it never seemed to make any difference. He was like an annoying little puppy, no matter how often you scolded him, he always came back for more.

Eddie had obviously briefed Shannel about the day's activities because the hostess gathered the contestants together once the cameras were up and running to explain how the day would go. Everyone was invited into the dining room at the house where the long table was set with twelve place settings, one for each contestant. The men were instructed to each stand behind one of the chairs around the table. Once everyone was in place, Shannel explained the first challenge.

"I hope you all like to eat! A big part of survival in Alaska is being able to find enough to eat. As you know, Alaska is home to a booming fishing and seafood industry. Many people make their way up to our fiftieth state to make a living off the abundance of seafood in our rivers and seas. Today, your challenge is courtesy of Humpy's Great Alaskan Alehouse right here in Anchorage. It's called the Six Pound Seafood challenge. Yes, you heard me correctly. Your challenge today is to eat six pounds of seafood as fast as you can. The restaurant has their own name for this, they call it the Kodiak Arrest Challenge. For our challenge today, the two men who finish their six pounds the slowest will be leaving the show and won't have the chance to be crowned Extreme Alaskan. If there are more than two people who can't finish all their food, we will weigh whatever is left to see who'll be leaving. In this case, the two men who've eaten the lowest number of pounds of food will be going home.

"On the menu today are three pounds of luscious King Crab legs, a one-and-a-half-foot-long fresh reindeer sausage, seven salmon cakes, mashed potatoes, mixed vegetables, and for dessert, one berry crisp. You have no time limit to eat everything, but remember, the two people who finish the slowest and eat the least amount of food will be leaving. Does anyone have any questions?"

Kina laughed silently as she looked through her camera lens and saw the looks of dismay on most of the men's faces. Six pounds was a lot of food, especially considering they hadn't been warned about the food challenge. They'd most likely eaten a large breakfast to prepare themselves for the day.

The men all sat down and their plates were loaded up with the platters of food from the servers at Humpy's. This was great publicity for the small alehouse and they'd donated the food for free. Again, Kina thought Eddie could be a jerk, but he definitely knew his business.

As the bell rang for the contest to start, the cameras rotated around the table. Every slurp, every burp, and every bite of food was immortalized on camera for the world to see. Kina wondered for the millionth time why anyone ever agreed to be on a reality show. If only they could see what she saw through her lens. Oh, Kina knew much of it would be edited out, but it was still disgusting. She never wanted to see herself on the big screen. She was perfectly happy in the background.

After about thirty-five minutes Nash was the first one finished with his plate of food. He triumphantly raised his arms and declared himself, "Done!"

Kina nearly snorted out loud. She wasn't sure that finishing all that food first was something to crow about.

Shannel agreed that he'd finished and he was escorted to a platform behind the table to wait for the others to finish. Slowly, some of the others finished their portions. Darius, Roger, Cole, and Grant were the next four to finish. They joined Nash on the platform. There were seven men still eating. Finally, after ten more minutes, Slade and Julio joined the others. Now there were only five men left. It didn't look like any of them were going to be able to finish all the food on their plates.

When they'd all finally given up, Shannel motioned for the scales to be brought in so they could see who ate the least.

From the camera's perspective it was disgusting. The leftover food for each man was piled together in a bowl and placed on the scale. Kina made sure to get some good close-up shots of the uneaten food dripping down the side of the bowls. Yuck.

After all the weighing was done, Shannel gathered all the men in a room next to the dining room. They lined up and Kina barely paid attention as Shannel did a run-through of the contest. The hostess asked some of the men to discuss their strategy and to talk about what the hardest part of the competition was. When all was said and done Shannel dramatically announced that Zach and Drew had eaten the least and were declared the losers.

Kina followed Drew as he went up the stairs to pack, as Taylor followed Zach. The two men didn't say much, at least nothing that was dramatic enough to make it into the edited version of the show. The two men were escorted out of the building, with Kina and Taylor hot on their heels filming every aspect of their departure.

Meanwhile, back in the decision room, Jeff, Carl, and Jonathan filmed as Shannel told the remaining ten contestants to get some rest because the competitions would only get more difficult as time went on. She explained that the last two men standing should expect to spend a couple of nights out in the wilderness to complete challenges to determine who would be deemed the Extreme Alaskan.

* * *

Jonathan watched as Kina laid her head back on the seat in the car as they all headed back to the hotel. His fingers actually twitched to take her head in his hands and give her a massage to try to help her get rid of her headache. He didn't think she'd appreciate his familiarity. He knew she noticed that once again, he blocked Jeff's attempts to sit next to her in the car, but he didn't care. As far as he was concerned, this was assigned seating and he'd always get to sit next to Kina.

"How about we all get together and have a beer at the bar?" Carl asked as they neared the hotel.

"Sounds good to me," Jeff and Taylor agreed.

Jonathan looked at Kina, waiting to see what she wanted to do. When she didn't say anything he nudged her with his shoulder. "What do you say?"

Kina opened her eyes to look at Jonathan with surprise. "Oh, me too?"

"Hell yeah, why wouldn't you think you were invited?" Carl said with surprise from the front seat.

"Well, I just figured you'd want to hang out with the guys." Kina said honestly.

"You are one of the guys, Kina," Carl said laughing.

Kina heard Jonathan say under his breath, "The hell she is."

She looked toward him only to see a look of innocence on his face. She laughed out loud. He was too much. "Okay, I'm in."

Jonathan smiled back at her and agreed to meet them in the hotel bar as well.

Kina looked around at the men surrounding her at the table. They all had frosty mugs of beer in front of them and were recounting the day's challenge and laughing. She was relaxed for the first time in a long time. She found she really enjoyed having a smaller group of camera operators on the set. It made for a more family-type atmosphere, something she hadn't even known she'd like.

She didn't even care that she had a headache. It wasn't awful and it was better to be here hanging out with Jonathan than sitting alone in her room again. Yes, she could finally admit it to herself. She wanted to get to know him. He fascinated her. He seemed like a good guy and she was attracted to him. He wasn't really her type, but he was funny and courteous and had a bit of mystery about him. The attention he paid her was also very flattering and Kina found him very hard to resist.

She was so relaxed and mellow with the good company and good beer that she missed seeing the burly local man saunter up to their table. The first inkling she got he was there was when she actually felt Jonathan tense at her side.

"Hey, sweet cheeks, can I buy you a beer?"

Kina looked down at the still half-full beer mug sitting in front of her. This guy had a lot of nerve, coming up to their table when she was sitting with four other men.

"Uh, no. I'm good," she told the man easily.

He obviously wasn't adept at taking no for an answer, as she'd found most men weren't, and asked again, in a voice that wasn't really a question.

"I'll buy you a beer."

Before Kina could say anything in return Jonathan had stood up and was chest to chest with the man. Words were said between them, too low for Kina to hear. The man turned around and left without a word and Jonathan sat back down. Kina immediately was pissed. What the hell?

"What the hell was that?" she asked nastily.

"I just let him know that you weren't interested." Jonathan answered calmly, taking a sip of his beer.

Kina saw red. Matt used to do the same thing all the time. Make every decision for her and not take into account what she wanted. She wasn't going there again, no way.

"How do you know I wasn't interested? Maybe I would've liked to have had a drink with him. You don't know anything about me and you don't own me. Understand?"

Jonathan looked at his woman evenly. He didn't understand where her attitude was coming from. He'd only been protecting her from harassment. He didn't want to think of anyone else's hands on her, but if she really wanted to have a drink with that bozo he wouldn't stand in her way. But he also didn't want her doing it just to make a point.

"I'm sorry, Kina. I honestly thought you'd be more comfortable hanging here with us. I didn't think you'd want to have a drink with him. If you're really interested in him I'll go and apologize." Like hell he would, but he didn't think telling her that would get him very far in his quest to win her heart.

Kina struggled to control her temper. Jonathan wasn't Matt. He wasn't trying to control her. She took a deep breath. "No, it's okay. Just don't do it again. I like to make my own decisions."

Jonathan nodded and noticed they had an audience. The other camera operators were looking on with extreme interest. He would've liked to have talked to her more about it, but knew he wouldn't get any further in front of the others. He desperately wanted some time alone with her, but didn't know how to go about it. Maybe he'd push his luck tonight and simply ask if he could talk to her alone. He didn't know if she'd go for it, but it was worth a shot. She was worth it.

Jonathan hoped she was ready to go. He didn't want any other trouble tonight and Kina was just too beautiful to sit in the bar any longer without attracting more attention. It looked like it was true that there were more men than women in Alaska, at least in this bar it was.

"You about ready to go?" Jonathan asked Kina, gesturing to her beer with his chin, hoping like hell she'd say yes.

He sighed in relief when Kina nodded, even though she'd rolled her eyes while doing it. They scooted out of the booth, saying their goodbyes to Taylor, Carl, and Jeff. As they walked toward their rooms, Jonathan asked, "Can I talk to you for a second?" When she hesitated and sighed, he said quickly, "I won't take much time, I swear. We can go to your room or mine, I just want to talk to you without the others hearing for a second."

Kina considered his words. She didn't want the others overhearing whatever it was that Jonathan wanted to tell her, either. It wasn't because she thought he'd tell her something bad, it was simply because on the most basic level, she wanted to be near him. As much as she didn't like his overprotective attitude, she liked him.

Kina nodded and decided she'd go to his room. It was a gamble, but that way she could leave whenever she wanted. It would be harder to kick Jonathan out of her room if he didn't want to go.

Jonathan opened his door and gestured her in. Kina was surprised to find his room was spotless. She'd halfway expected him to be a slob, but she admitted to herself that was because Matt hadn't bothered to clean up after himself, so she just expected all men to be that way.

Kina watched as Jonathan puttered around the room for a moment before finally settling on the chair in the corner. He looked nervous. It put her even more at ease. Had any man ever been nervous in her presence before? Nervous in a good way, not nervous because he thought she'd rip into him. She didn't think so. Most of the time they were arrogant assholes who thought she'd do whatever they wanted her to.

Jonathan took a deep breath then said baldly, repeating what he'd already said once. "I like you, Kina." He'd decided to go for it. Kina was a no-nonsense type of woman and he figured she'd appreciate his candor more than his beating around the bush. It could backfire on him, but he couldn't stand being around her and watching her flirt with other men and generally not know he had feelings about her. When she didn't say anything but only looked at him incredulously, he continued, "I know, I know, it sounds crazy, but it's true. I admire you and want to get to know you better."

Kina was floored. That was so not what she'd expected him to say when she agreed to come into his room. Before she thought about it she blurted out, "Are you drunk?"

He laughed. "No hon, I'm not drunk. I just wanted to get it on the table so you'd know where I'm coming from. I don't expect you to reciprocate in kind yet, but I feel like you have the right to know."

"Since when?" Kina said, still waiting for him to laugh and say, "Gotcha" as if it was all a big joke.

"Since Arizona," Jonathan answered honestly. He always wanted to tell her the truth. He didn't believe any kind of relationship could flourish if there wasn't honesty between two people.

"Wh-what?" Kina was completely floored. She knew she wasn't the type of woman to inspire thoughts of lust and the immediate "like" that Jonathan was claiming he felt for her. "I-I don't know what to say," she managed to stammer out.

"Please, don't say anything. I hope to Christ you'll give me a chance to show you I'm a good guy. Just get to know me over the next weeks and I'll prove it to you."

Kina shook her head. This was crazy, but deep down inside something unfurled in her gut. Could he be for real? She'd have to guard her heart just in case, but God, it was such a heady feeling. She didn't really think he'd want to be with her, not after hearing all about her messed up history with men.

"You're in charge here, Kina," he told her unexpectedly. "If you want to talk to me, let me know. If you want to hold my hand, take hold. If you want to kiss me, I'm all for it. But, you're in charge. I won't push my luck, but I will try to convince you to give me a chance. Be forewarned, hon."

Kina hadn't ever been in charge of a relationship. In all of her disastrous relationships, she'd been pursued and then subsequently dumped. Maybe that was the problem. Maybe she needed to take control of what she wanted for once. She liked that idea. The more she thought about it, the more she liked it.

"Okay, Jonathan. I'm in charge, huh?"

"Yes, ma'am," he answered, smiling, looking like he didn't know what to expect.

"Then goodnight, I'll see you in the morning." She spun and headed toward the door.

Jonathan's laugh followed her out the door.

Chapter Four

The next morning, Kina didn't know what to think about Jonathan and their conversation from the night before. She'd almost convinced herself he didn't really mean it. But when they all met to get in the car and go to the set, he walked right up to her, took hold of her hand and brought it to his lips. He gently kissed the back of her hand, all the while not breaking eye contact.

"Good morning, Kina," he murmured, and slowly let go.

Holy crap. He was intense, and hot, and she loved it. She wasn't sure why she loved it when he acted that way, but had hated when *Matt* did the same thing. She tried to remind herself that she was in charge. Kina wanted nothing more than to throw Jonathan down to the ground and hump him like there was no tomorrow, but unfortunately that wasn't going to happen anytime soon. She so wasn't ready for that.

She pulled her hand back. "Thought I was in charge?"

"Just saying good morning."

That grin was lethal. Kina climbed into the SUV trying to turn her thoughts to the upcoming job. She was only partially successful.

Filming for the next two days wasn't going to be very exciting. The next challenge wasn't scheduled for a while because apparently Eddie still had to set it up. So, while he hadn't wanted to bother with a lot of filming on set, they really had nothing else to do while they were there. Besides, there would need to be some filming done in the house, the entire show couldn't just be about the challenges.

Kina was hyper aware of Jonathan all day. He didn't break his promise to her; he was letting her call the shots in whatever relationship they may or may not have. It was driving her crazy. She didn't know how to be in charge of a relationship and she still wasn't convinced she even wanted one with Jonathan. She couldn't deny he was hot as hell and that she was attracted to him, but…there was always a but. She wasn't good at relationships. From her high school boyfriend to Matt, that had been made clear over and over.

In order to have a good relationship, there had to be trust, and Kina no longer felt she could trust anyone. Time and time again, any trust she'd given to someone had been broken.

Jonathan was having a good day. He felt relieved he'd told Kina how he felt. It would be the hardest thing he'd ever had to do, to not immediately try to plow right over any objections she might have about their relationship, but he'd promised to let her take control. And he would, even if it killed him.

* * *

The next couple of days continued much as the previous ones had. The group got up in the mornings and went to the production house where they got some random shots of the men sitting around talking, playing pool, cooking lunch, or whatever they happened to be doing. Shannel was scarce, as her job was to play host, not babysit the contestants.

Eddie had been around, mostly to direct some shots that he wanted, but he was also busy setting up the challenges that would happen in the upcoming weeks.

After filming for the day, the group would go back to the hotel and have a drink and dinner. There were no more incidents with any local men trying to hit on Kina and even Jeff was behaving himself for the moment.

Jonathan took every opportunity he could to brush up against Kina or to just sit next to her and listen to her talk. He thought she was loosening up around him, but he couldn't be sure. All he could do was wait for her to give him a sign, or flat out tell him she wanted to be with him.

379

Kina was ready to give whatever it was between her and Jonathan a try. They'd been tiptoeing around each other for a while now, and she honestly wanted to get to know him better. That night, before they met up at the hotel restaurant for dinner, Kina decided to just go for it. She'd never know what kind of man Jonathan was if she didn't do as he said, take control. If it turned out he was a jerk, she'd deal. But there was a little voice in her head asking, *'what if he's not?'* She didn't know his brother Dean, but after being around their parents while the last show had been filmed at their animal refuge and seeing how Dean was with Becky, she figured Jonathan might, just might, be worth the effort.

"Hey Jonathan, wait up."

Jonathan stopped before entering the restaurant. If Kina asked him to lie down in the middle of the road, he probably would've.

Kina stood next to Jonathan and was suddenly tongue-tied. What if he said no? Oh, the hell with it. "Doyouwanttogosomewhereelsefordinner?" she said as fast as she could.

Inside Jonathan was doing cartwheels, but he stayed calm. "Sure. I'd love to. Got any idea what you want to eat?"

Kina shook her head. It was enough that she'd asked him if he wanted to eat with her. She hadn't thought so far in advance as to what or where she wanted to eat.

"Can I make a suggestion?" At her nod he continued, "There's a place I've read about called The Bubbly Mermaid downtown. I've heard they have excellent fresh seafood."

"Sounds good," Kina murmured, glad she didn't have to come up with a place to eat. She probably would've chosen a fast food restaurant or something equally lame.

"Let me go and see if Taylor has the keys on him. I'll be right back." Jonathan quickly squeezed her elbow before heading into the restaurant to find the other camera operator.

While waiting for Jonathan to come back out, Kina leaned against the wall in the hallway. Jonathan had acted perfectly with her. He didn't make a big deal out of her asking him to dinner. He could've been an ass about the whole thing, but he hadn't. She saw Jeff walking toward her. She smiled at him and said hello. His response stunned her.

"So, you finally made your move, huh? When you're done with him, I'd love a go."

Kina was stunned into silence for a moment, then what he said finally penetrated.

"What the hell, Jeff? You're an ass. It'll be a cold day in Hell before you get a 'go'."

She was going to say more when Jeff was suddenly flying backward. Jonathan had come back and grabbed Jeff by the collar of his shirt and flung him around. Jeff hit the wall on the other side of the hallway, but was able to regain his balance so he didn't fall.

"You heard her. Kiss off, Jeff. She's not going anywhere with you. She's mine. And if you so much as look cross-eyed at her again, you'll have me to deal with."

Kina was shocked to realize Jonathan was really pissed. He'd always been so mild-mannered and polite. She hadn't even realized he had it in him. She should be upset, seeing how Matt always got so jealous when she even so much as looked at another guy, but this was somehow different. He was standing up for her, not acting irrationally. He hadn't beaten the hell out of Jeff, which said a lot about his control. Besides she would've done the same thing if she'd been strong enough.

"Whatever, dude, she's not worth it." Jeff tried to recover.

"That's where you're wrong and why you'll never have anything as precious as her in your life. Keep movin'." Jonathan shot back as he took Kina's elbow in his large hand and steered her toward the door, making sure to keep his own body between hers and Jeff's. He walked them out and didn't say another word until he was opening the passenger door of the SUV for Kina.

"Are you okay?"

"Yeah, sure." Kina said, amazed that it was actually true. She was good. While she'd never be completely comfortable with someone sticking up for her when she could do it herself, it felt good to have Jonathan there next to her.

"He's a dick," Jonathan responded more to himself than to Kina.

Kina laughed. It felt good to release some of her tension. "Yup, he is."

Jonathan laughed as well and after she'd sat down in the front passenger seat, he pulled the belt of her seatbelt out and held it for her. Kina looked up at him as he stood there waiting for her to buckle herself in. No one had ever done that before. Oh, she'd had dates open her door, but never had someone pulled her belt out for her and handed it to her. It was sexy as hell. She took the belt from his hand and his fingers brushed against hers in the process. She shivered. God, he felt good.

Jonathan walked around the front of the SUV, trying to get himself back under control. His adrenaline was sky high. First, because of Jeff. He wanted to pummel him into the ground for disrespecting Kina. Now, because of the slight touch of her fingers against his. He was in big trouble if that was all it took for him to get excited around her. He'd never survive a kiss or anything more.

The drive to The Bubbly Mermaid was done in silence, but not an uncomfortable one. Kina relaxed into the seat. That was another thing different about Jonathan. He never felt the need to fill the air with unnecessary conversation. Again, he was very purposeful. He spoke when he had something to say and acted when it was necessary. Otherwise, he was content to just watch or listen.

When they pulled up to the restaurant and parked, Jonathan turned to Kina.

"Do I need to apologize for what happened back there?"

Kina knew he was referring to his actions with Jeff. "No." At the relieved look on his face Kina continued quickly. "As long as you don't make it a habit of knocking around men that talk to me. I hear a lot of crap, being a woman in this job. I can deal with it."

Jonathan took a deep breath and thought about how he could say what he needed to say and not piss her off. He held his hand out, hoping she'd put her own in his. When she slowly placed her hand in his, Jonathan was thrilled. He lightly wrapped his hand around hers and rubbed it with his thumb. "Kina, I'll do my best, but as long as I'm around, no one is allowed to be disrespectful to you. I can't just stand there and let them get away with it. I'll try to curb my reactions, but you don't have to deal with that crap by yourself anymore. I have your back."

Kina just looked at him. Was he for real? She couldn't remember a time in her life when someone "had her back." It'd always been just her. She couldn't process this right now. She'd have to think about it later, so she just nodded.

Jonathan smiled, squeezed her hand, and told her to stay put. He hopped out his side of the vehicle, walked around to open her door, and helped her out. As they walked toward the front door of the quirky restaurant, Kina decided to go for it and reached for his hand and twined her fingers with his. His large calloused hand wrapped around her smaller one felt nice. She looked up at him and he smiled down at her. That smile was worth any angst she'd had about taking his hand.

They were shown to a booth in the back of the restaurant and Jonathan gestured her into one side of the booth and when she was scooting in asked if he could sit on her side. Shocked, she could only agree. Again, that was something no date had ever asked before. They'd always sat across from her. Always. Even Matt did that when he'd take her out. Of course, after they'd been dating for a while, he'd taken her out less and less.

The restaurant had a large selection of oysters, but Kina didn't care much for them. She was more of a shrimp and crab girl. She ordered the King Crab cocktail and Jonathan ordered seafood chowder and a plate of Alaska oysters fresh from Halibut Cove and Kachemak Bay.

Now that they'd ordered and were settled, Jonathan turned to Kina.

"So, tell me about yourself."

Kina laughed. "That sounds like a cheesy pick-up line," she told him unabashedly.

He chuckled back at her. "I suppose it did, but I want to know about you, Kina. I want to know everything about you."

Kina sobered. "That's a pretty tall order," she said seriously, having no idea where to start.

"What if we play a game? You can ask me anything and I promise to answer honestly, and then I get to ask you a question. We'll continue until you want to stop. Remember, you're in charge here."

Kina laughed, "Yeah right. I don't think I've been in charge from day one."

They both smiled.

"Okay, you're on. I get to go first, though," Kina told him, picking up her glass and taking a drink of water, while watching him nod.

"Let's see….is this like truth-or-dare where if you don't like what I ask you have to do something crazy to get out of answering?"

Jonathan didn't even smile. "No, hon. If I feel like I can't answer you honestly, I'll let you know. If I'm uncomfortable with the question, I'll answer what I can, but I'll tell you that I don't want to answer it right now. I promise, however…" He paused and took a sip of his own water as if he was nervous, before continuing, "…I'll answer your question at some point while we're here in Alaska. I want you to trust me and it might be too early for you to hear all my secrets at this point."

God. Kina loved that answer.

"I don't know if I can trust you," she blurted out without thinking.

"I know." Jonathan answered immediately, not looking surprised or upset in the least. "I can tell it's hard for you to trust people and that's okay. I'm perfectly happy with you taking your time. I want to know everything about you and all about who made it so hard for you to put your trust in someone. But I'd rather have your honest and complete trust whenever you decide you can give it to me, than force you to lie to me now and say something when it's not true."

Seriously, everything that came out of his mouth just got better and better. Was he for real? All right, she had to think of some good questions to ask him.

"Okay, wow. Hmm. Let's see. I'll start out easy. What's your favorite color?" She wanted to start out simple to break the intensity in the conversation.

"That's easy. Blue. My turn."

Kina squirmed in her seat. It seemed like a good idea when she was the one that got to ask the questions. It wasn't as much fun being on the other side.

"Are your toenails currently painted?"

Huh? That was his question? "That's your question?" she repeated what she was thinking incredulously.

"Yup. I've been imagining what your delicate feet look like for days. And thinking about your cute little feet led me to think about your toes. Then I got to wondering if you were the type of woman who liked to paint her toenails a sexy red or maybe with a sheer coat of pink…believe me, I've spent a lot of time imagining what you look like with naked…feet."

Kina blushed hotly. Jesus. She squirmed in her seat. He was good. "Uh, no. Just plain toenails. No color," she squeaked out.

Jonathan picked up her hand and ran his thumb idly over the back of it. She was so cute. This was fun. "Your turn again, honey."

"Uh yeah, okay. Um. I heard you telling Carl this was your last job as a camera operator. Why?"

He answered without hesitation, hiding nothing from her. "I hate it." At her raised eyebrows and obvious shock he continued, "I've been living in Los Angeles for the last few years and the people there are so fake and jaded. I thought maybe filming for reality shows would be better, but it's not.

I've had enough. My brother Dean, you met him on the last show, is going to let me come and work with him. I'll be able to be near him and Becky, as well as my folks. I can't wait. I've missed my family."

Wow, Kina would love to have a place she could call home. She'd never really thought about it. All she'd known for the last few years was moving from one set to another. But to have a place where you belonged, where you could put down roots, was something she'd always wanted, but hadn't been able to hold on to.

"Tell me how you got into this occupation."

Kina thought about Jonathan's question for a moment. Her answer wasn't a quick and easy one, by any stretch. How much should she tell him? She looked at the man sitting next to her quietly, waiting for whatever she wanted to tell him. She made the decision to be honest.

"A while ago I was broke and homeless. I'd just left my boyfriend and didn't have any ambition, or anywhere to go. An old acquaintance of mine felt sorry for me and let me move into the basement apartment of a house she was renting out. She also got me in touch with someone she knew in the television business who needed a daytime janitor. I started working and the cameras fascinated me. I paid attention, got friendly with the people who worked there and learned all I could. One thing led to another and here I am. I took the job with Eddie because it got me out of that crappy little town and allowed me to move around. I don't have any family and Matt had made sure I didn't have any friends, so there was nothing for me there."

She looked down at the hand Jonathan was holding and winced. He'd been squeezing it harder than was comfortable. Just as she went to pull her hand away he suddenly loosened his fingers and put them in his lap. She could see his fists were clenched. His voice, when he spoke however, was calm.

"I'm sorry you had to go through that, but I'm glad you got out of that situation and you're here now. I have about a million more questions I'd love to ask about some of what you just shared, but I hope you'll tell me when you're ready. This was supposed to be a lighthearted game so we could get to know each other better."

Kina put her hand over Jonathan's in his lap. She could feel the tension. It warmed her inside that he was trying to hide it from her. This definitely wasn't like her. In the past she would've warned him away from caring about her at all. But now, it felt right.

"I didn't mean to go there, but I'm not sorry I told you. Matt, my last boyfriend, did a number on me. I'll admit it. He tried to control everything I did. He told me what I could eat. He alienated all my friends. He made me dependent on him for everything and I hated it. I hated myself when I was with him. I can't ever go back to that sort of relationship. I don't know if I even have it in me to trust any man again after what he did."

Jonathan consciously tried to relax. Every muscle in his body was tense and he wanted to go and beat the hell out of this Matt person, but he had to keep himself in control. He knew Kina wasn't the type of person who wanted or needed that kind of man. She was independent and he loved that about her. It wouldn't be easy to tone down his protective instincts when it came to her, but he'd try. He turned his hand over and captured hers in his now relaxed grip.

"Thank you for sharing that with me. I know it wasn't easy. I swear I don't want to control you. I want to be with you. I want to stand next to you, not in front of you. If you allow me to spend time with you I'll show you that you can trust me. I won't let you down."

Kina opened her mouth to say something, she wasn't sure what, when the waiter arrived with their meal. Saved by the food!

Jonathan was content to let the serious subject drop for now. Kina had opened up to him and he was more than pleased. It had to mean she was beginning to trust him a little bit. He could wait.

Throughout dinner they continued their game of asking questions, although none were as intense as before.

"Which do you like better, chicken or steak?" Kina asked.

"Steak. What's your favorite scent?"

"Hyacinths. They smell so good! If you could be any animal what would you be?"

"Hippo."

Kina laughed at his answer, not expecting it. "Hippo? Who chooses that? Why a hippo?"

"No one messes with a hippo. Think about it. If you saw a hippo, what would you do? I'll tell you, you'd run the other way." Kina had to agree. God, he was hysterical. It was his turn.

"What's the most embarrassing thing you've ever done?"

"If I told you, I'd just be embarrassed all over again!" They both laughed.

He let it slide and asked another question instead. "What do you think of men with long hair?"

"Easy," Kina said easily reaching over to finger the end of the long ponytail hanging down his back. "I never thought I'd like it, but now I think it's sexy as hell."

Jonathan almost spit the water he'd been drinking across the table. Good God. He was hoping for a positive answer, but that was way more than he could've hoped for. He smiled at her, changing the subject to keep himself from kissing the hell out of her. "Your turn."

Their questions eventually turned into a game Jonathan used to play with his brother all the time. They called it, 'Would you rather.' He thought he remembered reading somewhere that it'd been made into an actual game people could buy, but he could only remember the fun times he'd had with his family playing it. The object was to pick one of two equally horrible choices. It was hilarious and Kina got into the spirit of the game without hesitation.

"Would you rather be bald or excessively hairy?"

"Would you rather break an arm or a leg?"

"Would you rather eat breakfast foods for the rest of your life or only dinner foods?"

They sat laughing and talking until they finally noticed they were the only people left in the restaurant. They'd been there for hours and Kina couldn't remember having a better time with anyone in her entire life. Jonathan was fun to be around and she felt no pressure. He was being true to his word and letting her set the pace of their relationship.

They apologized to the manager for staying so long, paid their bill and made their way to the SUV. It was late and dark. Kina felt Jonathan's hand at the small of her back as he steered her toward their parking spot. She noticed him constantly scanning the area as if looking for trouble. He didn't run to the car, but he also didn't waste any time. He was protecting her, and she couldn't get upset with him. When Matt used to do stuff like that it annoyed the hell out of her, but she knew it was because he felt as if she belonged to him and was just looking for a reason to beat the hell out of someone. She honestly believed Jonathan was doing it because she was important to him and he wanted to make sure she was safe. She had no idea how she knew that, but she did.

Once again he opened the door for her and when she was settled into the seat he handed her the seat belt. God, why that made goosebumps break out over her body, she had no idea. Kina decided she liked it when Jonathan looked after her.

After they were on their way back to the hotel Kina asked, "Would you rather have to rollerblade everywhere you went or skateboard?" Jonathan smiled. She liked the game they had played with one another. It was intimate and personal. Hell, she just liked Jonathan.

Chapter Five

It was time for another challenge. Eddie was upping the ante with this second challenge and the men were going to have to do something a bit more physical. Their task this week was to split logs. Alaskans who didn't live in cities usually used wood stoves to heat their homes. They had to split a lot of logs to keep warm throughout the long brutal winters.

Kina laughed. She didn't think any of the contestants had ever had to split logs before. This would be funny.

The men were loaded into two separate vans along with Shannel and Eddie and some of the other producers. The camera crew took their own SUV. Eddie didn't care about having any shots of the men in the car on the way to the venue.

They drove south of the city to Chugach State Park. The Park Rangers had cleared a small section of the park for them to film in. The men were given a lesson on the safest and most efficient way to use the axe. Many times people would use a wedge to assist them in chopping, but Eddie thought that was too wimpy for the show. After donning safety glasses and gloves, each man was allowed to practice chop one log to get the hang of it.

After safety had been taken care of, the show could start. Eddie lined all the men up and let Shannel do her hosting duties. She explained the premise of the contest, that the men each had ten minutes to chop as many logs as they could. Big trees were already chopped up into sections. Each section had to be cut up by the contestants into pieces that would fit into a typical wood stove. Each one would be measured and should be around six to eight inches in diameter. Anything larger would be thrown out.

The man who'd chopped the most legal sized pieces, the quickest, would win. The two men who chopped the least, the slowest, would be going home.

In order to save some time, the men would be competing two at a time. It was going to take probably around two hours to get through everyone as it was. Making sure camera angles were appropriate and each area was cleaned up between contestants was also important. Kina knew that when people were watching the show it would only take around ten minutes for everyone to get through their turn because of editing, but in reality it took hours because of having to re-do the set for each man. Not to mention safety procedures and questions that might arise during the filming.

Taylor and Kina were placed around one chopping area and Jonathan and Carl were set around the other. Jeff was a 'floater,' meaning he had to walk around and film the reactions of the other contestants and other interesting shots as the chopping was occurring.

The first men to go were Slade the lawyer, and Darius the chemist. They each set up at their block of wood and when Shannel blew the whistle, they were off. Darius completely missed with his first swing of the axe. Slade wasn't much better; but at least he hit the wood with his first strike, but then he couldn't get the axe out of the chunk of wood. And so it went.

Kina tried not to laugh as each group of men took their turn. It was obvious Julio, the web site developer, had never even held an axe before, because despite the instruction they'd had, he first tried to chop the chunk of wood with the blunt side of the axe. Roger and Trent were a bit better, but not by much. Kina was shocked at how good Benedict was. He'd obviously had some experience in the past, because he actually had a stack of something that resembled firewood at the end of his ten minutes.

It was during Ian and Nash's heat that the first injury occurred. Nash was furiously trying to chop the wood as fast as he could and when he swung the axe upward to take another hit, it flew out of his hands. Kina saw it go flying right toward Jonathan. She was supposed to be watching Ian through her lens to get the best shots, but she couldn't help but see the deadly weapon flying straight toward Jonathan. Luckily, he was paying attention and stepped out of the way of the missile at the last minute. When it landed, blade first, it hit a rock and a piece came flying up and hit Carl on the side of the head.

Carl was too much of a professional to stop filming. He kept on rolling until the ten minutes was up. Kina tried to pay attention to Ian, but all she could think about was if Jonathan hadn't stepped out of the way, he could've been hit with the axe. It was bad enough to see the trickle of blood coming from the side of Carl's face, all she could think was that it could've been Jonathan's skull bleeding.

After Eddie finally said "cut" after the time was up, Trent, a nurse, went over to Carl to see if he could help. Carl tried to blow off the whole incident, but for once Eddie was being a stickler for safety. Everyone gathered around Carl while Trent bandaged the slight cut on the side of his head. He absolutely refused to go to the hospital and Eddie actually made him sign a piece of paper that said as much.

Nash tried to apologize profusely, but Carl wasn't having it. Kina tried to get herself back into the swing of filming again, but it was hard. She didn't like to think of anyone being hurt, especially a friend like Carl, but the close call for Jonathan was never far from her mind. She knew Jonathan was trying to catch her eye, but she refused to look at him. She had to get herself together.

Finally, each of the ten contestants finished with their chopping. Shannel lined them all up again to announce the verdict. Benedict was the overall winner, which wasn't surprising to anyone. He'd done a great job. In the end Julio and Cole, the security officer, had chopped the least amount of wood. Because they weren't back at the production house, they had to "pretend" to leave. Jeff filmed them walking toward the van and getting in. Kina knew they'd splice in a shot of the van leaving later. But for now, some of the contestants joined Julio and Cole in one van and everyone else piled in the other to go back to the house.

Kina was glad she didn't have to be in the van; the men had been sweating profusely. It wasn't actually warm outside, but the exertion of chopping the wood plus their nerves, were enough to make them quite odiferous.

Eddie told the camera operators they had the rest of the day off. Nothing was going to go on back at the house, except for Julio and Cole packing their stuff and leaving the set. Eddie had learned his lesson in Arizona and each of the men, after leaving the show, were brought to a different hotel until the end of the show. That would assure that no one knew who won, but it was also protection for the contestants themselves in case someone didn't agree with the results of the competitions.

The camera crew piled into the SUV, ready to head back to the hotel to get their own showers. Kina leaned over the seat toward Carl.

"Are you really okay, Carl?"

"Sure, Kina, it really only winged me, not a big deal. Besides, you know I have a hard head."

Kina tried to joke with him, "Impressive you didn't drop the camera!"

Carl mock bowed and tipped an imaginary hat in her direction.

They all laughed. It actually was amazing he hadn't stopped filming.

Kina sat back and let the conversation and good natured ribbing continue around her. She looked over at Jonathan for the first time since they'd climbed into the car. She didn't know what she expected him to say, but she never thought he'd make light of the situation.

"Would you rather be hit by a flying axe or a flying hammer?"

She didn't want to laugh, truly she didn't, the situation wasn't funny in the least, but she couldn't help it. Dammit. Why'd he have to be funny on top of everything else?

"Ha, ha, very funny, twinkle toes." At his smile she continued. "How'd you know that thing was coming at you since you were watching only through the camera lens?"

Jeff sat sideways and put his elbow on the back of his seat. "Yeah, that was actually pretty impressive, Baker."

Jonathan waved his hand as if waving off any kind of praise. "I saw him trying to grip the handle on the few swings he took before that one. He was losing his grip on every swing; I figured it was only a matter of time. I was already planning on moving to a different vantage point when he let it fly. I guess I was just lucky."

"Damn lucky, if you ask me," Taylor called back from the front seat. Kina had to agree.

When they got back to the hotel, Jonathan waited until the others had left to go up to their rooms. He lightly grasped Kina's elbow and asked. "Want to do something today?"

"I thought you were going to let me be in charge?" she told him teasingly.

Jonathan grinned. God, she was cute. "Okay, so what do you want to do for the rest of the day?"

Kina laughed. How he ever thought he'd be able to let her make all the decisions she'd never know. "What did you have in mind?" She knew he had to have something up his sleeve or he wouldn't have asked her.

"What about the Alaska Native Heritage Center?"

Kina didn't know what to say. She thought he might say the name of another restaurant or something. She never thought he'd be into something educational. She blushed. She'd stereotyped him, and she didn't like that about herself.

"Sure, sounds interesting."

As Jonathan pulled the keys out of his pocket, Kina looked at him. She smirked; he'd had it planned the entire time. The rat.

As if Jonathan knew what she was thinking, he said, "I asked Taylor for them earlier. He said he didn't mind if we took the car again today. He said he was going to call home and then take a nap."

Jonathan settled Kina into the front passenger seat and once again handed her the seatbelt. Kina loved it.

When they were on the road to the Heritage Center she asked him why he'd chosen it.

"I just thought if we were going to spend six weeks in Alaska, I'd like to get to know more about the culture of the people and the history. It's fascinating to me how the Eskimos and Native people have lived for hundreds of years, doing things the same way, passed down from generation to generation. I thought we'd get an appreciation of the Native people and their traditions and history of the state."

"I'd like that." Jonathan was a lot deeper than Kina had ever given him credit for. He was like an onion, the layers just kept peeling off one by one, revealing more and more of the man underneath. She was liking what she'd seen so far.

Jonathan parked the SUV and they strolled into the Center, hand in hand. Kina didn't even hesitate to grasp his hand when he held it out to her as he helped her from the car. Holding his hand was almost as natural as breathing. She didn't even try to think about how fast he'd become important to her. She just accepted it, and hoped like hell he wouldn't break her heart. He'd just started to thaw it out, she didn't want to imagine what would happen if he broke her trust now.

They walked around and checked out the different exhibits. There were a lot of fun things for kids to do. There were traditional dances that were held at the center as well, but none were being performed that day. It didn't matter. They were enjoying just being with each other and learning about a different way of life and culture. Talk eventually turned to work.

"What do you think of the show?" Jonathan asked Kina. "You were with Eddie in Australia. Do you think he's changed at all?"

Kina thought about it before answering. "Yes and no. Yes, this show is different in that Eddie isn't trying to hook anyone up. I think he learned his lesson from Arizona. But I also think he's still Eddie. He'll still try to manipulate anyone he can in order to make the show a success. He has even more to lose now after not being able to air the Arizona show."

She paused. Not knowing if it was really appropriate to ask her next question, but she remembered what Jonathan had said at dinner, that he'd tell her the truth if he could. She figured if he didn't want to answer, he'd tell her. "Can I ask you something?"

He didn't hesitate to reassure her. "Of course hon, anything."

"How is Becky doing? I feel so horrible about what happened to her back in Arizona. I had no idea those guys would attack her at the hotel. I was in the limo when she was dropped off. I just feel like maybe I should've done something…" Her voice trailed off.

Jonathan stopped their stroll and pulled her over to a bench against a wall. They sat and he put their clasped hands on his thigh and put his other hand over the two of theirs. "She's okay, Kina. She's been seeing a therapist and working through her issues. She and Dean are so in love, it's almost sickening." He said that with a smile so she'd know he was kidding. His voice got serious again. "Remember how I told you I don't sleep well? That I get nightmares?" At her nod he continued. "It's because of what happened to her. I should have stopped it. I had every chance and I didn't."

"I don't believe that," Kina said without even asking what he meant. "Seriously, Jonathan, I don't know how you think you could've done anything, but I know without a doubt you did everything right that night. You couldn't have done anything differently."

Jonathan gave her a sad smile. "Thanks hon, but you don't know…"

Before he could continue Kina interrupted him. "I do know. Jonathan, my God, there's no way you'd have let anyone get hurt on your watch. You need to let this go."

"I can't," he said simply.

"Have you talked to someone about this?" Kina asked him seriously. "I know most men think they're too macho to need any help getting through horrible things that happen to them, but it sounds as if you need to talk it through."

At his shake of his head she said boldly, "I'm here if you want to talk to me about it."

Jonathan grasped their hands tighter and bowed his head. "I'm afraid if I tell you what happened, you'll not want to see me anymore."

Holy crap. Kina hadn't ever seen that kind of deep honest emotion from a man. Kina pulled their clasped hands up to her mouth and kissed his knuckles. "I might not know you that well, Jonathan, but I do know you're one of the good guys. You didn't hurt Becky. You didn't cause her to be hurt. Some idiots did that all on their own. Hell, you won't even let some guy say jerky things to me and you don't even really know me. There's no way you'd stand aside and let someone your brother loved get hurt. I'd love for you to talk to me. I'd love for you to tell me everything. If you think I'll turn my back on you, I'll prove you wrong. I don't think this is the time or the place, but maybe once we get to know each other better, you'll trust me."

Jonathan's eyed glowed as he looked at her. "Believe it or not, I do trust you, Kina. I trust you more than I trust myself. I'll tell you, but you're right, not now. Will you take a rain check?"

Kina simply nodded, too choked up with emotion to talk. She'd never had a guy open himself up to her like Jonathan just had. Every boyfriend she'd ever had was a macho jerk who never really allowed her in, emotionally. She hadn't really known Jonathan that long and he'd already opened himself up more to her than anyone ever had before. She really hoped he was serious.

They continued making their way through the Heritage Center. It was an amazing place and Kina hoped one day to be able to come back and see some of the demonstrations. It was a small glimpse into a fascinating culture.

As they walked out of the building toward the car, Kina asked Jonathan, "Would you rather be stuck for five hours in an elevator or on a ski lift?" Thus began their hilarious trip back to the hotel.

Chapter Six

Jonathan thought this was one of the most boring shoots he'd ever been on, but that actually worked in his favor with Kina, because it made her more willing to talk to him as well as giving them more time to talk to each other. Since there was no competition on the show, other than the actual contests, the men had been quite well-behaved. As much as Jonathan hated the drama of men fighting for women or men competing for a woman's attention that always happened on dating shows, at least it was interesting for the camera operators. There was always someone and something interesting to film.

This was torture. All that happened between contests was everyone sitting around. Jonathan had heard rumors that Eddie was trying to speed up production and he was all for it. The sooner they got done here, the sooner he could go home and start his new career.

The only problem with that, was Kina. He wanted more time with her. He wanted more time for her to get to know him. She was his One. If Jonathan didn't break through her emotional barriers before they left Alaska, he didn't know if he'd ever get a chance to. He wanted her. He wanted her more than anything he'd ever wanted in his life. All the other women he'd known paled in comparison to Kina. It wasn't just her looks, although she was beautiful to him, it was her. Her larger-than-life personality, her zest for life, and just her all-around demeanor.

He loved that she'd taken right to the silly game of 'Would you rather.' Some of the best times they'd had, had been a result of the answers and conversations they'd had over the questions they'd come up with. He didn't want to lose her. He knew he had to talk to her about what had happened in Arizona, but he was honest when he told her he was scared of losing her. Even though Becky had told him time and time again that she didn't blame him, he blamed himself. He wasn't sure he could get over it. He was trying, but it was difficult.

There were only six men left on the show. The last contest had been a few days prior. The men had been challenged to see how many fish they could catch in a net. The catch was that they were in a stream that was freezing. It wasn't like they could just stand on the bank and fish, either. No, they had to get right out in the middle of the fast-moving water and catch as many fish as possible. As far as 'extreme' went, it wasn't very, but Jonathan knew Eddie was saving the harder challenges for the upcoming competitions. Slade and Grant were the last two men to be sent packing. They'd caught the least number of fish and were currently thanking their lucky stars that they were sitting in nice warm hotel rooms, waiting out the rest of the show.

This next contest was the first one where the contestants would be "roughing" it outside overnight, and thus, the first time the camera operators would also be roughing it. Jonathan was worried about who would be paired up. He desperately wanted Eddie to put him and Kina together, but he also didn't want Kina to think he'd put Eddie up to it. He wouldn't protest if they weren't together, only if Kina was paired with Jeff. He didn't trust Jeff as far as he could throw him. He'd been behaving after their altercation in the hallway, but he'd learned from those jerks on the Arizona show never to underestimate someone's need for revenge. No matter how pissed Kina got with him, he wouldn't allow her to spend the night out in the wilderness with Jeff.

Eddie wanted to have a meeting with all the camera crew before they were sent off. He wanted to explain the rules of the contest to everyone. He figured the camera operators could act as the 'officials' so no one would cheat.

"Here's how it's going to work. We'll be in the Chugach National Forest. There's a lake there called Eagle Lake. The men will be paired off around the lake. They shouldn't cross paths, but everyone will be in one general location. There are only five of you, so we'll split up into pairs and then there will be only one of you with one of the groups of contestants." He shrugged. "That's just the way it has to be."

When no one disagreed with him or otherwise protested, Eddie continued.

"The men will be given basic provisions, flint, an emergency blanket, an axe, one MRE for the two of them, and one extra pair of socks. We'll set them up with some cold weather gear before they head out, jackets, long underwear, etc. They'll be expected to set up camp and be out for three days and two nights. In a few hours, we'll drop everyone off and pick them up around noon on the third day. Their task will be to build a raft they'll have to actually use. When we come to pick them up they'll have to demonstrate their raft floats by paddling out three hundred yards into the lake, then turn around and come back to their campsite. Whoever builds the least water-worthy raft, or if they can't paddle the six hundred yards, will be going home. If more than one group can't make it the entire way, whichever group goes the shortest distance will be leaving.

"Your jobs, as constant observers, will be to make sure there's no cheating going on. You'll all be equipped with a radio just in case. You'll each have your own tent and provisions. No fires, though. Only the contestants are allowed to start a fire. If you light a fire the men might be tempted to use it instead of building their own. This is about them, not about you. And another thing…I don't want anyone getting hurt, is that clear? If these pussies can't handle the weather and get frostbite or if they cut off a limb, contact me immediately. If they just want to quit, too bad. They can't. That makes for great TV. People love to watch men, who think they're tough, be miserable and whiny. We haven't had enough of that on the show yet. Everyone understand?"

Jonathan shook his head. Man, Eddie was a jerk. He wondered how the man had made it this far in his career, but he supposed you had to be heartless to be a producer of reality shows.

Eddie continued. "Okay, so I've decided who will be with who."

Jonathan held his breath. He really hoped he didn't have to get all macho alpha in front of Kina.

"Jeff, you and Carl will be with Trent and Ian."

Jonathan let out his breath. Thank God. He could live with wherever Eddie put him now.

"Jonathan and Kina will be with Roger and Darius, and Taylor, you'll be by yourself with Benedict and Nash. Anyone have any problems with that? Taylor, you all right with being on your own?"

Taylor nodded, as everyone expected he would.

"Okay, you'll all be given a small tent and a sleeping bag to stay in while out there. There is, of course, no sharing those with the contestants. They have to figure out how to stay warm on their own. If you run into any situations out there, as I said, just use the radio to call back. For the next hour we'll be getting the men outfitted in their gear and you all can meet back here for Shannel to explain the contest to the men and we'll get headed out.

Jonathan was thrilled he'd be spending the next two nights with Kina. He couldn't have planned it better himself. He sensed someone coming up to stand next to him and turned to see Kina standing there, looking furious.

"What the hell?" She hissed at him. "Did you set this all up? Did you go to Eddie and tell him you were trying to get me in bed and to put us together?"

"Hang on, Kina. I didn't say anything to Eddie about us. What's happening between us is just that, between us. I'd never disrespect you that way."

Jonathan watched as Kina's breath heaved in and out of her chest. God, she was magnificent. He wished she hadn't immediately thought the worst of him, but he couldn't deny she was glorious when she was worked up. He tried again to soothe her when she didn't say anything. He stepped closer to her and was thrilled when she didn't take a step back. Whether she'd admit it or not, she was beginning to trust him on some level.

"I'd never do anything to jeopardize your career. I know how important it is for you to be seen as 'one of the guys.' Unless your safety was at stake, I'd never go behind your back. But just so you know, full disclosure and all that, if Eddie had tried to pair you with Jeff, I would've said something. There's no way I'd have you suffer two days with him."

He waited for the explosion. He was amazed when his words seemed to have the opposite effect on her.

Kina tried to bring herself under control. She knew Jonathan wouldn't go behind her back and ask to be paired with her just to get her in bed. She'd just automatically been a bitch to him, it was what she usually did. She didn't know how she knew he wouldn't try to set her up that way, but she knew it. He'd had plenty of times to make a move and he still hadn't even kissed her. Kina tried not to be upset about that. She knew Jonathan expected her to be upset with him for saying what he had about Jeff, but the truth was that she would've gone to Eddie herself and asked to be reassigned if he'd put Jeff with her. So she couldn't get mad that Jonathan would've done the same thing.

She brought her hand to her forehead and closed her eyes. "Crap. I'm sorry. That was bitchy of me to think, let alone say. I know you wouldn't have done that. I wasn't thinking."

Jonathan put his hand under her chin and watched as she opened her eyes and looked into his. "It's okay, hon. I don't know half the things you've probably gone through in your career to get where you are. I know most men in this industry are sexist. Just know I've got your back. And thanks for not being mad about the Jeff thing."

"I would've done the same thing," Kina told him honestly, echoing what she'd thought a moment ago. "I don't want to be alone with Jeff, forget being side-by-side with him, for three days in the wilderness."

Jonathan dropped his hand and they both laughed; glad the tension had been eased between them.

"I do have a question, though," Jonathan asked, unable to hold it back. "Would you rather be stranded in Alaska in the cold or Africa in the heat?"

Kina laughed.

* * *

Kina and Jonathan watched as Roger and Darius tried to figure out what to do first to set up their camp. Kina was watching Roger through her lens and Jonathan had Darius. She supposed the men weren't doing too badly, but it was obvious it was going to be a long two and a half days for them. Darius' profession as a chemist and Roger's vocation as a teacher weren't going to help them much in the Alaskan wilderness.

They knew enough to try to set up their sleeping quarters first. Kina didn't know much about wilderness camping either, as she wasn't really a camping kind of girl, but she didn't think the flimsy shelter they'd constructed would do them much good when it got dark and cold. But her role was to observe, so observe was what she was doing.

Kina and Jonathan continued to watch and film off and on while the guys tried to start putting together their raft. Their idea was to gather as many big logs as they could and attach them all together with the rope that Eddie had allowed each pair to have in their packs. On the surface it seemed like a good idea, but Kina wondered if the two men knew anything about what knots they should use, or how to lash the logs together, or even how many they should use. She mentally shrugged. It wasn't as if she knew those things either.

Jonathan put down his camera and leaned his elbows on his upraised knees. They'd sat down a while back because it was hard work to stand all day filming. They'd used one of their emergency blankets for a barrier between the cold, hard ground and their backsides. He looked at Kina sitting next to him, until she too put down her camera. He smiled at her.

"Think they have a chance at winning?"

"No way in hell," Kina answered, laughing quietly.

"Would you rather be stuck on a deserted island with four people you hate, or by yourself?"

"Easy. Definitely by myself." Kina told him. Jonathan agreed.

Kina tried to think of a really good question. "Would you rather have the hiccups for the rest of your life or feel like you need to sneeze, but not be able to, for the rest of your life?"

Jonathan laughed so hard Roger and Darius looked over at them. Jonathan waved at them in apology before answering. "Oh my God, both of those options are so horrible. But I'd have to say the sneeze thing because I hate it when I have the hiccups. I can't imagine having them nonstop forever."

Kina just smiled. She couldn't believe she was sitting here, in the middle of Alaska, on the job, enjoying the hell out of being with a man. She stared at Jonathan's lips, wondering what they'd feel like on hers.

"You'd better stop looking at me like that, Kina, or I won't be responsible for my actions," Jonathan warned her seriously.

"How am I looking at you?"

"Like you want to have your wicked way with me."

Kina turned back toward the men struggling to tie two logs together, still grinning.

Jonathan shifted. He was hard and he hadn't even kissed her yet. The look Kina had given him made him want to throw her over his shoulder and head off to their tent for the rest of the night. She was sexy as hell and he wanted nothing more than to spend hours worshiping her. He sighed. It wasn't the time or the place, dammit. But if he had his way, he'd taste her lips before the night was up.

Later, as the sun was setting and after they'd eaten their pre-packaged meal, Kina watched uncomfortably as

Darius tried unsuccessfully over and over, to light a fire. The men had gathered small sticks and some moss and had been trying to use the flint, with no luck. How anyone could fail at building a fire when they had a perfectly good flint was beyond her. She couldn't stand it anymore. The men were miserable. She looked around, as if someone would be standing in the woods spying on them, and leaned over to whisper to Jonathan.

"Do you think I should bring them a couple of matches? I mean, they look awful. I know Eddie doesn't want us helping them, but I hate just sitting here watching this."

Jonathan grinned at her. For all her brashness, she really was a softie. He whispered back, "I won't tell if you won't."

Kina smiled at him and walked toward Darius and Roger. She came back soon after, still grinning.

"Did they take them?" Jonathan asked, wondering if the men would try to play the game honestly or if they were too miserable to care anymore.

"They took them." Kina said simply. There was Jonathan's answer.

They watched as the fire the men were desperately trying to light suddenly came to life. The glow of the flames made its way across the distance to where Jonathan and Kina were sitting. There was no official rule that they couldn't go and sit with the men, but there was an unwritten one. Kina didn't really want to go and sit by the fire anyway, she was enjoying being with Jonathan in their own little dark world.

As darkness fell and the temperature got colder, Jonathan put his arm around Kina and pulled her into his side. He argued with himself on whether or not he should make the play, but in the end decided to go for it.

God, he loved this woman. He hadn't admitted that to himself before, but Jonathan knew it was true. Kina was hardworking, honest, and a softie deep, down inside. Thinking about what she'd said about her last boyfriend, he couldn't stand the fact that someone had tried to crush her spirit. There was no way he'd want to tell her what to do all the time. Jonathan knew he'd have to try to curb his natural tendency to protect her, but he wasn't as bad as his brother was with that. Dean was the true alpha in their family. Jonathan decided to try to keep things light between them for the moment.

"Would you rather be illiterate, but able to read minds, or just have the ability to read?"

Kina had to think about that one for a moment. At first it seemed like a hard question, but the more she thought about it the easier it got.

"Definitely just have the ability to read. Think about it, after a while you'd be so sick of hearing what others thought. 'Should I order the nuggets or the burger?' 'Look at how fat he is.' 'I have to poop.'" She shuddered, but teased as she continued, "But I'd love to know what you're thinking half the time when you're looking at me."

Jonathan looked at the woman snuggled into his side and told her honestly, "I'll tell you what I'm thinking. I'm thinking how beautiful you are. I'm thinking how much I enjoy being around you and laughing with you. I'm thinking how badly I want to sink my hands in your hair and taste your lips. I'm wondering if you'll taste half as good as I've imagined."

Kina's breath caught. Holy Mother of God, he was good. Goosebumps broke out all down her arms. He was never afraid to put himself out there, emotionally. Did she dare do the same?

"I've wondered the same thing." She dared.

Jonathan immediately stood up and called over to the other men without responding to Kina's words. "We're hitting the sack. If you need anything, emergency-wise, just let us know. Otherwise, we'll see you in the morning."

The guys nodded and turned back to their fire, huddling as close as they dared to try to keep warm and ignoring the two camera crew.

Jonathan held his hand down to Kina. "Ready for bed?"

$$Chapter\ Seven$$

Wow. Jonathan was looking at her in that intense way he had. Kina reached up to take hold of his hand. She had no idea what he had in mind, but for now, in this place, she trusted him. Was he going to escort her to her tent? Had what she said turned him off? Maybe this being honest thing wasn't working out after all.

Jonathan pulled Kina upright and headed to the two small tents they'd put up earlier. They'd set them up so they were facing each other and the doors opened toward each other. Jonathan walked around to the back of the tents, away from the other men and their fire. He never let go of Kina's hand. He stopped in front of the openings to the tents and turned Kina to face him. She really was tiny compared to him. He lifted her chin with one finger so she was looking into his eyes.

"There's nothing more I'd like to do than to take you inside one of our tents and make love to you all night long. I want to see your muscular little body more than I want my next breath. Unfortunately..." Jonathan blew out a long breath of air. They both watched as the chilly temperature turned it into a visible vapor. "It's way too cold to do what I want to do. To take the time, to do what I want to do."

Kina's breath was coming in pants. She couldn't hide what she was feeling because of the coldness of the air. Every little puff that came from her mouth was being broadcasted to Jonathan, loud and clear. She guessed her being honest worked after all. She wanted the same thing. The images his words brought to her mind were hot as hell. She could almost imagine him braced over her, his hair hanging down and brushing over her chest. She shuddered. How could she want this so quickly? She thought about it. Did she just want sex or was it Jonathan? She decided it was definitely Jonathan. No one else had made her feel this way in a long time.

Jonathan ran a finger down Kina's cheek and continued. "Even though it's too cold to make love to you tonight, I want you next to me. I want to feel you along my body. I want to hold you all night. I need to feel every inch of you curled up next to me. I'll understand if you think it's too soon. I won't force you, Kina, it's up to you. Just know I want this. I want this more than anything."

He stopped and actually took a small shuffling step away from her. He dropped his hands to his side. Kina was floored. He'd laid out what he'd wanted and was honest-to-God putting the decision in her hands. Matt would've just grabbed her and shoved her into the small tent.

She nodded at Jonathan. He took a step that brought him back in direct contact with her again. She could feel the heat from his body all along the front side of hers. He wasn't touching her, but if she took a deep breath she knew her breasts would brush against his chest. She craned her neck to look up at him.

"Say the words, hon."

Kina loved, and hated, that he wanted to hear her say what she wanted and he wouldn't just take a small nod from her as agreement.

"I'd love to spend the night curled up next to you," she told him simply and honestly. She had no idea where this was going, but for now she'd take it. It'd been so long since she'd cuddled with a man. She missed it. Matt hadn't been a cuddler. Once he'd gotten off, he turned over, with his back to her and went to sleep. Kina shook her head. She had to stop comparing everything Jonathan did to Matt. It wasn't fair to Jonathan or her. But then again, every time she did compare them, Jonathan always came out on top, so maybe it wasn't such a horrible thing after all.

Jonathan took her hand in his again and stepped toward his tent. He unzipped the opening and motioned for Kina to precede him into the small space. And it *was* small.

These tents were made to hold one person. It'd be a tight fit, but Kina supposed that was what Jonathan envisioned.

Kina entered the tent, sat down, pulled off her boots and put them by the door. She scooted away from the opening and lay down on her side to give Jonathan room to enter. She watched as he first unzipped the other tent and grabbed the sleeping bag. He tossed it into his tent and then he also sat and removed his boots before scooting back and zipping up the flimsy door.

Kina was nervous. She wasn't sure what to do. She should've known Jonathan would take control. He pulled off his outer jacket and placed it where their heads would be. He turned to Kina and reached for the zipper of her jacket as well. Kina watched as he unzipped her jacket. She sat up to help him remove the coat. After placing her jacket next to his, he lay down on his side and put his head in his hand and just stared at her.

"What are you looking at?" Kina said nervously, wondering when he'd start…whatever it was he was going to do.

"I'm savoring this moment. You have no idea how often I've dreamed about you in my bed." He chuckled. "Although this isn't really what I had in mind, but I'll take what I can get."

Kina didn't know what to say to that. He was so different from any man she'd ever met before in her life and she was so out of her element.

"Do you know how beautiful you are?" Jonathan asked quietly, still not moving to touch her in any way.

"I'm not beautiful." Kina told him honestly.

"You are," he insisted, finally moving. He took his index finger and ran it lightly over her eyebrows. Then he ran his finger down her nose and lightly traced her lips. Next, his finger roamed over her cheek to her ear. He continued tracing the contours of her face.

"Your skin is so soft. I've never felt anything like it. Your nose is small and slightly turned up at the end. Your lips are full and every time you speak I imagine what they'd taste like. You have cute little ears and your hair is your crowning glory. Oh, you're beautiful all right, Kina. So beautiful I have no idea how you haven't been snatched up by anyone else yet. But you haven't, and if I have anything to say about it, you won't be." He paused, looked away for a moment and then looked back into her eyes.

"What I'm about to say is probably going to freak you out, but I'm going to say it anyway. You're mine. Mine. I don't care how long it takes for you to realize it and understand that I'm not going anywhere. That I'll do whatever it takes to protect you from anyone who wants to hurt you. I'm not going to cheat on you; I'm not going to look elsewhere if you can't decide right away. I'll be here, waiting for you."

"Are you for real?" Kina couldn't believe what he was saying.

"I'm for real. *This* is real."

Kina closed her eyes. She was so confused. How could she even for a second want to hear that kind of thing from Jonathan? This wasn't the kind of woman she was. She couldn't deny his words made her feel good. More than good. They made her feel as if she finally had someone to count on. Who would be there for her? But at the same time, he was right, his words did freak her out. She wasn't sure what she was supposed to do with them. Her heart was beating what seemed to be a million miles an hour, she was scared, but his words also touched a place deep down inside of her. A part of her that wanted to be taken care of. That wanted to be wanted. She was confused and scared, but strangely, also felt safe. Here. With Jonathan. He wouldn't hurt her. He wouldn't rush her.

When she didn't say anything in response, Jonathan simply said, "Come here, it's cold and we need to get some sleep. Tomorrow will be a long day."

He turned over on his back and held his arm up so Kina could snuggle down against him. When she tentatively dropped down next to him, he grasped one of her arms and pulled it over his chest. Her head was resting on his shoulder and she could feel his arm go around her back. He reached over and pulled the extra sleeping bag over both of them.

Kina felt Jonathan's arm rubbing sensuously over her back. Up and down. Up and down. God, it felt good. She was warm, comfortable lying against his chest and content. She never wanted the morning to come.

"Would you rather gain fifty pounds or lose fifty pounds?"

Kina giggled. She loved this. She was so relaxed. It wasn't weird. It wasn't creepy. It was awesome. He totally got that she didn't want know what to say to his intimate words. He didn't push. He didn't insist she talk to him. He'd just changed the subject back to something light. They played the game for a while until she was so tired she couldn't stay awake anymore.

"This is nice," she said sleepily, losing the battle to stay awake. She was so comfortable.

"This is nice." Jonathan whispered back. "Sleep, hon. I'll be right here."

Kina smiled and fell asleep immediately.

* * *

Kina slowly became aware of her surroundings. It was still mostly dark outside and she couldn't understand what had woken her.

"No! Becky? Where are you? No!"

Kina suddenly remembered where she was and who she was with. She could feel Jonathan thrashing in the throes of a nightmare beside her.

"Becky?" he yelled louder, obviously distraught.

Kina put her hand on his chest. "It's okay, wake up, Jonathan." She spoke firmly, trying to break the grip the dream had on him.

"I'm sorry, I'm so sorry." Jonathan sobbed, still stuck in whatever he was seeing in his dream world.

"Jonathan," Kina said more firmly. "Wake up."

After saying his name a few more times Kina saw his eyes open in the dim morning light and the bleakness she saw there made her gasp.

Jonathan shut his eyes tightly. Crap. He'd had the damn dream again. He'd hoped he'd put it behind him, but it was obvious he hadn't.

"Talk to me," Kina said quietly, rubbing her hand over his chest soothingly.

Jonathan wanted nothing more than to get up and pace, to get away from the sympathy he could see in her eyes in the minimal light in the tent. Could he let her in? Was it too soon? Would she think badly of him? He knew he had to tell her, he'd just hoped it would be later.

Without opening his eyes, he put his hand over his face and scrubbed. "I'm not sure this is the right time to tell you," he told Kina honestly.

"If not now, when?" she asked stubbornly. She put her hand over his, resting on his face. "You said I was yours, I think I want that as well, but you have to talk to me. You have to let me in."

Crap. She was right. Jonathan knew Kina was right, but this was the hardest thing he'd ever had to do in his life. He hoped like hell she wouldn't look at him differently when he was done. His entire life felt like it was at stake. If she rejected him he didn't know what he'd do.

"You know what happened to Becky, my brother's wife, right?"

Kina simply said, "Yes, you know I do."

"I could have prevented it," Jonathan said bleakly, laying it right out there.

"Jonathan, you told me that before. I didn't believe it then and I don't believe it now."

He interrupted her before she could say anything else. He had to get this out all in one shot or he'd never be able to get through it.

"It's true. I went to the hotel that night. I knew something was wrong. I don't know how I knew it, I just did. I was worried about her. When the front desk clerk wouldn't tell me what room she was in, I let it go. He'd only connect me to her room via the phone and she didn't answer. I just left. I should've insisted. I should've called the police or something. I should've done more to find her. I left her there, for those men to hurt her." Jonathan said in anguish. "I left her there," he said again, in a whisper.

Kina came up on an elbow and leaned over Jonathan, getting in his face so he couldn't ignore her words. "It wasn't your fault, Jonathan."

When he didn't say anything she knew she wasn't getting to him. She tried a different tactic. "What did Becky say? Does she blame you?" When he didn't answer she continued. "What about your brother? Does he blame you for what happened to his woman? Did he tell you it was your fault?"

"No," Jonathan said softly.

"Why don't you believe them? Do you really think they'd lie to you? Do you really think Becky would be doing so well if they blamed you? If she still held some angst toward you?" Kina tried one last question to try to get through to Jonathan. "Would your brother still want you to come home and work with him if he thought you were in any way responsible for what happened to Becky?"

Jonathan didn't say anything. Kina leaned down and brushed her lips over his cheek, then his forehead, then finally his lips. She kept her mouth close to his and said resolutely, her lips brushing his with each word. "It. Is. Not. Your. Fault."

Jonathan didn't say anything, but his arms came up around her, knocking her off balance. She fell onto his chest and his lips claimed hers. He left her no room to back off, no room to say no. He conquered her mouth with his. His tongue swept inside her mouth, curling around hers and memorizing her taste, the feel of her. He ran his tongue over her teeth, around and over her tongue, and finally he drew back, nipping her lips with his teeth before curling his hand around the back of her neck and bringing her forehead to rest against his. He didn't apologize for the rough kiss he'd stolen. Her hair fell around them, cocooning them into their own private world.

He needed her more than anything he could remember ever needing before in his life. She was his. He wasn't going to let her go. He couldn't bring himself to apologize for the kiss, even if she hadn't wanted it or initiated it. He'd needed it.

"I dream I'm looking for her everywhere, but I can't find her. I'm calling her name over and over and I know she's there, but she's not answering me. I'm in a hallway and trying to open all the doors. I know she's behind one of them, but I don't know which one. All the doors are locked and I'm just going up and down the hall trying to get into the rooms yelling for her. Finally I get to a room and the door is unlocked. I open it and she's lying on the floor. Bloody and beaten. She opens her eyes and looks up at me. She says 'Why didn't you find me earlier?' She blames me in my dream. It's always the same. I never find her in time and she wants to know why."

Kina tried to concentrate. Holy hell, their kiss had knocked her socks off. It was so hot. Jonathan hadn't asked if it was okay, he hadn't let her take the lead, he'd stolen the kiss, and she'd loved every second of it. He took it from her and she'd gladly let him. This man was hurting and needed her. Her. No one had ever needed her that badly before.

"You have to stop torturing yourself," Kina whispered. "Becky and Dean wouldn't want this for you. You said it yourself, she's doing great. Yes, what she went through sucked, but she's happy now. No one blames you, but yourself. You have to forgive yourself, Jonathan. Look at it this way. If the same thing happened today, would you do everything the same as you did then?" She didn't even have to wait for him to answer. "No, you wouldn't. Learn from what happened and move on. For your sake, for their sake," her voice lowered even more, "for our sake, move on."

Jonathan's eyes opened and peered into her own. They were face to face. She saw the guilt burning in his eyes, but she also thought she saw hope. "I'll try, Kina. I'll try, but if I slip, I hope you'll be there to help me up."

Kina nodded. "I will, Jonathan. I will."

It was enough, for now.

"I'm sorry about the kiss, hon."

Kina smiled. This she could deal with. "I'm not."

"You're not?"

"How could I be? That was the hottest good morning kiss I've ever received. Hell, it was the hottest kiss I've ever received, period." Kina loved to see the smile come over Jonathan's face. Man he was hot, and for now, he was hers. She couldn't help but tease him, glad they were getting back to their lighthearted banter. "But you did say I could be in charge, remember?"

Jonathan smirked. He brought his hands up away from her body and clasped them together under his head in a relaxed pose. "By all means, take charge." He challenged her, hoping like hell she'd take him up on it.

Kina looked down at the broad chest she'd been lying on. The sun had finally started making its way over the horizon and allowed just enough light to admire him with. His long hair was spread out over their makeshift pillow and the sweatshirt he was wearing was stretched tight over his abs and chest. She licked her lips. This was going to be fun.

"You'll keep your arms there?" She asked innocently running one finger down the center of his chest toward his waistband. She swore she heard him growl.

"Careful hon, you might bite off more than you can chew."

Kina laughed. "Oh, I think I can handle what you've got." She bent down and nipped his chin. Yup, that was definitely a growl, but she was impressed with his control as he kept his hands clenched together under his head.

"Kiss me. God, please kiss me." He bit out.

Kina couldn't tease him anymore. She wanted Jonathan as much as he apparently wanted her. She leaned down and licked his bottom lip. Before he could do anything else she grabbed his lip with her teeth and pulled. That was it. His control was gone.

He sat up, grabbed her by the shoulders and spun her around in the small space. Kina found herself on her back with Jonathan leaning over her. He slammed his lips down on hers once again and they battled for control. Kina wasn't going to passively lie there and let Jonathan do whatever he wanted. She let her hands wander while their tongues dueled and their teeth nipped and pulled at each other. She worked her way under the back of his sweatshirt and under his T-shirt and let her nails lightly scrape their way up his back as far as she could get them to go. She whimpered when Jonathan drew back from her mouth to stare down at her.

He didn't say a word, but he flattened his hand and drew it down over her chest, over her breastbone, over her bellybutton to the button on her jeans. He didn't unbutton it, but worked her T-shirt out of her pants and moved his hand underneath. God almighty. His hand was chilly from the morning air and she could feel the callouses covering the palm of his hand. He worked his way upward, never losing eye contact with her, until he reached her belly button. One finger swirled around it and lightly pressed in.

She couldn't help it, the question just popped into her head and she couldn't hold it back. "Would you rather have an innie or an outie?" She watched as Jonathan didn't say anything, but smiled and dropped his lips back to hers.

As they kissed and continued to learn the contours of each other's mouth, Jonathan's hand moved upward again. He went as far up as the bottom of her bra then stopped, running his fingers over the underwire sensuously. Over and over, Jonathan's fingers caressed the skin just under her bra. Goosebumps rose all over her skin and she could feel his grin as he felt them too. Her nipples were hard and she swore she could feel them ache.

Jonathan's long hair was hanging around them and Kina imagined how it would feel to have his hair brushing over her bare chest, as he suckled at her breasts. Her breath came out in short choppy pants.

Kina dug her nails into Jonathan's lower back a bit harder, not hard enough to break his skin, but enough to let him know she was loving what he was doing to her body and what she wanted him to do to her body.

Just as Jonathan's hands started to skim over the cups of her bra they heard, "Good morning!" ring out from across the clearing. Damn.

Jonathan raised his head from hers and they both stilled. Kina couldn't help but giggle. Jonathan shook his head and smiled down at Kina. "I did say last night, this wasn't what I wanted to happen, but I can't be sorry. You feel so good, hon. I can't wait to get you alone."

Kina slowly removed her hands from Jonathan's skin soothing him where she'd dug her nails in and brought one hand up to his scruffy face. "I can't wait either."

Jonathan reluctantly slid his hands back down her belly and smoothed her T-shirt down. He cupped her cheeks in his and leaned down to give her a sweet kiss on the lips. "As much as I want to feel your heat surrounding me, we'll take our time. You deserve to be wooed."

"Wooed? Who says that?"

"I do," answered Jonathan with a smile. "Now, how about we get this show on the road? Eddie would have our heads if we didn't get the guys' morning routine on film."

Kina nodded. As much as she wanted to stay in this little tent with Jonathan all day, they had a job to do.

<h1 style="text-align:center">Chapter Eight</h1>

To give Roger and Darius credit, they didn't say anything when Kina and Jonathan got out of the same tent that morning. Kina figured they were just too miserable to care what the camera operators were doing. Their shelter had held up through the night, but it wasn't very much protection from the biting wind and the cold weather. They'd managed to keep the fire going throughout the night and it was blazing when Kina had finished brushing her teeth and using the little girl's "tree."

Kina had never liked keeping her distance from the contestants. It just seemed cold to watch people day in and day out and not talk to them. She'd tried to refrain from getting to know Sam, from the Australian reality show, but that didn't last very long, especially after Sam had saved her life. The two of them had forged a close friendship that she treasured today. Kina hated what Eddie had done to her and Alex and was so glad they'd managed to end up together despite the underhanded tricks Eddie played on them both on the set and during the editing process.

While Kina knew she'd never be close to Darius and Roger like she was with Sam, she still made the effort. She wandered over to their fire and held her hands out. Even though she'd been snuggled up to Jonathan all night, the air this morning was chilly and the flames felt good on her fingers.

"What's up for the day, gentlemen?" she asked politely.

"Trying to get that damn raft to float," Roger answered for them both. "We've tried everything we can think of to get the darn thing to stay together when we put it on the lake, but the knots we've tied always come undone. Got any advice for us?" he asked hopefully.

Jonathan piped in before Kina could say anything. "Sorry guys, that one's outside our expertise."

Kina looked over at him. She hadn't heard him come up behind her. She wasn't sure if he'd answered because he thought she'd jump in to help the men or what. She relaxed when she saw him wink at her. Okay, then.

The day actually went by pretty quickly after they ate breakfast. Darius and Roger headed down to the lake and Kina and Jonathan spent the better part of the morning filming their trials, and sometimes heated discussions, on how to get the raft to be seaworthy.

They took a break for lunch a few hours later. Jonathan and Kina wandered a bit away from the men to eat, simply because they didn't want to flaunt the fact that they had a nice well-rounded lunch, and the men only had the remains of their one MRE.

Jonathan found a flat rock in the sun and gestured for Kina to sit. He brought over their supplies and pulled out two oranges, bread, sliced turkey, slightly wilted lettuce, and two small bags of potato chips.

Kina peeled the oranges while Jonathan put together their sandwiches. Kina thought for what seemed the hundredth time, how well the two of them worked together. She hated to keep comparing Jonathan to Matt, but she couldn't help it. Matt would've made her do everything while he glared at her in displeasure as she did it.

There were so many differences between the two men it wasn't even fair to compare them. Jonathan had opened up to her that morning. He'd made himself vulnerable to her and shown her a side of himself she knew many people didn't get to see. He felt deeply. Jonathan wasn't the kind of man to let things go easily. On the surface he came across as a typical macho man who wanted to be in charge, but by his actions, he'd proven over and over to have hidden depths.

Jonathan held out a sandwich to her. They sat and ate in companionable silence. The sandwiches tasted awesome. Kina wasn't sure if it was because of where they were, but she knew she'd remember this little picnic for the rest of her life. Nothing with Jonathan was as she'd experienced before. So far she'd loved every second of her time spent with him. He was courteous and attentive, but not suffocating. He was also fun to be around.

"Would you rather have to eat nothing other than fruits or vegetables for the rest of your life, or only able to eat meat?"

Jonathan laughed. He loved the scenarios Kina could come up with. They always seemed appropriate to their circumstances. He noticed they'd both finished eating their sandwiches and had moved on to the oranges. He got a wicked idea.

Kina startled when Jonathan reached over and took her hand in his. He lifted it up to his mouth and put her index finger in his mouth and sucked the juice off. She could feel his tongue swirl around her knuckle sensuously. Gah. Two could play at that game.

She grabbed his hand that was holding hers and returned the gesture, only hers was much more suggestive of what she'd like to do to him later. She twirled her tongue around his finger and took the entire thing into her mouth down to the knuckle, then sucked hard. She watched, fascinated as his cheeks flushed, and his eyes dropped into slits. She probably shouldn't poke the bear, but it was so much fun.

Jonathan tried to get himself under control. My God, this woman was dangerous. She was lucky he was a gentleman and wanted to take his time the first time he had her.

"I've never been with someone like you."

Jonathan turned toward Kina and lifted his eyebrows. He'd wanted her to open up to him, but it wasn't something that could be rushed. Kina had to do it on her own and at her own pace. He was floored when she not only opened herself up, but laid herself bare. He grasped her hand, offering silent support, while she continued talking.

"When I was growing up, I never knew my dad. My mom worked really hard to keep a roof over our heads and put food on the table. She was a good parent, but just not there much for me, emotionally. We moved around a lot, she was always trying to find a better job and more money, but unfortunately, that always seemed out of reach. When I was sixteen, she had a heart attack and died."

"Where was your dad?"

"He wasn't around. Mom never talked about him much, only to tell me that once he heard she was pregnant, he left. He didn't want a kid and as far as I know he never even saw me."

Jonathan heard the pain in her voice. "That's his loss, Kina."

She nodded, then continued. "I moved in with a friend of mine from school until I graduated. I had one boyfriend in high school. I thought we were good. I'd been planning on trying to get into the same college he was going to attend. One day, I heard through the grapevine at school, he'd been cheating on me. When I asked him about it he just shrugged and told me what we had was never serious. It was only a fling and he couldn't believe I'd thought we were going to stay together. It hurt."

Jonathan's arm wrapped around her shoulders and pulled her into his side. Kina couldn't get distracted now. She had to keep going. He'd opened up to her this morning, she could do the same. "Then I met Matt. He seemed to be everything I'd ever wanted. He wanted to take care of me and I wanted to be taken care of. My mom hadn't done that great of a job at it and my high school boyfriend hadn't wanted me either. At first it was great. He was paying all the bills; he drove me where I wanted to go. He did stuff I thought was courteous and helpful, like get my phone messages for me and answer my phone. After a while he got more and more 'helpful.' He wouldn't let me go anywhere without him. I soon lost touch with any friends I did have in high school. He made himself the center of my world.

"He'd get crazy jealous whenever we went anywhere. If the guy bagging our groceries smiled at me, he'd threaten him. God forbid when we went out, if someone talked to me, he'd lose it. When we'd get home, he'd accuse me of leading men on. The sex became more and more scary. He'd hold me down and put his hand over my mouth to keep me quiet as he took me. He didn't care about foreplay or making sure I wanted any of what he was doing to me.

"I knew it was out of control. I didn't know how I'd gotten there. How did me wanting someone to take care of me, turn into that? Finally, one day when he'd gone to work, I wrote him a note, packed up what I could, and just left."

"Have you ever heard from him since, hon?"

"No, never. It was as if once I left, he forgot all about me. That's definitely a good thing." Kina paused, getting to the point of her story. "I can't go back to that, Jonathan. Matt taught me a lot about myself. I can't be owned. I might like having someone pay attention to me and do things for me, but being 'taken care of' isn't what I want anymore."

Jonathan turned Kina toward him. He looked in her eyes and hoped she could see his sincerity. "I don't want to control you, love. I can't deny I want to take care of you, but not like he did. I want to make sure you're comfortable. I want to be there for you when you've had a bad day. I want to make your lunch for you. I want to drive you places, but not to be controlling, but to just be with you for an extra five minutes of the day. When I say you're 'mine,' I don't mean as a possession. I mean you're mine to protect, to care for, to be with, to care about." Jonathan couldn't say 'love,' it was too soon. Oh, he meant that, but figured it was too soon for her to hear it.

"I'm not him. I'll do everything in my power to try to make that clear to you. I love that you can take charge. I love that you're independent. There's no way I want to decide what you should wear each day or even make all the decisions about what we should eat and when. I just don't want you ever to be too independent to not want me around."

Kina took a deep breath. "Just give me time."

"You got it, hon. As much as you need. You got it."

Jonathan leaned toward her and kissed her gently on the forehead. He then gathered up their trash and tried to get both of them back on an even keel. They still had a long day ahead of them and he knew they had to get going. After putting their lunch things away he looked down at Kina, pulled her hand up to his mouth and kissed it tenderly.

"Ready to go?"

At her nod he dropped her hand and they both grabbed up their cameras and headed back towards the contestants.

The rest of the afternoon was much the same as the morning. Roger and Darius had finally seemed to get the hang of the knots and lashings they needed to make their raft float. It was a good thing they'd only have one more night outside, however, because their tempers were flaring and it was clear they were ready to have a break from one another.

That night, the four of them sat around the fire for a while, talking about their lives back home and why the two contestants decided they wanted to be on a reality show. Kina wasn't surprised to hear they'd thought they'd be on a different kind of show.

"I agreed to be on the show because I thought it was a bachelorette type of show," Roger said. "It was only right before we were to leave to come up here Eddie told us the show had changed."

Darius agreed. "Yeah, I'm not really cut out for this type of thing. But I figured I'd already told everyone I was going to be on television, so I might as well still come."

"Did he give you a chance to back out?" Kina asked curiously.

"Yes, from what I understand, there were a few guys who refused to come, after hearing it was some sort of 'ultra man' challenge thing." Roger answered.

Kina nodded. She'd thought it was odd there were only twelve men to start with. That number seemed low. But Eddie obviously hadn't wanted to open auditions again so he went with what he had.

"So far," Darius went on, "the show's been kinda lame. The challenges haven't been too hard, especially since they're trying to make this show out to be some sort of macho man thing. But I suppose that's okay with us since we weren't really prepared for it."

Kina had to agree. After the sun started to set, Kina looked over at Jonathan. Would he want to sleep in the same tent tonight? She was so nervous. She wanted to sleep with him again, but only sleep. She wasn't ready for more…yet. She felt pretty raw after sharing how her relationship with Matt had been like with him. She didn't think Jonathan was the type of man to run scared after hearing something like that, but how well did she really know him after all?

Jonathan was waiting for Kina to look at him. He'd been ready to hit the sack a while back, but was enjoying the camaraderie Kina had with the two men. She was fascinating to watch. Her natural, bubbly personality made people want to confide in her. He gestured with his head towards their tents, asking nonverbally if she was ready. She nodded and picked herself up off the ground.

"We're going to head off to sleep," she said half-apologetically, knowing she'd be warm and relatively comfortable tonight, while they'd have to sleep on the hard ground and in the cold again.

Jonathan was feeling pretty mellow until Roger opened his mouth.

"Yeah, wish I could have me some of that," he said not too quietly.

Jonathan was in his face before anyone could react. "You want to say that again?"

"Ah, no, sorry," Roger stammered, obviously taken aback at how quickly Jonathan had gone from friendly cameraman to pissed-off in-his-face male.

Jonathan glared at him some more and said before turning back toward Kina, "No one disrespects my woman. Especially not in front of me…got it?"

He watched as Roger nodded furiously and dropped his eyes to the ground and away from him.

Satisfied, Jonathan reluctantly turned back toward Kina. He had no idea how she'd react to his actions. After all she'd told him, he figured she'd probably be pissed. She'd told him often enough how she hated to be treated like she couldn't take care of herself. But when he'd heard the crude words coming from Roger he just reacted. He couldn't have sat there and allowed him to diss Kina like that. No way.

When Jonathan turned around he saw Kina standing with her arms folded across her chest…grinning.

Thank God.

Jonathan didn't say anything, but put his arm around her and rested his hand at the small of her back before steering them toward their tents. He waited to hear what she had to say. It didn't take long; they hadn't even made it ten steps when she said, "God, that was hot."

He smiled.

"Would you rather have a guy fight for you or over you?"

He wasn't expecting an answer, but heard Kina say under her breath, "For me."

* * *

As Jonathan lay in his tent with Kina in his arms, he thought about what would happen after the show was over. He knew he was headed back to Arizona for good. He was telling Kina the truth when he'd explained that he wasn't cut out to be a camera operator anymore. He was excited about his new career. He didn't know what Kina thought was happening between them, though. Sure, he'd told her she was his, but he didn't know if she really understood what that meant or what he'd meant by it.

They'd had a lot of serious talks lately, but he figured he might as well start one more. He hated to disturb the sweet feeling of her lying in his arms. Kina fit him perfectly and he could imagine them falling asleep this way every night for the rest of their lives, but that was the problem. He had no idea if *she* also could see that, or even if she wanted it.

"You awake?" he asked Kina softly.

"Yeah," she murmured sleepily.

"What are your plans for after this show is over?" he asked bluntly, not beating around the bush. He might as well throw it out there. Jonathan knew Kina would rather he be upfront and honest than prevaricate.

Kina was tired and half-asleep, until she heard the seriousness behind Jonathan's question. She had no idea how to answer him. She knew what she wanted, but she wasn't sure what he wanted to hear.

She decided to tread carefully. "Eddie's offered to sign me on for another three show contract, but I'm not sure I want to keep working for him. I'm not thrilled with the way he treats people and what he's done to the contestants on his shows in the past."

She squirmed when Jonathan didn't answer right away.

"What if I asked you to come back to Arizona with me?" he finally asked.

God. Kina didn't know how to answer him. It was way too soon for her to be thinking about moving to a different state for a man…wasn't it?

"I don't know what to say," she told him honestly. And she didn't. She wanted to jump up and scream 'Yes!' but the more practical side of her said she didn't even know him.

"Say yes," Jonathan urged, but said no more.

"What would I do there?"

Jonathan wanted to tell her that she didn't have to do anything but love him, but he knew that'd sound crazy. And besides, Kina was the type of woman who needed to do something; she needed to feel like she was contributing. She'd never let him earn all the money.

"I don't know," he said honestly, "but I'd help you find whatever it was that you wanted to do there. All I know is I want you with me. I don't want to leave in a few weeks and never see you again. You're all I've ever wanted in my life. More than I ever thought I'd have. I want to introduce you to my folks as mine, have you see how happy they are on the animal refuge they run. I know you saw them when you were there for the last show, but I want you to know them. I want to have double dates with my brother and Becky."

"You're smart, Kina; if you want to stay in television, I'm sure you'll find your way to do that. We have lots of TV stations there, with your experience, someone will snatch you up quickly. If you want to do something else, we'll figure that out too. I just want to share my life with you, however you'll let me."

Kina teared up. She was thankful it was dark in the tent and Jonathan couldn't see her. "I'll have to think about it," she finally said, once she had her emotions under control. "I've been at the mercy of a man before, I told you about that," she told him honestly. "I don't know if I can do it again." She felt him nod, but he kept silent.

"I'm not asking you to be at my mercy, hon. If anything, I'm at your mercy. You could tell me you wanted to live on a nudist colony and I'd be helpless to deny you anything. If you wanted to get your own place, I'd understand. I want you to feel comfortable and not feel like I'm smothering you. It would kill me to have you living there and not in my arms every night, but I understand why you'd need that. I do."

Quiet settled over them. They both had a lot to think about.

When Kina didn't think Jonathan would say anything else before they fell back asleep, he surprised her.

"All my life I've heard from my dad about how he met my mom. He told me and Dean stories about how when we found the woman for us, we'd know immediately. We'd take one look and know she was the One. Kina, I swear I thought he was crazy. There was no way anyone could do that. It wasn't logical. Dean and I always laughed at him behind his back. Then Dean met Becky. He told me it was exactly as Dad had explained to us. He met her and knew she was it for him. He was done. Period. I still didn't really believe the whole thing. I mean, it's ridiculous...Then I met you."

Silence filled the tent again. What was he saying? Was he saying…no.

"Jonathan," Kina started. She had no idea what she was going to say, but Jonathan interrupted her by putting his fingers across her lips. His fingers were warm against her mouth. She felt his lips skim across the top of her head.

"Don't say anything, love. I know it's crazy and hard to believe, hell, I didn't believe it and I had the proof in my dad and ancestors right there in my face my entire life. But you're it for me. If you don't want to go to Arizona, I'll go wherever you want to go. I'll follow you around as you advance your career. I don't care. I'll stay at home and clean and cook and do your laundry. Whatever it takes. I won't lie, I was looking forward to working with Dean and living near my family, but you mean more to me than all of that. You think about it. Whatever you want to do, I'll be there, if you'll let me."

Kina didn't like it. Not at all. She didn't want to be his One. She wasn't good enough for him. How could he feel that for her? She had so many questions and so many doubts. It was too much pressure.

Jonathan sighed. He knew it was too soon for him to reveal his feelings, but he couldn't help it. He loved her. Period. He'd let Kina think about what he said and hope like hell he hadn't just chased her away for good.

He put his hand on the back of her head and held her to him. "Shhhh, don't say anything. Just go to sleep. No pressure, hon. I swear. Just sleep. We'll talk about it later."

He felt her nod. Neither fell asleep right away.

Chapter Nine

Kina woke up first in the morning. Jonathan had slept peacefully through the night and hadn't had any more nightmares, at least none that had woken her up. She lay there waiting for the day to start, enjoying the feeling of being held tight. Even in his sleep, Jonathan hadn't loosened his hold on her. It felt…good. Not stifling, as it would have felt if another man held her like that. Kina breathed in Jonathan's smell. He hadn't shaved in the time they'd been out there, and the beginnings of his dark beard were sexy as hell. She would've gotten up, but somehow knew if she moved, he'd immediately wake up. She was enjoying being close to him and listening to him lightly snore.

She thought about everything he'd told her last night. She'd been way freaked out, but this morning, lying in his arms, she'd mellowed. She had no idea why, but she believed him. She'd seen Dean with Becky. She'd even seen his parents with each other. There was something about their relationships that seemed magical. She never saw any of them being overbearing or too controlling. Yes, Dean was protective, but Becky never complained. The more Kina thought about it, the more the tight ball of doubt in her stomach began to loosen.

Eventually, Jonathan began to stir. The real world would intrude on their idyllic time soon enough. She looked in his eyes as they opened for the first time.

"What time is it?" he mumbled sleepily.

"I have no idea." She decided to go on as if their emotional discussion the night before hadn't happened. There'd be time to re-hash it and figure everything out later. "Would you rather have to wake up at six am every morning no matter what, or not be able to go to sleep until one am?" As far as a "would you rather" question, it was kinda lame, but Jonathan laughed anyway. He squeezed her once and stretched.

"I'll go out first, give you some time to get changed, unless you want to go first?"

Kina nodded and waved him on. He was always looking out for her, never forcing her to do things his way. Would that annoy her down the line? Would it get old? She wasn't sure. She wasn't submissive, but it was nice to be taken care of now and then. She'd been honest with Jonathan about that. She figured it had a lot to do with her childhood, when she'd not really had anyone to take care of her. She sighed. She was worrying herself to death. Kina decided to take the day as it came and not worry about anything other than getting the best shots for the show.

Darius and Roger were actually still sleeping by the time she and Jonathan had finished getting ready. Kina filmed some quick shots of them sleeping that could be spliced into the final version of the show, then helped Jonathan pack up their tents. They'd be picked up today and the competition would commence to see whose raft floated the best in the lake.

Not too much later, the two men woke up and started their morning. They didn't have any food left, having eaten it all in the days before, and they hadn't found anything else to eat near the campsite. They were grumpy and tired, and it showed. Kina tried not to laugh. It wasn't nice, but she knew it'd make for great reality TV.

Precisely at noon, Eddie strode into the camp area. Kina had no idea where he came from, but thought it was funny he just sort of appeared out of thin air. He asked Darius and Roger if they were ready to go and simply nodded when an emphatic 'yes' was the answer.

They all trudged down to where a boat was waiting on the lake. It had Benedict and Nash in it already, along with Taylor. The plan was to collect everyone and meet Shannel back at a rendezvous point. They'd film some of the ceremony there and then make the rounds to each of the campsites where the men would show off their rafts and attempt to make the six-hundred-yard round trip, to prove their raft was seaworthy. Of course on television, it would be seamless and the traveling from campsite to campsite wouldn't be shown. More of the magic of editing and television.

It was a pretty sad group that gathered with Shannel. Trent and Ian apparently weren't speaking to each other because of something that happened back at their campsite. Roger and Darius weren't too bad, although Roger looked like he had a three-week beard instead of just a three-day one. Benedict and Nash looked like they hadn't slept at all in the last three days.

Shannel went around the group, asking the men how they fared, whether they'd had anything to eat besides the one MRE they were given, and if they were able to light a fire with the flint they were given.

Kina was scared that Roger and Darius were going to spill the beans about how she'd cheated and given them a few matches, but she should've known better. There was no way they were going to let anyone know what had happened. They were too thankful they'd had fire to give her away.

The others had also managed, from what they'd said, to light their fire. It seemed that was the best thing that happened to any of them, however. Trent and Ian fought over every aspect of their time out in the wilderness. Trent had wanted to build the raft one way and Ian disagreed. So they'd spent the first day and a half arguing about it. They didn't want to cooperate with each other in building a place to sleep because they were so mad at each other, so they suffered as a result of that as well. Since Ian was a restaurant owner, he had all sorts of ideas about how to find food, but Trent's occupation as a nurse made him wary of eating anything that wasn't packaged and safe. All in all, it sounded like they'd had a perfectly miserable time. Kina knew they would be highlighted pretty heavily in the airing of the show. While Eddie might not like drama personally, it made for great television.

Kina thought Roger and Darius' recounting of their time by the lake was actually pretty boring, especially compared to Ian and Trent's. She knew Eddie would cut most of it from the show. There just wasn't anything fun to watch about two people getting along and not having anything dramatic happen.

Benedict and Nash had a close call with a bear while they were sleeping one night. Apparently Nash hadn't put away the trash from their MRE very well and they'd heard a bear around their site. They panicked and didn't know what to do, but Taylor had taken one of his camera lights and shone it at the bear. Luckily, the bright light scared it enough, that it ambled away. Of course Taylor hadn't gotten that part on film, much to Eddie's chagrin, but he did manage to get some footage of the bear walking away into the woods surrounding the lake. It was a good shot, just enough drama to use as a teaser for the show.

The contestants were all loaded up into one boat with Shannel, Eddie, and Carl, and the rest of the crew climbed into another. They headed off to Trent and Ian's campsite and raft first.

Jeff couldn't control himself and just had to act like an ass, while they were headed away from the dock.

"So…you two have a good time out in the wilderness?"

Jonathan didn't answer, trying to control himself for Kina's sake, but glared at Jeff instead. Kina could've told him that wouldn't shut the other man up.

"Seriously, did you use body heat to keep warm? Wish I was paired up with you, baby, I would've found some creative ways to keep you warm a-l-l night long."

Before Kina could put a hand on Jonathan to keep him calm, he'd taken Jeff by the collar and was holding him over the side of the fast-moving boat. Crap!

"If you ever lay a hand on her, you'll regret it. Hear me?"

Kina quickly put her camera down and instead of pulling on Jonathan, she knew that wouldn't do any good, she leaned over Jonathan, putting her hand on the small of his back to steady herself and put her face right up next to Jeff's.

"As if I'd let you anywhere near me Jeff. Stick with your groupie chicks, you'll never get any of this!"

Jonathan realized what he'd done the second he felt Kina's hand on his back. Ah, crap. Oh well, it was too late to take it back. It was the third time he'd acted without thinking when someone had spoken crap to Kina. She'd forgiven him twice; he wasn't sure how long his luck would hold out if he kept it up. He was shocked to hear Kina's scowled words at Jeff. Although he supposed he shouldn't be. She could hold her own, he knew it, but there was no way he'd leave her to fight her own battles. She was his. He'd protect her no matter who or what was threatening her. And Jeff's words were definitely a threat.

He pulled back, bringing Jeff upright with him, and Jonathan could still feel Kina's hand on his back. She was lightly rubbing in little circles, as if to calm him down. And surprisingly, it was working. Just her touch alone could ground him.

As soon as he had his balance, Jeff shrugged off Jonathan's hold. "I was just kidding man, jeez!"

They all knew he hadn't been joking, but in order to let it drop, they all backed off. Kina picked her camera off the bottom of the boat and waited for them to arrive at the campsite. She wasn't sure why she wasn't more pissed. If it had been any other man, or even if this had happened before she and Jonathan had spent those two days and nights talking and sharing emotional experiences, she would've gone off. She was perfectly able to speak for herself and put Jeff in his place. But now, knowing Jonathan the way she did, she felt warm inside. It was obvious he was trying to tone down any he-man tendencies he might have, but to have someone so willing to stick up for her was a heady feeling. One she was very afraid she could get used to.

* * *

It was decided the camera operators for each pair of contestants would film their portion of the raft contest, so Kina and Jonathan could just watch from a distance as Benedict and Nash tried to paddle the six hundred yards on their raft. Kina thought they just might have a chance. Their raft seemed to be very sturdy and at first, they were doing great. They'd made it three hundred yards out and had started back toward the shore when it started tipping.

Nash tried to compensate for Benedict's weight sliding toward the water but couldn't quite recover the raft. It made for an excellently framed shot. Benedict fell into the water with a huge splash and the raft tipped all the way up. This, consequently, literally threw Nash from the tallest point on the raft, head-over-heels into the water. The raft flipped completely upside down. If the contest was being held in Florida this wouldn't have been a big deal, but because it was Alaska, in late September, it was a serious situation.

The water was not warm. Everyone standing around knew the men didn't have a lot of time, before they'd start freezing, literally. The motorized boat was there, ready to fish the contestants out of the water if needed, but first it was obvious they wanted to try to get back on their raft and finish the competition. After a few attempts, everyone standing on the bank watching knew it wasn't going to be possible. Every time Benedict tried to get back on, the raft tipped almost vertically so he couldn't manage it. They got smart and Nash tried to balance it out on the other side, but as soon as Benedict got halfway on and Nash tried to get on as well, it would tip.

After about five minutes of the men gallantly trying to board their craft, the medic on the boat called it quits. The two men were fished out of the lake and their sad little raft was towed back to shore.

Kina wasn't one to laugh at anyone's misfortune, but they had looked pretty funny. She was just glad it wasn't her in the cold water. While everyone else was warm and dry on the bank, Ian said just loud enough for those standing around to hear, "What doesn't kill you, makes you stronger."

Kina almost lost it when Jonathan leaned toward her and whispered for her ears only, "Except for bears, bears will kill you." It was especially funny since they were all currently standing in prime bear territory. It was funny, but not funny at the same time. Kina mock-glared at Jonathan and said primly, "Shhhh, behave!"

They shared a smile at the joke.

When the men got back to shore, everyone could see the medic had provided them with emergency blankets to warm their core body temperature. The men were fine health-wise. Wet, cold, and upset they couldn't make it back to shore on the raft, but fine.

Everyone re-boarded the boats to make their way to Roger and Darius' camp so those two could try out their home-made raft. Apparently, making a raft from scratch was harder than it looked. Roger and Darius started out well, just as Benedict and Nash had, but they had issues even before they'd made it to the three hundred yard mark. There wasn't anything dramatic about the failure of their raft, they just suddenly started sinking. One minute they were there on the lake paddling hard, the next they were up to their waists in water, then everyone saw logs floating all around them and all that could be seen of them was their heads bobbing above the waterline.

They were quickly hauled into the safety boat as well. Benedict and Nash high-fived each other. Because they'd gone further than Roger and Darius, they'd be staying on the show. It was up to Trent and Ian to beat the benchmark that had just been set by Roger and Darius.

Shortly after everyone arrived at their campsite, it was pretty obvious that Trent and Ian would be going home. Their raft looked like it had been built by a bunch of kids. There were large spaces between the logs they'd tried to lash together, which by itself wouldn't necessarily mean the raft wouldn't float, but the lashings were unevenly spaced and the knots didn't look right. Kina figured if she, someone who knew nothing about what a knot on a homemade raft was supposed to look like, thought they looked weird, then the duo was doomed.

Kina was amazed the raft actually made it about forty yards offshore before suddenly coming apart. Much like Roger and Darius' raft, one moment Trent and Ian were sitting on the logs paddling and the next, there were logs floating all around them and the men were treading water. Unlike Roger and Darius, the two men immediately started yelling at each other and blaming the other for their failure.

Because they were so close to shore they weren't picked up by the emergency boat, but they simply swam back to where everyone was standing instead. The second they could stand, Ian threw a punch at Trent. Apparently, Trent saw it coming and ducked, but instead of taking the higher road and ignoring his partner, he swung right back at Ian. The fight was definitely on.

Kina didn't bother picking up her camera to film; she figured Jeff and Carl had it under control. She noticed that Jonathan subtly took a step to his side and was half-standing in front of her. Again, if someone had done that even a month ago, she would've blown up and gotten pissed. She could take care of herself and made sure everyone knew it. But Jonathan protecting her? She was all over that. She actually liked it.

When Ian and Trent's fight brought them closer to where they were standing, Jonathan took hold of Kina's elbow and backed her up, while somehow still staying in front of her.

Jonathan wanted nothing more than to break up the fight, but since he wasn't a part of the show he couldn't. He knew Eddie would be beyond pissed if any of the staff cut in. Fighting was classic reality TV and usually brought huge audiences. Jonathan knew this wasn't cool and the men could really hurt each other. He caught Roger's eye. Roger was a teacher and probably had some experience in breaking up fights before. Jonathan gave him a chin-lift toward the two men.

Roger obviously got the gist of what Jonathan was trying to tell him. The staff of the show couldn't break up the fight, but the other contestants could. Roger grabbed Darius by the shoulder and the two of them made their way over to Trent and Ian who were still trying to pulverize the other. Benedict and Nash saw what they were doing and went over to help as well.

"Yo! Enough!" He tried to reason with them first. When it didn't even faze the two men slugging it out, Roger and Benedict grabbed Ian and Darius and Nash grabbed Trent. For a moment Kina couldn't see anything but elbows and fists. When the dust settled Trent was on the ground on his stomach and Ian was being held back with a man holding each arm.

"You, dick!" Ian yelled at Trent. "We could've won if you'd have just listened to me!"

"Whatever, Ian!" Trent returned. "If we'd gone with your idea, we wouldn't even have made it as far as we did!"

"Enough!" Nash said loudly. "Jeez. Just enough." He couldn't seem to come up with anything that would really convey his disgust with the other two men.

Kina looked at Eddie who was watching from the side with a look of glee in his eyes. An unplanned fight like this was reality show gold. Usually producers would have to ply their contestants with alcohol to get such a great fight. Not here. It was obvious he loved it. Kina shook her head. One more reason she didn't want to work for him anymore. Eddie cared more about ratings than the people on his shows.

The trip back to the rendezvous point was quiet. When they pulled up to the shore everyone got out and went to their positions for the official ceremony. They all knew who'd be going home; it was just a matter of having it said officially for the show. After Shannel's speech Trent and Ian had to climb into the same van to be driven off the impromptu set. Kina could only chuckle at that. Given how pissed they were at each other, it had to be an interesting drive back to the production house to pack!

The rest of the contestants and Shannel were quickly hustled into another van and all of the camera crew got into their SUV to head back to their own hotel. They were looking forward to having the next day off. After their long three-day outdoor adventure, it'd be great to be able to sleep in and be lazy.

Chapter Ten

Kina knew what she wanted to ask Jonathan, knew what she really wanted, but she was scared to death to actually ask. She knew it'd be up to her, he wouldn't bring it up. As they all gathered their camera equipment from the back of the SUV, Kina thought about the best way to bring it up.

Ah hell, there *was* no good way. Jonathan had always been honest and up front with her, so there was no reason she shouldn't be the same way with him. She lagged behind the others, knowing Jonathan would hang back with her. He was never far from her side nowadays and she liked knowing he had her back.

Softly, as they walked toward the hotel, Kina said, "Would you rather sleep by yourself, or in the warm arms of a friend?"

Jonathan stopped in his tracks and stared down at Kina. Holy crap, had she really just said that? "Ask me," he demanded. He had to make sure she was serious and wasn't just playing their game with him.

Kina looked him right in the eyes and asked, "Do you want to sleep over tonight?"

"Hell yes, honey. I wanted to ask. I've gotten used to having you in my arms, but I didn't want to push. I told you that you'd be in charge and I was determined to make sure you knew I meant it. Thank you for wanting to be with me. Thank you for trusting me."

Kina smiled at Jonathan. God, it was heady to have this strong alpha man thank her for something as simple as asking if he'd spend time with her.

"Let's get cleaned up and meet the others downstairs for some good, hot food. See you in about forty minutes?"

Kina smiled and nodded. "Thank you for not making this any weirder for me than it already feels."

He leaned down and kissed her temple. "Go get clean. I'll see you in a bit."

Jonathan smiled as he entered his room. He was thrilled Kina wanted to be with him. He hadn't lied to her. He'd slept better with her in his arms than he had in the last couple of months since Becky had been hurt. Jonathan debated not shaving off his three day beard, but in the end decided he wanted to be able to feel Kina's soft skin on his face rather than have his scruffy whiskers get in the way. Eventually, when he had his way, he didn't want to scrape up her sensitive skin either.

Kina climbed into the shower and noticed in the bathroom mirror the goofy grin she was wearing as she stepped in. God, had she ever been this giddy around a guy before? She didn't think so. There was something special about Jonathan, but she couldn't put her finger on it. He was so different from any man she'd ever been around before. He was sensitive and not afraid to put his own feelings out there, but at the same time he was as alpha as anyone she'd ever met. Alpha in a good way, not an asshole way like Matt was. He was quick to protect her and make sure no one gave her any crap. But he'd also let her do her own thing, as long as he was sure she wasn't in any danger. It was heady. Kina still had no idea where anything was going with them.

He was going back to Arizona in a few weeks and she had to decide what she was going to do. A part of her wanted nothing more than to drop everything and follow Jonathan, but the other, more independent part of her, didn't want to be one of those women who blindly followed a man. It was so confusing.

Jonathan and Kina met outside their rooms about forty minutes later. They were both showered and cleaned up. Jonathan leaned down and kissed Kina on the cheek. He lingered a bit and nuzzled the side of her neck, breathing in deeply.

"God, you smell good, honey."

"It's just soap."

"Yeah, but it's soap on you, so it smells like nothing I've ever smelled before."

Gah. See? He was awesome.

Jonathan grabbed her hand, as if he had no concerns about who'd see them holding hands, and led her down the hall to the small elevator. They were meeting the others in the hotel restaurant to have a hot meal.

Dinner was fun. They were all in great moods. The fight between Ian and Trent was interesting and everyone knew their camera work would make for great TV. Being warm and clean was also a big boost to everyone's feeling of well-being.

Carl brought out his smart phone and started showing off pictures of his girls. Catherine was a very cute dark-haired five-year old. He related a story about Catherine getting home from her first day of all-day kindergarten a couple of months ago. When she arrived home she stood in the hallway with her hands on her hips and declared loudly, "You fooled me! School is hard!" Apparently, going from a part time day-care/preschool to an all-day kindergarten was tough for a little kid. Kina could almost picture the outrage on her little face.

Carl also told them all a story about a time when Celeste saw an old picture of John Lennon with colored eyeglasses and insisted she get a pair too. She was only six years old and the only kid in her elementary school to have blue-tinted glasses, and according to Carl, she rocked them!

Not to be left out, Taylor got in the action. He bragged about his girls and tried to outdo Carl's stories. The funniest story was about Phyllis. They'd been hanging out at Taylor's mom's house and listening to old songs from the seventies. Phyllis was around six years old and loved singing and dancing. After a morning spent playing games and listening to music, Phyllis disappeared. When they found her, she was in the front yard of the little house, dancing all over and pretending she was on stage. She was belting out the words to Shake Your Booty by KC and the Sunshine

Gang, as loud as she could. Taylor recalled the neighbors standing on their porches laughing hysterically and clapping for his little girl. She'd misunderstood the words to the song and had been entertaining the entire neighborhood by singing "Shake Your Booby" over and over. They still hadn't let her live it down.

Carl's other daughter, Beth, was adorable. She was tall and skinny and apparently, sometimes clueless. He gave an example of how, once when she was young, they were in a public restroom and Beth repeatedly was running her hands under the faucet at the sink to wash her hands. She looked up at Carl with tears in her eyes and said, "It's broken!" Carl leaned over and turned the knob. Beth had assumed it was an automatic faucet.

Kina laughed at the men's stories. It was obvious they were madly in love with their kids. She'd never been sure she even wanted kids, but listening to the two men talk about their families with such devotion and love made her wonder if she should re-think her decision. She didn't have a close-knit family growing up and never really knew families could be like this. Hell, she didn't really know how to be a mother. She'd learned how to be a hard worker from her mom, but any maternal instincts she had were buried deep. Her dad, not being around, was also a factor. Kina wondered, for a moment, if her life would've been different if he'd been there. Would he have been protective of her, or only annoyed she was underfoot? She had no idea, but shrugged off the bad mood threatening. She couldn't change the past and besides, Kina thought she'd turned out all right in the end.

Jonathan squeezed her hand. She looked up at him. He wasn't looking at her, but she knew he'd somehow felt her mood change. How had he gotten to be so perceptive?

After a couple of hours of good food and good company, they decided to call it a night. Kina didn't want it to be obvious that Jonathan would be sleeping in her room, but she also didn't really want to hide their relationship. She surprised herself with that thought. Relationship. Yes, she admitted to herself, she was in a relationship with Jonathan.

It was different from anything she'd had before, and that made it more special.

She'd never had a relationship with a guy and not slept with him. She didn't sleep around, but she was also very cautious. She always kept men at arms' length emotionally, until she decided she was ready. Nothing about this relationship with Jonathan fit the pattern she normally followed. Mentally shrugging, she reflected it was also, so far, the best relationship she'd ever had, so she might as well go with it. She knew it was soon, but spending such close quarters with someone, day in and day out, had a way of speeding up relationships. She'd seen it over and over on the shows she'd filmed. She supposed she and Jonathan were no different, really.

Kina had no idea whether they'd have sex tonight or not. She wanted it with him; there was no doubt about that. It was obvious they had sexual chemistry, but she was also enjoying the intimacy they had, without the pressure of sex to go with it.

As they neared the end of the hallway where they were staying, Carl and Taylor said good night and entered their rooms without looking back. Jeff put his hand on his doorknob and looked back at Jonathan and Kina. Jonathan had taken her hand again and was holding it as Kina dug the key to her room out of her back pocket. Jeff had been quiet; he hadn't made any snide remarks all night about the intimacy the two of them obviously shared. Kina braced herself. She figured he couldn't hold out forever. He had to make some sort of comment. She figured he'd burst if he didn't.

He surprised both of them by simply raising one eyebrow and then mock-saluting them as he entered his own room and closed the door.

Kina looked up at Jonathan and asked skeptically, "Do you think that's the end of that?"

"Frankly hon, I don't care. He can think whatever he wants, as long as he doesn't disrespect you."

Kina just shook her head. How the hell could he just get better and better?

"I'll give you some time to get ready. Half an hour okay? I'll come back over, if that'll work for you?"

Kina leaned up toward Jonathan. He was perfect. Seriously. "Sounds good."

She kissed his lips briefly then turned and opened her door. She smiled at him as she shut it softly behind her. The second it closed she whirled around to face her room. Oh my God! How in the heck had she gotten it so messy in the short time she'd been there? She hurriedly started throwing clothes into drawers and tidying up. She only had thirty minutes to make the room presentable and to figure out what she was going to wear to bed.

* * *

Exactly thirty minutes later, Kina heard a soft tap at the door. She smoothed her hands down the sleep shirt she was wearing. She didn't own anything sexy and figured Jonathan had better get used to her like this. She'd never understood how people could sleep in long slinky nightgowns or even skimpy little tops. Both of those would annoy her to no end while she was sleeping. Nightgowns tended to get twisted around her body and the sexy little tops were usually made with a lot of lace and other uncomfortable materials that would rub and irritate her skin all night.

A thought struck her for the first time. Duh, maybe people didn't actually sleep in those things, they only wore them for their partner and then they came off and they slept nude.

Kina opened the door and smiled shyly at Jonathan. How the hell did the man look sexy as hell in everything he wore? He was wearing a pair of sweat pants and a T-shirt that looked molded to his body. She stood back to let him enter her room. What was she doing? He was so out of her league. He'd said she was beautiful, but he was the beautiful one.

Jonathan could tell Kina was starting to freak out. She looked sexy as hell standing there in a huge T-shirt with her feet crossed over one another. He entered the room, closed the door behind him and turned, then took her face in his hands and leaned down, tilting her face up to his. He kissed her, keeping it light, even though he wanted nothing more than to throw her down on the bed behind her and strip her out of that shirt.

When he lifted his mouth from hers, he didn't let go of her face. He asked teasingly, "Would you rather sleep with a basketball team or a chess team?" She laughed, as he'd meant her to. "Relax, Kina," he scolded her gently. "It's just me."

"That's what I'm nervous about," she answered, giggling nervously.

"Come here." Jonathan wrapped Kina up in his embrace. She fit against him perfectly. He just held her for a long moment. He let go, just enough for her to lean back to look up at him, but kept his hands clasped at her lower back.

"There's nothing I want more, than to strip you out of this sexy-as-all get-out shirt and make love to you all night long." At her nod he kept going, not letting her speak. "But I don't want to rush us. I know you're mine. I know I want you for a lot longer than a quick fling while on location. I was serious the other night when I told you I wanted you to come with me to Arizona. I won't bug you about it, but know what's between us is more than just here and now. You're more than just some itch to scratch while I'm here. Whatever you need, I'm here. For now, can we just hang out, get to know each other better, watch some TV, and get a good night's sleep?"

Kina was speechless, probably for the first time in her life. It was like Jonathan could reach right into her brain and pull out her innermost thoughts and desires. Yes, she wanted him. She wanted to see first-hand what was underneath the tight clothes he was wearing, but she also wanted to feel as if he wanted her for her, not just for her body.

"I'd like that," she told him with a smile. They made their way to the bed. Kina pulled back the covers and they crawled in. She nestled against him. Neither moved to turn on the television.

"Tell me more about your family's animal refuge."

Jonathan spent the next ten minutes talking all about the coyotes they helped rescue and the work that went into the refuge keeping the animals happy and healthy. Kina thought Jonathan was lucky to have such great parents and such a great legacy in his family.

After a moment's silence Jonathan asked, "Would you rather have a perfect sense of direction or a perfect sense of time?"

After laughing and having a thorough debate on which would be better, Kina said, "I don't know if I've told you this or not, Jonathan, but I like you."

Jonathan gave her a squeeze. "Good. You know, I like you too."

As Kina fell asleep in his arms, she thought it was one of the best days she'd had in a long time.

Chapter Eleven

The next few days were crazy for the camera crew. Eddie suddenly decided he wanted the four men who were left on the show to be filmed practically all day, every day, which was ridiculous because they weren't doing anything at the production house. A schedule was worked out between the five camera operators so that two of them would be at the house at all times. That meant long hours of work for all of them. Long, boring hours.

Kina tried not to be upset at not being able to sleep in Jonathan's arms. It was ridiculous. She'd been sleeping by herself for a long time now and she wasn't the type of person who needed to sleep in a man's arms in order to get a good night's rest. And while she was sleeping well at night because she was exhausted, a part of her, deep down, admitted to like being in Jonathan's arms at night. She worried about him. Was he still having nightmares? Was he sleeping all right? Gah. It was crazy. Of course, he was just fine. He was a guy. Guys slept with different women all the time. Right?

Kina tried to convince herself that was true of Jonathan as well, but she knew he was different. She wasn't sure how she knew, just that she did. They'd seen each other briefly in passing, one morning that week. Jonathan was coming back from his shift at the house, just as Kina was headed out. He'd walked right up to her and clasped the back of her neck and brought her head to rest on his chest. He always did that. Hauled her against him with a hand behind her neck or head. She should hate it. She should protest it. But she didn't and couldn't feel the need to. She wound her arms around his waist and held on.

Jonathan hadn't said much, but she could feel every muscle in his body relax once she was in his arms.

"Are you okay?" she'd asked him quietly. "Are you sleeping all right? Any more nightmares?"

"I'd sleep better with you in my arms. No more nightmares. Thank you for being concerned about me. I don't think anyone I've ever dated wanted to know about my well-being before. It means a lot to me, hon."

He kissed the daylights out of her, backed her up, kissed her forehead briefly, then said as a goodbye endearment, "Would you rather never get enough sleep, or sleep so much you're only awake for a few hours each day?"

Kina smiled. God, he was cute. "Get some sleep, Jonathan," she murmured, letting go of him and stepping back. "I'll see you soon."

"Be safe."

Those two words stayed with Kina the entire time it took to get to the house. Jonathan had begun to tell her that when they separated. He didn't say, "Have a good day", or "I'll miss you," it was always, "Be safe." She figured it had something to do with Becky, but that wasn't all of it. He truly wanted her to be safe when he wasn't there with her, when he couldn't be there to protect her himself.

Today's shift promised to be another boring day. Unfortunately, Jeff was her camera wing-man for the day. To be fair, he'd been behaving himself recently, but Kina had worked with him long enough to know there was no way he'd be able to control himself much longer. She knew he was bursting to say something snide and/or sexist to her.

Their shift in the house started out with the men sitting around eating breakfast. It was quite boring. Even the contestants themselves seemed bored out of their skulls.

It was Darius who came up with the bright idea of sneaking out of the house, which was surprising, since he was the stereotypical, serious chemist. Kina wouldn't have thought he had it in him to be such a rebel. But she supposed the "Alaskan sickness" that sometimes came over the residents of Alaska in the winter didn't discriminate against those who were only visiting.

Knowing they had to take the cameras with them, the men decided to take the fifteen passenger van, instead of the small rental car Shannel and Eddie traveled in.

Kina rolled her eyes at the men. They were acting more like teenagers who didn't want to get caught sneaking out after curfew than grown men.

She didn't particularly like the fact they were leaving the house, but what choice did she have? She'd just have to roll with the punches. Kina tried once to convince the men they shouldn't leave, but she was quickly overridden. They were on a mission. Even Jeff got in on the act and told her she was being a kill-joy and she should just go with it.

Benedict was voted to be the driver, Jeff sat in the front seat filming the men while Kina sat in the back, off to the side, so she wouldn't be in Jeff's shot when he turned his camera around. They were driving around aimlessly. The guys had no idea where they were or what they wanted to do, they only knew they were "free" for the moment.

Because Benedict was driving, he saw the strip club first. Of course the others enthusiastically agreed, it was the best idea to stop in for a while. Kina rolled her eyes again. Jeez. Could they really want this little visit to be on national television for all to see? She knew Eddie would be pissed they'd left the house, but he'd still use the footage, especially if they did something dumb. And this was as dumb as they could get.

Benedict parked the monstrous van and everyone climbed out. It was ten in the morning, not exactly prime time for this type of establishment, but it was still open. Kina laughed to herself, knowing the types of women who would be dancing this early wouldn't be the best the place had to offer. Those women worked the night shift, where they could make more money when there were more customers.

The first issue materialized as soon as they walked inside. The manager came storming over, demanding the cameras be turned off. Kina couldn't blame him. The place was horrible. Even in the dim light in the room she could see the tattered curtains, the worn and stained carpets, and the sad little stage where the strippers would dance. It smelled of stale cigarette and cigar smoke and something funky Kina couldn't place. One of the only good things about the venture was the fact that there were only two other customers in the place.

Jeff actually stepped up for once and calmed the manager down. He explained they were not from a documentary, or anything that would show his esteemed establishment in a negative light, but rather they were filming a reality show. He agreed they wouldn't film any of the women dancing, but only the men on the reality show. Kina saw Jeff slip the sleazy manager a hundred dollar bill, which seemed to be what the guy was waiting for. Jerk.

The men got a table and enthusiastically ordered beers. Kina was disgusted. Beer wasn't her alcoholic drink of choice at any time, and certainly not so early in the morning. She tried to turn off the logical side of her brain and turn on her camera side. She had to get the men in the best light so the shots would be usable on TV. She couldn't use the light on her camera, that would ruin the ambiance of the shot.

For the next hour she and Jeff rotated around the table, filming the guys getting hammered and hitting on the waitresses. They hooted and hollered at the two strippers who occasionally took the stage for short, rather uninspired, pole dances. Finally, figuring she had enough shots of the men being idiots, she motioned to Jeff, that she was going to go outside for a break.

Being smart, she left the camera inside with Jeff. She wasn't going to risk bringing the expensive electronic equipment outside, in the rather questionable area of town, but she needed to get outside into the fresh air.

It was still cold, but it felt great after the stifling atmosphere of the strip club. The cloying smell of perfume mixed with all the other disgusting smells was nauseating. Kina looked around. She knew Alaska was beautiful. She'd seen it firsthand on her outings with Jonathan and during the filming of the show, but this street was not beautiful at all.

There was trash all around, as if no one cared about actually trying to put it in a garbage bin. There were plenty of used cigarettes strewn everywhere on the ground. She could just imagine the employees and customers alike stepping outside, smoking their cigarette down to the nub to get that last bit of nicotine before throwing it on the ground, stepping on it briefly, then disappearing back inside the dark building.

Kina looked up and down the street. There were a few other businesses, but they were all currently closed, except for the liquor store at the end of the road. There weren't many people around, but those that were had their heads down and were rushing from one place to another. There was a bus stop across from the strip club that had one rather unsavory looking character waiting for the next bus, at least that was what Kina assumed he was doing.

She was startled to see the man was watching her. He was wearing black cargo pants and black boots, the kind she imagined soldiers wore. She couldn't see what type of shirt he was wearing as he had on a long black coat which was buttoned up to his chin. Kina shivered. She was a pretty worldly woman, and she'd lived in some pretty scary places growing up as a child, so she could tell this guy was bad news. Break-time was over. Kina slipped back inside the rundown building regretfully. Even with the creepy bus stop guy, she'd much rather be outside in the fresh air than in there.

For the first time since she'd arrived, Kina started to feel uncomfortable. She was truly on her own now. She saw Jeff had also put down his camera, and was doing shots with the guys. Unbelievable.

Kina marched over to the men. "What the hell, Jeff?"

He mocked her and responded, "What the hell, Kina?"

All the men thought it was the funniest thing they'd ever heard in their lives and erupted in laughter. Great. Just great.

She reached down and hauled Jeff up by the collar of his shirt. He wasn't expecting it and his arms pin wheeled as he tried to regain his balance. As the other men continued to laugh, Kina yanked Jeff away from the table toward the door. When they'd gotten far enough away so that the others couldn't hear them, she lit into him.

"Seriously? You know we aren't supposed to hang out with the contestants! And drinking this early in the morning? We have to get them out of here and back to the house!"

"Shut up, Kina. Serioushly," he slurred, "haf some fun for once. You're alwaysh so uptight. Have a drink with ush. Maybe then you can schow us what you're schowing Jon-boy."

Kina shoved Jeff away from her as hard as she could. Jesus, he was an ass. She left him standing by the door and wandered over to the bar. She hauled herself up on one of the stools and refused to look back at the table of idiot men. The bartender came over to where she was sitting.

"Can I get you anything?"

"I'd love a bottle of water, if you have one," Kina told her. She wasn't going to drink anything out of a glass. Who knew what germs she'd get.

The bartender nodded and turned away to get the drink for her. When she returned, she asked Kina, "So, what's the deal?" and motioned with her head toward the table of idiots Kina had come in with.

Kina figured, at this point, she had nothing to lose. The bartender was surprisingly pretty. The woman didn't seem as worn down as the other waitresses and dancers in the place. "Those idiots are on a reality show and busted loose from their leash today. As a part of the camera crew, I had no choice but to follow along. The other camera guy over there, is just an imbecile."

The bartender laughed. "Well, you just sit here as long as you need to. We'll just let them have their fun." She got serious and leaned over the bar toward Kina. "As long as they're in here, they'll be all right. They'll be poorer for it, but safe. But don't let them wander around outside when they leave. It's not a safe area for a bunch of drunk men who think they're invincible."

Kina nodded. "Yeah, I kinda got that in the five minutes I was standing outside taking a break." She thought about calling Eddie, but figured the men would soon get bored and they'd be heading back to the production house.

Unbelievably, the men hung out at the strip club all afternoon. Food was scrounged up from somewhere to feed them and to help keep the alcohol flowing and their buzz continuing. Kina didn't bother filming anymore. It was pointless. When the place started getting more crowded, the bartender let Kina put both the cameras behind the bar to keep them safe.

Kina considered calling Jonathan, but talked herself out of it. This wasn't his problem. She was an adult and a professional, she could handle it. All she had to do was get the drunks back to the van and back to the house. Easy.

Not so easy. First, the men didn't want to leave. Kina supposed she couldn't blame them. The strippers that had come in for the second shift were much better-looking than the ones who had been working when they'd arrived. Second, the guys were so drunk they couldn't think clearly. And third, they knew what awaited them back on the set. Boredom, and most likely they'd be in trouble for sneaking out.

Finally after around seven hours in the bar, Kina had enough. They were leaving. She considered ditching them all there, but knew that wasn't cool and they'd only get in more trouble if she left. She begged the new manager on duty to help her get all of the men to the van. Reluctantly he agreed, after all, they'd been spending a lot of money all day and he didn't want to lose his best customers.

Kina had to stand and wait for each of the men to say goodbye to their waitresses and the dancers they'd been feeding money to all day. Kina rolled her eyes for what seemed like the hundredth time that day. She watched as they groped the women's breasts and slapped their asses for good measure. Good God, they were pathetic. The waitresses just laughed, knowing they'd made a boatload of money off the group. "Extreme Alaskan," Kina's ass, more like "Pathetic Losers."

The group stumbled toward the van, laughing loudly and exclaiming the day had been the "best ever" and how they'd all be best friends forever. They were acting just like drunk college women. Kina and the manager somehow were able to get all the men inside the van safely. At least the guys were happy drunks. It would've been worse if they'd been mad or angry when drunk.

At the last minute, Kina remembered their cameras. Crap. It was a good thing she hadn't left them at the bar. That would've meant another trip back to this awful part of town to retrieve them.

"Can you please stay here for just a minute and watch them to make sure they don't do anything stupid?" she pleaded with the manager. She didn't want to leave them there for even the two minutes it'd take her to run back inside and grab the cameras. Thank God she had the keys to the van in her pocket. At least they couldn't drive drunk or leave her there stranded.

When it looked like he was going to decline, Kina sighed and reached into her pocket and brought out a twenty. "Would this help convince you?"

Smirking, the manger pocketed the money and said, "This'll hold me for five minutes. Better hurry, sweet cheeks."

Ugh. Another jerk, in a long line of jerks she'd had to deal with that day. Running back into the building she'd hoped never to have to enter again, she rushed over the bar The bartender saw her coming and lifted the little wooden door, granting her access to the area behind the bar.

"Thanks Shirley, appreciate it. Have a good night."

She and Shirley had gotten on a first name basis since Kina had been there all day, and she waved as Kina backed out of the bar area with a camera in each hand and headed back toward the front door.

Stepping back outside was like sucking in oxygen, after being underwater for too long. Even though the area of town they were in was crappy, the air smelled fresh and sweet. She loved Alaska for that fact alone. Kina fast walked toward the van. She could hear the men inside singing a song about a lumberjack. She smiled, thinking how ridiculous the entire situation was. She only had to deal with the drunken louts for another half an hour or so, then she'd be free.

Kina should've been paying attention to her surroundings and not thinking about the warm bath she wanted to take that night. She suddenly found herself sprawled on the ground, looking up at two men. They were tall, but not very muscular and they smelled horrible. Kina could smell them from her position on the dirty ground. They smelled like body odor and pee. Gross. She didn't have the time or the patience for this. All she wanted to do was get back to the hotel and get clean and sleep. She sighed.

Kina hoped the cameras weren't broken. She'd taken a hard tumble and had both hands full with the cameras so she couldn't break her fall. One of the guys had shoved her hard from behind. She picked herself up off the ground and faced the men. She glanced quickly at the van, although she could still hear the drunken singing coming from the men, they weren't paying any attention to her.

"You don't want to do this," she told the thugs honestly, knowing she could kick their butts. She hadn't had self-defense training for nothing. Although typically in self-defense one was supposed to do just enough to get away, she had to get to the van and get out of there. These guys wouldn't let her calmly open the van door and start up the engine nonchalantly. She had to convince them she wasn't a pushover and to leave her alone.

"Hand over the cameras," the taller of the two men growled.

"Like hell," Kina answered, not thinking.

"Hand 'em over," the second man growled, not expanding on his threat.

Kina didn't wait to hear anything else. She'd learned in her classes to use every body part she had to hurt the other person. Her head, her elbows, her knees, her feet. As the first man came toward her, she aimed her foot at his knee. She figured most men would think a woman would go for their family jewels first, so she aimed for another basic pressure point. She kicked him as hard as she could, not holding back in the slightest. Sure enough, as soon as her foot made contact with his knee, he went down, hard.

Seeing his buddy rolling around on the ground seemed to galvanize the other creep. He roared and grabbed Kina from behind. Kina took a deep breath, turned her head to the side and slipped right out of his hold, just like she'd practiced in class. He was so surprised at her quick escape, he didn't manage to block the heel of her hand as it slammed into the fleshy part of his face. He howled in pain and staggered away from her. He blindly swung his fist in her direction and before Kina could duck, managed to nail her in the cheek.

Damn, that hurt. Holy crap. Getting hit in the face hurt. She'd never been hit before. On television, actors always made it look like it wasn't that painful. Shit. She'd had no idea how much it would hurt. She blinked hard. She couldn't break down now.

Kina ignored her throbbing cheek for the moment and reached down to grab the cameras and get the hell out of there. Before she could reach the damn equipment and head for the van, the first guy was on his feet again. Kina sighed. She was done with this, dammit.

He grabbed Kina's wrist and said confidently, "Try getting away now, bitch."

Really? He thought holding her by her wrist was keeping her secure? That was the easiest hold to get out of, if someone grabbed you. Kina looked down and yanked her arm towards herself, right where his thumbs and fingers met. It was like slicing butter with a warm knife, her wrist came free so easily. She brought her knee up quickly and slammed it into his groin this time. He fell to the ground, swearing profusely.

She turned and delivered a roundhouse kick to the other guy who'd recovered and was coming at her. She hit him right in the femoral artery, which worked just as well as nailing him in the groin. He went down hard.

Not waiting for either of them to recover again, she snatched the cameras up and headed for the van at a dead run. Damn the other guys for not being sober enough to be aware of what was going on and come help her. And double damn that manager. He was leaning against the van watching her. Watching. Bastard.

Kina briefly thought about Jonathan and how there was no way he'd simply stand against a van and watch a woman, or anyone, fight. He'd be right there helping. It wouldn't matter if he knew the people in the fight. She couldn't think about him right now. She had to concentrate on getting out of there.

She snarled at the manager as he strolled away, but didn't bother wasting any energy on bitching him out. She didn't have the time. She practically threw the cameras into the van and vaulted up into the driver's seat. She ignored the comments from the guys, who still had no idea what had just happened right in front of their damn faces, and jammed the key into the ignition. She cranked the engine over and slammed the gearshift into drive. She watched as the two thugs in the parking lot came toward the van, albeit slow because of the injuries she'd inflicted on them, but coming toward her nonetheless.

She slammed her foot on the gas and everyone in the van was thrown backward in their seats. Again, she ignored the drunken comments from the men and concentrated on getting out of the parking lot, without flipping the van. She enjoyed watching the thugs leap out of the way. She would've hit them without a second thought if they hadn't moved. Assholes.

The back end of the van fishtailed as she turned onto the street. She regained control of the van and let out a sigh.

Holy crap. That wasn't fun. She reached a hand up to her face. She realized she was shaking, most likely from adrenaline. Her face also hurt. She figured she'd most likely have a black eye as well. That guy had gotten her pretty good when he'd hit her. She blinked her eyes rapidly, to keep the tears that were welling from falling. She wouldn't fall apart. She wouldn't fall apart. She wouldn't fall apart.

"Wooooooo, Kina, you're Mario An-An-An…whatever hish name ish," Nash drunkenly slurred from the backseat.

"You go, grrrrrrrl!"

"Shit, I hit my head."

Kina ignored the comments, concentrating on figuring out how to get back to the production house. Since Benedict had driven them out she wasn't exactly sure as to how he'd gotten them to the strip club in the first place. After driving around for a bit she recognized one of the main roads she'd been on with Jonathan and turned.

Jeff was surprisingly quiet, sitting in the front seat next to her. After what seemed like hours, but was probably only around twenty minutes, Kina pulled into the driveway of the production house. Eddie wrenched open the front door and stalked toward the van. Kina almost wanted to laugh at the look on his face, when the four contestants tumbled out of the van toward the house. At this moment, in their shared drunkenness, they were the best of friends. Any disagreement they'd had in the past were only memories.

"Where the hell have you been?" Eddie demanded of the group of drunks.

"Schrip Club." Darius slurred, not hiding anything. "It was aweshome!"

The others added their agreement and continued into the house, laughing and giggling like little girls.

Kina turned off the van and grabbed her camera that was lying precariously between the front two seats. She left Jeff's for him. She'd had enough of covering his butt for the day. She stepped down out of the van and headed toward the SUV to put her camera up.

"Where the hell do you think you're going?" Eddie scowled at her. Since he didn't have the men to yell at anymore, he changed his target to her. "Why the hell did you take these guys out without my permission?"

"I'm putting my camera up, then I'm going to go back to the hotel," she said without turning around. She'd had enough of annoying men for the day.

Eddie had come up behind her without her noticing and he grabbed her bicep and tried to turn her around to look at him.

Kina ripped her arm out of his grasp and whirled around to face him. "Keep your hands off me, Eddie. I've had a hell of a day babysitting your actors and Jeff. I don't want to talk to you; I don't want to look at Jeff. All I want to do is go back to the hotel and take a shower. You got a problem with that?"

Looking uncomfortable, Eddie stared at Kina's face, noticing for the first time the bruise on her face. "Uh, are you all right?" he said awkwardly and belatedly.

"No. My face hurts and I'm pissed off," Kina said shortly turning back around to place the camera in the SUV.

"Jeff," she called out. "I'll be in the car. Do whatever you have to do and I'll wait for you, but I'll only wait for five minutes. After that you're spending the night here."

Eddie turned to lambast Jeff, wanting to yell at someone, only to watch as Jeff stumbled as he climbed out of the van and tripped over his own feet. Kina and Eddie stared at the man, now lying in the dirt, as he laughed uncontrollably over his clumsiness. Kina sighed, and ignoring the man trying to climb to his feet, went back to the van and grabbed Jeff's camera. If she didn't take it with her, it would sit in the van all night. Jeff was in no shape to even remember he was a cameraman, much less remember to pick up the camera and bring it with him.

On her way back toward the SUV, she said, "Eddie, help him into the backseat. I'll take him back to the hotel and get the tapes from today back to you tomorrow."

Eddie, knowing by the look on her face that she was
at the end of her rope for the day, amazingly did as she
asked. He stood back after he'd closed the door on his drunk
cameraman and watched as Kina pulled away from the house
without looking back.

Chapter Twelve

Kina pulled up to the hotel, dreading trying to get a drunk Jeff up to his room. As soon as she pulled into the parking lot, she saw Jonathan waiting for her. Crap. She had no idea how he knew when they'd be back, but maybe he'd just been hanging out in the lobby waiting for her. On one hand, Kina was glad he was there so she didn't have to deal with Jeff on her own, but on the other hand she knew he was going to lose his shit over her face.

She'd checked it out in the car mirror before she left the production house. She was right, she had the beginnings of a black eye and the cheek would definitely bruise. Luckily, the guy hadn't hit her nose. The last thing she wanted to deal with was a broken nose. Kina didn't think she needed to go to the hospital, nothing was broken, she'd just be sore for a while. It definitely could've been a lot worse. All in all, she'd been lucky.

She parked the car and rested her head on the steering wheel for just a moment. That moment was long enough for Jonathan to open her door. She raised her head and turned to look at him. She knew the moment he realized something was wrong. The look in his eyes turned from gentle and welcoming to hard and angry.

"What the hell?"

Kina held her hand up and closed her eyes. "Can this wait?"

"Hell, no!" She felt his hand brush against her bruised face lightly. "Talk to me."

"Can we please get him to his room, first?"

Jonathan looked in the back seat at Jeff, who'd finally passed out on their way to the hotel. "No. I need to take care of you first. He can wait here," he told Kina resolutely.

"I'm fine, Jonathan; we have to get him upstairs."

Since the SUV had high seats, Jonathan was able to block her from getting out of the driver's seat simply by stepping closer to her. "What happened?" he said, holding on to his temper, by sheer force of will. "Tell me."

Kina sighed. She decided to give him the condensed version so they could get out of the parking lot. She also needed his touch, to feel connected, so she leaned her forehead against his chest, and grabbed hold of his T-shirt at his waist. She needed the connection with him, even if he would be mad at what she told him.

"The guys decided they were bored and wanted to go out. Since we were tasked with filming them, we went too. They found a strip club and spent the day drinking and having fun. On the way out of the joint, I was asked to give up the cameras by two 'gentlemen' in the parking lot. When I declined, they tried to convince me. I beat the crap out of them, we left, and here I am."

Jonathan had so many questions racing through his mind, he almost couldn't decide where to start. He stroked her hair from the top of her head down to the middle of her back where it ended, then brought his hand back up to her head to do it again. "Where were the guys when those thugs tried to convince you to give up the cameras?"

"In the van."

"Did they see what was going on?"

"I have no idea."

"Give me the keys."

Kina was startled by his request. She raised her head and looked at his face. What did he think he was going to do? "Uh, no."

Jonathan held out his hand again. "It wasn't a request, give me the keys."

"No, Jonathan. I don't know where you think you're going, but, just, no."

Jonathan leaned in close to Kina. "You don't get it. They should've taken care of you. You never should've been in that position."

"You're right, I shouldn't have been," Kina agreed but at the same time trying to reason with him. "But I was. And you know what? I took care of it myself. Just like I've been doing for most of my life."

"No, you don't get it. You're mine, now. If someone doesn't treat you the way you should be treated, it's my job to take care of it."

Kina was pissed now. "No, it's not. Jeez, Jonathan, I can take care of myself. Look at me! I took on two grown men and I'm just fine. They're hurting more than I am!"

Jonathan was still pissed, but his hand was gentle as he cupped her cheek and ran his thumb over her bruised cheek. "No, you're not fine. They touched you. They never should have touched you. They hurt you. I'm just going to have a word with the men at the production house and explain."

"No!" Kina yelled, smacking his hand away from her face and not wanting his gentleness while he stood there and metaphorically beat his chest like a caveman.

"You're not! Listen to me, Jonathan. You can't do this. I can't be with you if you're going to do this. What are you going to do when I trip over my own feet? Beat the crap out of someone standing next to me? What if someone accidentally elbows me in a store? You gonna knock them off their feet, yell at them? It's ridiculous. You knew I could take care of myself before you met me. What makes you think now is any different? You're acting like Matt. He used to beat the crap out of people he imagined looked at what was his too."

Jonathan tried to tamp down the hurt and fury her words caused him. "You're shaking, honey. You're hurt. I can't ignore that and not do anything."

"It's the adrenaline, Jonathan. I'm fine. Seriously. All I want to do is go upstairs and take a shower and lie down."

"Give me the keys and you can go and do that. I'll be back later."

Kina couldn't think of anything else to say. He wasn't hearing her. He was going to do what he wanted to do, just as Matt always did. She'd thought he was different. It was breaking her heart, to know he wasn't. She handed Jonathan the keys and waited for him to get out of the way. When he finally stepped back, she jumped down and opened the back door. She got the cameras out of the back.

"Will you please help Jeff up to his room before you go?"

Without waiting for his answer, Kina turned toward the hotel doors.

"I'll let you know when I'm back and maybe we can get something to eat?"

Kina ignored him and entered the hotel without looking back, blinded by the tears coursing down her cheeks.

* * *

Jonathan knew Kina was pissed and upset, but she was asking too much of him to ignore what had happened to her. He was damn proud of her for being able to get herself out of the situation, but she shouldn't have had to do it. And that was the crux of the matter. The other men were right there and were too drunk to help her. She could've really been hurt.

He wanted to be with her, to help her clean up and take care of her face, but it was more important to him to go to the production house. He had to talk to the men. They had to know what they'd done. After Jonathan was done with them they wouldn't let a woman face two thugs on her own again, that was for sure.

After dragging Jeff up to his room and leaving him passed out on his bed, he'd deal with him later, Jonathan drove to the production house. Eddie and Shannel weren't around anywhere. He went up the stairs to find the men still on the show. He'd teach them a lesson on how women should be treated that they'd never forget.

* * *

Kina heard Jonathan knocking on her door. She ignored him. She was broken by his refusing to listen to her. She knew he was an alpha and felt the need to be protective of her, but she'd begged him to let it go and he didn't. She wasn't sure she could spend her life with him watching over her like that, ignoring her wishes.

She couldn't go through it again. It had taken her months to get over the pain Matt had inflicted on her, she wasn't sure she'd ever get over it from Jonathan.

Jonathan knew Kina was in her room. She was obviously pissed at him. She couldn't seriously think he'd just leave it alone. No man in his right mind would ignore what happened if it had happened to his woman. He thought about what his brother would've done if this was Becky. He'd have lost his ever-loving mind. The only reason the two men who attacked his wife were still alive and breathing was because the police caught them before Dean did.

"Please let me in, Kina," Jonathan said softly at her door.

Kina bit her lip. It took everything she had to not answer him. He sounded so sad, but she couldn't give in. He'd hurt her. No, he'd devastated her.

"Did you get some ice for your face?"

God, why did he have to be so concerned and so darn nice?

When she still didn't answer him, after a while she finally she heard him say, "Okay, I'm right next door, hon. If you feel like talking later, please don't hesitate to come over. I'll see you tomorrow."

She turned her face into her pillow so he wouldn't hear her cry. She was so disappointed in him. She'd had such high hopes for their relationship and now she didn't know if she'd be able to trust him again the same way she had before.

* * *

The tension in the SUV was ratcheted high the next morning on the way to the production set. Kina had skipped breakfast so she didn't have to talk to Jonathan. She knew he was waiting for her and wanted to talk to her, because he'd stopped by her door on his way down to breakfast.

"Kina? Are you awake? I'd like to talk to you before breakfast."

When she didn't answer, she'd heard him sigh. "Okay, you're still mad at me. You know what happened to Becky. I couldn't let this go. If the same thing happened to you, I'd lose it. I wouldn't be able to handle it. I'd hoped to be able to talk to you and explain what happened when I went over to the house yesterday." When she didn't answer him after several moments, he said, "I'll talk to you downstairs."

Kina sat fully dressed on her bed and listened to him walk away. She'd started to second-guess herself. Was she overreacting? His bringing up Becky's experiences had made her think. She knew how devastated Jonathan had been when Becky had been hurt. She knew. He'd opened himself up to her and told her everything. Had yesterday brought on flashbacks for him? Did he sleep all right last night? Oh, crap. She had a bad feeling she'd done him a disservice. She hung her head and closed her eyes. This was too hard. This was why she wasn't good at relationships. She tended to only think about what she felt, what she wanted. Knowing she had to face him at some point, she took a deep breath and made her way downstairs.

Jeff obviously wasn't feeling well that morning. He was hung-over and hurting. Kina didn't have any sympathy for him. He'd definitely overstepped his bounds as a camera operator yesterday. She wondered for a moment if he'd regretted it, then decided he probably didn't. For the first time since they'd gotten to Alaska, there was silence in the car on the way to the set. Taylor and Carl had no idea what was going on, but with the bruise on her face, they knew something was up. They stayed silent, but gave her concerned looks as they traveled toward the set.

Eddie was there to greet the SUV as they pulled up to the house. As soon as Jeff stepped out of the vehicle, Eddie asked to speak with him. Kina, Taylor, and Carl looked over at them with curiosity, but Kina noticed Jonathan seemed to be ignoring them altogether. Eddie and Jeff were still talking, as the four of them walked into the house.

Not too long after that, Eddie entered the production house and closed the door. "Jeff won't be joining us on the rest of the show. It'll be up to the four of you to cover the competitions and to finish the filming. I understand, Kina, that what happened yesterday wasn't your fault, but I do expect in the future that if something like this happens again, you'll notify me immediately. You shouldn't have been put in that position and the men shouldn't have left the house, no matter how bored they were."

Kina could only nod. She was shocked. She'd never thought Eddie would've been that cool about the entire situation. If anything, she figured he'd be a jerk about it and either fire her or at the very least scold her. It was hard for her to believe he'd actually fired Jeff. Why had he fired Jeff and not her? It didn't make any sense.

She looked sideways at Jonathan, he wouldn't meet her eyes. Hmm. Kina wondered if he had anything to do with it. Maybe she should've talked to him this morning, after all. She looked at Jonathan carefully for the first time that morning.

He had no outward cuts or bruises that would indicate he'd gotten in a fight the night before. That didn't necessarily mean anything, though. The other four guys were pretty drunk and they most likely couldn't defend themselves very well.

She looked at Jonathan's hands. If he'd decked any of the men, his knuckles would be bearing the marks. Nothing. They were as smooth as they had been the last time she'd seen him.

Eddie continued talking to the camera crew. "As you know, there are four contestants left. We'll begin having single-elimination contests from here on out. We'll obviously have two more competitions before the final event. The single eliminations will be handled with short challenges, and the final, for the 'Extreme Alaskan' title, will be another overnight assignment. I'll explain what that is when we get to it. In the meantime, I'll assign each of you to film one of the men. Stick with them, film everything they do. After recording today, I expect you all to check out of the hotel and stay here. The pressure will be on and I want to get all of their reactions on film. If you have any problems with that, you can talk to me later, but I expect no one will. You're all professionals here, make sure you act like it."

Kina winced, knowing he wasn't really talking to her, but feeling bad all the same. She knew she should've called Eddie yesterday as soon as the men said they wanted to get out of the house, but she hadn't.

Kina caught the sympathetic look in Jonathan's eyes and looked away. She wasn't ready to deal with him. She knew he'd done something, but couldn't figure out what.

Jonathan was frustrated that he hadn't been able to tend Kina's face the night before. She was too pissed at him to let him into her room. He would've made sure she kept ice on it and hopefully that would've lessened the pain and the bruising. He hated that she had to take care of herself, but he'd had to go to the production house the night before. He just had to.

Jonathan winced at the condition of the four contestants as they entered the room after all the cameras were set up. They looked extremely hung-over and uncomfortable. He didn't have much sympathy for them, but he could still feel for them.

Jonathan thought back to the night before. He hadn't fought anyone, that wasn't his style. But he'd slain them with his words. He made sure they knew what could have happened to Kina. He explained in great detail what a woman goes through when she's raped. What it does to their self-esteem and what kind of life they had afterward. He made them think about their moms and sisters and friends. Would they sit around and watch as someone precious to them fought for her life or fought to protect herself?

He'd ground them into dust with his words. He knew they'd never do it again, and that was what he was going for. He'd also sat down with Eddie and let him know all about the issues he and Kina had with Jeff. It wasn't that he was a bad worker or necessarily a bad person, but the chip on his shoulder was huge and the night before had been the last straw for Jonathan.

Eddie reassured him that he'd take care of the issue and Jonathan was glad to see this morning that the man *had* dealt with it. Jonathan had wanted to talk with Kina before breakfast and let her know what he'd done and how he'd dealt with had happened to her, but she wouldn't talk to him. It disappointed him, but he supposed he couldn't blame her. She'd been burnt before by a man who'd taken over and acted way too macho and controlling. He'd just have to give her time, she'd come to him when she was ready…he hoped.

Chapter Thirteen

Kina watched, with no sympathy, as the four men competed in the next competition. They were all miserable, but she couldn't care less at the moment. Her face still hurt from the blow she'd taken the day before. She also knew she was sporting a nice bruise as well. Kina didn't bother to try to hide it with makeup. She wanted the guys to see what had happened to her. The pain wasn't anything that would keep her off the set and not working, but she still knew it was there nonetheless. None of the men would really look at her after seeing her black eye for the first time. She again wondered what Jonathan had said to them yesterday.

None of the four men looked like they'd been beaten up, at least from what Kina could see. It just didn't make sense to her. She knew Jonathan had been over to the house last night, but she couldn't fathom him just sitting down for a chat. Then again, that apparently seemed to have been just what happened. Crap. She'd expected Jonathan to beat the hell out of the men, that was what Matt would've done. She thought about how she'd obviously misjudged Jonathan…again.

Kina knew the competition today was geared toward punishing the men. Eddie was good at coming up with things like that. As he had Shannel explain, part of living in Alaska was being able to be self-sufficient. They were brought to a local homestead in the middle of nowhere. The owners, Mr. and Mrs. Morrell, had a pretty big farming operation, as well as an extensive garden. They were completely self-sufficient during the winter and had fresh eggs, milk, and enough vegetables to last them throughout the harsh season. They'd spent the entire summer working on killing enough game to freeze and growing the fresh food in their gardens.

Thank God, Eddie wasn't going to have them go out and hunt for anything. Kina knew someone would probably have blown off a foot or something if they had to actually shoot live animals for the competition.

It seemed that today's challenge would be to milk a cow and fill an entire bucket with milk, gather a dozen eggs, behead a chicken, and pull weeds out of a section of the garden. It didn't seem that hard of a challenge, but with all of the men being hung-over, it'd be tough.

Kina was in charge of filming Darius. Overall, she found her attention wandering throughout the challenge. She kept thinking about Jonathan. She'd been so mad at him last night; mad enough to never want to talk to him again, but now she was second-guessing herself. He'd been so calm this morning, saying he wanted to talk to her. He hadn't even tried to get her alone today. He was giving her space. She didn't know if she should be upset about that or not.

In her experience, men would try to get her to listen to them and didn't care if she wanted space or not. They just barged their way in and made her listen to what they had to say. Jonathan wasn't like that. He was giving her space, space she wasn't sure she wanted anymore. Oh, she figured she'd talk to him before the day was out, but for now she couldn't think about him and do her job.

She focused on Darius as he chased a chicken around a pen. He had to catch the thing then bring it to the block of wood they were using as a chopping block and cut its head off. Kina didn't even want to watch it through the lens of her camera; she couldn't imagine what the men felt like, actually doing it. The worst thing about it was the chicken running around without a head after the axe had been used. Kina always thought that was just a saying, 'running around like a chicken with its head cut off', but it was apparently true…gross.

The competition was a timed one, as all of the men were expected to finish all of the tasks. The slowest man to finish would be the one to leave. Kina swore the men were deliberately trying to throw the competition. What did it say for your show when no one wanted to stay and they all wanted to be kicked off?

Kina watched the other men with only half an eye. She barely noticed when Roger went off into the bushes to throw up, after watching Nash cut the head off the chicken and get sprayed from head to foot with its warm blood.

Finally, the torturous day was over. All four of the men had finished the tasks. Shannel and Eddie lined the men up next to the pen which held the cows. Now they had to stand there and smell the cow manure and wait for Shannel to finish with her speech. Kina swore the hostess made it extra-long on purpose. Finally, she was done and it was time to name the slowest competitor for the day. Benedict had completed all of the tasks the slowest and would be leaving the show. Kina tried not to laugh at the look of relief that crossed his face. Even funnier was the looks on Roger, Darius, and Nash's face when they realized they'd be staying for at least one more competition.

The ride back to the production house was quiet. Everyone except for Eddie and Shannel were now traveling in the same van, since they all fit.

Kina put her head on the seat behind her and closed her eyes. She was tired. Tired of trying to figure out where she and Jonathan stood, and honestly just tired of the whole camera operator gig. She never thought she'd feel that way. She remembered how much of a high it used to give her and the way she'd loved moving from show to show and getting the best shots. She thought about the joy she felt, watching the shows she'd worked on when they aired on television, recognizing her filming, being able to tell it apart from that of the other camera operators.

Now she never watched them. She'd lost the excitement she'd used to feel about her job. That made her sad. She felt lost. If she couldn't do this, what could she do?

Nash's words broke the silence in the van.

"I'm really sorry, Kina. We shouldn't have broken the rules, but more importantly we shouldn't have dragged you along to that shithole."

Darius chimed in when Nash quit talking. "We had no idea what was going on. We wouldn't have left you to deal with those assholes if we weren't so drunk. I know it's not an excuse, but we're sorry."

Kina expected it and wasn't surprised when Roger added his apology to the others'. "We hope you can forgive us, Kina. We were stupid and you paid the price."

The mood was solemn in the van until Nash broke the tension. "Although, we heard you kicked their asses."

Kina smiled. She had kicked butt. She just wanted this all to be done. She didn't want them to keep bringing it up. She wouldn't lie; she was glad they were sorry and that they'd apologized. Hopefully they'd learn from it, but she also wanted it done.

"It's okay, guys. I know how stir crazy it can be, cooped up in the production house. If you ever do anything like that again, I'll bring out the pictures I took of you all with those skanky strippers."

At their horrified looks, she let them off the hook. "Kidding. But you'd better hope Eddie doesn't want to use the footage we did take before the day got too crazy."

Everyone got out of the van after arriving at the house. Privacy was at a premium since everyone was now staying at the set. Kina knew she had to talk to Jonathan. He'd been quiet, too quiet. She didn't like it. She'd prefer him to be talking to her and joking. She missed it and she didn't like the awkwardness that surrounded them both.

"Can I talk to you, Jonathan?" she asked as they walked towards the house, honestly, not knowing what he'd say.

"Of course."

She should've known he wouldn't play games with her. "My room, after we get our cameras put away?" Since she was the only woman on the crew she had her own room. The guys all had to share a room. It was the only place she could think of that was guaranteed to be private. She desperately wanted things back the way they were between them, but wasn't sure how to get them there.

* * *

Jonathan took a deep breath. Thank God, Kina was going to talk to him. The day had been torture. He was glad the men had apologized. He knew he'd guilted them into it last night, but it was the right thing to do. He just hoped he could get Kina to listen to him, because he'd never be able to sit back and let her get hurt or disparaged and not do something about it. It'd be a change for her, but that's just the way it was. He couldn't change the person he was, just as he didn't want to change who she was.

He knocked on Kina's door about ten minutes later. He opened it when he heard her call for him to enter.

Kina was sitting on the edge of the bed looking uncomfortable. He opened his month to say something, he wasn't sure what, when she beat him to it.

"I'm sorry, Jonathan. I was out of line."

He shook his head. "No, you really weren't. I don't want you thinking you can't disagree with me. There'll be times when we don't agree, hon. Hell, I love that you can stand up to me. I don't ever want you to think that you can't. I'd even venture to guess we'll probably disagree a lot. You're passionate and I love that about you." When Kina opened her mouth to say something, he interrupted her again.

"But, you have to understand the way I am. I know you can take care of yourself, if you couldn't, you'd most likely be in the hospital because those guys would've done unspeakable things to you. But you don't have to do it all by yourself anymore. I know you're independent and strong as hell, but that doesn't mean I won't protect you. I still don't think you understand this yet, but you're mine. No one disrespects you and gets away with it. Let that sink in. I told you before and I'll keep saying it, until you get it."

Jonathan watched Kina as she sagged back on the bed. He stared at her, willing her to understand.

"When I was with Matt, we went out one time to have dinner. The waiter was cute and was harmlessly flirting with me. Matt didn't like it. He yelled at me all the way home, about how I was acting like a whore and didn't I know

I was his? When we got home, he said he was going out and would be back. When he got home later that night, it was obvious he'd been in a fight. I found out later he went back to the restaurant and waited for the waiter to get off work. He beat the hell out of him right there in the parking lot, just to prove to himself that I was his and that no one flirted with his property. It embarrassed the hell out of me and I felt so bad for that poor waiter. He hadn't done anything wrong. It made me feel like I'd done something wrong, when I hadn't. It also made me realize I never wanted to be in a relationship like that again."

As much as he hated to hear her story, Jonathan got it. "I didn't touch them, Kina."

"I know. I figured that out, but I didn't know that this morning when you wanted to talk. I should've known you weren't like Matt, but I was stuck in the past. I heard you call me 'yours' and I was afraid you'd be like him. I'm sorry, Jonathan. I know you aren't like him. I do. I swear."

Jonathan walked over to Kina and knelt in front of her. He took her hands in his and stared up at her. "I'm not like him, hon. But you have to know, I'll protect you with my life if I have to. I want to stand next to you, not in front of you, but again, if I need to, I'll shove you behind me so fast, you won't know what hit you. If you want to flirt with a waiter, go for it. It's not going to make me lose control. I'll just know at the end of the night, you're going home with me, and you'll be in *my* bed. In fact, I encourage you to flirt with whoever you want, just know any time you do, I'll find a way to remind you that you're mine, while you're flirting." He smiled at her, imagining running his fingers up her thigh under the table while she smiled at a waiter.

He got serious again and repeated what he'd just told her. "I didn't touch them last night, Kina. I made it very clear that what they did was seriously messed up. They weren't too happy with me, but they understood where I was coming from. They were mortified about what happened to you and what could've happened to you. They had no idea what you went through and I think that was what finally got to them the most."

"What about Jeff?"

He sighed. He figured this was coming. "I had a talk with Eddie as well." He put his finger to her lips, knowing she'd protest. "Listen, please. Jeff had it coming. You know it as well as I do. He wasn't fired for good. I just explained to Eddie, how Jeff had no respect for any woman. That he wasn't good for the camaraderie of the camera crew. Since it's the end of the show and he didn't really need him, Eddie agreed to move him off the show. I should've shared this with you before I did it, but I saw red when I saw you'd been hurt and I hadn't been there. Not only did Jeff not do anything about it, but he'd joined the other idiots in getting hammered. It wasn't cool of him and although on some level, it wasn't cool of me to do what I did, again, I couldn't just let it go. I hope you understand."

He held his breath until Kina nodded. She opened her lips and licked his finger still resting there. Jonathan moaned, actually moaned. God, she was so sexy and holding himself back from her was killing him.

Kina smiled. She knew they had more to talk about. She was putting off having the conversation about what she was going to do after the show was over. She desperately wanted to let Jonathan know she'd come to Arizona with him, but she was scared. She wasn't a hundred percent sure it was what she should do, but at the same time she finally knew she wanted a change. She was ready to get away from filming reality shows.

She watched as he drew in a harsh breath. The little moan she'd heard from his lips was sexy as hell. It was getting harder and harder to not jump him, especially when she knew he felt the same way about her. She glanced at his manhood, prominently displayed between his legs as he knelt there. She winced. It looked uncomfortable.

"Are you staying here tonight?" she shyly asked.

"Ah, love, there's nothing I'd like more, but if I do, I think we both know what'll happen. I want you more than you know, but I also want our coming together to be because we know it's a permanent thing. I'll wait for you to know for sure. I don't want to just be an itch you want to scratch. But I warn you now, when you do come to me, I'm keeping you. I won't let you go. When that's what you want, come to me. I'll spend hours making sure you don't regret your decision."

Holy crap. Kina squirmed on the bed. That was hot. She knew when they did finally get together they'd be explosive.

She watched as Jonathan leaned toward her to take her lips with his. He plundered her mouth; there was no other word for it. He tasted and caressed every part of her. It was over long before Kina was ready. He leaned back and put his hand on her cheek. "Thank you for not letting this be the end of us. I'll see you in the morning."

Dazed, Kina could only nod. He was dangerous, that was for sure.

Chapter Fourteen

Kina tried not to laugh as Darius, Roger, and Nash were fitted with crampons. Their last challenge to determine who the final two contestants would be was a classic Alaskan rite-of-passage. They would be trekking across the Portage Glacier, hitting checkpoints along the way. Of course, since the men would be trekking across the glacier, that meant the camera crew would too.

Eddie had actually gone all out and hired a local sightseeing company to fly a helicopter overhead and film the men walking along. Taylor, the lucky duck, was chosen to be the one who'd film from the air.

The men would be, of course, timed, and whoever was the slowest to get to the final checkpoint would be leaving the show. To up the ante, and the drama, the men would be leaving at different times, so they'd have no idea how long the others were taking.

They'd seemed to collect themselves after the last challenge and they all seemed as if they actually wanted to be there again. Kina had been worried after Benedict had left. It would certainly be a let-down of the entire show, if all three contenders bagged the last few competitions. She wasn't sure what had happened to make them change their minds, but the days they'd spent together in the house waiting for the next competition obviously did them good.

Kina wasn't looking forward to the day. She was in good shape, but knew it'd be tedious and somewhat dangerous to walk on the glacier while filming at the same time. She'd have to watch where she was putting her feet, but she couldn't do that with one eye glued to the viewfinder of a camera.

She was assigned to Roger for the day. She didn't really have a preference for one man over another. They were all pretty decent guys, the strip club incident notwithstanding. She glanced over at Jonathan. He'd be with Darius for the day. Darius didn't look too sure about having Jonathan following him all day, but she knew he'd get over it as soon as he started concentrating on completing the challenge.

Jonathan had held her hand the entire trip to the glacier. Before they'd gotten out of the van he'd leaned over and whispered in her ear. "Stay safe today, hon."

She got goose bumps every time he'd said that to her. He wasn't just saying it; it was obvious he meant it.

She and Roger were second to start the competition. Carl and Nash were first, and Jonathan and Darius were the last to leave. The trek across the glacier wasn't too strenuous, but there were some large crevasses they had to get around. At each checkpoint the men had to do an activity. At one stop they had to prepare a fish for eating, including scaling it and taking out the guts. At another stop, they were to braid a series of ropes together that could be used in rappelling. And at the last stop, they were supposed to build a sort of snow shelter that would be the type used if they were ever caught out in a snowstorm. For the last activity, Eddie had flown in truckloads of snow to use. The glacier just didn't have the snow needed, on the surface, for that kind of task.

Roger did pretty well at all three of the check points. They were well on their way to the finish line when he stupidly got too close to the edge of a large crevasse. Because of the summer heat and the melting of the top layer of ice all summer, it wasn't stable. Kina saw the ice start to break off under his feet, before Roger even felt it.

"Look out!" she called out, not even thinking about keeping quiet for the sake of the show.

Roger whipped his head around to look at her and she could see the second he figured out what was happening. The panicked look on his face spurred her into action. She dropped the camera, without a care to its value, and leaped toward Roger. Luckily he threw his body at her at the same time. She landed on her butt and grabbed his wrists with her hands. She dug her crampons into the layer of ice just at the side of the gaping hole widening under Roger alarmingly.

Roger was kicking at the empty air beneath his legs as he frantically tried to get back to more stable ground.

"Dig your shoes into the ice!" Kina called to him, trying to back herself, and Roger, away from the hole. "Do it!" she commanded, seeing he was losing it and panicking. Thank God she had the little spikes on her boots. They allowed her to grip the ice and give them some leverage. Without them, they'd both have been on their way to the bottom of the big crack in the ice by now.

She sighed in relief when she saw Roger listening to her and doing as she said. She was strong, but Roger was a big man, and he was wearing a large backpack which was weighing him down. She wasn't going to let go. She couldn't.

Kina strained backward at the same time Roger tried to use his legs and feet to gain purchase and push himself toward her. Just as she felt her hands slipping off his wrists she felt them slowly making progress. Inch by precious inch they backed away from the cold gaping hole that had tried to swallow Roger. When they'd scooted far enough away that his feet were no longer dangling into space, Kina finally let go of the death grip she'd had on his wrists and watched as he scrambled to his hands and knees and crawled away from the hole in the glacier.

She quickly crab-walked backward at the same time and scooted on her butt to a safe distance away from the unstable ground. When they were both well away from the danger of being sucked back into the hole, they collapsed on the ground.

"Holy shit," Kina said under her breath. "That was close."

She was totally unprepared for Roger to surge upward, grab her hand, and pull her into a huge bear hug. She knew how he felt. She'd felt the same way in Australia when Sam saved her from the poisonous snake. When you see your life pass before your eyes, you're just so grateful to have another chance at living.

"Jesus," Roger exclaimed. "Thank you. Shit." He couldn't seem to form a coherent sentence.

Kina smiled and held him just as tightly. She had to admit to herself that she was probably just as freaked as he was. She patted him on the back, trying to help both of them regain their equilibrium. Finally pulling herself back together, she asked, "You ready to get off this godforsaken piece of ice?"

Roger pulled back and looked Kina in the eyes, not ready to let it go yet. "Seriously, thank you. I don't know what I would've…"

Kina interrupted him. "I know, Roger, I *know*. I'm glad I was here. You're okay. Let's go?"

They both picked themselves up off the ice and headed toward the finish line. The camera she'd so carelessly dropped as Roger had started being sucked into the hole miraculously seemed to be all right. Kina noticed Roger was being a lot more careful about where he walked. He also kept his pace slow and steady, so Kina could easily keep up with him.

As expected, Carl and Nash were already at the finish point when they arrived, but that didn't necessarily mean they'd been faster than Roger and herself. Since they'd left in waves, there was no telling whose time was faster. Kina didn't say anything about what happened to her and Roger; she just went over to where Carl was standing and joined him. Not too much later, Jonathan and Darius arrived. Jonathan looked relieved to see her as he came into the finish line area. Kina felt the same relief at seeing him. She understood a bit more about why he felt the way he did about her, because she felt that same protectiveness toward him.

It finally struck her. If she felt that way about him, his feeling that same protectiveness about her couldn't be wrong. She knew he wouldn't want her to protect him, but the feeling was still there. It made sense. She got it. Finally. He'd protect her, just as she'd protect him. Knowing what had happened to her and not knowing whether Jonathan was all right as he trekked across the dangerous ice made it all too clear. It wasn't like she wanted to hold him back, or own him; she just wanted to make sure he was safe.

Shannel got the men all lined up the way she wanted and began the ceremony. She went around to each man and talked about their experiences on the glacier. Kina tensed, knowing what was coming. She wished Roger would keep his mouth shut, but knew he wouldn't. His feelings of gratitude were still too raw and new.

"I almost died out there today," Roger said solemnly. It was almost comical how everyone's head whipped toward him as he spoke. Kina kept her eyes on Roger through her lens. She couldn't look at Jonathan right now, finally understanding how he'd be feeling. She knew she'd feel the same way, if Nash dropped a bomb like the one Roger just lobbed into the group.

Of course Shannel encouraged Roger to keep talking.

Roger told everyone how he'd been admiring the bright blue color of the glacier inside the crevasse and how, before he even knew something was wrong, it was collapsing under him. He described how Kina had grabbed hold of him and prevented him from falling to his death. Without lifting her head from her camera, Kina felt Jonathan's hand at the small of her back. He pressed into her, but didn't say anything or further distract her from her job.

Roger embellished the telling of the dramatic story, but the underlying emotion was real. She really had saved his life. She knew it, he knew it, and now everyone else knew it too. Kina watched as Roger broke out of his place in line and started toward her. Jonathan lifted the camera out of her hands, she briefly saw the emotion in his eyes, and then Roger was there. He brought her into his arms and just hugged her, again, grabbing on tight. The retelling of the story had obviously made him emotional again.

Kina closed her eyes and leaned against him. He was a decent guy who'd had the scare of his life. She felt happy; he was man enough to show emotion and not care who was watching. She had no idea if this would show up on TV, knowing how Eddie felt about the contestants mixing with the camera crew, but she didn't care. She was glad she'd been there at just the right time.

When Roger had himself under control, he pulled back and kissed her on the cheek and made his way back toward the other men and Shannel. Kina cleared her throat and reached for her camera, which was still in Jonathan's hands. She risked looking up at him, not knowing what his reaction would be. She had no idea if he'd be pissed or upset or what.

She watched as he leaned toward her and said in a low voice. "I'm so proud of you, Kina. If this wasn't going to be shown to millions of people right now, I'd kiss the hell out of you."

Kina blushed and couldn't say anything. Wow. Just wow.

She picked up the camera and filmed the rest of the ceremony. Nothing remotely as exciting as what happened to Roger had gone on with the other two contestants. They had funny stories to tell about braiding the rope and on trying to get the scales off of the fish. When Shannel finally read off the times for each of the contestants, Kina wasn't surprised to hear that Roger had the slowest time overall.

Roger didn't seem to mind either. His final words for the show said it all. "Even though I'm leaving the show today, I'm leaving with my life, so I feel like I've won anyway."

Because they were on a glacier, Roger couldn't leave the same way the other contestants had. They all had to hike off the glacier to get to the van. Jonathan didn't even flinch, which Kina appreciated more than she could say, when Roger took hold of her hand and held it the entire way back to the van. They didn't exchange any more words about what had happened up on the glacier, but Kina knew they'd created a bond that would never fade.

Kina thought about how close she and Sam were, and understood what Roger was feeling. She could feel Jonathan walking close behind her, keeping watch over her and it warmed her heart. He was letting Roger hold her hand, but she was still aware of him. It was like he'd warned, even though another man had her attention and was close to her, she knew he was there, knew she was his and his alone.

Kina exchanged contact information with Roger before he left the production house. She knew she'd always keep in touch. It was like the old Chinese proverb, if you saved someone's life, it was yours forever. She didn't even startle when she felt a hand curl around the back of her neck. Jonathan. She'd missed that.

"Are you all right, hon?" He seemed to know how emotional she was over what had happened. "You want to talk about it?"

"I'm good." At his skeptical look, she turned toward him and looked up. "I swear, I'm okay."

She fell even more for the man standing in front of her, when he simply nodded. He pulled her toward him and gathered her close. She loved when he did that. It made her feel so cared for, so safe, so loved. Holy cow. She didn't want to go there, not yet.

"Would you rather spend a month alone with your lover in a cabin high in the mountains surrounded by snow, or on a deserted tropical island?"

Kina laughed and didn't take her head from his chest as she answered, "If that was an invitation, my answer is that it doesn't matter as long as we're together."

Chapter Fifteen

This was it! The final competition for the show was here at last. Kina knew everyone was ready for it to be over. The weather had gotten colder and the daylight was getting shorter and shorter. Kina had the utmost respect for anyone who chose to live in Alaska year-round. She knew it was beautiful in the summer, with the long summer light and the mild weather, but staying there all-year-long took a special kind of person. She knew she couldn't do it.

Darius and Nash also seemed ready to be done with the show. They were nervous about what they'd have to do for the final competition, but ready to be done with it. Kina didn't think either really cared if he was named the "Extreme Alaskan," but it was more that they wanted to get home to their own space and friends and family again.

She and Jonathan had worked out an easy camaraderie. They hadn't spent the night together again, knowing what it would lead to if they did. Kina wanted to make love to Jonathan more and more each day, but she also liked that they were taking it slow. It was great getting to know him without the pressure of being naked thrown in.

They did spend the evenings in each other's arms watching TV or just hanging out with the others. They shared some scorching kisses, but tried to keep it at that. They both knew the end of the show meant some decisions would have to be made.

Kina still hadn't decided what to do. On one hand, she wanted to be with Jonathan, but she was honestly scared to death to think about giving up her job. She hated not being able to make a decision one way or another. She didn't want to be a camera operator for reality shows anymore, but she did want to stay in the business. She didn't know how that would work if she moved to Arizona to be with Jonathan. If she started at a new television station, she knew she'd have to start at the bottom and work her way up again, and that definitely didn't appeal to her.

She knew Taylor and Carl were ready to go home as well. They'd started talking more and more about their adorable little girls and she knew they missed their spouses as well. Taylor had been with his partner, John, for over fifteen years and Carl had been married to his wife for ten. While they understood the life of a camera operator meant a lot of time away from home, it was never easy.

Eddie had worked hard to make sure the final competition between the two men would be dramatic. He'd chosen to have another overnight adventure, but this time it would be on Bear Island. Bear Island was located southwest of Anchorage in the Katmai National Park and Preserve. It was an actual island on Kukaklek Lake. The best, and quickest, way to get to it from Anchorage was by helicopter.

The island was known to have a large population of brown bears, it wasn't so far from the mainland that the bears couldn't easily swim to it. They found the island to be a perfect place to nest and raise their young. Part of the reason was because the food was plentiful and the predators few. The brown bears had mostly been stuffing themselves with food during the summer, but the danger of an attack was never really gone. The men, and subsequently the camera operators, would have to constantly be on the alert for the massive animals.

Native Alaskans knew to keep clear of the bears, especially this time of year. They were unpredictable and many people were killed each year from bear attacks. Because it was so dangerous, Eddie brought in an Alaskan ranger to talk with both the camera operators and the contestants to go over some basic bear safety.

Kina listened intently as the ranger explained how brown bears were able to run in short bursts up to forty miles an hour and they were also very good swimmers, so it was unlikely a human would win in a foot race. Darius and Roger were both given bear boxes, which were bear-resistant containers and they were instructed to put any leftover food in, to string up in trees to prevent the bears from entering the campsite after smelling food.

Basically, the ranger told everyone that bears don't like being surprised, they should never be crowded, and they're always looking for something to eat. Kina looked around and saw everyone was paying close attention to the ranger. They all knew Bear Island could be dangerous and they wanted to stay safe.

Kina muffled her laughter when Jonathan leaned over and asked quietly in her ear, "Would you rather be mauled by a hungry bear or a hungry lion?" She shivered as he nipped her ear quickly before facing the ranger again and pretending he hadn't just made her quiver and wish those teeth were nipping somewhere else.

The plan was to drop off the two contestants with two camera operators filming each man on either side of the island. They weren't supposed to interact with each other, but Eddie and the production crew would be stationed on another part of the island. As long as they kept their interactions with each other off camera, it wouldn't be an issue. Each pair of camera operators would have a radio for safety purposes.

The contestants would spend another two nights on the island, in much the same time frame as their last overnight contest. They'd be dropped off around noon and picked up around the same time on the third day. This time the difference was that each man wasn't given anything to eat, it would be up to them to find their own food. They were to make their own shelter, find their own food, and generally just survive while out on their own. They were given one match, one fishing hook and they were allowed to dress as warm as they'd like.

Kina didn't know what the actual competition was from Eddie's brief explanation, and obviously the men were confused as well. Most of the activities in the past had been based on time or some other type of quantifiable outcome. Finally, Eddie got to the point.

"In order to win and be called the 'Extreme Alaskan', you'll be judged by one of the local rangers. Whichever of you is deemed to have the best campsite, will win. The ranger has a checklist of things she is going to use to see if your site is deemed 'Alaska-worthy.' She'll check to make sure your shelter is solid, you have a good food supply, you have a good place for your fire, etc. We can't tell you all of the criteria. It's up to you to figure out how to make your site a place you, or anyone else, could actually survive in if they were there for a long period of time. Use what you've learned over the course of the last weeks and what you know from your previous experiences. Be safe, have fun, and we'll see you in a few days."

Eddie broke everyone up into their groups. Kina wasn't surprised she and Jonathan were together again. While she was a bit embarrassed, she was also glad. Obviously Eddie wasn't dumb, and after his talk with Jonathan about Jeff, he'd obviously figured out they were together. He could've been a jerk and separated them deliberately, but he hadn't. Another surprise.

Taylor and Carl winked at Kina as they set off with Nash. Kina would've been happy being with either of the other men; luckily, they all got along extremely well, especially now that Jeff was no longer with them.

Kina and Jonathan set off after Darius. He was given instructions on how to get where he was to set up his camp. It started out as a quiet trek because Darius didn't have another contestant to talk to, but remembering what the ranger had said about bears and how they didn't like to be surprised, he started to whistle while he walked. Making noise was a great way to let bears know you were there so they could keep their distance.

Kina would've loved to have been able to make some noise of her own. She was a bit paranoid about the whole bear thing. She had no desire to run into a bear in her lifetime. But since the cameras would pick up any extra noise they made, both she and Jonathan had to keep silent.

After a forty-five minute walk, they arrived at Darius' spot on the other side of the island. It was breathtaking. They were looking south over Kukaklek Lake and the sun was hitting the lake and glistening off it like a million diamonds sparkling on the water. It was beautiful. Kina thought if it was only about fifty degrees warmer, it could almost be a tropical paradise and a place she'd like to come to. Almost.

Darius got right to work. Kina almost felt sorry for him. As a chemist, he hadn't had too much need to run around the woods collecting firewood and trying set up a camp according to some obscure standards he'd be judged by.

Jonathan leaned over and tapped Kina on the shoulder. She stopped filming so he could talk to her.

"Do you want to set up our camp, or continue to film Darius?"

Kina smiled.

"What are you smiling for?" Jonathan asked running his index finger down her cheek lightly.

"Because you asked me which I'd rather do," Kina answered honestly, loving his hands on her. "Most men would've just assumed they'd have to put up the tent while I filmed."

Ignoring her sexist comment, Jonathan instead chose to concentrate on two words she'd said. "The tent? We did bring two, you know."

"I know," Kina said blushing. "You can set up the tent; I'll follow Darius for a while."

Jonathan looked around to see where Darius had gone. He was across the clearing, not paying any attention to them, instead he was trying to set up a lean-to with some branches. Jonathan hooked his hand behind Kina's neck and pulled her toward him.

Kina loved that it seemed to be his favorite way to bring her toward him for a kiss. His palm on the back of her neck was like an instant aphrodisiac for her. Her brain knew what was coming and she was instantly ready for him. The kiss, as usual, was intense. It was way too short for Kina's liking, but they both knew they were working and had no time to make out like two horny teenagers.

Stepping back from her, Jonathan said, "Okay, I'll set up our tent. You follow Darius, but be safe."

Nodding, Kina headed toward Darius to get some good close-up shots of him setting up his camp.

The rest of the day went by relatively smoothly. Darius managed to get his lean-to set up and miraculously, he was able to start a fire. Kina almost laughed out loud at the victory dance he did after he got it to a safe level. Watching him hoop and holler and skip around the area was just too funny. Kina thought once again how great his actions would be for television. He also managed to catch a small fish in the lake. He didn't have to worry about any leftovers because he ate the entire thing. She was actually pretty impressed at how well he'd done. She knew she wouldn't have been half as successful as he was. Thank God, she was filming and not on the show itself.

After Jonathan and Kina ate and the sun went down, it was still way too early to head to bed. They'd gotten some good nighttime shots of Darius lying under his shelter gazing up at the sky and other generic nighttime shots that could be edited into the show wherever Eddie would like to put them in. Both Jonathan and Kina were more than happy to sit around the fire Darius had built and relax for a bit.

They'd all gotten to know each other pretty well over the last weeks, not to mention the recent drama with the strip club, so they were all comfortable hanging out for a while. Kina was going to start the 'Would you Rather' game, but then decided she liked it being just between her and Jonathan.

They sat around and talked about nothing important, just the weather, what Darius had planned for the next day and what he'd do when the show was over.

"Maybe after the show airs, you'll be so famous some hot chick will look you up."

Kina and Darius laughed at Jonathan. Kina picked up where Jonathan left off.

"Yeah, even though this wasn't a dating show, it could still work out for you."

Darius laughed. "I'll just be glad to go back to my nice, plain, boring life. I think I'll tell anyone who'll listen to not apply to be on a reality show. It's not all it's cracked up to be."

They all laughed. After about two hours or so, Jonathan stood up.

"Thanks for letting us share your fire, Darius. We're going to hit the sack. We'll see you bright and early in the morning."

Darius nodded at them and didn't even make any comments about the two of them having only one tent set up. Kina figured after Jonathan's talk with him there was no way he'd chance being disrespectful in any way toward her. It was obvious they were "together" and Darius didn't seem to have any issues with it.

Climbing into the tent felt awkward this time. The last time they were on site outside it seemed more natural. Kina figured it was because there was more sexual tension in the air now and they were more aware of each other.

She settled down on the sleeping bag Jonathan had put down and waited for him to join her. Jonathan had taken the ranger's words to heart and had put their MREs inside the bear-proof container and strung it up over a tree about fifty yards away. He didn't want to take any chances of a bear wandering into their tent looking for food. That was one of the most dangerous situations people could get into with a bear. The ranger told everyone several horror stories about campers who'd either been in their tent when a bear got curious, or who'd gone into their tent, believing it would protect them from a bear. There was nothing to do but fight if that happened. Kina didn't want to have a fight a bear in such close quarters as this little tent.

Jonathan zipped up the door flap and shut off the flashlight, leaving them in total darkness. It was intimate in a way that being in a bed together hadn't been. Kina felt him take off his boots and then strip off his jeans. She sighed as he gathered her into his arms and drew the second sleeping bag over them. God, she loved being in his arms like this.

After a moment of silence Jonathan said softly, "I've missed this."

Kina had too, but they both knew why they hadn't been sleeping in the same bed. It was the big hairy gorilla in the room they'd both been ignoring. He'd said he wanted them to get to know each other before making love, but he'd also said he wanted to wait until she was ready to give herself to him. To be with him. He wanted her to be able to say with one hundred percent conviction that she wanted to be with him.

"I've missed it too," was all she could say in response.

Jonathan didn't let the subject drop as Kina hoped he would.

"Have you thought anymore about coming to Arizona with me, once the show is over?"

Kina shifted in his arms until she rested her chin on his chest. She could just make out his face. As much as she wished they didn't have to have this conversation, she knew it was time. Hell, it was past time to have it. "I've thought about it," she hedged, still not knowing what she'd tell him.

"What's holding you back, hon?" Jonathan asked tenderly. "Talk it though with me, let me help you, ease your fears."

"But you'll find reasons for me to move, no matter what I say," Kina said in frustration. "How can I talk it through with you when I know you'll try to convince me to move down there no matter what reasons I come up with for not wanting to'?"

Jonathan was silent for a long while. Kina turned back on her side and rested her head on his shoulder again, keeping her arm thrown over his rock-hard abdomen.

"I want you with me, Kina," he finally said. "I want you with me more than anything. I'd do just about anything to get you there with me, for you to want to be there with me. But I don't want you to agree and then regret it later. I want you to move to Arizona and be sure it's where you want to be. I could tell you the streets were lined with gold there and I know you'd still only come when you're ready."

Kina chuckled. It seemed like he did know her after all.

"I love you, Kina." Jonathan threw it out there like a grenade. It sat between them, scary and exciting at the same time.

After hearing no response from her Jonathan continued. "I want you to know. Just as I told you earlier, you're mine, and I want to make sure you know how I felt. I'm not asking you to move and change your entire life on a whim. You're it for me. Period. If you want to do the long-distance thing for a while, I'll do it, but know I ultimately want you with me. In my house. In my bed. You're the one for me. You're my One. I want to marry you. Spend the rest of my life with you."

Kina started to panic. She wasn't ready for this. She hadn't known Jonathan long enough. She tensed.

Jonathan ran his hand over the small of her back soothingly. "Don't freak, hon. God, I wasn't going to go there tonight, but I don't know how else to make sure you know I'm serious. I'm not some young college kid who wants a one-night-stand. I want you. Just you. All of you. But only when you're ready."

Kina was still silent. She couldn't get any words out. On the one hand she wanted to immediately say yes to whatever he suggested, but the more logical and stubborn part of her was screaming at her to slow down, that this couldn't be real.

Jonathan kissed her forehead gently and kept his lips on her skin. She could hear him breathe in deeply, as if inhaling her essence into his soul. "Shhhh, just relax, love. No pressure. Let's get through the rest of this show and then we can talk again if you need to. I won't bring it up again, but I'm not sorry I told you how I felt. Sleep now. I'm right here, I'm not going anywhere."

Chapter Sixteen

Kina came awake slowly the next morning. It was still dark, as the sun rose much later in the morning than she was used to. She lay still and enjoyed being in Jonathan's arms. They were in much the same position as they had been when they fell asleep; there wasn't much room in the tent for much moving around anyway. Jonathan was on his back with his arm around her waist and she was using his shoulder as her pillow and was on her side with one arm curved over his stomach. Kina heard his light snoring as he breathed in and out. She moved her head a fraction and took in a deep breath. God, he smelled good.

Oh she knew most people probably wouldn't agree, after all they'd spent the day hiking and working, and then part of the night in front of a smoky camp fire, but those smells intermingled with his natural scent was heady. He smelled strong, like he could conquer mountains and slay dragons. She wished she could wake every morning with his smell in her nostrils.

Kina paused. Hell. She could, if only she was brave enough. Ultimately, that was what it came down to. Was she brave enough to take the leap and trust Jonathan? She was scared. It was a frightening thought to think about leaving what she knew, her career, and leaping off a cliff into the unknown. But she knew Jonathan would be there for her. He was her parachute. So, what was holding her back? Why wasn't she jumping at the chance to be with him?

It was because of her past. She hadn't had good luck with relationships and she was terrified this would end up the same way, no matter what Jonathan said. She couldn't really remember, but she knew she'd probably thought she felt the same way about Matt before she moved in with him too. She tightened her arm around Jonathan and snuggled deeper into his side.

She felt him stir and clasp her to him as he woke.

"Good morning, love," he said sleepily. "What time is it?"

"I have no idea."

"Have you been up long?"

Kina shook her head. "No, just lying here enjoying being in your arms." She decided to be honest with him.

Jonathan gave her another squeeze and kissed the top of her head. "I haven't had any nightmares in a while," he said unexpectedly.

Kina raised her head. "What?"

"I haven't had any nightmares since we talked," he repeated. "I heard what you said about it not being my fault. I even called Dean one night and had a long talk with him. I told him how I was feeling and he reacted the same way you did. I took your words to heart and decided to believe you." Jonathan laid it all out there, holding nothing back.

"Thank God," Kina said fervently. "It wasn't your fault. You're so protective with me; I know you were the same with Becky."

"Thank you, Kina. Thank you for believing in me and helping me get through that."

Kina blindly raised her mouth to his, not thinking for a second about morning breath or what she might smell like, only needing to feel his lips and tongue on hers. Jonathan obliged her and devoured her mouth with his. Soon, that wouldn't be enough, but for now, here, it was perfect.

They slowly made their way out of the tent and into the chilly morning air. Darius was already awake and sitting next to the fire. He'd most likely not slept that well and that was why he was up already. Kina wandered off to do her morning ablutions and Jonathan wandered in the opposite direction. They met back at the tent and gobbled down a quick MRE. They didn't want to flaunt their food in front of Darius, but they had to eat to have the energy to haul their cameras around all day and to keep up with whatever Darius had planned for the day.

Darius spent most of the morning fishing. He remembered the ranger saying they had to have enough food to last for a while, so instead of worrying about berries and other grasses he could collect, he concentrated on getting protein.

Overall, he was a very good fisherman. He seemed to have mastered the art of using the hook he'd been given. He tied it to a long thin stick using some of the flexible weeds that grew around the shore. He walked out into the lake a little ways and was very patient. He'd either gotten used to the cold water or he was numb. Either way, he'd captured some little crawfish that were along the shore to use as bait and had stood in the water for a long while catching fish.

Kina watched as the pile of fish on the shore grew. She glanced at Jonathan nervously. She put her camera down and waited until Jonathan noticed and had done the same.

"Do you think that's okay?" she said pointing at the pile of fish lying on the rocks. She was worried about bears. Would they smell the fish and think it was a free lunch?

"I have no idea." Jonathan answered, looking around. "What if we move over there?" He pointed at a rock sticking out a bit over the water, away from where Darius was fishing.

Kina nodded in agreement. She was all for getting away from anything that might attract a bear. "Should we say something?"

"Normally, I'd say no, we aren't supposed to interfere with the show, but I think this is a safety issue."

Kina agreed and Jonathan called to Darius to let him know their concerns. The other man called back that he was almost done and would come into shore and deal with the fish in a moment.

Jonathan and Kina moved to the rock and continued filming. They watched as Darius caught another fish and moved toward the shore. He waved at them, letting them know he was done. Jonathan helped Kina off the rock and they both moved toward Darius.

Kina froze. Holy crap. Her worst nightmare was coming true. A brown bear was ambling down the shore right toward Darius. Without thinking she grabbed Jonathan's arm and yelled out at Darius.

"Darius! Behind you!"

He turned and as soon as he saw the bear, he forgot everything he'd learned from the ranger. He dropped the makeshift fishing pole and the fish he was carrying and turned and ran straight for them.

The bear, used to chasing his prey, immediately roared and gave chase. Darius ran past them as fast as he could. Jonathan grabbed Kina and held her in place.

"Don't run, Kina," he warned.

Kina couldn't run. She was frozen in place. The bear stopped ten feet from the two of them. It stood on all fours and swung its head from side to side. Kina heard it clacking its teeth together as if practicing biting down on their tender flesh.

"Spread your arms out," Jonathan said, not trying to lower his voice. "Make yourself appear as big as possible."

Kina did as Jonathan instructed. Neither one had thought to drop their cameras. She watched as the bear stood there, still swinging its head and opening and closing its mouth. Crap. She had no idea what that meant in bear language, but it couldn't be good.

"Now, start walking backward," Jonathan continued to instruct. Kina noticed he kept himself between her and the bear. No, no, no, no. This wasn't happening. She suddenly remembered all the times Jonathan had told her how he'd protect her and stand in front of her, if necessary. She'd never been so scared in all her life. She was scared for herself, of course, but she was also scared for Jonathan.

The bear didn't seem impressed with them at all. It made a growling noise and followed them as they backed up. Suddenly the bear was done playing nice. The smell of the fish and Darius running had obviously made all of its protective instincts kick in.

It came at them suddenly and before Kina could do anything, it took a swipe at Jonathan. He still had his camera in his hand and used it to block the bear's attack. A swipe from a bear could kill an elk or deer with one blow, so Kina knew Jonathan was in big trouble. The camera went flying from his hand and landed with a thud fifteen feet away. That was way too close. Thank God it hit the camera and not Jonathan. Kina leaned forward to hand her camera to Jonathan for extra protection when the bear came at them again.

Jonathan saw Kina lean forward at the same time he saw the bear's paw come toward them again. He didn't have anything else in his hands to protect her with so he simply pushed her backward with one strong shove on her chest and stepped into the space she'd just been standing in. The bear's paw struck him right across the lower stomach. It would've hit Kina in the chest had she still been standing there. Jonathan fell to the ground without a sound, clutching his stomach.

Shit. That hurt. Jonathan looked around frantically. He was on the ground now, not a good place to be when confronted by a brown bear. Brown bears were part of the grizzly family and he knew he had very little time to do something to save both himself and Kina. He grabbed a handful of dirt and rocks from next to him and threw it at the bear as it came toward him again.

He heard Kina yelling at the bear and frantically trying to talk to him at the same time. He couldn't answer her; he was concentrating on the bear coming right for him. Suddenly, Kina's camera was dropped in his lap. He grunted with the pain of it landing on the wounds from the bear but he grabbed it and held it up just as the bear went to hit him again.

Once again the bear's claws hit the camera and it went flying.

Adrenaline flowing through his body, Jonathan crab-walked backward as fast as his abused body would let him, still trying to grab handfuls of the loose sand and throwing it at the bear's head. He saw sticks flying from behind him as well. Kina was still there, throwing whatever she could get her hands on to try to get the bear to retreat.

"Get the hell out of here, Kina!" he yelled at her, hoping like hell she'd follow his instructions.

No!" she yelled back, continuing to throw things at the bear.

Finally, as the two of them backed toward the trees, the bear stopped following them. It stood there and growled and clacked its teeth together as Kina tried to pull Jonathan's arm to help him move back out of its way. Jonathan gritted his teeth. He was in severe pain. He knew it was bad, but he had to get them away from the bear in case it decided to charge them again.

After they'd moved about twenty feet away, the bear turned around and headed toward the pile of fish Darius had left on the ground. Jonathan could feel Kina trying to pull him upright. He used all his strength, and most of hers as well, to climb to his feet and stumble along beside her. He had no idea where she was taking them, but as long as it was away from that damn bear, he was happy.

Kina dragged Jonathan along beside her as far as her strength would allow. Jonathan was practically dead weight way before she got back to the camp. They weren't going to make it back to the tent and the first aid kit they'd brought along. She eased him to the ground, looking around nervously. She looked down at Jonathan. He'd dropped down on his back and his eyes were closed. Kina took a closer look. Oh, shit. His shirt and hands were covered in blood.

Kina reached down, noticing her hand shaking uncontrollably, and lifted the bottom of Jonathan's shirt. After taking a look she quickly dropped it and pressed her hands hard to his stomach. She ignored his inhalation of pain at her actions. She tried not to throw up. She concentrated on breathing in through her mouth and out through her nose. She thought she'd seen what might have been his intestines. He was hurt. Bad. She had to get him help.

"Darius!" She screamed into the still forest. She couldn't leave Jonathan because she was literally holding his life in her hands. "Darius!" She yelled again. He'd better still be around. God, what if that bear smelled Jonathan's blood and came back for more? What if there were other bears around. She had no idea how that worked, but fresh blood in the forest couldn't be good. Crap. Crap. Crap.

"Would you rather…" Kina heard Jonathan say in a breathy voice, "…be mauled by a bear… or a lion?" Kina saw him smile weakly. "I'm thinking neither, at this point." He answered his own question.

"Shut up, Jonathan. Just be quiet. You're going to be fine. Just fine." Kina sniffed, desperately trying to keep herself under control. Crying wasn't going to help Jonathan at this point.

Jonathan hurt. He knew it wasn't good. "No guilt, love, promise me."

Kina shook her head in denial. She knew what he was doing. "No, just no. You shut up. You're going to be fine. Darius!" She screamed one more time. Where the hell was he? She needed him. Now.

Jonathan laid his hand over hers lying on his ripped-open stomach. He couldn't look down, but could feel it was bad. "Love, remember what I said. I'd do anything to protect you. Anything. I'm glad it was me."

Kina's eyes filled with tears again. Shit. She hadn't believed him. She knew he said he loved her but this was too much. No one had ever done anything like what he'd done for her today. Her father hadn't even wanted her born. Her high school boyfriend didn't respect her and Matt had just wanted to own her. She knew he never would've given his life for hers. "I never asked for you to do this," she said brokenly, not being able to stop the tears coursing down her face and dripping onto their joined hands over his stomach.

"That's what love is. Not having to ask."

Kina watched as Jonathan's eyes closed and his hand went lax and fell off of hers. No. This wasn't happening.

Darius finally came running through the woods toward her. She had to get help.

"Kneel down here and put your hands where mine are," she ordered curtly, once again gaining control over her riotous emotions.

"What happened?" Darius asked.

"What the hell do you think happened?" Kina snapped. "He was mauled by a bear. The same damn bear you ran from and led right to us." Darius had no response. "I have to get back to camp and get the radio. He needs help. Whatever you do, don't let go. Keep the pressure on his stomach. I don't care if that bear comes back. You. Do. Not. Move. Got it?"

At his nod Kina lifted her arms and waited until Darius had a good strong grip on Jonathan. Before running off, she leaned down and kissed Jonathan's lips. "I'll be right back, please don't die on me," she whispered and then was gone through the trees.

Kina ran as fast as she could back to the camp and snatched up the radio. She frantically radioed the production camp and explained between harsh breaths that Jonathan was badly hurt and they needed a helicopter. Eddie hadn't wanted to believe her until she cussed him out and threatened a lawsuit if he didn't get someone out there soon.

Eddie obviously had planned for some sort of emergency care in case someone needed it because within twenty minutes, a helicopter was landing on the same shore Darius had been fishing at and where the bear had attacked them. Kina had taken over holding Jonathan together while Darius went to meet the chopper at the lake. He led the paramedics back to the forest where Kina was kneeling on the ground. They took one look at the amount of blood on her hands and on the ground underneath Jonathan and packed him up and got him on the stretcher and headed toward the helicopter. They didn't spend any time trying to put in an IV in while they were in the wilderness. They just packaged him up and were on their way.

There was no room in the chopper for Kina so she could only watch as Jonathan was taken away. He'd never regained consciousness. Left with Darius in the clearing, the silence was heavy. They could no longer hear the whoop whoop whoop of the helicopter as it sped toward Anchorage.

"I…" Darius started to say and stopped as Kina's hand came up.

"No." Kina said as she started gathering up the pieces of the ruined camera equipment strewn about the area. She had to get to the hospital, but she still had a job to do. The attack ran through her mind like a record spinning over and over. Picking up the pieces of equipment was like picking up pieces of Jonathan.

She got everything back to camp and radioed Eddie. He was pulling Carl off of Nash's campsite and sending him to hers. He'd take over the rest of the filming so she could get to the hospital and Jonathan. Kina shouldn't have been surprised that Eddie wasn't going to stop the show, but she was. Why she'd thought his camera crew meant more than the show, was beyond her.

After all her back and forth with herself about whether she should quit or not was now a moot issue. She was done. So done. There were times during the filming she'd thought maybe Eddie was changing and perhaps she'd sign up to continue to work with him. But now there was no way in hell.

Carl gave her a big hug when he got to her campsite. Kina noticed there were two rangers carrying shotguns who arrived with him. At least Eddie had sent along extra security. At least she wouldn't have to worry about the rest of them out at the lake while she was with Jonathan at the hospital.

She didn't say a word as she sat in the helicopter Eddie had to arrange to take her to the hospital. He'd made a token protest at the cost of flying her back separately from the rest of the crew, but quickly shut his mouth at her ferocious words again threatening all sorts of lawsuits.

As soon as they landed at the Anchorage airfield, Kina took out her cell phone. Thank God she finally had service. The first thing she did was call Dean, Jonathan's brother. She didn't have his parents' numbers, but Jonathan had programmed his brother's number into her phone for emergencies. She supposed this was definitely an emergency.

"Hello?" Dean answered after the first ring.

Kina got right to the point. "Dean, this is Kina, I'm working with Jonathan in Alaska. There's been an accident. Jonathan's in the hospital."

Kina could hear him moving around quickly. "What happened?"

"He was swiped by a bear. I have no idea how bad it is, but I think it's bad. They flew him off the set and to the hospital here in Anchorage. I'm on my way there now, but I don't know anything." Her voice cracked. "I don't know if they'll talk to me since I'm not related to him, so you'll want to get here as soon as you can."

"I'm on my way, Kina. I'll call the hospital and give them permission to talk to you. Keep me up-to-date. I don't know how long it'll take me to get there."

"Do you want me to call your parents?" Kina asked, hoping like hell he'd say no.

"I'll take care of it. You just get to my brother. If you talk to him, tell him we're on our way."

Kina agreed and hung up. Thank God Dean would be there soon. She flagged down a taxi and headed to the hospital.

* * *

Kina stood off to the side of the waiting room. The last twenty-four hours had been the longest she'd ever experienced in her life. Dean had arrived, as had the rest of Jonathan's family. Becky, his mom and dad, and even some

505

of the people who worked on the refuge, she'd recognized them from the shoot they'd done there. They all showed up to support their son, friend, and brother.

Kina felt completely out of place, but she couldn't go anywhere until she knew Jonathan was going to be all right. The doctors had come out periodically to update the family on his condition. They'd explained the extensive injuries Jonathan had and how the bear's claws had actually perforated his bowel as they'd swiped across his abdomen. They'd gotten him sewed up, but their main concern now was infection. Not only were the bear's claws covered in bacteria and dirty as hell, the waste material from his bowels had leaked into his body, so it was a double whammy.

Jonathan was fighting as hard as he could, but it was just a matter of time to see if he'd pull through. Kina teared up. God, now she understood more what Jonathan had been talking about when he'd talked about his feelings of guilt when it came to Becky. The one nap Kina had managed to squeeze in, ended abruptly with her jerking awake because she'd been reliving the exact moment Jonathan stepped in front of her to take the bear's swipe. Guilt. It was an insidious emotion. Nothing anyone could say would assuage it.

She thought back to their brief moment in the woods before he'd passed out. Jonathan had tried to tell her not to feel guilty. He knew she would. She knew he'd be pissed at her for feeling this way and she tried really hard to tamp it down.

Jonathan's mom, Bethany, came toward Kina. His mom was the last person Kina wanted to talk to. She just knew the eagle-eyed woman would take one look at her and know this was all her fault. So she was completely shocked when the older woman walked right up to her and folded her into her embrace. Kina couldn't help it; she'd been strong for so long, but that one little bit of sympathy broke her. She burst into tears and buried her face in the other woman's hair and just cried.

When she finally came back to awareness she noticed she was sitting on a small couch in the waiting area with Bethany still holding on to her tightly.

"I'm so sorry," Kina said, pulling back to wipe at her face.

"What are you sorry about? You looked like you really needed that; both the shoulder to cry on and the cry itself."

"Well yeah, I just cried all over you and you don't even know me!" Kina said, shocked this woman would even want to take the time to comfort someone who was basically a stranger.

"I know you. And even if I didn't, you're Jonathan's One. That means you're family."

"Wh-what?" How did she know that? Had he talked to his mom about her?

Bethany sighed. "Has he told you about our family?"

"Uh, yeah." Kina drew out the word in confusion. She thought she knew where Bethany was going with this and it was a bit awkward.

Bethany didn't take offense, but instead just smiled.

"So, he did tell you, but you don't really believe it. Let me tell you a story, Kina. In my family," Bethany gestured behind her at her husband and other son, "the men have one woman who is meant to be theirs. One. They go through life knowing this, but not really believing it until they meet her. It happened with Robert, my husband. He was going on his merry way, saving lives, then boom! He met me at the scene of an accident and knew I was his one and only love. Dean was the same way. He was a ladies man. Never settling down because it never felt right. Then he met Becky. Obviously you know their story. It wasn't easy, but Becky was his One. This has happened over and over throughout our family history. We have story after story of our ancestors who never thought they'd get married, never thought they'd find that one person who completes them, until one day they did. The same thing happened with Jonathan. He hadn't really talked to you on the set until he went to all of the crew to see if any of you could help Becky. He talked to you and knew. Kina, you're his One."

Kina was shocked and confused. Jonathan had told her he loved her and had told her the story of her being his One, but she'd pretty much blown him off, thinking he was just being romantic. She couldn't understand how Jonathan's mom knew about her, though.

Bethany must have seen her confusion. She took hold of Kina's hand and held it tightly. "He told us, dear. As soon as he came back to the house after meeting you, he came bursting in the room and said 'I've found her!' He's been wooing you. It can be a hard thing to hear and believe. It sounds crazy, but I see you already knew some of this already. He trusted you enough to tell you."

Kina looked up from their clasped hands to see Becky and Dean standing in front of them. She turned and saw Robert, Jonathan's dad, standing to the side, watching his wife carefully.

"It's true, Kina," Becky said softly. "I know it sounds crazy, but the Baker men would do anything for their One. I know you're feeling guilt about what happened to Jonathan, but, stop it right now. Seriously. He's been through this too and I've told him over and over that I don't blame him nor do I want him to blame himself. You haven't told us what happened out there and how he came to be hurt exactly, but we can guess. He was probably protecting you, right? Somehow he was hurt instead of you."

Kina looked down at her hands. God, hearing it out loud was so much worse than thinking it in her head.

Dean took over for his wife. Kina noticed the protective hand he had at Becky's back and how she was curled into his side. "We're protective. It's in our genes. Jonathan isn't quite as alpha as I am, but if you were in trouble, or Becky, or our mom, or really any other woman, he'd do anything in his power to protect you. I can imagine you were filming and a bear came up on you. He probably stood in front of you and took that bear on."

"Close enough." Kina mumbled, completely floored by what this family was saying.

Dean went on. "He loves you, Kina. You're his One. He'd do anything for you, just as I suspect you'd do for him. Don't feel guilty. Put yourself in his shoes. God forbid it was you lying in that bed, would you want him to feel guilty for you protecting him?"

Kina sat up straight on the couch. Oh crap. Dean was right. He was so right. That was just what she needed to hear to give her a kick in the pants. She'd be pissed if the tables were turned and Jonathan was feeling guilt about her getting hurt while protecting him. She'd been telling him over and over about how she could take care of herself, and now, look. Loving someone, having someone love you, wasn't about being independent and moving through life on your own, it was about protecting each other. Being there for each other when needed. She'd helped Jonathan through some hefty guilt he'd been feeling just as he'd helped her with that damn bear. She had to get her act together.

Kina stood up and hugged Dean as hard as she could. Of course she couldn't even get her arms all the way around him, he was so big. He uncurled his arms from around Becky and held Kina tight for just a moment. He put her away from him and looked into her eyes. "You're okay, now?"

"I'm great." Kina said with steel in her voice. She had things to do and people to talk to. She'd make this right, once and for all.

* * *

Jonathan gradually became more and more lucid over the next couple of days. It wasn't until his third day in the hospital that he was awake enough to recognize anyone. Dean happened to be in the room when he came to.

Because he still had a breathing tube in, he couldn't talk. He was agitated and Dean saw the panic in his eyes. He put a hand on his brother's forehead and one on his chest. He leaned down to speak into his ear. "Settle, bro. You're fine.

509

Kina's fine. You're in the hospital, but you're healing and we'll get that tube out of your throat so you can talk, all right?"

Jonathan looked up and saw the honesty in his brother's eyes. He wouldn't lie to him. Dean knew what Kina meant to him. He knew. Jonathan relaxed and closed his eyes. He'd believe his brother, but he still wanted to see Kina.

Two days later, Jonathan was leaving the hospital and he still hadn't seen Kina. She'd disappeared. He heard all about his mom's conversation with her, but no one had spoken with her. It was if she'd vanished into thin air. It was killing him. He'd let her run for now, but he'd find her. He wasn't giving up on her. He couldn't. He needed her.

He pushed the hurt down. He was hurt she hadn't come to see him in the hospital. Surely, after everything they'd been through, she'd want to make sure he was going to be all right. He tried to put himself in her shoes. She was scared and feeling guilty. She probably thought she was being noble or something and thought leaving him was the best thing she could do for him. Well, screw that. He'd make sure she knew how much she meant to him. As soon as he got back on his feet, he'd find her and somehow make her understand how much he loved her. She had to. Without her, he was nothing.

Dean and his dad had arranged for him to get home via a chartered plane. Jonathan knew it had to cost a whack, but he also knew he'd never make it if he had to fly commercial. He'd argued to stay in Anchorage and recuperate, but his family wasn't having any of it. The only reason he wanted to stay in Alaska was Kina. He thought maybe if he stayed there, she'd come see him and let him convince her she was his world.

The doctors signed all the papers and put him in the care of his family. Dean and Becky drove him to the airport so he could lie down in the back seat, and his parents took a taxi. The few friends who had flown up when he was first hurt had already left a few days ago. They'd headed back to

Arizona to make sure the refuge was taken care of. Jonathan was wheeled onto the plane and settled himself into the cot that had been set up for him. He was quiet. All he could think about was leaving Alaska and Kina. Where was she? Was she all right?

The plane ride was uneventful and soon they were on their way to his parent's animal refuge and home. He hadn't had time to find a place to live yet. He'd been planning on doing that after the show as over, and hopefully with Kina. He wanted to find a home she'd feel comfortable in.

After the long trip, Jonathan finally gave in and took a pain pill. He was in quite a lot of pain and only wanted to sleep. That was a lie, he only wanted Kina, but after that he wanted to close his eyes and let the fog of the pain medicine take him. As he settled into the queen bed in his parent's guest room, he felt someone at his side. He cracked his eyelids open, hoping against hope it was Kina. It wasn't.

Becky sat down at Jonathan's bedside and took his hand in hers.

"You'll find her when you're better." She knew.

Jonathan took a deep breath. "What did she say to you, Beck? Do you know where she went?"

Becky shook her head. "I don't know, but I have a feeling she'll find her way to you. She was dealing with some pretty heavy stuff in the hospital. She was feeling guilty you were hurt protecting her." At Jonathan's shake of his head she hurried on. "We told her she shouldn't feel guilty. Dean even hinted to her that she'd do the same thing if the tables were turned."

"Did she get it?" Jonathan asked, tortured by the thoughts of Kina feeling bad for one second about what he'd done. He hated the thought of Kina being the one hurt and lying in a hospital room, but he knew she'd protect him in a heartbeat if she had to.

"I think she did. She got a weird look on her face and ran out of the waiting room like a fire had been lit under her. She loves you, Jonathan. I'd bet my life on it. You should've seen her. She was magnificent. She got hold of us and helped arrange for all of us to get to the hospital. She kept us informed about what was going on with you until we could get there. I know you don't remember this, but at one point the doctors weren't sure they wanted to do surgery because you were so weak. She knew if they didn't do it, there was a high chance you wouldn't survive. From what the doctor told us, she browbeat them into agreeing it was the only thing to be done, and you were in surgery before we even arrived."

Jonathan smiled weakly. He could imagine Kina doing just that. "I can't keep my eyes open, but tomorrow I'm going to find her."

Becky smiled. She had no doubt Jonathan would do just that.

* * *

Kina sighed. The last two weeks had been so frustrating. She'd gone back to the production house intending to talk to one of the producers, but she'd forgotten no one was there, they were all still on Bear Island. She had no way to get out there, and honestly didn't want to. She had way too many bad memories to want to ever lay eyes on it again.

She had to wait another two days for Eddie and the others to get back. Taylor and Carl wanted to know how Jonathan was. Since she hadn't been back to the hospital she could only say that he'd be fine. She didn't know the particulars, but was thankful Dean had been texting her and keeping her in the loop.

Dean was the only person in Jonathan's family who knew what she was planning. She hadn't wanted to tell anyone other than Jonathan, but she also wanted to make sure at least one member of his family knew she was coming back. She wasn't deserting him. She just had some things to take care of first.

Kina sat down and met with Eddie. The meeting was a long one, but after it was over Kina knew her life had changed, hopefully for the better. She'd taken a risk. She hoped, but wasn't one hundred percent sure, that Jonathan would think what she'd done was a positive thing. Only time would tell.

Before sitting down with Eddie, she'd had a long talk on the phone with Dean. She didn't want to go behind Jonathan's back, but she had to secure her future before she could involve him. She knew Jonathan would do whatever it took to get her to Arizona, and she appreciated it, but she had to do this on her own. For her to have any feeling of accomplishment, she had to make this happen herself.

Dean, at first, wasn't too sure about having anything to do with Eddie. He'd never gotten over what had happened to Becky, and Eddie wasn't on his list of favorite people. After talking it over with Becky and having his lawyers look over the paperwork she'd faxed to him, he'd finally agreed. Kina smiled, remembering how he'd told her in a disgusted voice, "I'm only agreeing because you're family." Family. Maybe she'd finally get the loving family she'd always dreamed of.

It was time to get to Arizona and to Jonathan. She'd heard from Dean that Jonathan had been snarky and grumpy and downright annoying. God, she missed him and hated like hell that she hadn't been able to talk to him, but it was time to face him and let him know what she'd done. She only hoped he still wanted her in Arizona with him.

Ironically, she was at the airport at the same time as Darius and Roger. She hadn't seen Darius since that day on the island and she was honestly glad to be able to say good-bye to him. A little bit of her was still pissed at him for his role in what had happened to Jonathan, but after she'd thought about it for a while, she realized she probably would've run the same way he had. If Jonathan hadn't been there with her, telling her to calm down and stay still, she probably would have taken off right after Darius. She had to forgive him for being too scared to think straight.

They were all on separate flights, making their way home, but managed to have time to sit down for a drink before they had to leave.

After giving Darius a big hug and telling both men all about what had happened to Jonathan and how he was recuperating in Arizona with his family, she couldn't resist asking, "So…who won? Who is the 'Extreme Alaskan?'"

"Oh no, we're not telling you, sorry," Darius said teasingly. "You'll have to watch the show with the rest of America. You know we're under contract to keep silent."

"You mean after everything we've been through together, you're seriously not going to tell me?" Kina asked, annoyed. "You owe me!"

Both men laughed at her.

"Consider this payback for all those horrible shots you took of us," Roger told her, only half-kidding.

Kina got over her snit quickly, because honestly she didn't really care who'd won in the long run. She gave each of the men another big hug before heading off to her gate. "Thanks for being pretty cool about everything," she told them. "I've been on shows with some pretty horrible people, and you guys are all right."

They knew she was teasing and told her they'd see her later.

Kina knew they wouldn't, but it was a nice sentiment.

A few hours later Kina's nerves were getting the better of her. She was more nervous at what would happen next than she'd been for her first job interview as a camera operator. Dean had assured her Jonathan wanted her with him, but until she saw it for herself firsthand, she just wasn't sure.

After getting the rental car, Kina checked the map on her cell phone for the tenth time. She couldn't believe she was just going to show up at the refuge where Jonathan was staying with his parents, but she just wanted to get it over with. She couldn't go another day without seeing for herself that Jonathan was alive and well. Kina could still remember the feel of his warm blood seeping through her fingers, as she frantically put pressure on his stomach, while they were in the woods on the island.

Every now and then she'd have a nightmare where he'd be walking toward her holding his intestines in his hands, and asking 'why.' She shivered. Yeah, it was time to see him for herself and make sure he was okay.

Jonathan was sitting at the dining room table talking with his mom and making a list of places to start looking for Kina when the doorbell rang. Bethany got up and went around the corner to the front door. Jonathan didn't get up, he still wasn't moving very quickly these days and he was concentrating on his list.

He heard the surprise in his mom's voice when she opened the door, but couldn't hear her actual conversation with whoever was at the door. He steeled himself to entertain another one of his parent's friends. They'd been coming by at regular intervals to check on him. It was annoying, but sweet at the same time.

Jonathan couldn't believe his eyes when his mom returned with Kina in tow. He was stunned. He'd been all ready to set off to find her and here she was!

Jonathan slowly stood up and held himself steady with one hand on the tabletop. He simply stared at his One, as she stood in the doorway.

Neither noticed as Bethany disappeared into the back of the house.

Kina shuffled her feet. God, he looked like crap, but so good. He was standing in front of her, alive, and whole. Not knowing how he'd take her being there, she didn't move.

Jonathan had no such hesitation. He stepped toward her unsteadily. He had to have her in his arms right now.

Kina saw him falter as he came toward her and that loosened her feet. She lunged at him and they met halfway across the kitchen. She wrapped her arms around his waist carefully and leaned against him. God. How could she ever have thought for a second about not coming here to be with him? She only felt whole in his arms. She felt his hand come up and cup the back of her neck as he always did. It felt heavenly.

Jonathan let out a shaky sigh. Kina was here. She'd come. "Thank God," was all he could get out. "Thank God you're here."

Kina nodded and couldn't help the tears that coursed down her face and soaked into his chest. "I wasn't sure you still wanted me to come."

Jonathan drew back and took her chin in his hands. He hated to see her cry, but he had to make sure she understood his next words. "I was making plans to come find you, love. I wanted you here. I would've spent the rest of my life searching for you so I could convince you to stay with me." When Kina buried her head against his shirt again he couldn't help but tease her. "Would you rather have a beautiful woman wipe snot on you after crying or have her sneeze on you?" She laughed as he meant her to.

Jonathan shuffled with her, still snuggled in his arms, over to the couch. He carefully sat, not jostling his abdomen too much, and settled into the cushions with her in his arms. After she'd stopped crying, he finally asked, "Why'd it take you so long to get to me?"

Kina sat up part way and rubbed her hands over her face. Gah. She knew she had to talk to him, but she wasn't a pretty crier. Some women could cry crocodile tears and not mess up a speck of their makeup, not her. She got blotchy and her eyes swelled up terribly. When she looked up at Jonathan, he was looking at her as if she was the most beautiful woman in the world. God, she loved him. Yes. Loved. Him.

"I love you." She couldn't hold it back anymore. Being here in his arms was a miracle. She hadn't known if she'd ever feel the strength in his arms again. That bear had scared the crap out of her and made her understand just what she had in Jonathan.

"I love you too, Kina."

Kina nodded. "I know." She smiled sheepishly at him. "I should've told you before now, but I was scared. I wasn't sure how you could love me. Me. I'm nobody important. I haven't done anything important in my life. No one will remember my name. I didn't understand. Then you got hurt and I was literally holding your life in my hands and I knew. We don't have to do anything, we don't have to be famous, we can just love each other and be happy together. I wanted that. I wanted that more than I wanted my next breath, but you were lying under me and I was holding your intestines in my hands. I was scared to death."

Jonathan interrupted her, "But you did what you had to do, didn't you, love?" Kina nodded. "You did what you had to because you're strong on your own. You don't need me to be strong; you're independent and a hell of a woman. Any other woman might have fallen apart and panicked. You did everything right, Kina. I'm here. I'm alive. You're a hell of a woman. My woman."

Kina smiled. "Hey, this is me talking, not you." Jonathan smiled and nodded as if to say 'go ahead.'

"So there you were, lying unconscious in a hospital bed and I had to bully the doctors into not giving up on you, because I knew deep down, you'd fight. You'd fight to get back to me. And you did. Once I knew you were going to pull through, I had to make it so I could move down here and be with you." At the look in his eyes she hurried on. "I know, I know, I could've quit my job and sat around eating bon-bons and you wouldn't care."

She loved watching him laugh. She didn't love the wince that came along with the laugh, though. Obviously, laughing pulled at his still-tender stomach muscles.

"I went to see Eddie. I had to wait until he'd finished filming on that damn island. Then he gave me hell and negotiated with me for a few days before we could sign our new contract."

Jonathan scowled at her. "New contract? Wait a minute…"

Not letting him continue, she put her hand over his mouth to shut him up. She felt his tongue caressing the palm of her hand and she pulled her hand back. "Don't distract me!" she scolded him, "or I'll never get to tell you."

Jonathan pulled her hand back to his mouth and kissed the palm. "Go on love, I'll be good, but this story had better end with you living with me and spending every night in my bed and in my arms, or I won't like it."

Kina shook her head. Every now and then his alpha tendencies would come out. She tried to tell herself it was annoying, but the truth was, she loved it.

"I didn't want to move here and not have anything to do. I actually like being behind a camera and I'm good at it." Kina said the last with no pomposity in her voice. She was a good camera operator and she knew it. "I talked with Dean…"

Jonathan interrupted her for what seemed like the millionth time. "You talked to Dean? You mean, he knew where you were this entire time?"

Uh-oh. She didn't mean to get Dean in trouble. She tried to hide her smile. Jonathan was so cute. "Uh, yeah, but anyway…" Jonathan growled and pushed Kina backward until she was reclining on the couch. Kina didn't fight him because she wasn't sure how hurt he still was. She giggled.

"I've been going out of my mind trying to figure out how to find you and my brother knew where you were and was actually talking to you this entire time?" Jonathan asked again, in a mock-gruff tone.

"Yeah, but I didn't see you texting me at all. I would've answered."

"Are you kidding me?"

Kina shook her head. She hadn't meant to hide away from him, and she was telling the truth. She would've texted him back in a heartbeat if he'd contacted her.

"Why didn't you text me?" Jonathan asked, hurt.

"I wasn't sure whether you were pissed at me or not, and when Dean told me you were all right and not mad at me, I figured it was better if I just came here and talked to you in person. Besides, the more time went by, the more awkward I felt about contacting you out of the blue. I convinced myself you were better off healing on your own and didn't need my issues holding you back."

Jonathan shook his head in amazement. "I can't believe I didn't think to just pick up my phone and shoot you a note. I'm an idiot."

Kina put her hand on his face. "You're my idiot." She leaned up and kissed him briefly on the lips. Before he could deepen it, she pulled away. "Do you want to hear the rest of this or not?"

"Not."

She laughed and pushed at his chest. Jonathan briefly laid his forehead on hers. Then he sighed in mock aggravation. "Okay, okay, please continue. But as I said before, I hope this story ends with you living here in Arizona with me."

Kina decided to just get it out so they could move on to more pleasant things. "I consulted with Dean and we worked out a deal with Eddie where I'd film documentaries on women who are in need of security, and their stories. I wanted to tell the world about the plight of people who are stalked and to try to see if we couldn't help change the stalking laws in this country. I figured, the more we highlight the personal side of these women, the more people will see they're just regular people who happen to have had the wrong kind of person get obsessed with them. Do you know that in a typical one-year-period there are six point six *million* people over the age of eighteen who are stalked? And over a lifetime, sixteen percent of women and five percent of men feel they've been a victim of stalking or thought that they, or someone close to them, would be hurt or killed? That's crazy! People are crazy!"

Jonathan could only smile in wonderment at his love. She was so passionate, he was lucky to have found her.

Kina continued, "And not only that, but I told Dean he needed to look into helping not only women, but men too. Did you know that twenty four percent of stalking victims are men? That's a quarter of all victims! There are crazy women out there terrorizing people too. Women aren't the only victims!"

Jonathan couldn't stop himself from kissing the hell out of his woman.

Kina was surprised, but quickly joined in with enthusiasm. She'd never take this for granted again. Jonathan's lips were devouring hers and she loved it.

He pulled back and between nips of her luscious lips and asked, "Is there more?"

Kina tried to remember what she'd been talking about. Oh yeah. Stalking, Dean, Eddie, her job. She summed up the rest of her story quickly. "So I have the job of filming you guys as you help out stalking victims and working with Eddie's company to get the documentaries produced and aired."

"And you're here for good?"

"Yes, if you want me."

"I want you."

Kina smiled up at the most handsome man in the world. Her man. If someone had told her a year ago she'd meet the man of her dreams while working, she'd have said they were crazy. Her heart had been as frozen as Alaska was in the winter. She'd never thought she'd meet anyone who could thaw it out and make her love him as much as she loved Jonathan. As she thought back over the last year, she reflected on how she'd almost died in Australia, had spent a crazy couple of months filming a show that would never air, and finally, came face-to-face with a bear and lived. Most importantly, she'd met Jonathan, her One.

As she settled back onto the cushions of the couch and reached up to her man, she knew she'd finally found paradise.

Sam, Becky, and Kina sat around the small table in the bar just off the beach and raised their glasses toward each other.

"To life-long friendship!" Becky said a bit too loud. Since this was their tenth toast to nothing in particular, none of the friends seemed to notice the volume of her toast.

"To life-long friendship!" Kina and Sam repeated, then downed their shots.

After moving into their small house, both Jonathan and Kina wasted no time in settling down. Kina didn't think his parents had forgiven them yet for running off to Vegas to get married, but Kina had never dreamed of a big wedding. Truth be told, she never thought she'd ever get married in the first place. So they'd followed Becky and Dean's example and headed off to Nevada. They'd had a quick wedding with just Dean and Becky, and Sam and her husband Alex there as witnesses. It was perfect.

Kina had missed Sam and was happy they were able to at least see each other now and then, but they made sure they kept in touch via weekly phone chats to just catch up.

Kina loved traveling with Jonathan and Dean when they went to help set up security for someone who was being stalked. Dean was true to his word and had started including men in his business as well. He told her he'd honestly not even thought about a man being stalked, but after talking to some of the victims, he'd changed his mind pretty quickly. Women were just as crazy as men, and sometimes even more so, when they were stalking someone.

Kina loved being married to Jonathan. It was inevitable that they'd fight, as they both had such strong personalities, but making up was so much fun.

The first time Kina had seen Jonathan's scars, she'd broken down. She'd traced them over and over with her fingertips and with her mouth, trying to reassure herself he was whole again. They'd had another long talk about guilt afterwards. Kina admitted she still felt guilty that he'd been the one who had been hurt when she felt it should've been her. They'd even gone to see the same counselor Becky had seen after she'd been violated, and it seemed to help both of them. The woman had talked them through their feelings and they'd both agreed to let it go. They were both here and alive and together. It was enough for them both.

They'd never found out who was ultimately named the "Extreme Alaskan." Their last paycheck arrived in the mail and that was the last either thought about the show. As far as Kina was concerned, Jonathan had more than earned that title all by himself. Her friends were amazed she didn't care who won, but they respected her wishes to not talk about it. All it did was bring back bad memories for Kina. She was way too busy with her documentaries and helping out on the animal refuge to give it any thought, anyway.

The couples' weekend had been thought up by Becky and Kina one night. They'd had a tough week and decided they wanted to get away. Knowing their husbands wouldn't let them go by themselves, they let them come too. Kina thought about Sam and asked if she and Alex could come as well. Becky had agreed wholeheartedly. She'd met them while her reality show was filmed and liked them on sight. Sam had given her some great advice and she was happy to get to know her better.

So now, they were sitting at a bar on the beach, ignoring the looks from the men at nearby tables and drinking themselves silly. They knew their men weren't far away, watching over them. They'd had a conversation once after the last time they'd all gotten together and compared notes. They realized that none of their men ever got drunk when they did. Kina asked Jonathan about it and he'd responded that the guys agreed to let them have their fun and they'd be there to make sure no one harassed them and to keep them out of trouble, if it came to that.

It was overprotective and sweet at the same time. The three women also realized how good the sex was after their nights out. It was as if the men looked forward to them going out simply because of the uninhibited sex that happened afterwards. They'd all laughed and shrugged. They loved their men and loved the long, lovemaking sessions after their nights of drinking just as much.

"I think we should give ourselves a name!" Becky said excitedly. "We all met because of stupid Eddie and his reality shows…let's call ourselves the 'Reality Chicks'!"

"No, the 'Reality Bitches'," Sam said, laughing herself silly, thinking it was the funniest thing ever.

"You guys know what?" Kina said semi-seriously, hammered, but wanting her friends to know how much they meant to her. "We're bound together because of reality shows. That's amazing. I'm so glad I met you all. We're like the six shades of reality."

Kina felt Jonathan's arms around her waist before she could see him. He leaned down and put his cheek against hers. "Having fun, love?" Kina turned and blindly sought his lips with her own. How long had it been since she'd had him? She couldn't remember, but it had to have been too long. The feel of his hand curling around the back of her neck never failed to make her melt.

Alex picked Sam up and sat down on her stool, holding her tight in his arms. She giggled and wrapped one arm around his neck, but kept hold of her drink with the other. She leaned in and latched onto his neck, sucking hard. "Hey! Watch it!" he told her, knowing she'd ignore him. She loved marking him, especially when she was drunk. She always said she had to put her mark on him so no other woman would get any ideas.

Dean turned Becky and stepped into her space. She spread her legs, inviting him to stand between them. He put his forehead against hers and just held her. She was his life and he felt like the luckiest man alive having her in his. He knew how precious life was and how easily it could be taken away.

Kina turned back toward the group. She loved this. She loved all of them. She cleared her throat and raised her glass. She waited until everyone did the same. Becky had to lean over and smack Sam on the back of the head to get her to pay attention. After everyone's giggles died down, Kina said as solemnly as she could, seeing as she was three sheets to the wind, "To reality shows!"

Sam said "Reality Bitches!"

Jonathan added his own toast, "To all of us...friends forever—beyond reality!"

Discover other titles by

Susan Stoker

<u>SEAL of Protection Series:</u>
Protecting Caroline
Protecting Alabama
Protecting Fiona
Marrying Caroline (novella)
Protecting Summer
Protecting Cheyenne
Protecting Jessyka
Protecting Julie (novella)
Protecting Melody
Protecting the Future

<u>Badge of Honor: Texas Heroes Series</u>
Justice for Mackenzie
Justice for Mickie
Justice for Corrie (Mar 2016)
Justice for Laine (novella) (Apr 2016)
Shelter for Elizabeth (July 2016)
Justice for Boone (TBA)
Shelter for Adeline (TBA)
Justice for Sidney (TBA)
Shelter for Blythe (TBA)
Justice for Milena (TBA)
Shelter for Sophie (TBA)
Justice for Kinley (TBA)
Shelter for Promise (TBA)
Shelter for Koren (TBA)
Shelter for Penelope (TBA)

<u>**Unsung Heroes: Delta Force**</u>
Rescuing Rayne
Assisting Aimee (novella) Loosely tied to DF
Rescuing Emily (TBA)
Rescuing Harley (TBA)
Rescuing Kassie (TBA)
Rescuing Casey (TBA)
Rescuing Wendy (TBA)
Rescuing Mary (TBA)

<u>**Beyond Reality Series:**</u>
Outback Hearts
Flaming Hearts
Frozen Hearts

<u>**Writing as Annie George:**</u>
Stepbrother Virgin (erotic novella)

<u>Connect with Susan Online:</u>

<u>*Susan's Facebook Profile and Page:*</u>
www.facebook.com/authorsstoker
www.facebook.com/authorsusanstoker

<u>*Follow Susan on Twitter:*</u>
www.twitter.com/Susan_Stoker

<u>*Find Susan's Books on Goodreads*</u>
www.goodreads.com/SusanStoker

<u>**Email**</u>: Susan@StokerAces.com

<u>**Website**</u>: www.SealOfProtection.com

About the Author

New York Times, *USA Today,* and *Wall Street Journal* Bestselling Author Susan Stoker has a heart as big as the state of Texas where she lives, but this all American girl has also spent the last fourteen years living in Missouri, California, Colorado, and Indiana. She's married to a retired Army man who now gets to follow *her* around the country.

She debuted her first series in 2014 and quickly followed that up with the SEAL of Protection Series, which solidified her love of writing and creating stories readers can get lost in.

If you enjoyed this book, or any book, please consider leaving a review. It's appreciated by authors more than you'll know.